AF445458

MAKE YOU MINE

USA *Today* Bestselling Author

jenna hartley

Editing: Lisa A. Hollett
Cover: Qamber Designs

to keeping hope alive
even during the
darkest of times

jenna hartley

NOTE FROM THE AUTHOR

Dear Reader,

Make You Mine is a story about finding love after loss, and as such, it explores the complicated emotions that come from losing a spouse unexpectedly. That said, it is ultimately a story with a happily ever after, and it is my wish that you will find not just love but hope within these pages.

As the main character, Bryn, comes to realize herself, growth is possible even when everything seems bleak. Hope is possible even in the darkest of times.

Sometimes it is difficult to balance two competing emotions, especially when we are grieving the loss of someone or some place we loved, an ideal we held dear. We might even grieve the person we used to be or the life we thought we'd have. But learning to coexist with joy and grief, hope and fear is what makes us human. What makes us incredible.

I did my best to handle these topics with care, in the hopes that others would feel less alone when navigating such a difficult situation themselves. As always, if this is a sensitive subject for you, please feel free to reach out for clarification. Or if you need to skip this story for your mental well-being, I completely understand.

With much love and hugs,
Jenna

NOTE FROM THE AUTHOR

To my fellow hockey fans—I did my best to make this story as accurate as I could. That said, timings may have been adjusted for the purposes of the story. I may have condensed the number of teammates to create a tighter bond in a world that was easier to follow.

Go Hawks!

HOT AS PUCK

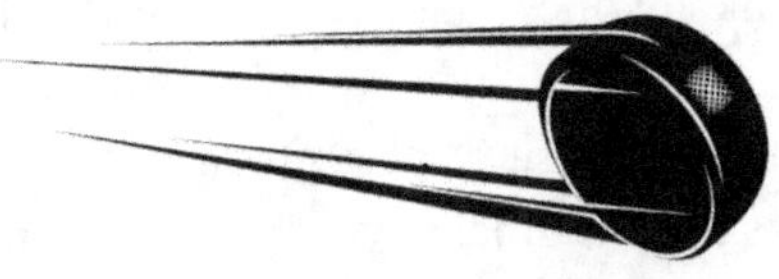

Original Air Date: April 30
@ The Hive Sports and Entertainment

Logan: Well, it's official. The season's over for the Hawks. Thoughts on last night's game?

Levi: You know, sis, it would be easy to be disappointed by the way the game ended. I certainly was. I was rooting for the Hawks—they were the underdogs. And considering all the changes they've had in recent years, both good and bad, they should be proud of their performance. They're in a bit of a rebuild cycle, but they're definitely going to be a team to watch.

Logan: For sure. LA definitely had their work cut out for them this year. First year with a new head coach.

Levi: Declan Cross is a fucking legend, and I can't wait to see what he'll do with the team. Especially now that they're getting Holden Hansley.

Logan: Holden freaking Hansley. Handy-man Holden. That guy is a beast on the ice. A GOAT. I wouldn't be surprised if he landed in the Hall of Fame someday.

Levi: I don't think anyone would be surprised by that.

Logan: So you think Hansley's going to bring the magic sauce the Hawks need to finally win the Cup again for the first time in twenty years?

Levi: I certainly think he'll add a lot to the team.

Logan: Obviously. Last season, Hansley was the league's leading goal scorer with forty-one goals in fifty-two games. He's won the "Rocket" Richard Trophy two years in a row, and he has one hell of a shot.

Levi: We all know the stats. He's a superstar, but hockey is a team sport. And even if you have all the best players, you gotta have—

Logan: Good chem.

Levi: Exactly.

Logan: There's also talk of bringing Carson Kovalsky more into the fold. I'd like to see how that plays out. He's got a lot of potential.

Levi: Potential as what? An influencer? I'm not sure he's ever met a camera he didn't love. He should focus more on his stick work and less on social media.

Logan: Ouch. Okay, Mr. Old-School.

Levi: Call me Old-School, but I'm not okay with putting my entire life on the internet.

Logan: Maybe not, but the fans are eating it up. And doesn't that seem a little hypocritical? I mean, you do co-run a player pod with behind-the-scenes looks at what's going on in the NHL and PWHL.

Levi: That's different. And the fans might be eating up Kovi's shenanigans, but I wonder how management feels about it. If Kovi's not careful, he's going to be seen as a liability.

Logan: Anything else you want to add? About the Hawks, not just Kovi?

Levi: We can't mention the Hawks without mentioning Derek Morgan. His death last season was a huge blow to the team—both on and off the ice.

Logan: Absolutely. Derek was a talented defenseman. His death certainly led to a lot of soul-searching for the team. I think he would be proud of what they were able to accomplish.

Levi: Which is why the Hawks' performance this season was even more impressive. The team certainly could've gone one of two ways in the wake of the tragedy. But they clearly chose to let it bring them together, strengthening their bonds. No one expected much of the team, but they rallied.

Logan: It's incredible, and hopefully that will only continue into the next season. Any other changes you anticipate for the Hawks? Any thoughts on the off-season? Plans?

Levi: No. Hopefully the team stays healthy and strong, especially Frasier Holmes. Fizzy was on fire this season, barely letting in any goals. Have you seen his stats?

Logan: Record number of goose eggs. The Hawks fans certainly had fun, going all out with their tradition of tossing plastic eggs onto the rink.

Levi: I can't remember a season with more shutout games. And that's due in huge part to Fizzy's aggressive butterfly style of play.

Logan: I've never seen anything quite like it. Some of the saves he made were unreal.

Levi: Right? He will do anything in his power to block the biscuit from hitting the back of the net.

Logan: True. His hips have got to hurt.

Levi: The game is always a grind, but this season, it felt like Fizzy had something to prove.

Logan: Maybe he did.

CHAPTER ONE

Frazier

"Oh my god. Seriously?" Bryn tossed her phone down on the bed with a huff. Biscuit lifted her head from the dog bed in the corner briefly before lowering it once more. "My sister is going to push me over the edge."

"Is this about the wedding?"

"What else?" Bryn rolled her eyes.

I surveyed Bryn's guest bedroom, grabbing a set of screws from the floor. She sank down on the edge of the mattress, still in her scrubs. Her hair was pulled back in a ponytail, the wavy blond strands falling like silk over her shoulder. She looked younger than her twenty-seven years, though she'd certainly been through a lot in the past eighteen months. We both had.

But life went on, whether we liked it or not.

It was strange to celebrate without Derek. First, it was a game the team had won. Then Christmas and New Year's. Then his birthday. The end of the season. And now, Bryn's sister's wedding.

"What's going on?" I asked.

If Bryn complained about her family, it was usually

because they were so close that it was inevitable. And if they smothered her, it was only because they cared.

I got it. I was close to my own family. Or at least, I used to be. Now, our relationship was strained—and in some cases, nonexistent.

But my found family? They'd all rallied around us after Derek's death. They and our friends, my current teammates, and even some former ones. Everyone had been hurting, but they'd stepped up to help Bryn. To support her—and, to a lesser extent, me—through the tragedy as best as they could.

"Allie said she feels like 'the light's gone out of me.'" Bryn used air quotes, rolling her eyes as she relayed her sister's sentiment.

Oof. I winced.

"And what do you think?" I had to bite my tongue to keep myself from saying a few choice words about Bryn's sister's comment.

"I think that my husband died and my life got flipped upside down and I'm doing the best I can."

I placed my hand on Bryn's knee, our eyes locking. "You're doing great."

I understood that Allie was trying to help, and I knew it was coming from a place of love, but she wasn't here day in and day out. She was supportive, as much as she could be from afar. But she hadn't witnessed Bryn's progress in the same way I had. Allie didn't see the good days and the bad days. And as much as I hated seeing Bryn in pain, I was so fucking grateful that she allowed me to be there for her.

"Thank you." Bryn dropped her head, gaze on the floor, before murmuring, "To be honest, most days, I'm just making it through."

"Give yourself some credit," I said, not willing to let her downplay what she'd survived or the progress she'd made. I gnashed my teeth. *I could kill Allie for making Bryn doubt herself.* "You're healing."

"Yeah," Bryn acknowledged reluctantly. "Okay. Maybe I was just making it through before, and I still sometimes have days like that. But I'm doing better."

I gave her knee a squeeze before releasing her. "What's really bothering you?" I asked when she started gnawing on her lip.

"I think..." Bryn blew out a breath, calmer now. "I think my family is worried the wedding will remind me of everything I lost."

Everything we'd both lost. My chest ached at the reminder.

Her husband. My best friend and former teammate. A talented hockey player and an even better man. It was still hard to believe Derek was gone. It just didn't make sense—his sudden death. I wasn't sure it ever would.

"She hasn't said it, but I get the feeling that my sister feels guilty that she found her happily ever after when we all know how my love story ended," Bryn continued, breaking me out of my thoughts. "But she shouldn't. I'm thrilled for her."

I knew that Bryn was genuinely happy for Allie. But that didn't mean Bryn couldn't also be hurting. If I'd learned anything over the past year and a half, it was that grief was complex. It often required you to juggle two conflicting emotions simultaneously—anger and sadness. Joy and heartbreak. And none of it was easy.

"Have you told her that?" I flipped my hat backward to keep my hair out of my face.

The length was starting to drive me nuts, but I'd been waiting for Georgia to come back from vacation. She was the team's stylist, and I wouldn't let anyone else touch my hair.

"Of course I have." Bryn stood and started pacing. "But I

feel like she's not listening at all lately, and she's not the only one."

I arched one brow, not liking the sound of that. "What does that mean?"

"People keep trying to set me up on dates, despite my telling them I'm not interested. And I'm sick of it."

I swallowed hard. *What?* I lifted my baseball cap, smoothing back my hair before shoving the hat on my head —again. *Fuck.*

"For the wedding, or in general?" I asked, trying to keep my voice calm. Even.

I hadn't realized that Bryn was ready to date or even interested in the idea. She'd stopped wearing her wedding ring months ago, but... I shook my head. No. Surely she wasn't...

Not that I was judging her. I just didn't know what to make of it.

"For the wedding. My future. They love to tell me what Derek would want." She scoffed. "Derek would want you to be happy. Derek wouldn't want you to be alone." She affected a different tone, as if to mimic another woman's voice. "Even Derek's *mom* told me that."

I didn't disagree with the sentiment, but I also knew that Bryn had to do what felt best for her. Sure, maybe she needed a push. But we also had to know when to give her space. It was one of the hardest things I'd ever had to grapple with.

"And it's not just them. One of my coworkers has been trying to set me up with someone." She shook her head. "They say it's about what Derek would want, but it's about them. *They* don't want me to be alone."

I gnashed my teeth, annoyed they were overstepping.

Be honest, a little voice said. *That's not the only reason you're annoyed.* But I shoved it away. She'd been married to my best friend. And despite how I felt...it didn't matter. I needed to focus on Bryn—what she wanted, what she needed.

"What do you want?" I asked.

"A time machine," she answered bluntly, though it didn't escape my notice that she'd avoided my question.

"Bryn," I sighed. "If I could buy you one, I would."

"Thanks, Bear. I just..." She sighed. "I don't want to be the center of so much attention for something so awful anymore. Especially not on a day that should be a celebration. I'm tired of the pitying looks, the curious whispers. I'm tired of being treated like I'm made of glass."

Losing your spouse had to be painful enough, but to have her greatest tragedy become national news? To have to grieve his loss so publicly? And yet to show so much strength and grace was a testament to her character.

I honestly didn't know how she did it. As Derek's best friend and teammate, I'd certainly been asked my fair share of invasive questions about the man, his loss, his legacy. But she'd been his *wife*.

Many times, I'd wanted to punch someone in the face solely for asking a question about Derek. Yet anytime Bryn spoke about Derek, she was full of poise, representing Derek's legacy with grace.

Bryn leaned back on her hands and stared up at the ceiling. And as always, she took my breath away. She had been to hell and back, and she was one of the strongest people I knew. And that was saying something, considering my teammates were some of the most elite athletes in the league, in the nation.

When her attention turned to me, I glanced down, hoping she hadn't noticed me staring. How could I not? She was gorgeous—blond hair, blue eyes, dark lashes, pouty lips.

But it wasn't just about her looks. She was also wicked

smart. She assisted doctors who performed literal brain surgery. On *children.* That took guts. And mental strength.

She cared about her patients, going above and beyond. Most of them sent her holiday cards long after they'd been discharged because she'd made such a positive impact on their lives. Hell, I'd seen her comfort Derek's fans when they should've been consoling her. She cared about everyone. Sometimes I wondered if she cared too much.

"You could skip it." I was joking, mostly. If skipping her sister's wedding would protect Bryn's mental peace, then I was all for it.

Bryn gave me a flat look. "She's my sister. And I'm a bridesmaid. Though, thank god, I'm not the maid—" She furrowed her brow. "Matron? Of honor. At least I don't have to plan the bachelorette party, the bridal shower. All I have to do is show up, and even that sounds like too much effort."

I shrugged, trying to act calm when all I wanted was to wrap her up in my arms and protect her. "Feign illness at the last minute."

"That would definitely ruin Allie's day. And I want to be there for her. Of course I do. But, ugh…" She flopped back on the bed, and I didn't look away fast enough. Now I couldn't tear my eyes away.

Even in her cornflower-blue scrubs, I could see the outline of her curves. Her breasts and hips were fuller now that she'd gained back some of the weight she'd lost after Derek's death. That was a relief. But she was still thinner than she'd been. I was just grateful she was eating, even if she lacked the passion she used to have for food.

Bryn was still talking, and I caught back on at the tail end, just as she said, "And then I just *had* to tell her I had a date to the wedding."

The idea of Bryn with another man had my gut tightening, the air being squeezed from my lungs.

"Who?" My voice came out as a growl.

"That's just it." Bryn rolled to her side, propping her head up on her hand. She blew out a breath, pink tingeing her cheekbones. "I lied."

A dark chuckle threaded through me, along with a potent dose of relief. *Thank. Fuck.*

Our other Bernadoodle, Bacon, wandered into the room as Bryn slapped my chest playfully before settling into a cross-legged position on the floor. Bacon climbed in her lap, as he had ever since he was a puppy. It was as if he thought he weighed twenty pounds instead of forty-five.

Both Bryn and I had each always wanted a dog. But until recently, neither of us had been in the place to take care of a pet full time on our own. When we'd jointly adopted Bacon and Biscuit, Bryn's grief had still been fresh, and I was on the road a lot for games. I'd hoped that a dog would bring us both comfort after losing Derek, and caring for them together had seemed like the perfect solution. Now, a year in, I couldn't imagine our lives without Bacon and Biscuit.

She gave Bacon some behind-the-ear scratches, and then he heard a sound and went to the window to investigate. Bryn groaned and flopped back on the floor, draping her arm over her forehead. "This isn't funny, Bear."

The dogs went over, licking her face until she was giggling. The sound was so light and full of so much joy that I closed my eyes as if to capture it in my mind. It was damn good to hear her laugh. I couldn't help but join in.

Bryn sat up, paused, then lifted her hand as if to touch my cheek. Everything in me reached out to her as I held my breath, waiting for the moment her palm connected with my skin. When she hesitated, I remained still, trying to be patient.

"I forgot how handsome you are when you actually smile." She blushed then, lowering her hand to her lap as she added, "It's difficult to see your lips through all the fur covering your face."

"Ha-ha," I deadpanned, mostly to stop myself from begging her to touch me. "You're not the first person to say that to me."

The guys loved to give me shit for my play-off beard, and I laughed off their good-natured ribbing. Play-offs were over. Done. And yet, I couldn't seem to make myself shave.

Florida had hoisted the Cup last month. And for some reason, I was still hanging on to my play-off beard as if it would bring me luck. Or change something. Fuck if I knew.

"I bet if you shaved," Bryn said, breaking me out of my thoughts, "you'd be out with some woman instead of spending your off-season keeping me company."

"Not likely," I muttered.

It didn't matter how many women hit on me—and the beard and long hair certainly didn't deter them. There was only one woman I wanted.

"I still can't believe you've been in LA for almost two years and haven't dated anyone," she said.

I had zero interest in dating someone. At least someone who wasn't Bryn.

But it was difficult not to think of her as Derek's wife. She'd been married to my best friend. My former teammate. My gut twisted with guilt.

I smoothed my hand down my beard. Derek, like the other guys on the team, would've given me shit for it. The thought made me smile, and I was grateful for times like this when I could think of him without feeling like I'd taken a frozen puck to the chest.

"Haven't had time," I said in answer to Bryn's comment about my lack of dating, which was partially true.

The life of a pro hockey player was intense, especially during the grueling eighty-two-game regular season. Not many people could understand the hours, the travel, the dedication involved. It might be the off-season now, but that didn't change anything—at least not for me and my interest in a romantic partner.

I'd been friends with Bryn for nearly a decade. It was only in the past year that things had changed for me.

"Do you have time for hookups?" she asked.

"Why?" I leaned forward. "You offering?"

I couldn't believe I'd just said that. *Why the fuck had I just said that?* But it wasn't as if I could take it back now.

She laughed. "I'm sure you have your fair share of puck bunnies to choose from." She rolled her lips between her teeth then admitted, "I wish I could do casual sex, but I'm not sure I could keep my emotions out of it."

That didn't surprise me. Bryn and Derek had been a couple since her first year of college. For nearly her entire adult life, they'd prioritized their relationship through undergrad, through her extra schooling, and when he'd gotten drafted. She was definitely a relationship person, and that was why part of me couldn't be too mad at her family for wanting her to find love again.

"And you still didn't answer my question," Bryn said.

I tried to remember what we'd been talking about. Right. Puck bunnies. "That lifestyle quickly loses its appeal."

At least, it had for me. I'd tried a few hookups early in my career, but I'd only ended up feeling worse about myself.

Puck bunnies were only interested in bragging about the players they bagged. They didn't care about me as a person. They cared about my status as an NHL player. Sure, I'd been using them for something too, but the entire experience made me feel...cheap.

"So does that mean you're looking for a relationship?" Bryn asked, surprising me further.

"What's with the interrogation?"

"I don't know." She ducked her head. "Just curious. You never talk about anyone, and I wondered if you were still hung up on Sheree."

I barked out a laugh. Sheree and I had dated for a year while I'd lived in New York. But when I'd gotten traded to LA, I hadn't asked her to move, and she hadn't offered. Our relationship had run its course. Fizzled out.

"I'll take that as a no."

"You know it's a no," I said, still wondering what was behind this fishing expedition.

"So then, why don't you date?" Bryn asked.

"I told you. Don't have time."

"Mm." She eyed me skeptically.

"What?" I nudged her foot with mine.

"You don't have *time* to date—" Bryn nudged me back with her foot "—because you're always with me."

"I'm not *always* with you."

Bryn narrowed her eyes at me, arms crossed over her chest. "Don't get me wrong, I love spending time with you. And I appreciate everything you've done for me, truly. But I don't want you to feel like you have to put your life on hold for me."

"Bryn," I chided.

"I'm serious." She narrowed her eyes at me.

She really had no idea how I felt about her, did she? Not that I should've been surprised. We'd grown close in the last year and a half, and at some point, I'd realized that she was so much more to me than just a friend. But I'd never crossed that line, despite being tempted to. God, I was so fucking tempted.

Bryn tilted her head. "What?"

I love you.

I was tempted to blurt out the truth in that moment. It wouldn't have been the first time I'd been tempted, but I also knew a conversation like that would require some finesse. Even if you ignored the fact that her late husband had been my best friend and teammate, *Bryn* was my friend. She was important to me, and I was scared to ruin what we had for something she might not even want.

So, instead of confessing my feelings, I tried to get a sense for where she was coming from. Why was she asking me these questions? And why now?

"*What?*" she asked again, pressing when I still hadn't responded.

"You're annoyed with your family for bossing you around, trying to get you to date. And yet you're doing the exact same thing to me."

She looked away quickly. "That's different."

"How?" I scoffed, crossing my arms over my chest.

She lifted her shoulder. "I already had my love story. You haven't."

I blinked a few times. It felt like watching a teammate get injured on the ice—gut-wrenching and brutal. Everything stopped, the world quieting around me.

She doesn't truly believe that, does she?

But the longer we sat there, the more it sank in. The more I realized how convinced she was that she'd never love again.

I... I rubbed the back of my neck. *Christ.*

Her admission shattered something inside me, especially the way in which she'd delivered it with complete and utter sincerity. With just a few simple words, she'd upended my entire world.

CHAPTER TWO

Bryn

I popped up from the floor, unable to handle the intense way Frasier was looking at me after my admission. His expression was the same one he wore when he faced down an opponent on the ice. It said, *I see you, and you can't get anything past me.*

"I'm going to go make some dinner. Do you want to stay and eat with me?"

"Sounds good." He returned his attention to attaching the fan blades to the motor.

He was always helping with something around the house. I'd told him I could hire someone, but he always insisted on doing it himself. He was a fixer. If he saw a problem, he wanted to solve it. And I suspected that working on projects, helping me, helped him process his own grief.

I went to the kitchen, Bacon and Biscuit on my heels. I crouched down beside them, giving each of them a good scratch behind their ears. Then I stood and washed my hands so I could prepare dinner. Their nails scrabbled against the floor as they raced over to their food bowls.

I grabbed my tablet and pulled up one of my favorite

recipes from Maggie, the team's nutritionist. I was glad Frasier had agreed to stay because it pushed me to cook an actual meal. As I washed and chopped the vegetables, I thought back on my conversation with Allie. I knew my sister wasn't trying to be hurtful, but her words had still had that effect.

It feels as if the light has gone out of you.

I'd wanted to rail at her, but deep down, part of me worried that she was right. For the past year and a half, I'd been in survival mode. And it was exhausting.

My sister could empathize all she wanted, but she'd never truly understand what it was like. And I hoped she never would.

But now, I'd gotten myself stuck in a situation. Her comment had made me feel defensive, deflated. So when she'd pushed about bringing a date to the wedding, I'd lied.

"I have a date," I'd blurted, hoping my tone didn't betray the anger and hurt, the defiance coursing through me. The lie.

"Who?" She'd laughed. "Frasier?"

"Yes," I'd snapped. I'd been just... so over it.

"And he's your date. You guys are together." She sounded so smug. So skeptical.

"Yes," I gritted out. She'd pushed me too far.

"What?" Allie shrieked. "Is that why you've been so annoyed anytime I suggested dating someone? Why didn't you just tell me you were in a relationship with Frasier?"

"Because..."

Crap. Crap. Crap. What had I done?

I wasn't dating Frasier. But the fact that she thought I was meant she—and others—would finally stop pestering me to "be happy" and "find love again." It was also one hundred percent not true.

That would've been a good moment to course correct, but instead, I dug my heels in even deeper. "Because it's new," I said, scrambling for an excuse that made sense. "And we're not really telling anyone."

"But you're bringing him as your date to the wedding." It wasn't a question, but it sounded like one, like maybe she didn't believe me. Like she was trying to catch me in the lie.

I cringed. I'd told her that Frasier was coming, when I hadn't even asked him if he would.

Instead of saying yes, I tried to backtrack a little. "It's new, so please...don't tell anyone that we're together for now. Not even Kit."

"Why not?" she'd asked. "Everyone will be so happy. This is great news, Bryn!"

Yeah. Great.

"I just..." I blew out a breath. I'd really done it now. "People might think it's weird—me dating Derek's best friend."

It would be weird, right?

Frasier entered the kitchen, and I nearly dropped the knife I'd been holding.

He furrowed his brow. "You okay?"

"I was lost in thought. You startled me, that's all." I smiled brightly.

He placed his hand on my arm, somehow making me feel both calmer and even more unsettled. "You sure?"

Frasier was so tall I had to tilt my head back to meet his eyes. Six-foot-two and 190 pounds of muscle. I nodded. He held my gaze for a moment then, seemingly satisfied, he went over to the sink to wash his hands.

As I saw it, I had two options. Tell my sister I'd lied. Or confess everything to Frasier and ask him to go with me to the wedding as my pity date. Both options were embarrassing in their own way. And besides, could I really ask Frasier to do that? It was the off-season, and he deserved a well-earned break.

What would he even think?

I knew how guarded he was about his privacy. He didn't like being photographed in public, and he was famously tight-lipped about his love life. If there was even a whisper of a hint that we were dating… I cringed.

I didn't want to rush into anything, so I decided to think on it over dinner. I was still thinking on it as we moved outside to let the dogs run around after we'd eaten and cleaned up.

"Bryn," Frasier said, and I turned to look at him. I sensed that he was nervous, but I didn't know why. "This might be overstepping, but…"

Frasier sighed, lifting his favorite Dartmouth hat to drag a hand through his hair. The brim was fraying, but it was still his favorite. He'd had the hat since college, and it was so faded it was almost gray.

His hair was long, so long that it curled up at the nape of

his neck. He looked like an ad for a wilderness survival guide. A man who was strong and rugged. Capable.

"Do you want me to go with you to your sister's wedding?"

"I—" I blinked a few times. Here he was, handing me the solution to all my problems, and he didn't even know it. Selfishly, I wanted to say yes. But I shook my head instead. "I can't ask you to do that for me. Not when you've already done so much," I added in a softer voice.

He was silent, and I couldn't get a read on him. And so, instead of pausing to let him speak, I rambled on. "Besides, I know it's later in the off-season," I continued. "So you have to think about training more seriously."

Frasier searched my eyes, and it felt as if he were peering into the depths of my soul. The man's intensity was unnerving, especially when it was directed solely at me.

"Bryn," he chided. "Come on."

"I hate asking you to give up precious vacation time to go to my sister's wedding. You're always over here, helping me, when I know you have better things you could be doing with your time."

A muscle in his neck jumped. "First of all, you didn't ask me to go with you. I offered. And there is nowhere I'd rather be. Nothing I'd rather be doing."

"Yeah, but—"

"*Nowhere*," he said in a solemn tone that quieted me.

"Thank you," I said, but it didn't feel like enough.

Frasier was one of the few people who got it. Who knew what it was like to have a spotlight turned on your pain. He'd been nothing short of amazing since Derek's death.

He'd been one of the first people to show up after Derek's passing. One of the few people who continued to show up. His friendship had kept me going, and the memories we shared had been a huge source of comfort.

People acted…funny when someone died. It was as if they didn't know whether to talk about the person, and it felt so lonely at times. But Frasier and I always talked about Derek, kept his memory alive. And I knew that Derek's parents appreciated that just as much as I did. I still met up with them regularly for dinner, and they still treated me like a daughter.

"What are the dates?" Frasier asked, pulling out his phone to check his calendar.

I relayed the info as I used my phone to search for the Huxley Grand Anguilla. I navigated to the resort amenities section and handed my phone to Frasier. "And it looks like they should have everything you need to train. Plus, they have a spa with massage therapists since I know how important rest and recovery are to your off-season training."

"Wow. That's…" He blinked a few times as if stunned. "Thank you for considering that."

"Of course."

He handed my phone back to me. Then he removed his cap, smoothed his hair back, and replaced his cap on his head with the bill facing backward. It made him look both boyish and hot. I did my best to ignore that sizzle of awareness his movements invoked.

He was attractive; he always had been. But it was the first time in a long time that I'd allowed myself to notice. And now that I had, I couldn't seem to stop.

He actually seemed to be considering this.

Tell him.

I should tell him that my sister thought we were dating.

Instead, I said, "If you go, you'll get an all-expenses-paid vacation to Anguilla. Plus, I'll owe you. Big-time."

I wasn't sure what Frasier could possibly want from me, what I could offer him in return, but it would be worth it not to have to go to my sister's wedding alone. This would be the first wedding I'd attended without Derek, and I had no idea how I was going to react. I loved Allie, and I desperately wanted to celebrate life and love—not dwell on everything I'd lost.

Sometimes that was the hardest part of losing someone—realizing that life moved on. Even when you didn't want it to. Even when you weren't ready.

"*If* I go, you're not paying for my trip," he said.

"You're right. My sister's fiancé is." I grinned, knowing Frasier wouldn't fight me on that.

We both knew Kit had more money than he knew what to do with. He was paying for the wedding but also travel and accommodations for all of his and Allie's immediate family. It was incredibly generous, but that was just the type of guy Kit was.

"You don't have to decide right now," I added. "You can think about it if you need to." I wanted Frasier to agree to it because he wanted to go with me, not because he felt like he should. And if I told him my sister thought we were dating, he'd *definitely* feel obligated to go. "I know I sprung this on you."

"I don't need to think about it."

"Right, but…maybe you should. I don't want you to do anything you're not comfortable with."

Frasier gave me the strangest look. But before I could even try to decipher it, his expression shifted to something more neutral. "As you said, it's only for a handful of days. How bad could it be?"

"You did what?" Georgia shrieked from the other side of the clothes rack.

She was helping me shop for my upcoming trip to Anguilla. And since it was a destination wedding, my sister had decided to cram everything into a five-day span. Bachelorette party. Rehearsal dinner. Wedding. It was going to be a lot, but at least Frasier would be there with me.

I glanced around the store and then glared at her over the top of the rack. "Jeez. Keep it down. It's not a big deal."

"Not a big deal?" She scoffed, wide amber eyes meeting mine as she joined me on my side. "Sweetie." She patted my arm. "You asked Frasier to be your date to your sister's destination wedding. On a romantic island." She held my gaze as if waiting for me to connect the dots.

"No. *He offered* to be my *plus-one*," I clarified, thinking there were no dots to be connected.

"But your family thinks you're dating."

"Right," I said. "Well, just my sister. And I swore her to secrecy."

"Mm-hmm." Georgia threaded her hand through her strawberry-blond tresses. In the years I'd known her, she'd been a platinum blonde, a redhead, and now she'd gone strawberry-blond. She was always changing her look, like a chameleon who jumped from one thing to another just so they could experience a new color.

"She's not going to tell." *She better not.* "I gave her some very compelling reasons to keep her mouth shut."

"You blackmailed her?" Georgia arched one eyebrow.

"No." I laughed, though that wasn't a terrible idea. "I may have used some emotional guilt to persuade her."

Georgia laughed. "Bryn!" She held a hand to her chest. "I didn't know you had it in you."

"There's gotta be some benefit to your husband dying," I

joked. Georgia didn't even bat an eye. She knew that morbid humor could be part of the healing process, at least for me.

"And Frasier?" she asked. "What did he say when you told him your sister thinks the two of you are together?"

"I…might have left that part out."

Her eyes bulged out of her head like one of those squeezy toys the dogs loved. "He doesn't know?"

I shook my head. "And he doesn't need to."

She furrowed her brow. "Won't he think it's odd when you're suddenly more affectionate?"

I lifted a shoulder, hoping she didn't see straight through my nonchalant attitude. "I told my sister it was new, and we were keeping it quiet. So I don't think she'll be surprised by the lack of PDA."

"Mm," was all Georgia said.

"Yeah. Okay. It's not the perfect plan, but it'll be fine."

"I get why you lied to your sister. But are you sure you should leave Frasier in the dark?"

"I don't want to complicate things."

She barked out a laugh. "Not complicate things. Yeah. Right."

"Come on," I said. "You know if I told him the truth, he would've felt obligated to go with me."

"When it comes to you, I'm pretty sure that man would say yes to anything."

That wasn't true, was it? But the more I thought about it, the more I realized that Frasier would do anything for me. And I would do anything for him. Because we were friends.

Georgia and I continued perusing the clothing racks, and I hoped that was the end of it.

"At least you picked a good one for your first—and hopefully only—fake relationship since Derek."

I laughed, feeling lighter. "Fake, one-sided relationship. Do you think I'm pathetic?"

"No." Her tone was firm. "I think you did what you had to do to protect yourself." My shoulders relaxed. "And I'm sure Frasier would understand if you told him."

Was that a not-so-subtle push to fess up?

I hung my head. "I'm sure you're right, but he's already doing so much for me. I just need to tell Allie the truth." I straightened, resolved. "I *will* tell Allie the truth." Before this gets even more out of hand.

"Sometimes I still don't understand how Frasier's single. You've seen what he looks like under the mountain-man aesthetic he's currently sporting, right?" she asked. "Because I have. And Frasier is a total hottie."

My sternum burned, and I wondered if you could get heartburn from oatmeal with a banana. I pressed my lips flat.

I had no reason to be jealous. Not that I was. Georgia was the team's official hair stylist, and she sometimes traveled with the Hawks to away games. Considering how much she loved to change her own color and style, it surprised me that she'd taken a job cutting men's hair. But she often used the off-season to take on other clients.

"I've known him since college, remember?" I'd watched him grow into the man he was today. "And besides, I thought you weren't into hockey players."

She wasn't interested in Frasier; I knew that. But her words had certainly provoked a strong reaction in me.

"I'm not," she said in a firm tone. "And even if I were, my brother would never allow it."

One of Georgia's older brothers, Daniel, was the general manager for the Hawks, one of the youngest in the league. Overprotective. A tad overbearing. A shark in business, but a softy when it came to his sister.

"So you're not attracted to him. Like, at *all?*" Georgia asked as I looked through the dress options.

I kept my eyes firmly trained on the dresses in front of me. "He's an attractive man. Objectively speaking," I added.

Who was I kidding? Frasier was hot.

"*I* know he's attractive." She wagged her finger at me. "The entire world can see how attractive he is. But I asked if *you* were attracted to him."

I shrugged, returning my attention to the clothes and hoping Georgia would do the same. But I could feel her watching me, practically bursting.

"Come on," I huffed. "Out with it. I know you want to say something." I knew Georgia well enough to suspect she had something on her mind.

"You know why your sister didn't question this surprise relationship with Frasier, right?" she asked.

"Because she wants it to be real."

"Maybe, but you and Frasier have good chem. Are you sure you both want to be just friends?" Her amber eyes bored into mine.

Good chem. That was such a hockey thing to say. The guys were always talking about which defensive and offensive pairs had good chem.

But when it came to Frasier, I didn't know what to think anymore. He didn't date. And after our conversation the other night, I knew he wasn't hooking up with anyone. But then I thought back on his comment—asking if I was offering to hook up with him. It made me wonder... Was he attracted to me?

And it wasn't just that. There were little moments when I'd catch him staring at me, or he'd let his touch linger. Anytime we watched TV, he'd place his arm around me, letting me cuddle into his side. Because we were friends, right?

Instead of answering Georgia's question—because I couldn't—I tried to deflect with humor. "We're not hockey players." I draped a black dress over my arm, adding to my pile of things to try on.

"No, but I'm sure he'd be happy to body check you." She grinned, removing the black dress I'd just selected and replacing it with another, more colorful one.

I pulled a face at her cheesy pun.

She laughed, not at all bothered. Then her expression turned more serious as she placed her hand on my arm. "Hockey jokes aside, you and Frasier are good together."

"Yeah. As friends."

"Oh, come on, Bryn." Her eyes danced with mischief. "I see the way he looks at you, and it's not like a friend."

I opened my mouth, ready to argue. It wasn't anything I hadn't heard before. Everyone was always trying to read more into Frasier's and my friendship than there was. Teammates. Family members. Friends. The internet.

"Stop shipping us," I teased.

I may have stopped wearing my wedding ring, but I was still very committed to my husband. I'd planned to spend the rest of my life with him, and just because his life had been cut short didn't mean my love ended.

Georgia watched me, giving me a cryptic smile. "You know it would be okay if you weren't *just* friends, though, right?"

"I—" I cleared my throat and glanced at the floor. I wasn't so sure about that. "I just don't see that happening."

"Why not?" Her tone was laced with curiosity and free of judgment.

I sighed, a million reasons racing through my mind.

Derek, for starters. What the hell would he think? What would his parents think? This wasn't just me dating another man—it was Derek's best friend.

And even if you ignored all that, I wasn't sure Frasier was interested. I wasn't sure it was a good idea to go there. What if Frasier and I tried to be something more, and it made everything awkward? What if I screwed up one of the most important relationships in my life?

Ultimately, I shook my head.

"Because you're not ready to date anyone? Or because you're not interested in Frasier?"

"I'm not sure I'll ever be *ready* to date someone, but also..." I swallowed hard around the boulder lodged in my throat. I didn't even know how to say it.

"You still have needs," Georgia offered.

"I, um... Yeah," I said, grateful that she understood.

God, it felt good to admit that. Freeing.

I didn't just miss my husband, I missed being held. Touched. I missed sex.

Georgia wrapped her arm around me, hugging me tight. "Of course you do."

I released a heavy sigh, giving her a quick squeeze in return. "Thanks for always understanding."

Georgia—like Frasier and my other best friend, Logan— had been my rock. I'd had to survive one of the most painful life experiences in a very public way, and she'd been there for me every step of the way.

When I'd been living in a haze of shock and grief, she'd whipped into action. She'd fixed my hair and makeup many times, making sure I looked fabulous even when I was falling apart. And she'd stood by my side at his funeral, at the tribute games, holding my hand when I needed extra support. The games had been deeply moving and beautiful but also profoundly painful.

For now, I mostly preferred to watch the games on TV from the privacy of my living room, cuddling with Bacon and Biscuit while Georgia did her nails and Logan yelled at the screen, at least when she wasn't playing herself in the PWHL for Minnesota. Sometimes Kylie joined us. Georgia had recommended that I reach out to her to help me with PR after Derek's death, and Kylie and I had since become close friends.

Sitting in the WAGs suite with the other wives, girlfriends, and partners was…unthinkable. And even though everyone had been nice, I felt "other" somehow since losing Derek. I wasn't a wife; I was a widow. It was a completely different club—and one I'd never wanted to be a part of.

"Hey," Georgia said, placing her hand on my arm. I startled from the contact. "You okay?"

"Honestly?" I swallowed back the emotions, willing the tears away. "No. But I don't really want to talk about it either."

Crying wouldn't change anything. Nothing would bring back Derek or the dreams we'd shared for the future.

No one knew that Derek and I had been trying to conceive when he'd died, not even my closest friends. And now, it would never happen.

Georgia's frown deepened. "You sure?"

"I'm sure," I said, eager to move on. I was twenty-seven, and I'd already found and lost the love of my life. It was… a lot.

"You know I'm always here if you want to talk." She hugged me. "Or not talk."

"I know. And thank you. I appreciate it more than you'll ever know."

She released me, and I gestured to the dresses draped over my arm. "I'm going to try these on."

She trailed me to the fitting room, taking the one next to mine. We were quiet apart from the rustle of fabric as we changed. I ruled the first dress out before I'd even zipped it up all the way. My body had changed, and I was still getting used to what looked good on me now. What fit my life now.

The next one was definitely better. It was the dress Georgia had picked.

"What do you think?" The fabric flowed around my legs as I stepped into the hallway. It was beachy, and I already felt like I was on vacation.

Georgia pulled her curtain aside. "Love it. That color is great on you, just as I knew it would be."

"Thanks." I grinned. "I like that on you too," I said, admiring the pink jumpsuit she was wearing.

She grabbed another dress from a nearby rack. "Try this one next."

I jerked my head back. It was gorgeous, colorful and flowy, but also…sexy.

"Really?" I asked, studying the low neckline. Lower than anything I'd worn in a while, though I mostly lived in scrubs or yoga pants these days.

"Yes, girl." She handed it to me before shoving me back toward the fitting rooms. "Be colorful. Live life. Have fun."

That used to be me. Colorful. Carefree.

As I stared at myself in the mirror, the dress held up to my front, I realized that I wanted to be that girl again.

CHAPTER THREE

"**W**hat do you think about Kovi joining the team?" Gabe asked, clearly trying to strike a balance between being discreet since we were in the weight room at the Atlas Center and being heard as music blasted through the speakers.

I grunted in response, then pushed up the bar, grateful my teammate was spotting me so I didn't drop it on my face. When I reached the top of the move, he helped me maneuver the bar to rest in the cradle.

"Thanks." I sat up, toweling off my face and grabbing some water.

Carson Kovalsky had spent the past few years in Nashville before he'd been traded to the Hawks. Kovi was a cocky motherfucker, but he was talented. He'd been part of the USA Hockey National Development program, playing for a few years in London after that, before being drafted to the NHL.

"He has a lot of potential," I said, wanting to be fair. I didn't know the guy all that well. It wasn't his fault he'd been brought in to fill Derek's position on the line.

"Let's hope he lives up to it," Gabe said.

I only hoped that Kovi and Boone, one of our D-men, would have some good chem once they spent more time on the ice together. Because so far, the only thing they seemed to be doing effectively was annoying the shit out of each other.

Training camp would be starting before we knew it, and I was easing back into my workout routine in preparation for the season. A few of the guys were in the weight room at the Atlas Center, including Boone, Zayn, and my backup goalie, Quinn.

I knew what it was like to be in Quinn's shoes. To feel the constant pressure of keeping your spot so you weren't sent back down to the AHL. I'd spent a few years in the AHL, honing my skills before landing a one-way contract to New York.

"What do you think about him?" I asked.

Gabe was a talented left winger and one of my closest friends on the Hawks. If I was known as a bear—grumpy and reserved—he was the NHL's golden boy—charming, well-liked, at least off the ice. On the ice, he was known for his elite offensive play. He was not only reliable but high energy, often bringing a sort of golden retriever vibe to the team.

"He could be a huge asset on the ice but a potential liability off it."

I shook my head. "You've been listening to the *Hot as Puck* podcast again, haven't you?" I teased.

Gabe grabbed some plates, carrying them back over. "What makes you say that?"

I chuckled. "Because that's almost exactly what they said on a recent episode. Would you really want your new teammates judging you based on the opinion of a rival player who clearly has an axe to grind?"

"Yeah. What is the story there?" Gabe asked, referring to

the way one of the Hot as Puck podcast hosts, Levi, had referred to our new teammate.

"How would I know?"

"I just figured…" He lifted a shoulder. "Since Bryn is besties with Logan, she'd have the inside info."

I laughed. "Logan might be one of Bryn's closest friends, but I rarely ever see her."

Logan lived in Minnesota and played for the PWHL. And she was always busy—training for her own season, playing hockey, running camps, or watching a game for the podcast.

"Maybe I'll ask her." He pulled out his phone.

"Do you want her to high-stick your balls?" I joked. But I wasn't joking, not really. Logan was tough. "And how do you even have her number?"

"I don't. I was going to DM her."

I barked out a laugh. "Good luck with that, Goldie."

"What?"

"DM her? Do you know how many DMs she probably gets a day? And you're counting on the fact that she'll actually check them."

"She'll respond," he said with a certainty that was either enviable or delusional. I couldn't quite decide.

"You are such an optimist. I guess they don't call you the Golden Boy of the NHL for nothing."

He rolled his eyes. "Yeah. Whatever. No one's perfect."

"You have one of the cleanest reputations in the league."

"Well, that's not that difficult, considering the competition." He grinned.

I chuckled, thinking of some of our teammates who loved to party. Loved to fight—both on and off the ice.

"What about you?" he asked.

"What about me?" I gulped down some water.

"Going to try to beat your record for goose eggs?"

Last season, I'd played my best season ever since joining

the NHL. I'd had more goose eggs than ever—games where the Hawks got a shutout and allowed zero goals against our net. And the fans liked to celebrate—by tossing plastic eggs on the ice like the ones the Easter Bunny had left for us as kids.

"That's always the goal."

He rubbed his hands together. "I can't wait to see what the fans come up with this year."

I chuckled. The fans had gotten more creative this past season, tossing more colorful and elaborately decorated eggs. Sometimes the maintenance staff had even discovered items hidden inside the eggs. Often it was a name and a phone number, but sometimes it was candy or even a mini canvas painted with my likeness or one of my teammates.

We ate that shit up, though we had to pretend as if we were unaffected since management hated it. Or at least, they claimed to. But if it kept the fans engaged and the seats filled, management couldn't be too pissed about it.

After that, we stopped chatting so much and focused on our workout. My muscles were screaming at me by the time we finished, but it was Bryn's words that continued to haunt me. Pushing me harder with every rep. Every exercise.

I already had my love story.

I could understand why she might believe that—her husband had died. But she held on to this deep-seated conviction that she would never be happy in love again. And the idea that she'd convinced herself it was true made me incredibly sad.

"Ice bath then sauna?" Gabe suggested.

"Sounds good," I said, even though we both knew it would hurt like a bitch.

When we reached the treatment room, we stripped down to our compression shorts.

"Audiobook?" he asked.

I held up my phone, gritting my teeth at the missed call notification. Someone had left a message from an unknown number, and I had a good feeling I knew exactly who it was.

"You good?" Gabe was watching me with a concerned expression, and it was then I realized how hard I was squeezing my phone.

I loosened my grip and tried to release my anger as well. *He's not worth it.*

"I've got *The Order of Time* cued up," I said.

I tapped play, and the sound of Benedict Cumberbatch's rich, velvety voice filled the room. As he explored the nature of time, Gabe and I climbed into our respective ice baths. I eased into the cold water, feeling the bite of the chill with every inch of my body that was submerged. I took a long, deep breath.

Most people's first instinct when climbing into an ice bath was to stop breathing, but that was the opposite of what you needed to do. Slow, controlled, deep breaths were key.

"Ten minutes?"

"Fifteen," I said, focusing on my breathing. I'd already set a sleep timer on the audiobook, but I glanced at the digital clock on the wall, noting the time. And then I let go.

I thought about the upcoming season. About Bryn. About Derek.

For over a decade, Derek and I had shared the dream of hoisting the Cup over our heads. First as college students, hoping to make it to the NHL. Then as pro athletes, following each other's careers from opposite sides of the country. And finally—for a short time—as teammates once more.

But now, he'd never see that dream materialize. It was up to me to make it happen—for both of us. And I knew many of my teammates felt the same way. That additional pressure to make every game matter—for Derek.

We were a tight team, and his death had been sudden, unexpected, and absolutely devastating—to me, Bryn, the team, to everyone who'd known him.

I could remember that morning. We'd played my old team, New York, the night before, and we'd won in overtime. I'd texted Derek to see if he was coming down to breakfast. It wasn't unusual for him to skip, so I hadn't thought much of it at the time. But after he'd missed breakfast, I'd pounded on his door to get him to wake the fuck up because he was going to be late for the bus. Then the texts started from Bryn, asking if I'd seen Derek. And then Coach's ashen face delivering the news that Derek was gone.

My best friend had died in the night, alone in a fucking hotel room. And none of us had had a clue until it was too late.

Gabe shook my shoulder, and I realized then that he'd climbed out of his tub and was standing before me. "Time's up." He tapped the edge of my tub, and I noted he already had a towel wrapped around his waist.

The room was silent. I didn't know how long it had been since the audiobook had shut off. I pushed myself upright. Water sloshed against the edges of the tub, my body confused by the sudden change in temperature. My skin went from freezing cold to burning hot in mere seconds. I breathed through it, knowing the worst of it would pass soon. I just had to make it through.

It felt like that had been my mantra the past year and a half. *Just make it through.*

Hockey had helped. My teammates. Bryn.

But I didn't want to just make it through. Not anymore.

Gabe handed me a towel. "Where's your head at?" he asked as I wrapped it around my waist.

Where it always was. When I wasn't focused on hockey,

my thoughts were on Bryn. It was a problem, especially lately.

When I didn't immediately answer, Gabe peered into my eyes, scanning them as if checking for a concussion. When he tried to hold his hand up to my forehead, I shoved him away playfully, laughing as I said, "Fuck off."

He seemed to think that because he had an undergrad degree in biology and watched a ton of medical dramas that he was a doctor or something.

"I may not be a doctor, but I know something's wrong," he said, turning serious. "What's bothering you, Fizzy?"

What was bothering me?

I was tangled up in fucking knots. I was grieving my best friend while falling in love with his wife. She didn't have a clue how I felt about her, and I was about to spend five days with her on a romantic island for her sister's wedding.

What have I gotten myself into?

I opened the door to the sauna, and Gabe followed me inside. We sank down on opposite benches, the heat seeping into my pores and making me relax. Gabe was silent, and I knew he was still waiting for me to tell him what was going on.

Maybe it was the endorphins from the cold plunge followed by the sauna—the startling contrast. Or maybe it was the warm, enclosed space that felt sacred, like a confessional. But somehow, I found myself admitting, "Bryn's sister is having a destination wedding, and I offered to be her plus-one."

He leaned back on his elbows, watching me. "Interesting."

Gabe was the one person who knew how I felt about Bryn. He'd caught me smiling at a text from her on the jet one night toward the end of the season. When I wouldn't tell him who I was texting, he'd grabbed my phone. His eyes had widened in shock and then landed on mine in understanding. He hadn't said anything more about it then or since, but I'd figured it was only a matter of time.

Apparently, I'd given him the opening he'd been waiting for because he said, "Her plus-one or her date?"

"Plus-one," I said in a firm tone, warning him not to push it.

"Holy shit." A smile formed on his lips. "This is a golden opportunity,"

I frowned. "How do you figure?"

He nodded, and I could see the wheels turning. "Time to get out of the friend zone, baby!"

"I—" I shook my head. "You're—"

Gabe held up a hand. "Don't try to deny it. And don't try to make this about Derek either. He was a good man and a good husband. I miss him like hell, but that won't change the fact that he's gone."

He's gone.

Sometimes it was still difficult to wrap my head around that fact.

I knew Gabe wasn't trying to be harsh or hurtful. He was trying to be honest. Even so, I didn't want to talk about this anymore.

"I'm done," I said, shaking my head.

Gabe continued, undeterred by my surly attitude. "No, Frasier. *I'm* done. I'm done standing by and being silent. I can't keep watching you tear yourself up over this."

I clenched my fists. "You're overstepping," I bit out.

"Am I?" he asked, not willing to back down. "Because I thought we were friends. And friends are there for each other."

"I'm in love with my best friend's wife. Does that sound like something a good friend would do?" I growled.

Gabe slicked his hair away from his face. "The fact that

you love her doesn't take away from the friendship you had with him."

"Doesn't it?" I asked, more annoyed with myself than anything else. "Isn't it a betrayal of our friendship? Isn't it *wrong*?"

Gabe sighed. "If anything, it's…" He seemed to search for the right word, eventually settling on, "Understandable."

"Understandable," I scoffed, my gaze focused on the floor.

I smoothed my hair back from my face, sweat dripping down my forehead. I grabbed one of the peppermint-scented towels and draped it over the back of my neck, hoping it would soothe my frazzled thoughts as quickly as it was cooling my skin.

"You've known Bryn since college. She's always been a part of your life, but especially since…" He sighed. "Anyway, it's understandable that something so tragic would bring you even closer together. And knowing Derek, I think he'd be grateful."

"Grateful," I spat. What a fucking joke.

"He would," Gabe said, not backing down. "I think he'd be grateful that you've been there for Bryn. That someone he was so close to loves her."

I heard him, but I wasn't sure I agreed. At least not entirely. I knew Derek would appreciate everything I'd done to help Bryn. I knew he'd want her to be happy. I just… "Fuck." I clenched and unclenched my fists at my sides. "Why is this so hard?"

"Grief sucks, man." Gabe leaned back against the bench on his side. "It fucking sucks."

"Yes, it does," I echoed.

We were quiet after that, finishing out our remaining time in the sweat box before it was on to the showers. I might not agree with everything Gabe had said, but I was grateful for his support and his friendship. I resolved to be a better friend, and not just a better teammate, to him as well. I knew that I'd closed myself off after Derek's death, and I knew that Gabe—like many of my teammates—had tried to be there for me.

I padded out to the stalls to grab my clothes and then stopped. Sometimes it still caught me off guard, seeing someone else's name on the stall next to mine where Derek's should've been.

The first skate, the first game, without him had been gut-wrenching. Even now, I still sometimes found it difficult to be at the rink without him. We'd shared so many memories together—both on and off the ice—and I felt closer to him at the rink than anywhere.

Gabe placed his hand on my shoulder, a silent show of support as we stared at where Derek's name had been. Neither of us spoke of it again until we were headed out to the parking lot.

I thought about what Gabe had said. About Bryn. About Derek. There had been a period of time after Derek's passing when I hadn't been sure I could lace up my skates again and get on the ice. But then I'd think about how pissed Derek would be if he knew I'd stopped.

The fact that I kept playing the game we'd loved without him didn't diminish the time we'd played together. Was it different? Yes. But he would've wanted me to continue playing.

And while my relationship with Bryn wasn't comparable, the thought certainly gave me pause. Maybe there was some-thing to what Gabe had said. Maybe my relationship with Bryn now—and the one I wanted to have with her going forward—didn't have to take away from what they'd shared.

If losing Derek had taught me anything, it was that life was short. Don't live with regrets. Even so, I was conflicted. I might not want to live with regrets, but I wondered what I'd regret more—pursuing Bryn and risking our friendship or always wondering.

Gabe seemed to have a plan for that, but I'd cut him off. And now that I'd calmed down some, I couldn't stop wondering about what he'd been going to say.

"What did you mean earlier?" I asked Gabe, my mind circling back to our conversation. "About this being a 'golden opportunity'?"

The corner of Gabe's mouth tilted upward ever so slightly. "This is your chance to show Bryn what it looks like to be more than friends. To show her exactly how you'd treat her if she were yours."

"I *do*," I said, annoyed he didn't see that.

Every day. Bryn was the first thing on my mind when I woke and the last when I went to sleep. We texted throughout the day. I brought her coffee at the hospital. I helped with stuff around the house.

"No." Gabe's tone was firm. "You do all the things a brother might do—take the car for repairs, fix things around the house."

"I—" I opened my mouth to protest but then closed it.

Was that what Bryn thought? Was that how she saw me? As a brother? I cringed.

He pointed at me, a shit-eating grin splitting his face. "Now you're getting it."

"And you think the wedding is my chance to 'show' her?" I asked, using air quotes.

"Yes." He nodded emphatically.

"I don't know," I hedged. All the same reasons for not pursuing her were still there. What if I ruined everything?

"Dude, it's the perfect solution. Totally safe. If she's not into it, apologize and say you got carried away with the vacation vibes or the romance of the wedding. But if she is..." He lifted his shoulder, a smirk on his face as if to say, "Well..."

It sounded great. In theory.

In reality, I had some major reservations.

"It feels…dishonest."

"Think of it as a way to test the waters."

Or to fuck myself over in the process.

"She's not ready to date. And even if she were, who's to say she'd be interested in me?"

"You're joking, right?" He stared at me. "Of course she's interested in you."

I jerked my head back. "She told you that?"

"She didn't have to, Fiz. It's written all over her face. Both your faces, actually, any time you're together."

I shoved my hands into my pockets, my mind spinning. I thought about the way she looked at me sometimes, her pupils darkening. I thought about the things she did, the effort she put into my needs. Sharing the dogs, making meals, immediately considering what I might need if I went with her to Anguilla.

My ex had assumed that the off-season meant I was *off*. Sheree had always griped that I'd had to continue training and focusing on my recovery. But Bryn not only understood my needs, she had gone out of her way to make sure they'd be met.

"Did she tell you she wasn't ready to date?" Gabe asked.

"Not in so many words." I wasn't going to betray her trust by telling him how Bryn really felt about it.

"What exactly did she say?"

That she was sick of her family trying to set her up on dates. And she'd already had her love story.

He waved his hands in the air. "It doesn't matter. What matters is that she was with the same guy for almost a decade. She hasn't dated in a long-ass time. She probably doesn't even remember what a date is."

I rolled my eyes, though I knew there was some truth to what he said.

"I know you guys hang out a lot, and that's great. But maybe you need to do a little more wooing."

"Wooing?" I coughed on the word.

"My sister forced me to watch *Bridgerton* with her after her last breakup. It was brutal. Point is, wooing works."

I chuckled. "Wooing," I said again. "I'm not sure Bryn wants to be wooed."

"Every woman wants to be wooed."

"Right. And you know this because you're such an expert," I teased. Gabe had been single for as long as I'd been, maybe even longer.

"Let me ask you something," Gabe said. "If something weren't working for you on the ice, what would you do?"

"Ask for help from Price." The goalie coach. "Practice more."

"Yes, but..." Gabe huffed. "If someone kept scoring on you. Say, in the five-hole, would you just keep doing the same thing? Or would you change it up?"

"I'd change it up." *Obviously.*

"So, with Bryn. Has your approach been getting the results you want?"

I frowned. We both knew the answer to that. I shook my head.

"Then maybe—" he clapped a hand on my shoulder and stood "—it's time to shake things up."

Gabe was right. It was time to shake things up. No more "just getting through." No more regrets.

CHAPTER FOUR

Bryn

"Five days until my wedding!" my sister squealed through my earbuds. "I'm so excited that I get to see you tomorrow!"

Allie had called me a few days ago, and we'd been playing phone tag. Until now. Okay, honestly, I'd been avoiding her until I could put it off no longer. I'd waited until the very last minute.

Allie had to suspect that I was upset, right?

I knew she was preoccupied with the last-minute preparations and excitement. Just like I knew I needed to tell her the truth about my relationship with Frasier, but I'd been dreading it.

Also, I was still hurt by what she'd said about the light going out of me. And while I wanted to gloss over it and just enjoy the wedding, I was a wreck. The closer we got to the actual trip, the more nervous I grew.

It was a good thing Allie was keeping me busy with all her color-coded spreadsheets. My sister's "Bride Tribe" group chat had been blowing up this past week, and I had a feeling things would only continue to intensify as we approached the big day.

I loved Allie, and I would always be there for her. But I had to wonder…had I been this over the top before my wedding?

Honestly, I couldn't remember. And part of me hated that I couldn't remember. So much had happened since then. If I could go back in time, I'd tell myself to slow down, really take it all in.

Every moment with Derek. Every look and touch. I swallowed hard. All of it. Gone. Over far too soon. In the blink of an eye.

One night, I'd gone to bed happily married. The next morning, I'd woken up to my worst nightmare—my husband was dead.

It felt like I'd lived a lifetime since my wedding day, even though it had only been three years. At this point, I'd been a widow almost as long as I'd been a wife.

You can't go back. You can only move forward.

It was something my therapist and I had discussed a lot. And yet, I often found myself wondering what I could've done differently. Wondering if I should've known. If I could've somehow changed the outcome.

It was a futile exercise; I knew that. But sometimes, I couldn't seem to make myself stop. I often lay awake at night, imagining if I could've somehow saved Derek.

Everyone—even my fellow medical professionals—told me there was no way I could've known, nothing I could've done. But I was his wife, damn it. And I worked in the medical field. Shouldn't I have realized something wasn't right? Shouldn't I have sensed it?

There was a knock at the back door, and my mood instantly lifted when I saw Frasier standing there, hand raised in greeting. Bacon and Biscuit trotted over, tails wagging, eager to greet him.

I didn't know when it had happened, but slowly, Frasier and I had fallen into a bit of a routine the past year. Frasier would come over Thursday nights after practice. He'd work on a project. We'd eat dinner and watch a movie, and then he'd leave the dogs with me since I had Fridays off. They'd stay with me through the weekend or any time he had an out-of-town game.

It was nice. Cozy.

Sometimes we talked—about Derek or the team, about my work, or whatever else was on our minds. Sometimes we didn't. And that was okay too.

I beckoned Frasier inside, holding up my phone to signal that I was in the middle of a conversation. Frasier stepped inside, closing the door softly behind him. His baseball cap shadowed his eyes, making him look more dangerous than he was. His hair curled at the nape of his neck. It wasn't as long as it had been, but he was still rocking the beard.

"And you packed everything for the bachelorette party, rehearsal dinner, and wedding?" Allie asked, reminding me that I was still on the phone with her.

"Yes. I promise. You have nothing to worry about," I said in a tone I hoped was reassuring.

I knew Allie was stressed, and I knew we'd need to discuss my hurt feelings at some point. But for now, I wanted to keep the focus on her wedding. She deserved to enjoy this moment that she'd been looking forward to and planning for so long. It was a big reason why I was even hesitating to tell her the truth about Frasier and me. There could be a lot of drama around weddings, and I didn't want to add to it.

"Okay. I just…" She sighed. "I really want everything to be perfect."

Ah. To go back to a simpler time when everything was easy.

I'd never admit it, but I envied my sister sometimes. Or maybe I just missed the girl I used to be—naïve, so unaware of how painful life could be. But happy.

I sighed. I wanted to be happy again. Genuinely happy.

I'd catch glimpses of it every so often—former me. The one who was carefree and joyful. But it felt like trying on an old piece of clothing that was two sizes too small.

Frasier tapped my foot with his. And when I glanced up at him, he raised one brow as if to ask, "You good?"

I nodded, smiling at his uncanny ability to communicate without words.

Some people found him to be grumpy, territorial, and off-putting—hence the nickname, Bear, which he'd gotten in college. But to me, he'd always been more of a giant teddy bear. Protective, fiercely loyal. And he gave some of the best hugs. I'd definitely needed a lot of them over the past year and a half.

To everyone else, he was Frasier, Holmes, Fizzy. His nickname "Fizzy" was a nod to both his first name and the fact that he didn't get shaken on the ice. He was known for keeping his cool. He didn't get rattled when the opposing team chirped or made a shot. He ignored it or brushed it off and focused on the next play. But to me, he'd always be Bear.

I opened my arms, and he pulled me into his for a hug. His hair was still wet, and god, he smelled good. Distractingly so. Or maybe I was distracted by the way his T-shirt clung to his chest, stretching across his powerful muscles.

What is wrong with me? I wondered as I pulled back. I was ogling my best friend.

Georgia's comments about how attractive Frasier was must have gotten into my head. At least, that's what I kept trying to tell myself. But lately, it felt as if something had switched back on inside me. A desire to live and have fun. It was as if my libido had come back online.

My therapist said that was a good thing. She was encouraged by how I was processing my grief, especially the shifts she'd noticed lately. I didn't disagree. Something felt… different lately. Lighter, somehow. Maybe it was that I'd survived the first year without Derek—the first Christmas and New Year's. Our first anniversary without him. My birthday and his.

Maybe it was the fact that I'd finally been allowed to grieve in peace. To get back to living my life and going through my routine without cameras constantly following me. I'd found my new normal, and Frasier was a big part of that.

Lately, my therapist had encouraged me to try to find more opportunities for fun, to seek out joy even in the small moments. She called them "glimmers." I loved that idea, and I'd been trying. But sometimes, it was easier said than done.

I'd redecorated my bedroom, though I later realized that I'd been using the project as a way to temporarily fill the void and regain a sense of control. I'd revisited old hobbies, like dancing. I'd taken up new hobbies, only to later quit them. I'd even bought some toys in an attempt to shake things up and do some self-exploration.

But both the desire for joy and my body's craving for physical affection and sex felt almost foreign at this point. As foreign as smiling or laughing had felt for months after Derek's passing. But I'd learned how to do those things again. Maybe I could learn to enjoy myself again, and not just for the sake of appeasing everyone else's worries.

My sister was still talking, and I continued to "mm-hmm" at the appropriate intervals.

I knew the wedding preparations were important to her,

and I wanted to be supportive. But after everything I'd been through, it all seemed so…trivial. A wedding was a big celebration, yes. But it was also one day. A marriage lasted a lifetime—or at least, it was supposed to.

Frasier pointed at my bedroom, and I nodded, knowing he wanted to work on his latest project—installing a custom shelving unit in my closet. The dogs trailed after him, and I was eager to wrap up my call so I could join them.

"So…" Allie started, and I hated when she prefaced stuff. It always made me nervous. "This thing with Frasier…"

Crap! I glanced down the hall, praying Frasier was out of earshot. And then I stepped out onto the back patio, closing the door behind me.

I kept my voice low, hoping it didn't betray my panic. "Please tell me you haven't told anyone."

No one could find out.

"Of course not. But… I don't get it, Bryn. Why are you being so secretive about it? This is exciting."

"I told you why," I said, annoyed that she was pushing me on it. But also, annoyed with myself for lying. Frasier valued his privacy, and here I was, threatening everything. I felt awful that I'd betrayed his trust and put him in this situation.

"If I were you, I'd be joyous. And you can bet that I'd tell everyone."

I should've been relieved by her support—not that Frasier and I were actually dating. But instead, I was angry. All I could think was, *but you're not me. And you have no idea how I really feel!*

So instead of telling her the truth, I said, "I should go," eager to get off the phone.

"Bryn…" She sighed. "Don't be like that."

Like what? I wanted to ask. But I didn't have the energy to deal with it. Sometimes lately, it felt as if she wanted to put a timeline on my grief. Like I'd been sad for too long. I'd become too much of a drag.

"I'll see you soon, Al."

"See you soon," she said in a resigned tone. "Love you." Her voice sounded small, far away.

"Love you too," I said, ending the call.

I stared out at my small yard, kicking myself for how that had gone down. Why couldn't she understand? And why hadn't I just told her the truth?

I took a moment to collect myself. When Derek and I had first moved in, we'd been excited to have some green space, a garden. But it had languished since his death, and I was surprised anything was still alive. Despite my neglect, a few flowers had still decided to bloom, showing that growth was possible even when everything seemed bleak.

Something fluttered down from the sky, and at first, I thought it was a leaf. But when I looked closer, I realized it was a butterfly. I smiled, lifting a hand to my mouth at the sight of it.

Hi, Derek.

I watched the butterfly for a moment longer, feeling calmer.

Not long after Derek's funeral, on a particularly low day, a bright-blue and black butterfly had landed on me. Ever since then, I'd associated butterflies with Derek. And once I'd made the connection, I felt like I saw them everywhere. Sometimes, it was a real butterfly like the one in the garden. Other times, it was a butterfly painted on a rock. A sign.

Anytime I saw one, it brought me comfort and made me smile. It was why I'd gotten my tattoo on his birthday. I turned my wrist to admire the design. At first glance, it looked like a butterfly. But when you looked closer, the butterfly was actually comprised of sixes in many sizes. The tattoo artist had played with the spacing and sizes until it had looked just how I'd wanted. And I loved that the sixes represented Derek's lucky number, the one he'd worn on his jersey.

I sighed. I might not like how I'd left things with my sister, but I also knew I wasn't ready to clear the air either. So, I shoved my phone into my back pocket and headed back inside.

CHAPTER FIVE

Bryn

I padded down the hall to my closet where Frasier was measuring the space. I couldn't stop myself from watching his forearms as they flexed. God, I loved a good forearm.

"Bryn?" Frasier asked.

"Hm?" When I met his gaze, he was watching me with a curious expression.

Crap. I'd been checking him out. *Again.*

His smile was bemused. "I asked what time you wanted to leave for the airport tomorrow?"

"I don't know. Maybe eight? Hopefully evening traffic will have calmed down some by then."

"Sounds good. Oh, I brought something for you. For the trip." He stood and dusted off his hands before reaching into his tool bag to grab something.

He handed me a package in brown paper. It was clumsily wrapped, but I was delighted by the surprise. It was the size and shape of a book, and when I tore off the paper, I gasped.

"How?" I gaped down at it then back at him.

Frasier lifted a shoulder as if it was no big deal, but the

tips of his ears were an adorable shade of pink. It was a huge freaking deal.

"But this is the new Meghan Hart and Penelope Glass book."

I turned it over in my hands, admiring the cover and scanning the back. Not only that, it was the special edition version with foil on the cover, printed edges, and custom interior artwork. It was gorgeous, and I couldn't wait to read it.

"It isn't even officially published yet," I said, astonished to be holding it in my hands. In fact, it wasn't releasing for another week or two. It wasn't even on the shelves.

I wasn't surprised that Frasier had been able to score an early copy. He was a celebrity after all, and it wouldn't take much to pull a few strings. But he rarely, if ever, used his status to get what he wanted. And the fact that he'd gone to the effort—for me... I blinked back a few tears, suddenly overcome with emotion.

"Check out the inside," he said in a gruff voice.

I opened the cover and froze when I saw what was on the title page. My heart was pounding as I read the words.

Bryn,

The best love stories have no end. Here's to your happily ever after.

Meghan Hart and Penelope Glass

The bridge of my nose stung at those words, scrawled in one of my favorite authors' hands.

The best love stories have no end.

It felt like a message from the universe.

When I glanced up at Frasier, he was watching me with a

wary expression. Was he worried about how I'd react? He shouldn't have been. Not only had Frasier gotten me an early copy of a special edition book by my favorite authors, but he'd had them sign it to me.

"Oh my god. Thank you." I nearly tackled him in my excitement.

He chuckled, and the dogs jumped at us, thinking it was playtime. Which had the effect of me tumbling forward and the four of us all but wrestling on the floor. Biscuit licked at my face, and I playfully tried to bat her away. And then Bacon joined in, and I couldn't stop laughing.

"Oh my god." I held my arms up to block my face, my stomach aching from laughter. Tears leaked from my eyes. "Stop."

When the dogs wouldn't stop, Frasier rolled so he was on top of me, shielding me from them. His muscular body was lined up with mine. Our eyes locked, and my breath caught in my throat.

Holy...

I licked my lips, and his eyes tracked the movement, his Adam's apple bobbing. He stroked the side of my face, dragging his hand slowly down over my jaw and neck. My eyes fluttered shut briefly. *Holy shit, that feels good.*

When I reopened my eyes, his gaze was searching, questioning. He leaned forward ever so slightly, and for a moment, I thought he was going to kiss me. Did I want him to kiss me?

He inched closer, so close I could feel his breath on my skin. I could see the golden flecks in his blue eyes. A starburst ring surrounded his pupil, and it reminded me of the time I'd seen a full solar eclipse. It had been beautiful and awe-inspiring, much like the man staring back at me.

One of the dogs barked, and I startled, nearly head-butting Frasier in the process. Luckily, he had quick reflexes, and he dodged me.

Frasier jolted upright. "I should take them out. I'll be right back."

It was almost as if he couldn't get out of there fast enough. He nearly tripped over Biscuit in his haste, and I wasn't sure whether to laugh or feel rejected. Because what the hell was *that*?

I stood and smoothed down my hair, trying to calm my racing heart. I wondered what would've happened if we hadn't been interrupted. I wondered—again—if Frasier had been going to kiss me, or if he'd simply gotten caught up in the moment.

I placed my hand on my neck, remembering the feel of his touch. The way he'd looked at me intently as he'd slid his hand over my skin. Sparks still danced from where he'd touched me.

I sighed and headed toward my bedroom. My hands were shaky as I placed my new book in my carry-on bag. I still couldn't believe he'd given me a signed copy of an unreleased book by my favorite authors. I couldn't think of a more perfect gift. And the fact that Frasier had known, had gone to the trouble, meant more than anything.

Why had he done that?

Because we were friends, and it was a thoughtful gift?

I was tempted to text Georgia to ask for her opinion, but I also didn't want to read too much into the situation. I hadn't dated anyone since college, and that was nearly ten years ago. I was out of practice. But Frasier's and my wrestling match had sent my brain into overdrive, and now I was over-thinking everything.

When Frasier returned a few minutes later with the dogs in tow, he said nothing and neither did I. He merely resumed working on the shelving, acting as if the almost-kiss had never happened. But my body was still tingling from his proximity. From the way he'd looked at me, hovered over me, his eyes heavy with desire.

I rolled my lips between my teeth. If the almost-kiss had made things this awkward, I could only imagine how bad it would have been if we'd actually kissed.

"That escalated quickly," I joked, feeling the need to say something about what had happened. "Sorry for tackling you." I laughed nervously.

He chuckled, and it dispelled some of the tension inside me. "Maybe you should join Logan on the ice if you're going to start body checking people."

"Not sure I'm cut out for that." I grinned.

"You're tougher than you look."

My chest warmed from his compliment. He always knew just what to say to build me up.

"Thank you again for the book." I met his eyes, wishing I could convey just how much it meant to me. "It'll be perfect reading for our trip."

We were scheduled to fly from LA to Miami. After that, we'd board another plane to Anguilla.

He kept his attention on the shelves when he spoke. "I'm glad you like it."

Biscuit nudged me with her head, begging me to pet her. We lapsed into a comfortable silence as I smoothed my hand over her soft fur. Frasier continued installing the organizers.

"This is going to look so good when it's done," I said, admiring the space. "It already does."

I'd moved Derek's clothes to the guest closet almost a year ago. I couldn't handle walking in to get dressed and being confronted with the memories every day. But a half-empty closet wasn't much better. Now, finally, the closet was going to feel intentional instead of sad.

Frasier nodded. "Hopefully I can finish tonight so you can put your closet back in order before we go."

"No rush," I said. "And you know you can come over just to hang out, right? You don't have to work on a project."

"I like doing projects."

"I know, but…" I focused on Biscuit, forcing out the words. "I don't want you to feel like I'm using you."

The corner of Frasier's mouth twitched. "Maybe I want you to use me."

Had I imagined it, or was there a suggestive undercurrent to his tone? Either way, his words and the way in which he'd said them had flooded my mind with lascivious images of all the ways I could *use* him.

But when I glanced up at him, I quickly dismissed the idea. Frasier was just being Frasier. It was playful banter, nothing more. Just like our tussle on the floor was playful, nothing more. *Right?*

"I just…" *I think I'm going crazy.* "I don't want you to feel like I'm taking advantage of you or that this relationship is one-sided."

"Bryn." He looked at me, his eyes piercing mine. "Do you feel like I'm taking advantage of you every time you make me a home-cooked meal?"

I frowned. "No. Of course not."

I enjoyed cooking, and it was more fun to cook for someone rather than just myself. After Derek's death, there'd been a stretch of time where neither food nor cooking sounded appetizing. It was easier now, but it wasn't the same. Food had become something that I ate because I had to, not because I wanted to.

I wasn't motivated to cook for myself, but I was happy to cook for Frasier. It made me feel useful, good, especially since I followed the meal plans from the team's nutritionist,

Maggie. And in doing so, I fueled my body with healthy, nutritious meals.

"What about when you keep the dogs or take them to the vet?"

Was he kidding? I loved Biscuit and Bacon. I loved spending time with them, caring for them. I'd been skeptical when Frasier had first proposed the arrangement, but it had worked out great.

"I like doing that. I'm happy to do that." More than happy. I loved Bacon and Biscuit; they made me feel loved and accepted and seen.

"Then trust that I like doing this for you. 'Kay?" He held my gaze, until I nodded.

"Okay," I said, though I still felt like he was a better friend than I was. Or maybe I just felt guilty about the fact that I'd conned him into attending my sister's destination wedding with me under false pretenses.

Tell him!

I can't tell him, I argued with myself.

I already had no idea how I was going to repay Frasier. Yes, he'd offered to go. And a free vacation to Anguilla wasn't exactly a hardship, but he didn't get much downtime. And he was giving up some of his very rare free time to do this for me.

He might be happy to accompany me to my sister's wedding, but he'd offered to go as my plus-one, not my fake boyfriend.

I sighed. I didn't think Frasier would be upset about what I'd done, but it was embarrassing. Not the idea of dating Frasier—anyone would be lucky to have a man like him in their life. But the fact that my sister's comments had gotten under my skin to the point that I'd responded in such a juvenile way.

I was acting like I was in middle school. Like the time

Jimmy Randall had teased me about my breasts being the size of mosquito bites. I'd been so mad and mortified, and I'd shot back that my boyfriend in Canada liked them just fine. And then, like now, I hadn't had a boyfriend.

I sighed. I was secretly hoping no one—besides Allie, of course—would ever find out that Frasier and I were "dating." Maybe that was wishful thinking, but I was rolling with it—for now.

"Want some help?" I asked Frasier, needing to dispel some of my nervous energy.

"No, but I'd love some company. Unless you have things you need to do."

I shook my head. I was almost done packing. Most of the stuff I had left were things that I couldn't pack until the day of. So, I sank down on the floor into a cross-legged position. Bacon and Biscuit settled down, one on either side of me.

I stroked Biscuit's fur as a sense of peace and contentment washed over me. This was my happy place—relaxing at home with Frasier and our fur babies. We'd gone to the shelter to find a four-legged friend, and we'd ended up with two.

"What do you want for dinner tonight?" I asked.

"Whatever's easiest for you. I'm sure you don't have a ton of groceries since we're about to go out of town."

"Actually, Maggie sent me a new recipe I can't wait to try. And I already have almost everything we need."

"Sounds good to me," Frasier said. "You know I'm not picky, and I always appreciate your home-cooked meals."

Frasier finished assembling part of the unit, sliding it into place with a satisfied expression.

It always impressed me—his ability to acquire new skills. His willingness to learn anything and everything. I wondered if it stemmed from his childhood and the fact that his family had owned a fertilizer and farm equipment business back in Canada. Or maybe it was just who he was.

He'd worked construction jobs during the summers in college. It was sexy that he knew how to work with his hands. That he wasn't afraid to get dirty.

Derek had always hired someone to take care of things, but Frasier was intent on working them out for himself. Neither option was wrong. It was always good to hire someone more experienced, especially if you knew that you were out of your depth. But I loved that Frasier pushed himself to see what he was capable of.

"Maybe you should buy a fixer-upper," I said. "Since you like projects so much."

Frasier's condo was nice, but it wasn't what I considered his style. It was modern, slick. It didn't need any work, and it didn't feel like a home.

"Maybe someday."

I wondered what he was waiting for. He certainly had the money to buy a nice house, but maybe he didn't want to commit to a mortgage until he'd met the person he wanted to share a home with.

"Waiting for Ms. Right?" I teased.

"Something like that." He kept his attention on the instruction manual, his tone disinterested.

I tried to imagine the type of woman Frasier would end up with. She'd have to be understanding of his schedule, something that had been an issue with girlfriends in the past. She'd have to love hockey and dogs. And she'd have to be okay with the fact that we were so close.

Though, obviously, things would have to change once he was in a relationship. I couldn't imagine any girlfriend being pleased about the idea of him spending so much time with another woman, even if we were just friends. The idea of my relationship with Frasier changing made me sad.

I sighed, knowing it was inevitable.

One day, Frasier would find someone and fall in love. He was such a catch, and he was a relationship guy. But the thought of him meeting someone and getting married sent a twist through my gut.

"Keep that up, and you're going to pass out from lack of oxygen," Frasier joked, startling me from my musings.

I jerked my attention to him. "What?"

"You keep sighing."

"Oh." I laughed, feeling self-conscious. "Sorry. I didn't even realize I was doing it."

"What's on your mind?"

I shifted. "Is it terrible to admit that part of me is dreading the wedding?"

"It's your date, huh?" Frasier deadpanned. "I hear he's a real douche."

I couldn't help it. I started laughing. I appreciated the out; I'd had enough introspection for one night.

"Really? I think he's a sweetheart." When Frasier looked up at me, I could feel my cheeks heating. But I pushed on. "I'm just worried he won't have a good time. You see—" I leaned in as if preparing to impart some huge secret "—I kind of roped him into going with me."

He leaned even closer, close enough for me to smell his cologne. "I'm sure he feels honored to be going as your date." His sincerity was as disarming as his proximity. "And I bet he's looking forward to spending time with you."

Something inside me warmed at those words, and I found myself smiling. "Ditto."

And that was how I knew everything would be okay.

CHAPTER SIX

Frasier

Bryn snorted from beside me, her shoulders shaking as she laughed silently. It had been a long day of travel, and the cabin lights were dimmed because it was evening. After an extended delay in Miami, we'd missed not only our flight to Anguilla but all of the few remaining flights from Miami to Anguilla. So, we'd been rerouted on a flight bound for Sint Maarten and would then have to take a ferry to Anguilla.

Most of our fellow passengers were already watching something on the in-flight entertainment system or trying to sleep, but I was too busy watching Bryn. It was good to see her laugh.

I leaned over the armrest, inhaling her rich, amber scent. God, she smelled so good. "What's so funny?"

"So, in my book…" And then she started laughing again, and I couldn't help but smile as she struggled to get herself under control. But every time she tried to tell me what was so funny, she started laughing all over again.

I got the feeling she was a bit slaphappy from exhaustion. Originally, we were supposed to arrive in Anguilla this afternoon, and now we wouldn't be getting there until well after dark. It wasn't ideal, but fortunately, it wasn't going to affect much, apart from our sleep.

Bryn bent forward, and her shirt slid up her back. Her yoga pants rested low on her hips, and I spied a sliver of her lacy underwear. *Fuck me.*

"Sorry. Sorry." She swiped away a tear. "It's funny, but it's not *that* funny. I think I just got the giggles, you know?" She looked as if she was still fighting laughter.

I nodded, bemused. Travel delays sucked, but I wasn't even all that bothered because it gave me more alone time with Bryn.

"I'm glad you're enjoying the book," I said.

My agent, Talia Winters, had definitely been intrigued by my request for an early copy, but it hadn't been difficult to make it happen. She'd reached out to Meghan Hart's team, and they'd asked for an autographed jersey in return. I'd thrown in some center ice tickets to a home game because I knew how much a signed, early copy would mean to Bryn.

I'd given her the book because it would make her happy. There were no strings attached. No expectations. But I'd be lying if I said it wasn't part of Operation Woo.

Selfishly, I wanted to show Bryn what she meant to me. But I also wanted to do this for her. To remind her that she deserved to feel loved and desired. She might have lost the man she loved, but she didn't have to spend the rest of her life alone.

Bryn grinned. "Like you wouldn't believe. But I should probably switch to something else." She closed the book before placing it in her bag. "Otherwise, I won't get any sleep, and I'll be exhausted when we land."

"Do you want to watch something together?" I asked because I had a feeling I wouldn't be sleeping anytime soon.

Maybe I'd pass out at some point, but I doubted it. I was often on planes, and I rarely slept.

"I'd love that." She grabbed her headphones. "What'd you have in mind? Nothing sad."

I scoffed. "Trust me. I know better. And I'm not Georgia."

"Right?" She laughed. "She always picks the tearjerkers."

When I'd scrolled through the entertainment options earlier, I'd already favorited a few that I'd thought Bryn would enjoy. "That new comedy you wanted to see is on there."

"Oh really?" Bryn perked up. "Let's do that. Let me just get set up."

She pulled a few things out of her bag, and I watched in fascination as she sprayed her face with something. Next up was lotion, and then she grabbed a blanket.

She turned to me, and when she caught sight of my expression, she laughed. "What?"

"You are very...prepared." Not that it surprised me. Bryn was always thinking ahead. It was one of the things I loved about her. One of the *many* things I loved about her.

"My skin-care ritual makes me feel calm and centered, especially when I'm traveling." She sighed happily. "I guess you could say it's a glimmer."

Ah. I should've known. *A glimmer.*

Lately, Bryn had been talking about glimmers a lot. It was a term she'd heard from her therapist. Bryn had explained it as a small moment of joy or peace that came from appreciating everyday experiences.

Every moment I spent with her was a glimmer. It didn't matter how mundane the task was; spending time with her brought me peace and joy.

She shifted in her seat so she was turned more toward me. "What do you do for self-care?"

I nudged her. "That's a bit personal, don't you think?" I teased.

Her cheeks flushed with color, as if she'd only just realized how that sounded. "I mean…"

I chuckled, wondering if it was wrong that I enjoyed watching her squirm a little. She grabbed the spray bottle and aimed it at me, spritzing me with cool liquid.

"Hey." I narrowed my eyes at her.

She was biting back a smile, and I wanted to kiss her so damn bad.

She held the bottle aloft once more. "Can I spray you for real?" When I didn't respond, she added, "Please. I just want to make you feel good."

I bit back a groan, imagining her saying that in an entirely different context. One with a lot fewer clothes. Maybe one where she was on her knees before me, pouty lips parted before my cock. *Fuck.*

"Sure." The word came out strangled.

She leaned closer, smoothing some of my hair away from my face. It felt so good. *Too* good.

She seemed to linger for a moment, and then she removed the cap, misting it over my face. I wasn't sure what I'd expected, but that felt…actually, really nice. Refreshing.

She opened the lotion. "Then, you need to moisturize," she said, smoothing the thick lotion over my skin. It felt so good—to be touched by her. Cared for by her.

"There." With her hands still on my face, she smiled softly. "How did that feel?"

"Amazing." My voice was gravelly, and my body felt like a live wire. "Thank you."

She smiled again, wider now. "You're welcome." She let out a happy sigh and settled back to her seat. Completely unaffected. "Now we can watch the movie," she said, covering herself with the blanket.

I laughed to cover my discomfort, cueing up the movie on my screen. When we were both ready, we hit play at the same time. One minute, I was watching the movie—more like watching Bryn's reactions to the movie—and the next thing I knew, I was blinking my eyes open.

I glanced around, surprised I'd fallen asleep in the first place. The plane's engine was still humming and Bryn was asleep, so I took the opportunity to study her. Her hair was up in a messy, high bun. Her lips were parted softly, and she looked so peaceful.

I lifted my hand as if to touch her cheek, imagining how it would feel to touch her freely. To not hold back anymore. And then I lowered my hand and shook my head. *What am I doing?*

I stretched out my legs then got up to use the bathroom. As I was headed down the aisle, I could see the moment it happened. That spark of recognition when a woman a few rows back realized who I was. There was that pause, the widening of the eyes, and then the knowing smile that came after.

I ducked my head but not before I'd seen her scan me from top to bottom, her eyes lingering on my gray sweat-pants. I continued on, hoping to keep a low profile. I'd gotten stopped by fans a few times at the airport in LA and Miami, asking for a picture or an autograph. I appreciated them and their support, but also...I just wanted to enjoy my vacation with Bryn.

And while I would never be rude to a fan, it was difficult to hide my annoyance when they inevitably asked Bryn to step aside and take their picture. She'd done so—graciously, of course. But I'd wanted her by my side, in front of the camera. Not hiding behind it.

I locked the bathroom door, taking care of business before washing my hands. I brushed my teeth, feeling more refreshed. When I emerged, the woman from a few rows back was standing outside.

I tried to tell myself that maybe she also needed to use the bathroom, but from the eager glint in her eyes, I feared that was wishful thinking.

"I've always wanted to join the Mile High Club," she said in a sultry tone. "What do you think? Want to make this trip *fly* by?"

You'd think after all these years I'd be used to that by now, but sometimes I was still caught off guard by how brazen people could be. And I cringed at the cheesiness of her lines. Because that's what they were—lines. She didn't care about me as a person; she just wanted to be able to say she'd fucked an NHL player.

"I'm not interested," I said, moving to bypass her. I wasn't trying to be rude, but I wanted to shut this down quickly.

"Oh, come on." She pouted, jutting out her hip.

Seriously? No meant no. That went both ways.

"I'm with someone," I said, though I didn't owe this stranger any explanation.

The woman stepped closer. "She's asleep." She placed her hand on my bicep. "It can be our little secret."

"Please remove your hand," I gritted out, just as a flight attendant joined us.

Of fucking course.

Her eyes bounced between us, taking in the scene. I could only imagine how this looked to her.

"Everything okay here?" she asked in an overly chipper voice.

"I was just returning to my seat," I said, hopeful the flight attendant wouldn't misconstrue the interaction. Regardless of what she thought she'd just walked in on, I was grateful for the interruption.

The rest of the flight passed without incident, but I didn't fall back asleep. After that encounter, my guard was up, and I couldn't seem to let it back down to relax enough to rest.

I was still tense when we waited for our luggage at the baggage carousel a few hours later. It didn't help that I had several missed calls from an unknown number, as well as one from my mom. I had a pretty good feeling I knew who was calling from the unknown number, but I'd been hoping the problem would just go away. Clearly, that had been overly optimistic. I sighed, resolving to call Mom back soon since it was past midnight.

We'd been warned that customs was running slower. They were short-staffed due to the late hour, and I was hoping they'd be as motivated to process us as we were to get out of here. I was more than ready to crash, and we still had to take a ferry to Anguilla.

I lowered my baseball cap, hoping no one else would recognize me. I tried to be kind to fans, but sometimes people could be so…invasive. One wrong move or statement taken out of context had the power to destroy my career.

"Is something wrong?" Bryn nudged me, and I hated that she'd picked up on my unease.

"Everything's fine."

When I spied my duffel bag, I tossed it over my shoulder before taking Bryn's bags in my other hand. "Come on."

"Bear," she chided. "You really don't have to—"

"Bryn." I leaned in. "I don't have to. I want to."

She didn't argue again after that, but I had a feeling her acquiescence had more to do with fatigue than agreement. Regardless of the reason, I'd take it as a win.

After waiting in line then clearing customs, we stepped outside, only to discover that the ferry to Anguilla had stopped running hours ago. And there wouldn't be another one until the morning. Bryn sank down on a bench and called the hotel, placing the phone on speaker. They promised to send a boat just for us and apologized profusely for the inconvenience.

At least that was settled. And our bags had arrived, which was a relief, considering the fact that we'd been rerouted.

As Bryn and I sat on the pier, waiting for our boat, she leaned her head on my shoulder. I wrapped my arm around her, holding her close. Just that simple contact had me feeling calmer.

"Well, this has been quite the adventure so far." She laughed.

"That's one word for it," I joked.

Her body was warm against mine, and I loved the way she felt in my arms. Like she belonged there.

Despite a long day of travel with numerous setbacks, Bryn hadn't complained once. In fact, she'd taken it all in stride just like she did everything else in life.

When a boat pulled up to the dock, a man in a Huxley Grand uniform stepped onto the pier. "Mrs. Morgan?"

"Yes. Thank you for coming to get us." Bryn smiled as if it were normal. And I supposed for her, it was. That was her name—Morgan. Derek's last name. Her married name. But hearing her referred to as *Mrs.* gave me a jolt.

I watched Bryn, but she didn't seem fazed. It was a powerful reminder that part of her would always belong to Derek. The wind pushed her hair away from her face, and I remembered the feeling of cupping her cheek. She'd looked up at me as if I were her whole world. And I held on to that feeling, realizing that maybe she could also belong to me.

"I'm James with the Huxley Grand Anguilla," the man said, interrupting my thoughts. "Allow me to load your bags, and then we'll be on our way. There are some waters and snacks on board. Please help yourself. It's about a twenty-minute ride to Anguilla."

During the ride, James told us about the history of the

island and the resort amenities. It was pleasant on the water, but more than anything, I wanted a shower to wash the travel grime off me and a comfortable bed. Judging from the looks of the resort as we docked, neither would be an issue.

I'd stayed at a number of Huxley Grand properties—they were the official hotel of the Hollywood Hawks after all. But never one like this. It was located in one of the most exclusive spots in the Caribbean. A tiny island only sixteen miles long and three miles wide that didn't allow cruise ships, high rises, or casinos. *Sounds like heaven.*

After debarking, we followed James up the path toward the hotel that looked more like a giant sandcastle rising out of the island. The cream-colored walls practically glowed against the night sky. And what a sky it was—full of stars that reminded me of being back in Canada, where there was way less light pollution than LA.

Waves crashed in the distance, and I could only imagine what this place looked like during the day. Magical was the best word to describe it. The hotel seemed designed to showcase the natural landscape, contorting itself to the land instead of imposing itself on nature. The sea air was a balm to my soul, and I found myself relaxing.

This was the first vacation I'd taken in years, and I got to spend it with Bryn. The idea had me smiling.

James stopped in front of a bungalow overlooking the ocean. Well, I assumed it had an ocean view based on the volume of the waves and the path we'd traveled from the dock, but it was too dark to see. "Welcome to your beachfront bungalow."

"Wait." Bryn frowned. "There must have been a mistake because I booked a suite in the main resort."

James smiled. "The happy couple gifted you with an upgrade."

"Oh. Oh wow," Bryn said, clearly surprised. "That's very...
generous."

"You are fortunate," James continued. "It's difficult to get a
bungalow, especially during the high season. And between
your wedding party and another one, the resort is full."

We followed James inside, and he set our bags down
before walking over to the French doors facing the ocean.
My attention was on the ceiling, where warm wood beams
followed the slope of the roof, drawing the eye up toward the
peak. The craftsmanship was beautiful, and I admired the
work that must have gone into it.

James opened the French doors, letting the ocean air
sweep through, ruffling the gauze curtains that pooled on the
floor and draped around the bed. The floor was comprised of
large tiles in varying sizes and shades of sand, from pale to
the richness of brown sugar. I wondered if the materials
were native to the area because they certainly seemed to fit
right in.

"Out here, we have a plunge pool or hot tub," James said.
Bryn and I followed him out to the deck, where a round pool
rested in the wood surface. There, he demonstrated how the
controls worked to make the water heated or cool. How to
turn on the lights.

The ocean was dark, but the sound of the waves was
comforting. The water ebbed and flowed, a constant in a sea
of change. But even that constant was never exactly the
same, the tides and the seashore always shifting, much like
my relationship with grief.

We headed back inside, back by that huge bed covered in
smooth, creamy bedding and the most luxurious-looking
pillows. I kept waiting for James to show us a second
bedroom. But he seemed more concerned with demon-
strating how the resort tablet could be used to order room

service, find out more about the resort amenities, or select from one of the many in-room workouts.

After pointing out the bathroom with its huge rain-head shower and freestanding bathtub with a giant picture window behind it, we returned to the main room. And it was then that I realized there *was* no other bedroom. I frowned, glancing around as if a door to another bedroom might magically appear. I must have misunderstood. Maybe my room had also been upgraded, and he had yet to show it to me.

Bryn thanked James with a tight smile. When he headed for the door, I grabbed my bag and moved to follow him.

"Can I help you with something else, sir?" he asked. "Would you like me to unpack your things?"

"Oh, I—"

"We're good, James," Bryn said. "Thank you."

I thanked James and paid him a generous tip before he left.

Now that we were alone, Bryn and I looked at each other and then at the bed. It was looming over us, and I had no idea what was running through her mind. She seemed just as taken aback by the sleeping arrangements as I was.

I dragged a hand down my face. I was exhausted from the long day of travel.

"I, uh..." Bryn seemed to hesitate. "When I booked the room, I selected a suite with two beds. In two separate rooms, actually." She glanced around, looking anywhere but at me.

I honestly hadn't given the sleeping arrangements much thought until now. Bryn had assured me everything was handled, and I trusted her. And while I could understand Allie wanting to give Bryn special accommodations, we were just friends. I was here as her plus-one.

She squeezed her eyes shut briefly, then let out a heavy

sigh. "I'm sorry about this, Frasier. I, um… Yeah." She glanced away, seeming to be at a loss for words.

I still didn't understand why Bryn's sister would upgrade us to a one-bedroom bungalow with only one bed. But Allie had, and now the resort was full.

"What do you propose?" I asked, wanting to focus on a solution.

Bryn went over to the sofa, inspecting it. "Maybe the couch has a pull-out mattress I could sleep on."

As if I would let her sleep anywhere but the bed.

"You'll take the bed," I said in a firm tone. This was not up for discussion.

The couch definitely wasn't a pull-out. This resort was far too swanky for something like that. As it was, the couch would be too short for her, let alone for my six-foot-two frame.

She furrowed her brow. "You'll never fit on the couch, and you need your sleep."

"And you don't?" I shot back.

She waved a hand through the air. "I'll be fine." But she wouldn't meet my eyes.

I frowned. What wasn't she telling me? She bustled about, unzipping her suitcase and pulling out some items.

"Bryn?"

"It's late." She gave me a wan smile. "We're both tired. I just want to shower and go to bed."

"Exactly. In *bed*. Not on a couch." I crossed my arms over my chest. On this, I would not yield.

"I…" She stopped pacing, dragging a hand down her face. "This isn't going to work—sharing a room. I'll just…I'll have to figure out something."

I dropped my arms, hands resting loosely at my sides. "Because of me?" My tone was cautious. I was scared to hear the answer.

I hated the thought that I made her uncomfortable. But I also knew it didn't make sense.

We were together almost all the time. She'd passed out on the plane. She'd fallen asleep many times during our movie nights. Her head on my shoulder, legs curled beneath her on the couch or her feet resting on my thighs.

"No, Bear." She dropped her head to her chest. "Because of me." She took a deep breath and let it out slowly.

"Because of your insomnia?" I asked, knowing that she'd struggled with it since losing Derek. But she hadn't mentioned it in a while, and she'd seemed more well-rested overall.

She nodded. "Sometimes it doesn't matter how exhausted I am, my mind will not stop spinning. It's not every night, and it's definitely gotten a lot better. But I never know when it will strike. And the idea that it *might* happen—that I might wake you up—stresses me out."

Wake me up? As if I cared about that.

She suddenly seemed so small. So fragile. I hated it.

I moved before I could think, crossing the room in a few strides and pulling her into my arms. Her cheek was pressed to my chest. Her head rested beneath my chin. Despite our height and size difference, we just…fit.

She fit. In my life. My world. My heart.

Slowly, she lifted her arms so they were wrapped around me. The ocean breeze whispered through the trees like a lovers' secret. And for a moment, everything felt right in the world.

"Thank you," she said, surprising me.

"For what?"

"That was a really good hug." She patted my chest, her hand stilling over my heart. "You always give the best hugs. Somehow, you always seem to know exactly what I need."

She lowered her hand and took a few steps back. When

she sighed, the sound filled the bungalow with such sadness. "I miss that—you know. Physical touch."

Was she saying what I thought she was? That she missed sex?

It wasn't a topic we'd ever broached before, but of course she'd miss sex, intimacy, connection. It was a huge part of any relationship, and she and Derek had been together for nearly a decade.

I didn't know what to say. I didn't know what would make her feel better or worse. But if she missed physical touch, then I was more than happy to hold her.

I opened my arms once more, beckoning her in. "Come 'ere."

She stepped into my embrace, and I held her close, resting my chin on the top of her head. Inhaling her scent. Closing my eyes as I soaked in the feeling of her body next to mine.

This wasn't about getting out of the friend zone or wooing her. This was about comforting Bryn and being there for her.

"I miss him too," I admitted.

She nodded against my chest. "I know. *I know,*" she said again, more softly this time.

We stayed there, holding each other. It wasn't the first time we'd clung to each other, but unlike other times in the past, the sadness didn't feel quite so heavy. If anything, it felt peaceful. As if we'd found our solace in each other.

"Part of me will always miss him," she whispered. "But I'm tired of feeling…stuck. I have to find a way forward."

I nodded. I knew the feeling well, and I hated that she felt that way too. But I was encouraged by the fact that she wanted to find a path forward. Because we both knew there was no going back. No matter how much we might wish to change the past, Derek was gone.

"We will." I rubbed her back, wanting to reassure her. "We

will find a way forward." I was certain of it. I had to cling to that notion, or I'd spiral into a grief so consuming that I feared I'd never surface again, just like I had when he'd first died. Hockey and Bryn had been the things to get me through it.

Bryn clutched my shirt, and when she peered up at me, the sight of her glassy eyes and pink cheeks, those dark, wet lashes, was nearly my undoing. There was something about seeing her like that. I hated that she was hurting, but I was glad she'd let me in.

The fact that she was letting me in on a moment of vulnerability stirred something deep inside me—a protective instinct. A sense of pride. Of gratitude.

"Together?" she asked.

"Together," I vowed.

CHAPTER SEVEN

Bryn

I grabbed a spare blanket from the armoire, lighter now that I'd confided in Frasier. For the first time in months, I felt as if I could breathe. I might not know what my path forward was, but I was confident that Frasier would be by my side just as he'd been for the past year and a half.

And the fact that I'd verbalized that I was feeling stuck, not just to Georgia but now to Frasier too, had released something in me. It was as if I'd taken that first step to unclog a plugged drain. I knew that things might only start flowing slowly at first, but at least they'd be moving.

I wandered over to the dresser where I spotted a gift bag with Allie and Kit's monogram on it. Inside, I found a tube of luxury sunscreen, some aloe vera, and a box of condoms. Leave it to Allie to put condoms in the welcome bag for her wedding party.

I returned everything to the bag then went to the double doors, letting the salt air caress my skin. The ocean waves crashed along the shore, and I peered up at the sky, enjoying the view of the stars. I'd taken a long, hot shower, and I was puttering about the room while Frasier took his turn in the bathroom.

Most people would be thrilled by the room upgrade. The huge bathroom. The privacy. The view. It was incredible. And maybe I would've been, under different circumstances.

But I'd reserved a suite with two separate beds. In two separate rooms. Not...I glanced around and let out a heavy sigh. A romantic bungalow with a hot tub. And a freaking king-sized bed with a canopy.

I dragged a hand down my face. *I'm in an only-one-bed situation with my best friend.*

It was like a scene straight out of one of Meghan Hart or Penelope Glass's romance novels.

Though, if we were in one of their novels, Frasier would exit the bathroom wearing only a towel, steam billowing out around him. I swallowed thickly at the idea. I was trying really hard not to imagine Frasier in a towel, droplets of water running down the defined ridges of his chest.

We're friends. Just *friends.*

And *friends* did not imagine their friends naked in the shower. So I didn't think about that as I lifted my hair off my neck and fanned myself. Nor did I think about the fact that we'd be sleeping in the same room, even if I insisted on taking the couch.

I pinched the bridge of my nose. I'd really screwed up this time. If I'd just confessed to Allie before the wedding, Frasier and I wouldn't even be in this situation.

I appreciated that Allie was supportive of my—albeit fake —relationship with Frasier. I was touched that she'd taken time out of her busy schedule to do something nice for me by upgrading this room. But I also couldn't help but wonder if there was more to it than sheer enthusiasm. If, deep down, she was relieved. Relieved that she wouldn't have to worry about me and my feelings on her wedding day now that I was in a new relationship. Or worse, a desire to not have my sadness dampen her celebration.

I tucked the spare sheets around the couch, laying a blanket on top. When the water switched off, I hopped under the covers, quickly closing my eyes and trying to pretend I was asleep. Trying to pretend I hadn't been thinking about my *friend* and what he looked like naked.

The idea that he might somehow know that I was imagining him naked was even more uncomfortable than the couch I was currently lying on. Still…I was going to try. It wasn't Frasier's fault that my sister thought we were dating and should be upgraded to a romantic bungalow.

I heard the door to the bathroom open. A moment later, his dark chuckle threaded through the night air, curling low and deep in my belly. I rubbed my thighs together as if to ease the ache building there, squeezing my eyes shut tighter still.

"Bryn," he rasped. "You better get your ass in bed."

My entire body went taut as a violin string at the command, the power in his tone. Even so, I tried to remain as still as possible, hoping he'd believe I'd fallen asleep.

I guessed that was too much to ask because the next thing I knew, Frasier was scooping me up off the couch as if I weighed nothing. I flailed around in my blankets, completely caught off guard. But his grip was firm. Unrelenting. A bit like the man holding me.

"Put me down," I hissed.

"Hold still," he bit out.

I blinked a few times at his commanding tone. He'd never spoken to me like that. Never taken that tone with me. It was…kinda hot.

He shifted so he was cradling me, and that was so much worse. His body was so warm—warm enough for me to feel the heat from his bare chest through the layers of blankets I was wrapped in. And he smelled so good, like cedar and citrus. If I closed my eyes, I imagined being wrapped up in his arms in a cedar A-frame cabin, eating orange slices together as we looked out over the snow. There'd be a Christmas tree in the background and music playing softly.

Where did that come from?

Frasier crossed the room, dumping me unceremoniously on the bed. I let out a surprised oomph. I was wrapped in blankets, swaddled like a baby. And there he was, looking hotter than he had any right to.

Shirtless. Hands on his hips. Athletic shorts sitting low on his waist. I could see the outline of every muscle, every... *Oh god.* I shivered.

I felt completely off-kilter. Something about his stern, controlling demeanor and those blue eyes glittering in the dim lighting was doing it for me. Oh boy, was it ever.

I was only just beginning to realize that our friendship might not be the same after this trip. Hell, it was already affecting our relationship.

I liked seeing this different side to him. And this sexy/stern combo was turning out to be my kryptonite.

I writhed and thrashed, fighting my way out of the blankets like a caterpillar emerging from its cocoon. Finally, breathless, I flopped back on the bed, chest heaving.

His jaw clenched. "The fuck are you wearing?"

I glanced down at myself and shrugged. "PJs."

I'd packed this silky matching short and camisole set, expecting to sleep alone. I'd anticipated having a room all to myself.

So much for using my toys. I sighed. Not that they were all that satisfying. I missed the connection that came from sex as much as the pleasure.

Frasier pinched the bridge of his nose before looking

down and away. The next thing I knew, a T-shirt was sailing toward me.

"Put. It. On." His voice was tight, almost pained.

I would not be bossed around. I'd had enough of my family trying to tell me what I should do or thinking they knew what was best for me. Hell, strangers on the internet loved to dissect my life and my choices. Frasier was my friend, and I respected him. But I also wasn't going to be pushed around by him—or anyone.

Besides, he was being ridiculous. So I threw it back at him —hard. "*You* put it on." If anything, he had on even less clothing than me.

His eyes met mine. "Bryn."

"Make me," I huffed.

Over the past year and a half, Frasier had become my best friend. But that was not how he was looking at me now. And I knew that wasn't how I was looking at him either.

He looked downright pissed. And the exhaustion from the day coupled with the absurdity of the situation had emotion bubbling up inside me until I burst into a fit of laughter. Which only made Frasier's glare deepen. And me laugh even harder.

"Oh, come on, Bear," I teased. I got on my knees, righting my silky pajama tank. His eyes darted to my chest then to the ceiling. "Relax a little." I planted my hands on his shoulders— both to steady myself and to get him to lighten up.

Once I was more stable, I released him, and he took a step back. He crossed his arms over his chest and scowled. He was too uptight. Too in his head. We both were after a long day of travel and then the situation with us sharing a room. And I knew exactly what I needed to do.

I grabbed a pillow from the bed and lobbed it at his chest.

His nostrils flared. And somehow, even that was a turn-on. Or maybe getting a rise out of Frasier was the turn-on. I wasn't exactly sure. But the sight of him, standing there in only his athletic shorts… My eyes lifted to his glorious chest and shoulders…the tats that wrapped around his ribs.

And my god, those abs.

I'd seen him shirtless plenty of times. But his muscles seemed even more defined. Or maybe I was just horny. Okay. Maybe both. But Frasier was undeniably hot.

I didn't know what was wrong with me, but I liked that he was a little unhinged. All goalies were. You had to be to stand in a net and watch as a frozen disk of rubber came flying at you at insane speeds, willingly putting your body into its path.

I picked up another pillow, unable to stop myself. I couldn't remember the last time I'd had this much fun.

"You sure you want to do that, angel?" He arched one eyebrow, and my knees wobbled. His tone. That endearment. The way he was looking at me…

It made me want to challenge him, to push back. Something sparked inside me, and I felt more…alive than I had in a while.

Bring it on.

I grinned and then launched myself off the bed, ready to smack him with the pillow. But he was too fast. Of course, he was. The man was one of the best goalies in the league. The reflexes he'd honed from years of drills and training were unreal. But that didn't make it any less fun.

He grabbed me around the waist, tossing me back on the bed. "Now, stay." He dusted off his hands as if that was the end of it. As if I would just do exactly what he'd told me to.

Ha! As if.

If anything, his words made me even more determined to defy him. I'd never liked being told what to do.

When I moved to get up, Frasier pounced. He braced his body over mine, hands pressed to the mattress on either side of me. "Bryn," he growled, breath coasting over my nose, my lips. Minty. Fresh. Warm. "Stay."

My nipples tightened, cool air flowing across one of them and making me realize that my pjs had slid out of place, revealing my breast. Had Frasier noticed? The idea only made me hotter.

My core clenched with need. Oh god. *Oh my god.*

It was in that moment that I realized what a colossal mistake I'd made. Thinking we could share this romantic hotel room. Thinking nothing would have to change.

Because I wanted him. I wanted *Frasier.*

His warm, citrus scent wrapped around me, and I could feel the heat wafting from his body. If he came any closer, we'd be kissing. If he leaned in at all…

I sucked in a breath when I felt something long and hard brush against my thigh. Oh my god. He was just as turned on as I was. And he was…*wow.* I blinked a few times, my brain struggling to process all this new information. Talk about stimulation overload in the best possible way.

I lifted my hand, cupping his cheek. His expression softened, his eyes still hooded. He turned his head, pressing the most delicate, tender kiss to my palm. I sighed, warmth coursing through my body. But then, he froze. His entire demeanor changed, his body locking up tight.

I didn't understand what had happened, but I could feel the shift as surely as if a cold front had blown in.

Frasier squeezed his eyes shut as if pained then pushed away from me, standing. He turned, the muscles of his back flexing as he adjusted himself. I remained motionless, in a daze.

Did that really just happen?

And what *exactly* had happened?

I sat there frozen. We'd shared a moment. And then he'd pulled away. *Why?*

I turned my palm up to inspect it, and that's when I saw it.

Oh. *Oh.*

The butterfly tattoo on my wrist.

Now I understood why Frasier had pulled away. And I was filled with both relief and disappointment.

I'd almost crossed a line with my husband's best friend, *my* best friend, that couldn't be uncrossed. And as much as my body might be ready, my mind and my heart were a different matter entirely.

I sat up, adjusting my shirt so I was covered once more. Heat scorched my cheeks, and my thoughts bounced all over the place.

"Frasier, I…" I didn't even know what to say.

I was so hot and bothered and confused. It felt as if Frasier and I were on the precipice of something important. Something dangerous. Like Alice stumbling through the looking glass, unsure where she was or how to get back home.

Did I want to take that next step? And did I want to take it with him?

My body was still reeling. My mind was in overdrive. God, I really needed a way to shift the energy in the room. Lighten the mood. Because it felt way too heavy all of a sudden.

"Go to sleep, Bryn," Frasier said in a softer tone. He still wouldn't look at me.

He grabbed the pillow I'd placed on the couch, fluffing it. There was no way I'd allow him to sleep on the couch, but he wouldn't let me sleep there either. And neither of us was willing to back down. In my mind, there was only one solution.

I pulled down the covers on the bed, climbing beneath the sheets. Frasier's shoulders visibly relaxed, and I had to bite back a laugh. As amused as I was, something warm unfurled deep inside me at that simple reaction. An unconscious movement.

Frasier always looked out for me, cared for me. He put me first, even when it was to his own detriment.

"Come on." I patted the empty spot on the bed beside me. "There's more than enough room here for both of us. Unless you're going to hog all the covers or pull a starfish on me."

"I don't…" He swallowed hard, his eyes focused on the ceiling. They bounced around, looking anywhere but at me. "I'm not sure that's a good idea."

I decided that the best option—the only option—was to confront this head on. We were both adults, and I wasn't going to let one nip slip or an erection ruin our vacation. It was a biological response to external stimulus.

Okay, it was more than that. At least for me. And while what had happened was hot, it was good we'd stopped when we did. I wasn't willing to lose our friendship for a temporary lapse in judgment.

"We're both tired, and we got a little…carried away," I said, trying to sound calm, cool, and collected, when I was anything but. "It's not a big deal."

Except it felt like a big deal. My heart was pounding. And it wasn't the first time something like this had happened. Although this time had definitely been different from when he'd shielded me from the dogs.

Frasier grunted but said nothing.

I didn't know what to say. What he wanted me to say. I just knew that I didn't want this to be awkward anymore.

Things were already tense with my sister after our last phone call. I'd replied to messages in the "Bride Tribe" group chat since then, but Allie and I hadn't communicated outside of that. And tomorrow, I'd have to face my sister and the rest of my family. I needed to know that Frasier and I were okay.

"Bear," I sighed. "I'm sorry."

He crossed his arms over his chest, nostrils flared. "You have nothing to apologize for."

"I do, actually. Because I'm pretty sure I'm the reason we're in this mess."

He furrowed his brow. It felt weird to have this conversation while I was in bed and he was sitting across the room. So I grabbed a robe from the closet and wrapped it around myself before I went over to sit beside him.

I rolled my lips between my teeth. "I think Allie upgraded us to this room because of something I told her."

The divot between his eyebrows deepened. "Why? What did you tell Allie?"

My heart was pounding, my stomach hollowed out. "Don't get mad, but…" I twisted the edge of the robe's tie between my fingers. "I might have told her we're dating."

I cringed, bracing myself for his reaction. My cheeks already felt like they were on fire.

"I'm sorry," I rambled. "I know it was stupid and imma-ture. But she just…" I sighed. "She kept pushing, so I pushed back."

"By telling her we were dating." I couldn't get a read on his expression. Was he mad? Annoyed? Amused?

I nodded. "But I swore her to secrecy. No one else knows."

He sank down on the couch. "Back it up. Tell me what happened."

So I did. And he listened patiently while I told him about my conversations with Allie and how she'd made me feel. Finally, he asked, "Why didn't you tell me this before?"

"At first, I was going to confess to Allie. But then, after I didn't…couldn't, I kept thinking that maybe my little lie wouldn't be a big deal. I didn't think it would affect anything.

But clearly—" I gestured to the room "—I was wrong, and I'm sorry."

"I'm not mad at you, Bryn." He placed his hand on my back, his words and touch filling me with relief.

"You're not?" I glanced at him.

He shook his head. "I'm proud of you for clearly setting some boundaries and expressing your needs." *He was?* "And I can understand why you said what you did."

My shoulders relaxed. I should've known he'd have my back. He always did. "Thank you."

Even so, telling him was a relief. Frasier was known for keeping his cool on the ice, and he rarely got ruffled off it. But everyone had their limits.

"So, what now?" he asked.

"What now?" I shrugged. "I confess to her in the morning, and we ask the hotel to find us alternate accommodations. Maybe I can room with one of the bridesmaids or my parents if I have to." Though neither prospect was very appealing.

"Mm." Was all he said in response.

Sometimes I felt like I knew Frasier well enough that I could decipher his cryptic remarks. This wasn't one of those times. I didn't have a clue what he was thinking, and it made me nervous.

"Or..." He rubbed the back of his neck. And then he said the last words I'd expected to hear from his mouth. "We could roll with it."

CHAPTER EIGHT

Bryn

M y phone buzzed, and I blinked my eyes open. I rolled over and stretched, my hand landing on...a piece of paper? Thick, crisp, and with a subtle texture.

Frasier's side of the bed was empty, and I picked up the note he'd left me on the hotel stationery. His scrawl was barely legible, but I'd always been able to decipher it.

Angel,

Hope you got some good rest. Went for a workout. Enjoy the spa. I'll see you later.

F

And then he'd doodled a little picture of a cartoon bear lounging on the beach. I rolled onto my back, laughing at the image of the bear. I didn't know how long he'd been gone, but the fact that my phone had alerted me of an incoming text message meant it was late. Or at least, late enough for my "Do Not Disturb" feature to have switched off.

Was it any wonder I'd slept in? After a long day of travel, Frasier and I should've crashed. Instead, we'd stayed up late into the night talking about his idea to "roll with it." To pretend we were dating. I still couldn't believe he'd suggested it in the first place. And even after sleeping on it, I wasn't sure whether it was a great idea or a terrible one.

Angel.

I could remember the way the pet name had rolled off his tongue last night. And now, he'd used it on a note. I wasn't sure what to think of it or anything.

My phone buzzed again, and I glanced at the screen. There was an update from the dog sitter, and I smiled at the pictures she'd sent Frasier and me of Bacon and Biscuit. They definitely seemed happy, and that was a relief. It wasn't often that both Frasier and I were unavailable. Then I opened my sister's wedding group thread.

(BRIDE TRIBE CHAT)

> Allie: See you all at the spa at ten!

> Elise: Can't wait!

I scrolled past the rest and then exited the group chat. Frasier and I had decided to skip breakfast with the rest of the wedding party, but I wouldn't be able to avoid my sister for much longer. Nor would I have Frasier as a buffer.

The bridal party was scheduled for a girls-only day of pampering and relaxation at the spa. Dad was planning to golf with a few of my uncles. Meanwhile, the groom and a bunch of the guys were spending the day at the pool. Both groups had invited Frasier to join, but he'd opted to spend the morning working out instead, which was fine by me. He barely knew most of them, and his training was important.

Besides, tonight, we'd all come together for a joint bachelor/bachelorette party at one of the island's well-known beach bars. And that would be when I really needed him by my side.

A new text from Georgia popped up on the screen.

Georgia: How's Anguilla?

Me: We got in super late, and I'm exhausted. But it's beautiful here!

I sat up and tried to snap a shot of the French doors with the view beyond.

Me: (picture attached)

Georgia: And how are things with your "date"?

Me: He's actually my fake boyfriend now. Thanks for asking.

I hit send before I could talk myself out of it. My phone immediately started vibrating in my hand. I answered it and put it on speaker mode before placing it on the mattress.

"Um. What? What the heck happened? I thought you were going to tell your sister the truth." Georgia asked.

"I was." I cringed. "But then things sort of spiraled out of control."

"That seems like an understatement," she mused. "Did something happen between you and Frasier?"

"I—" I cleared my throat. There had been the wrestling, the nip slip, and the erection. But I wasn't going to mention that. We'd stopped it before it could go any further. "No."

"Do you want something to happen?"

"No." *Yes. Maybe?*

"Okay, but then why are you fake-dating him?"

The silence that followed told me she was waiting for me to explain.

So I told her about my call with my sister before I'd left for the wedding. The surprise upgrade to the romantic beach bungalow and the fully booked hotel. Followed by my eventual confession to Frasier about our "relationship status."

"And then he suggested that we roll with it," I finished.

"That's what he said? 'Roll with it'?"

I nodded then remembered she couldn't see me. "Basically, yeah."

"Wow." Her tone was one of disbelief.

"I know!" I still couldn't believe it myself. It seemed so out of character for him.

"And you're okay with lying to your family? Well, continuing to lie to your family."

I could either tell my family the truth and admit why I'd lied. Or I could continue lying, and maybe I'd actually enjoy the wedding.

Besides, it really wasn't anything new. I'd gotten very good at hiding my pain from my family and friends. Frasier was one of the few exceptions, along with my girlfriends, Georgia, Kylie, and Logan. I couldn't have made it through all that I had without them.

"I don't love the idea, but it's only for the next few days. Then we'll go back home, and everything will go back to normal. In a month or two, I can tell my family we decided to just be friends."

"Mm."

I didn't like that mm.

"This is kind of a big deal," she said. "He hasn't dated in a while. And if anyone finds out, it's *going* to be a huge deal." She was quiet a moment, then said, "Maybe you should talk to Kylie. Give her a heads-up. Just…in case."

Frasier and I had discussed the potential for someone

finding out, but we were hoping that what happened on Anguilla stayed on Anguilla. Perhaps it was naïve, but I wasn't sure there was any way around it. If we were going to pretend to date, it was a risk we were going to have to take.

He didn't seem bothered by the idea. And considering the fact that we were on a small island, during the off-season, I was trying not to be too concerned. There was really no need to involve Kylie and my PR team for now. But as my friend, I wanted to tell her.

"It's just for the wedding. And we both know it's fake."

Georgia was quiet for a moment, and I could tell she wasn't entirely convinced. But then she said, "You know... this could be the perfect chance to work on getting those needs met."

My expression soured. "I'm not having sex with Frasier simply to have those needs met. I wouldn't use him like that."

"I wasn't suggesting that, but it's good to know that's what your mind immediately jumped to." I could hear the smugness in her tone.

I rolled my eyes, grateful she couldn't see the current shade of my face—bright, red, tomato.

"*You* know you're just friends," she continued. "But everyone else thinks you're a couple, right?"

They would soon enough, unless I told my sister the truth. "Yes."

"And you feel comfortable with Frasier. You trust Frasier."

I turned on my side, propping my head up with my hand. "You know I do."

"I'm not suggesting that you have sex. But since you're already pretending, maybe...lean into your role as his fake girlfriend. See what it feels like to date again in a safe, no-pressure way."

I furrowed my brow. "Lean into it...*how?*"

"Be more affectionate. Flirt. Have fun. See what it's like to imagine being in a relationship with someone again."

"I don't know," I hedged. This situation was already messy, and that could only complicate matters even more. Plus, I wasn't sure if I could keep my emotions out of it.

"Just think about it. Imagine the possibilities."

We ended the call soon after that since I had to get ready to meet the Bride Tribe at the spa. Frasier still wasn't back from his workout, and I was secretly relieved to have some time to myself to sift through my thoughts, as well as everything Georgia had said.

When I finally made my way over to the spa, I was still conflicted about the situation. I appreciated Frasier for suggesting what he had. But fake-dating your best friend seemed like asking for trouble.

Maybe I should just tell Allie the truth. I'd even said as much to Frasier last night.

I knew he'd offered to pretend we were a couple because he wanted to protect me. As pissed as he was at Allie for the things she'd said, he knew how important my relationship with my sister was to me. Even so, I wondered if pretending to be in a relationship with Frasier was really the best solution—at least where our friendship was concerned.

This trip was already pushing the boundaries of our relationship. Sharing a room, a bed. Not to mention the fight we'd had before that. He'd seen my nipple. I'd felt his hard-on. And I couldn't stop thinking about the charged energy between us.

By the time I opened the door to the spa, my stomach was in knots. Yes, I was hurt by the things Allie had said, but I could also admit there was some truth in them. The light *had* gone out of me. But lately, I'd felt some of that spark again.

Still, Allie and I needed to have a conversation about boundaries. She needed to stop trying to impose her timeline on me—either for my grief or how she thought I should handle my relationship with Frasier. But her destination wedding was neither the time nor the place to cause extra stress. I also worried that telling Allie I'd lied about my relationship with Frasier would cause drama. The only way to avoid that—at least as I currently saw it—was to keep my mouth shut. Both about my hurt feelings and my relationship with Frasier.

"Bryn!" Mom smiled, immediately coming over for a hug as I covered a yawn. "I'm so glad you made it. It sounds like you had a long day of travel."

I nodded. "Sorry we missed breakfast."

Mom leaned in, keeping her voice low. "Sweetheart, you don't have to explain anything. And if you need a break from some of the events, we get it."

"Thanks, Mom. But I'm good." I didn't want to make just my family believe it; *I* wanted to believe it too.

Allie was next in line, and then I greeted each of the bridesmaids. I knew some of them better than others, and it was nice to catch up. A hotel employee offered me a beverage, and I sipped my flavored water as I waited for my name to be called. I tried not to let my nerves show as one by one the bridesmaids were called back, leaving just Mom, Allie, and me.

I covered a yawn, another one. "Ugh. Sorry."

"Late night for you and Frasier in the beach bungalow?" Allie gave me a meaningful look.

The relaxing nature music was doing nothing to calm me. Especially when Mom's eyes darted between us, and I could see the wheels turning.

"Something like that." Though it wasn't what Allie thought.

"Wait…" Mom frowned. "Are you and Frasier…"

Allie said nothing, but I could tell she was close to

bursting from keeping the secret. I was tempted to shake my head and tell my mom we were just friends. But then I remembered how it had felt when Allie had said the light had gone out of me. How relieved she'd sounded when I'd told her I was dating Frasier. I saw the hopeful look on Mom's face, and I found myself saying, "Yes."

Allie let out a little squeal, and Mom broke into a huge smile. "That's wonderful. I'm so happy for you."

I fiddled with the tie on my robe then took another sip of my hibiscus-infused water. I hated lying to my family, but I wasn't going to go back on it now. Especially not when they seemed so happy.

"Does this mean we can finally talk about it?" Allie asked.

"Wait." Mom turned to my sister. "You knew?" And then she whipped her attention to me. "How long has this been going on? And why weren't we talking about it?"

"It's still new," I said, sticking with my story. "And I wasn't sure what people would think about the fact that he and Derek were so close. So we haven't been telling many people."

"All I care," Mom said, holding my gaze, "is what *you* think about it."

"Thanks," I said, just as Mom was called back for her facial. "Frasier makes me happy."

That was true, at least. Though, things had been... different between us since we'd arrived in Anguilla. Actually, before that, even. The signed copy of the new release came to mind. Followed by the almost-kiss.

Then there'd been our pillow fight last night after we'd argued over who was taking the couch. The assertive way Frasier had taken charge—picking me up and tossing me on the bed. Our push and pull. His body hovering over mine. His...

"What are you thinking about?" Allie poked me. Mom

was gone, and when I looked at Allie, she was wearing a knowing smile.

"Nothing," I answered quickly. Too quickly.

She poked me again. "Are you blushing?" she teased.

"Oh my god," I whispered, glancing around. "Would you cut it out?"

"Oh my god." She mimicked me as she leaned closer, grinning widely. "You are!"

"I am *not*," I protested. Why did we often revert to our childhood roles? "It's…warm in here. That's all." I pushed up the sleeves to my robe as if to prove my point.

"Nice tattoo." She grinned then added, "*Liar.* You were thinking about Frasier, weren't you? It's okay to admit it. You deserve to be happy again."

I crossed my legs, trying to hold it together as I said nothing. I was still hurt by our recent conversations—and the fact that she seemed able to so easily gloss over them. Or maybe she just didn't want anything to ruin her big day.

"Look, um—" She leaned in, lowering her voice. "I know you're upset with me, rightfully so. And I wanted to say that I'm really sorry about the things I said the other day."

Maybe I hadn't been as good at hiding my hurt as I thought, or maybe my sister was that good at reading me. I didn't want to cause drama, but since she'd brought it up, I needed to clear the air.

"Do you understand why I was upset?"

She sighed. "I know this is going to sound like it's about me, but it isn't. Not really. It's just so hard to watch someone you love go through something so awful. And I know there's no timeline on grief, but I'm worried about you. I just want you to be happy. Sometimes I feel like I don't know what to say, but I was genuinely trying to help."

"I get that," I said, appreciating her concern and the fact that she had understood and acknowledged the reasons for my upset. "But I'm trying. I've been going to therapy and I've tried new hobbies and I've pushed myself. You have no idea —" my voice broke "—how hard I've worked, every day. And it feels like your comments dismiss the progress I've made."

"Oh no." Her face crumpled. "That…" She swiped away a tear. "I'm so sorry, Bryn. That wasn't my intent at all."

"It might not have been your intent, but can you understand how it might have come across?" I asked. "It puts pressure on me to mask my pain or just get over it."

"I'm so sorry that it sounded that way, Bryn. I absolutely would never want you to feel like you need to hide your emotions from me. And the idea that I think you should get over it…" Allie shook her head. She looked so heartbroken and earnest that I couldn't help but soften.

"Thank you." I took a steadying breath, leaning my head back to blink away tears. "I appreciate your saying that. Just…" I toyed with the belt of my robe. "Can you trust me to do what I need to do for me instead of trying to push me into it?"

She cringed. "Like trying to set you up on dates?"

"Yes." I arched my brow. "Like that."

"I'm sorry. I just know how much you like being in a relationship, and I thought…" She lifted a shoulder. "Anyway. I promise I'll try to be better about listening." She leaned closer, taking my hands in hers. "I'm always here for you. You know that, right?"

"I know," I said, because I did. "I could never repay you for everything you did for me after Derek passed away. Thank you for being there for me."

"Brynnie, I'm your sister. I wouldn't be anywhere else."

I pulled her in for a hug, relief washing over me. I hadn't realized how much our rift had been weighing on me. But now, we'd both said what we needed to say, and I was ready to move on.

"Thanks for the room upgrade, by the way."

She grinned. "I thought it might be a nice surprise and… perhaps a good peace offering?"

Suddenly, she seemed so hesitant and unsure. And it made me realize that Allie had genuinely wanted to do something nice for me to apologize, but also to celebrate my new relationship with Frasier. It was really sweet.

I grinned. "Maybe we need to fight more often. I could get used to this."

She laughed but then seemed to hesitate. "Am I allowed to ask about Frasier now?"

I laughed, mostly to cover my anxiety. "Why? What do you want to know?"

"I just have so many questions." She seemed almost giddy. "How did it happen? When did you know you wanted to be more than friends? How long…"

"Whoa. Whoa. Whoa." I held up my hands. "Slow down, Al."

She laughed, leaning into me. "Fine. I guess you don't have to answer it all at once, but I've missed you."

Her admission made me feel even worse for lying about dating Frasier, but we'd just mended our relationship. I didn't want to risk damaging it again, especially not so soon.

So, I poked her in the side, and she giggled, pushing my hand away. "I've always been here."

"I know, but…" She sighed. "I've felt guilty, talking about my relationship with Kit or the wedding."

"Don't." I turned to look at her, taking both hands in mine. Regardless of my relationship status, I was thrilled for her. And I wanted to hear about everything—the good, the bad, the difficult. "I'm so happy for you. And I would never want you to dim your joy for me."

Allie nodded, sniffling. We'd always been close, and she'd really been there for me after Derek's death—she and her fiancé, Kit. They didn't live locally, but she'd stayed with me for weeks after he'd died. And I'd always felt their support, even from afar.

We were quiet for a moment, and I felt at ease. I might not be telling the truth about dating Frasier, but oddly enough, that lie had helped me repair the relationship with my sister.

"So…" Allie said, leaning in. "Is the sex as good as I'm imagining? Because hockey players are physically aggressive, and that's hot. And Frasier's so intense, especially when it comes to you."

He was?

And why would she think that? She hadn't even seen Frasier and me interact now that we were a "couple."

"Allie!" I chided, though it came out as more of a hiss since I was trying to be quiet.

"What?" She lifted a shoulder, completely blasé.

"You're getting married to Kit in a few days."

"And I had a huge crush on Frasier when you were in college."

"Oh god." I laughed, covering my face with my hands. "How did I forget about that? You were so obvious."

She gave my shoulder a gentle shove. "I was not."

"You totally were. You had a custom Dartmouth jersey with his name and number on the back of it."

She narrowed her eyes at me. "And if you mention that in your speech at the rehearsal dinner, I will kill you."

I smirked, enjoying the fact that I could hold this over her.

"Do you still have that jersey?" I asked.

"Why?" She nudged me. "You want to see how unhinged he'll be if he sees you wearing his jersey and nothing else?"

I rolled my eyes. "God. Sometimes I'm still surprised you didn't turn into a puck bunny."

She laughed. "Tempting, but trust me—" she leaned in "—Kit is the perfect guy for me."

"He definitely is," I said.

"Come on, Bryn," Allie pleaded, pressing her palms together as if in prayer. "Tell me if I'm right about Frasier. Tell me if my teenage crush lives up to reality." She batted her eyes.

"You are ridiculous," I said, but I was laughing the entire time. "But honestly," I said, knowing I needed to put an end to this line of inquiry, "I wouldn't know. We're sort of taking things slow."

She gaped at me. "You said it was new, not that you were taking it slow."

"It's both." I tucked my hair behind my ear.

"Whose idea was that? Yours?" She shook her head, dropping it to her chest in disappointment.

"His, actually," I said, thinking of the way he'd held himself back last night.

Frasier had looked at me with so much desire that it had nearly consumed me. And yet…he hadn't acted on it. Did I want him to act on it?

Part of me said, hell yes!

My body was ready, and I had a feeling Allie was right—a man like Frasier would be incredible in bed. The perfect mix of aggressive and attentive.

But another part of me freaked out at the idea of sleeping with someone who wasn't Derek. He'd been my first. My only. And I was scared to take that next step, though I knew without a doubt that I could trust Frasier.

"Really?" Allie was clearly skeptical. I didn't blame her, but I couldn't go back on it now. And it was true—at least, in part.

While the idea of pursuing something physical with him

was undeniably appealing. I was also scared to ruin our friendship. I couldn't risk losing him.

In the end, none of it really mattered because we were just friends who were pretending to date.

"Yes, really," I said.

"What do you want, Bryn?" Allie asked.

What did I *want?*

It was something I'd often asked myself in the past year and a half. For a while, I'd been so focused on the past, on everything I'd lost. But now, I found myself wanting to focus on the future, even if it was difficult to imagine one without Derek.

Before I could answer, my name was called, saving me from a response. I popped up from my seat, grinning at Allie as she narrowed her eyes playfully at me.

All thoughts and fears melted away along with my stress as the massage therapist eased the tension from my muscles. The conversation with Allie had definitely helped.

By the time the massage was over, I practically floated down the boardwalk to the bungalow. My mind was clear; my body was relaxed. I wasn't thinking about the past or the future. I was living in the now.

I had a few hours to chill before we needed to be at the combined bachelor/bachelorette party. Since it was a small guest list, Allie and Kit had invited everyone to bring their spouses or dates, even if they weren't a member of the wedding party.

I opened the door to the bungalow and called out, "Honey, I'm—" *Oh.* I cringed, stopping myself before uttering, "Home."

Frasier was sprawled on the bed, facedown. The sheets rested low on his waist. Sunlight filtered in through the French doors, the shadows of palm leaves rippling across his golden skin.

My mouth went dry at the sight of him. Of those strong shoulders and that muscular back. Of all that power and strength and control.

Not wanting to wake him, I tiptoed to my suitcase. I grabbed my swimsuit and changed in the bathroom before heading out to the plunge pool, book in hand. The spa was nice, but I much preferred to be outside. And I could use some alone time to recharge before tonight's festivities.

I sank into the water, double-checking that my hands were dry before picking up my book. Even though the story was captivating, I kept rereading the same words. My mind was preoccupied, and my thoughts kept drifting to the man inside asleep on the bed.

Eventually, I gave up, resting my arms on the deck to stare out at the ocean. My gaze caught on my tattoo, and I smiled. I wondered, as I often did, what Derek would think. About the tattoo. About life. About everything.

I knew he'd always want me to be happy. If the roles had been reversed, that's what I'd want for him. I'd hope that he'd honor my memory, of course. But I'd also want him to find happiness, love.

Even with your best friend?

I glanced down at my left hand. I'd stopped wearing my rings months ago. I'd loved them—the design, everything they had represented. But I'd grown to hate the inevitable questions. The pity.

Now they sat in a drawer at home, unworn. No longer a visible daily reminder of loss. A relic of a life once lived.

My tattoo was different. It was as if I were carrying a piece of him with me always.

I loved Derek, and I always would. But I was young, and I, hopefully, had a lot of life left to live. If his death had taught me anything, it was to cherish your loved ones and live life to the fullest. Because you never knew how much time you had.

CHAPTER NINE

"Frasier?" Bryn said, her hand on my shoulder. "Frasier."

"Mm?" Her hand was on my skin, and I briefly wondered if I was still dreaming.

"Sorry to wake you," she said in a soft voice. "But the party bus is leaving in thirty minutes. I figured you might want some time to get ready before we have to head out."

I blinked my eyes open, my face pressed against a pillow. "Thanks." My voice was gravelly from sleep. I pushed away the pillow and sat up, scrubbing a hand over my face.

When I glanced at Bryn again, I realized she hadn't moved. "You…" She gaped at me. "Bear…you shaved." Her eyes darted over my face.

Did she love it? Hate it?

I certainly felt different.

I wasn't clean-shaven by any means, but I'd asked the on-site barber to give it a good trim. Scruff now lined my jaw, and my skin was smooth and glowing after he'd steamed my face and wrapped me in a warm towel. I'd taken a picture mid-process for Bryn, knowing she'd appreciate my effort at self-care.

I'd left the barbershop feeling like a million bucks. Part of me wondered why I hadn't shaved sooner because I felt somehow both naked and free without the beard that I'd let go for so long.

Bryn lifted her hand, cupping my cheek. I loved the way she was looking at me. As if she was seeing me for the first time, and she liked what she saw. "It looks really nice. *You* look really nice." She smiled up at me, and it was like a punch to the gut. "And it looks like someone's been moisturizing."

I laughed, and she lowered her hand, taking a step back, eyes on the floor. It was as if the sun had retreated behind a cloud, and I hated how shy and withdrawn she was all of a sudden. This wouldn't do, not if we were going to convince her family we were a couple.

I still couldn't believe I'd suggested this charade. But when it came to Bryn, I'd do anything for her, even if she didn't realize it. Even if it cost me…everything.

"You were right," I said. "It does feel good to take care of my skin. But…" I inclined my head. "You might have to come up with a new nickname for me."

"Oh no." She laughed, shaking her head. "You'll always be Bear to me."

"Even without all my fur?" I joked, feeling as if we were on more solid ground once more.

She tilted her head, evaluating me. "You know why I call you that, right? And it's not because of the beard."

"Because I'm a grumpy bastard."

"No." She rolled her eyes, and it made me smile. "It's because you give the best bear hugs."

I couldn't believe that was the reason—at least, not the entire reason. But if she loved my hugs, then I would keep giving them to her. I opened my arms, and she stepped into them. I rested my chin on her head, taking a moment to center myself.

But the longer we stood there, the more I realized just how little clothing was separating us. She had on a robe, and I could feel her nipples, hard and brushing against my bare chest. And if I wasn't careful… I released her and took a step back before my dick could get even more excited.

I cleared my throat. "How was the spa?"

Her skin was glowing, and she looked rested and relaxed. Beautiful.

"Amazing," she practically moaned, which wasn't helping my situation. "You should definitely get a massage while we're here."

I chuckled. "I planned to."

"I'm almost ready. I can get dressed out here if you want to use the bathroom," she offered.

"You sure?" I asked.

She nodded, so I thanked her and grabbed my clothes and phone before shutting myself in the bathroom. I almost didn't recognize the man staring back at me in the mirror. I looked different…energized or refreshed or something. Starting my day with an intense workout had helped, as had being pampered at the barbershop, followed by a hot shower and a long nap.

I should've used some of that time to call my mom back, but I wasn't sure I was in the right headspace to have the conversation I assumed was coming. I could be wrong. But the timing of her call, coupled with the missed calls from an unknown number, meant I probably wasn't. My brother had this irritating habit of reaching out—if you could even call it that—at the worst possible times.

Not that any time was great. Not after everything he'd done.

I pulled on my pants, and I was buttoning my shirt when my phone chimed with an incoming message. I checked my phone, relieved to see that it was from Gabe.

Gabe: How's it going?

I knew he was referring to my relationship with Bryn, but I sent him a picture I'd taken of the beach before my morning run. I slipped on my watch and fixed my hair.

Gabe: Damn. Any progress on Operation GTFOOTFZ?

I stared at the screen, trying to decipher his long-ass acronym.

Me: Are you whiteboarding custom license plate ideas again? Because I've got to tell you, that one is terrible. Got foot fuzz?

Gabe: Operation Get the fuck out of the friend zone.

Gabe: You know…that golden opportunity we talked about?

Gabe: So…progress?

How the hell was I supposed to answer that? Did a fake relationship count as progress? In some ways, yes. But it also felt like two steps back.

Me: It's complicated.

Gabe: Then un-complicate it.

I clenched my phone, annoyed more with myself than my friend. Though his commentary wasn't helping matters.

For all my big talk of having no regrets, I clearly still had reservations. Not about Bryn, of course. I was crazy about her.

My heart and body were totally on board, but my mind… my mind wouldn't fucking shut up. I sighed, thinking of her tattoo. Of everything it symbolized. Seeing it on her wrist had been like being doused with a bucket of ice water.

Derek.

A man who had meant so much to both of us. Who *still* meant so much to us.

> Gabe: Stop playing it safe, Fizzy. You want it, you gotta go for it.

Oh, I wanted Bryn, all right. I just wasn't sure if I should go for it now that we were pretending to be a couple. I was afraid our fake relationship might only confuse things even more and make her question my true feelings.

That said, I was encouraged by last night. By the way Bryn had responded to me both then and when I'd given her the signed copy of the book. The chemistry was certainly there. Even though the situation wasn't ideal, I thought that maybe I had a real shot at turning this into something genuine.

A glance at my watch told me that it was almost time to go. I brushed my teeth and then

slid my phone into the pocket of my linen pants.

I cracked the bathroom door ajar without peering outside. "Is it safe to come out now?"

"You can come out," Bryn said.

I opened the door and my jaw dropped. She seemed to have a similar reaction, freezing in place.

She looked fucking phenomenal. I mean... *Damn.* She was wearing this colorful, patterned dress that wrapped around her waist, snatching it. It hugged her breasts, pushing them up. Then, it had this sexy little cutout that gave the most tantalizing glimpse of her cleavage and made me think she must not be wearing a bra.

It was hard to decide where to look. My eyes kept bouncing from her glossy pink lips to her bare shoulders.

Her hair was down in loose waves, and she looked sun-kissed and beautiful.

I strode over to her, admiring the dip of her waist, the expanse of skin revealed by the low back of her dress. It was a good thing everyone thought we were dating because I wasn't going to be able to take my eyes off her. And as much as I hated our fake relationship, it did have one thing going for it—it finally gave me an excuse to look my fill.

I took Bryn's hand in mine and gave her a spin before pulling her back in to me. "You..." I kissed her cheek. "Are stunning."

She dipped her head, cheeks turning an adorable shade of pink. "Thank you. So are you. I mean—" God, seeing her flustered because of me was gratifying. "You look nice. Handsome."

"Thank you." I slid my phone from my pocket. "Want to take a picture real quick?"

She looked at me, surprise lighting her features. "You hate being photographed."

I loved that she knew that. Knew that I endured it for the fans because I appreciated them. But I hated when people took a photo of me without my permission. I knew it was all part of the job, but it was a huge invasion of privacy. I would much rather someone have the balls to ask me for a photo than try to sneak one.

I lifted a shoulder. "Not when I'm with you."

I wrapped one arm around her then held up the other, phone in hand. The couple staring back at us on the screen was happy and relaxed. I snapped a few shots, hoping Bryn could see what I saw, before lowering my phone.

"Will you send those to me?" she asked.

"Of course," I said, immediately doing just that.

While Bryn went to grab her purse, I sent my favorite shot to Gabe to prove that I was trying to un-complicate things, as he'd said. A second later, my phone started buzzing with alerts. But when I glanced at it, it wasn't Gabe. The group chat was blowing up.

(Puck Dynasty Group Chat)

> Boone: Damn, Bear. What happened to your fur?

> Carson: Is that Bryn? She looks good. Where are you?

> Zayn: Doesn't look like LA.

> Boone: Wait. Are you guys together now? Is this a thing?

> Zayn: If so, fucking finally.

> Carson: Nah. We all know they're just "friends."

> Boone: At least when they finally admit they're more than friends, we'll have the perfect couple's moniker already picked out. Fryn

> Zayn: Brasier

While those jackasses workshopped our couple's moniker, I scrolled back up and saw that no… No. I hadn't accidentally sent the picture of Bryn and me to the group chat. Gabe had. *Traitor.*

I went back to our solo text.

> Me: What the fuck, man?

> Gabe: What? It's a good picture.

> Gabe: And you're welcome.

Me: For what?

Gabe: I helped you stake your claim.

I sighed. All the while, my phone kept buzzing. I didn't even bother to look this time. I didn't know what to say, so I decided it was best to say nothing.

"Everything okay?" Bryn asked.

Not wanting to let them get in my head, I switched off my phone. I wanted to be completely focused on Bryn. When I glanced up at her, she was watching me with a concerned expression.

"Just the guys talking shit." I showed her my phone screen now that it was blank. "They won't bother us now."

Bryn grabbed her purse, and we were about to leave when she stopped and turned to me. "Are you sure you want to do this?" she asked, uncharacteristically shy.

"Why? Are you having doubts?"

"About you?" She shook her head. "Never. I trust you."

"I know." It wasn't something I took lightly.

I brushed her hair away from her shoulder, loving that I had an excuse to touch her even though no one was around. She smiled, and I found myself smiling back.

"I talked to Allie earlier," she said, relief threading her words. "She apologized, and we cleared the air."

"I'm glad to hear that." I was grateful for it. "Do you feel better?"

She nodded. "I feel like she really listened to me."

"Good," I said, and I meant it. Because if Allie did anything else to hurt Bryn, we were going to have words. "What did you tell her about us?"

"Maybe it was wrong, but I decided to roll with it." She winked, and I chuckled. "So now she and my mom, and whoever else they've told, think we're dating."

I thought it was interesting that Bryn had decided that it was easier to pretend we were dating than tell her family the truth, but I kept that thought to myself. As I'd told her last night, I would do whatever she wanted.

"How'd your mom react?" I asked.

"She was so happy and relieved, even if she didn't say that. But Allie had a ton of questions, and now I'm worried that we're walking into this woefully unprepared."

I rubbed the back of my neck. "What kinds of questions?"

"Things like how long have we been together? How did this happen? Stuff like that. But hopefully, she'll be having too much fun tonight to pay us much attention."

I was skeptical. "Are you worried we won't be able to sell it?"

She lifted a shoulder. "I like to be prepared, and I feel very out of my element here."

Because of me? Because of the situation? Because she hadn't dated in a long time? Maybe a bit of all of it.

"This doesn't have to be difficult," I said, eager to ease her worries. "Try not to overthink it. Most people know we've been friends for a long time. This is just a natural progression of our relationship. Besides, we can let our body language do most of the talking."

"But if they do ask questions..." She rolled her lips between her teeth. "I think we should try to stick to the truth as much as possible."

As if I needed the reminder. The bigger issue was trying to remember that for her, at least, this was all pretend.

I gave her hand a squeeze, wanting to reassure her. I certainly wouldn't need to fake anything when it came to my feelings for Bryn.

She gnawed on the inside of her cheek, and I knew something was bothering her. But instead of pushing, I waited for her to speak.

"What if people think it's…weird?" she whispered, and I hated the uncertainty in her eyes. She glanced away. "That we're together because of…you know."

Because of Derek.

"Bryn." I grasped her chin, bringing her attention back to me.

"Yeah?" Her pulse was racing in her neck, eyes dilated. She seemed to like it when I took control. But that wasn't what I should be focusing on right now, so I pushed away those thoughts.

"How did your sister react when you told her we were dating?"

She laughed. "Not surprised. Like…*finally.*"

Similar to some of my friends, then.

"And your mom?"

"She said it was great news."

"That sounds really supportive to me. But regardless of what anyone else thinks, how do *you* feel when we're together?"

Her shoulders relaxed. "I feel…good. Calm and centered. I always feel safe with you."

My chest warmed at her statement.

"We enjoy being together, right?" I asked.

"Right." She grinned.

"So it's really not all that different from what we do at home. We've got this," I said, releasing my grip on her chin.

"Yeah." She exhaled quickly. "Yeah. We've got this." I wasn't entirely convinced she believed it, but it was a start.

I linked our hands as we made our way down the path that led to the front of the resort. It felt like the most natural thing in the world. We were almost to the main entrance when she stopped me.

She glanced around then pressed up on her tiptoes. When she spoke, her voice was low even though no one was around, apart from a few hotel employees. And they didn't seem to be paying us any attention. "What about PDA? We don't usually touch so much at home."

"Is this okay?" I asked, rubbing my thumb over the back of her hand.

She nodded. "Yes, but maybe we need a code word or something. You know—to discreetly check in or whatever."

I thought about it for a moment. Then I said, "What about a signal?" I tapped my finger twice against her hand. "Are you okay?"

"Yeah. Good idea." She seemed to relax a little then gave me two taps in response. "I'm good."

Two taps to check in. And two taps in response meant all was well. *Easy.*

"And if we need to slow down or stop?" she asked.

"We need a word," I said. "Something that might not ordinarily come up during conversation but is easy to remember. Maybe…Penny?"

"Penny?" she asked. "Like the coin?"

"Or one of your favorite authors." I rubbed the back of my neck.

She dipped her head. "I like that."

"I've got you." I tucked her hair behind her ear, savoring the fact that I could touch her so freely. "You know that, right?" I cupped her cheek. If I moved a few inches closer, we'd be kissing.

She searched my eyes before she nodded. "I know. You're always there for me."

I rested my forehead against hers. "Always," I vowed, moving my hand so that I was cupping the back of her neck.

I was so damn close to closing the remaining distance and kissing her. But at the last minute, I pulled back and pressed my lips to her forehead instead. I didn't want our first kiss to be under the guise of a fake relationship. When I kissed Bryn, I wanted her to know it was real.

So, for now, I'd continue to be patient.

She was important to me. She was *everything* to me.

We met the others out in front of the resort, where a small bus was waiting. I hung back, following Bryn up the steps, my hand on her lower back. Inside, the champagne was already flowing. Allie was holding a microphone and wearing a white top hat with a veil. She introduced everyone as they stepped onto the bus like an emcee at the Hawks game.

"Next up is my beautiful sister, my bridesmaid," Allie said in a dramatic, booming voice over the mic. "Bryn!" Everyone cheered. "And her handsome date, Frasier."

Allie winked at me. Kit stood by Allie's side, wearing his own black top hat. Her lipstick was already smeared on his cheek, and I'd attended enough parties as a young hockey player to know that we were in for one hell of a night.

Bryn sank down on one of the seats, and I joined her, wedging in close. She linked our hands, surprising me even more when she rested our clasped hands on her bare thigh. I blinked at her and then remembered why we were there.

Right. Our audience.

I could feel Allie's eyes on us, and it was time to put on a show.

I switched which hand was holding Bryn's so I could drape my arm over her shoulder, loving the way she nestled into my side. She smelled so damn good, and I was aware of every single place we touched, aware of the warmth of her skin. I pressed my lips to her temple, aching to explore more of her.

I double tapped her shoulder, and she double tapped my thigh, smiling up at me, eyes sparkling with mischief.

I knew that look. That look had led to countless acts of

daring. Like the night she'd convinced Derek and me to strip down to our underwear with her so we could all swim in a fountain on campus. Or the time she'd persuaded Derek and me to sneak her into the rink after hours.

I hadn't seen that look in a long time. Not since well before Derek's death. Not since college, really.

And even though I knew it meant trouble, I found myself smiling.

She was so fucking gorgeous. And I was determined to make her mine.

Bryn and I chatted with a few of the other guests during the ride. I'd met a couple of the guys earlier as I'd made my way around the resort, and they'd all seemed nice enough. Some of them were hockey fans, and they touched briefly on the upcoming season. But after that, everyone treated me like I was just like anyone else.

After a relatively smooth ride, we arrived at the beach bar. Bryn and I hung toward the back of the group. The place was poppin', and the live band had drawn a crowd. It was clearly a favorite spot of both locals and tourists.

Our group found a large table and ordered food and drinks. I kept an eye on Bryn, loving how carefree she seemed. And I could tell from the way her smile stretched to her eyes that she wasn't pretending for the sake of her family; she was genuinely having fun.

I ordered a drink, but I took my time sipping it. After a few drinks, everyone was singing along to the music. Allie and a few of the girls dragged everyone out onto the makeshift dance floor, which was really just a square of sand with colorful lights strung between the palm trees.

I watched on from the high-top table, nursing my drink. Bryn had always loved dancing, and she had this natural ability to move her body. I was in awe of her, as always.

She came over to the table, eyes bright and cheeks rosy. "Dance with me?"

I chuckled, allowing her to lead me out to join the others. The salty air was warm, the music had a sultry beat, and I glided my hands down her arms, guiding her hands to my shoulders. She watched me with rapt attention, draping her arms around my neck.

I hated that I had to question if what she was doing was all for show. But when I slid my hands down her back, I reveled in the way her pupils darkened in response. That was real, and I clung to the idea that her desire for me wasn't an act.

I placed my hands on her waist, guiding her, letting her feel the beat as I swiveled my hips. She followed along, arching one brow, clearly surprised that I was not only a willing participant but a skilled partner. *That's right, angel.*

She leaned in, her lips brushing my skin and sending a shiver of pleasure down my spine. "Where'd you learn to dance like this?"

"Lost a bet with Gabe."

She laughed, the sound light and full of happiness. "I think you could have a real shot at winning the Mirror Ball Trophy if you're ever on *Dancing with the Stars*."

Now it was my turn to laugh. "Yeah. That's never happening."

I'd enjoyed dancing more than I'd expected. I liked the challenge, of course. I loved anything that required me to be physical or challenged me mentally. But there was no way I was going to dance on live TV in front of millions in a tight-fitting sequined costume.

"Really?" She pouted.

"Angel," I chuckled, the endearment slipping out before I could stop myself. "You're the only partner I want to dance with."

She grinned. "That's sweet. But seriously? I would love to go on that show someday. The costumes. The talent. Ugh."

I chuckled. "I'll stick to the ice. It's enough that I learned a lot, had fun, and improved my agility." I did a maneuver to demonstrate.

"Clearly," she said. "I mean, damn, Bear. You've got some moves." She had no idea. Her cheeks were flushed, and I was dying to kiss her.

Shoot your fucking shot. Gabe's voice rang in my head.

I brushed Bryn's hair aside, meeting her gaze. Blue eyes full of trust and desire. The tension between us pulled taut. I leaned in. She licked her lips, and I wanted to taste them. She looked like she wanted me to taste them too.

But maybe what I'd mistaken for desire was actually just the effects of alcohol. She was buzzed and loose, her inhibitions lowered.

Regardless of the rum and our fake relationship, I knew she was attracted to me—last night had definitely shown that. But I needed to tread carefully. We might be pretending we were dating, but the last thing I wanted was to fuck up my chances with her and ruin our friendship. Because more than anything, that's what I feared. Losing Bryn for good.

"Bride tribe," Allie called out, waving her white top hat in the air, the veil fluttering behind it.

I leaned down and whispered, "Bride tribe?" in Bryn's ear.

She rolled her eyes, but she was smiling the entire time. "Oh yeah. I'm lucky Allie didn't make us wear the matching sashes she got us. Unfortunately—" Bryn adopted a sad expression, though I could tell she was trying hard not to laugh "—nobody could find them at the hotel."

"That is unfortunate," I said in a solemn tone.

She gave my arm a playful shove as we waited for the others to gather around for whatever announcement the bride was about to make.

"Okay, gang," Allie said. "The bus is here to take us back to the hotel."

"Already?" someone whined, clearly drunk.

A glance at my watch told me we'd been here longer than I'd realized.

"Don't worry." Allie linked her arm through Bryn's, and I was glad to see they were getting along and having fun. "The party's not over yet." Allie winked at me over her shoulder, her cheeks pink from the alcohol.

And Allie was right. Because the party kept going—on the bus, where the drinks continued to flow. Several of the couples were making out, including the bride and groom. Bryn and I kept stealing glances at each other, and then we'd laugh.

When we got back to the hotel, Bryn and I followed the others down to a fire pit on the beach. There were only a few open seats left, which left Bryn on the opposite side of the circle from me.

Every time I looked at her, our eyes caught and held briefly. And then she'd smile and look down into her glass.

I couldn't help but watch her. Hell, I couldn't take my eyes off her. She was like the puck in a play-off game, and my attention followed her at all times. Like it was my goddamn job.

Even when one of the other guests engaged me in conversation, my attention was still on Bryn. On the way the firelight flickered over her skin. Her musical laughter. The delectable color of her lips and cheeks.

Fuck me. I was so gone for this woman, it was ridiculous.

CHAPTER TEN

Bryn

"Who wants to go first?" Allie asked, holding her glass aloft. Some of the liquid sloshed over the edge, and she giggled as Kit reached out to steady her.

I laughed, sipping my own drink. I felt light and floaty—like nothing could touch me.

I was tempted to blame the buzz on the alcohol, but it was more than that. It was Frasier, and the way he'd touched me, watched me. All evening, he'd made me feel wanted and desired, and I thought I might combust.

I'd forgotten this sensation. Forgotten what it was like to crush on someone. And I found myself wanting to "lean in" to it, as Georgia had suggested. It might all be pretend—at least for Frasier. But if anything, that made it easier for me to let go.

"First for what?" one of the other bridesmaids asked, interrupting my rum-fueled musings. I kicked off my shoes, burying my toes in the cool sand.

Allie beamed. "Truth or dare, of course."

A few people groaned, including me.

After a fun evening at the beach bar, the party had moved

back to the resort. My body might be sitting in a chair in front of a bonfire, but my mind was still stuck on that dance on the beach. Talk about bringing the heat…

Holy shit, Frasier had some moves.

How that man was still single was beyond me. Sure, he could come off as intense, grumpy even. But beneath the intimidating exterior, he was a teddy bear. Definitely boyfriend material. *No.* Husband material.

He was kind and caring. He was loyal and generous. He'd always been there for me…and maybe *that* was the problem. Maybe *I* was the problem.

He was always too busy with hockey or me to leave time for anything else, like dating. He claimed that wasn't true, but I didn't see how it could be otherwise. I wanted Frasier to find happiness, but the idea of watching him with another woman sent such a visceral reaction through me that I thought I was going to be sick.

I am so screwed.

Because I was coming to realize that not only was I attracted to my best friend, but the feelings I had toward Frasier went so far beyond mere attraction. And I wasn't sure what to do about that. If I even *should* do anything about it.

When I glanced up, Frasier was watching me with a concerned expression. He looked as if he were about to get up and cross the circle to me, but I shook my head. His shoulders relaxed ever so slightly, but then he placed his hand over his heart. His eyes locked on mine as he tapped twice. *Are you okay?*

The bridge of my nose stung. I didn't know whether it was the alcohol or my emotions, but I loved this man for checking in with me. I loved that he knew me so well.

And even though I was far from okay, he made me feel like I could be. So I placed my hand over my heart and tapped twice. He nodded, seemingly satisfied—at least, for now.

"First of all, everyone put their phones in a pile," Allie said. "Or here." She stole Kit's hat and turned it upside down before passing it to the bridesmaid next to her. "Put them in here."

I didn't know whether that made me feel better or worse. At least no one would be able to record whatever was about to go down. But I wondered how far some of Allie and Kit's friends would take a game of truth or dare.

"You too, Allie," I said when I noticed she hadn't added her phone to the pile.

This was her bachelorette party, and I was willing to go along with some shenanigans. But I would never do anything that could risk Frasier's reputation or career. I knew how important it was to him. I knew how hard he'd worked for it, and how much his family had sacrificed for him and his brother when they were younger to make their dreams happen.

"I need my phone," she said. "I have a website that randomly generates the prompts."

"Isn't that cheating?" someone asked.

"Yeah," someone else chimed in. "I thought you had to come up with your own."

"More fun this way. More random," Allie said.

"We play this way all the time," one of the other bridesmaids said.

Seriously?

They were in their early twenties. Fresh out of college. And yet, it still surprised me that they were playing truth or dare.

"Aren't we a little old for this?" I asked as the hotel waiter delivered a fresh round of drinks.

"Just for that—" Allie grinned. "You're going first." Her

smile widened, her eyes taking on a wicked glint. *Oh boy.* "Everyone knows the rules. If you don't want to do the truth or dare, you take a shot. So, Bryn." She looked at me. "Truth or dare?"

I held my sister's gaze, not even sure I wanted to engage. But then I remembered that I was done with being sad and serious. And I figured, what the hell?

Maybe it was the ocean air—more likely, it was the rum punch. But I could certainly use more fun in my life. And so far, this trip had been fun. Frasier made it fun.

"Truth," I finally said, thinking that might be more intimidating than a dare.

Allie glanced down at her phone, where the website had randomly generated a question. "What's the last lie you told?"

I tried not to look at Frasier.

Don't look. Don't look...

I swallowed. Hard. "The last lie I told..." I glanced around the circle, trying to buy myself some time.

I couldn't admit that I was lying about my relationship with Frasier. But when my eyes inevitably landed on him, I found myself blurting, "I've been lying about our relationship, saying that we were just friends when we're so much more."

It was the most honest thing I could've said.

We might be playing a game, but in that moment, my words were meant solely for him. Frasier's eyes widened ever so slightly, and he rubbed the back of his neck. I wondered what he was thinking. I wondered if he realized just how truthful I'd been.

Because we were so much more than just friends. Frasier was my rock. But I was coming to realize that maybe friendship wasn't enough anymore. And somehow, that idea didn't scare me as much as I'd expected.

Allie laughed. "I'm pretty sure everyone knew you were

lying about that one, Brynnie." Kit nodded, which surprised me somehow. "But we're glad you finally admitted it."

Tension eased out of me as the game resumed. I finished my drink and ordered another. One of the bridesmaids ended up in the pool on a dare. One of the guys had to tell us the most hilariously awful, embarrassing story involving nudity or a sexual experience. By the end of his tale, we were all laughing so hard, I nearly peed my pants.

My cheeks ached, and I was struck by a realization. I wasn't pretending to enjoy myself; I was actually having fun. Maybe Georgia's suggestion hadn't been such a terrible idea after all.

But as Frasier's turn neared, I braced myself. Sure, there were no phones, but he was still a celebrity. If we'd been hanging out with other guys from the team, I wouldn't have been concerned. And while I didn't think anyone here would intentionally harm Frasier or his reputation, fame did funny things to people.

I smoothed my hand down my throat, enjoying the way his eyes lingered on my every move. I double tapped my collarbone. If he wanted out, now was the time. I could make some excuse, and we could leave the party, head back to our room.

But after tonight—the alcohol, the dancing, the flirting, the touching—I wasn't sure I could trust myself to be alone with him. I hadn't been able to take my eyes off Frasier all evening. The prospect of being alone in our room thrilled and terrified me in equal measure.

With his hand on his thigh, he double tapped his response. *Okay, then.*

"Frasier," Allie said. "Truth or dare?"

I held my breath, and then he said, "Truth."

Allie tapped her phone then grinned. Several people around the circle "oohed" in anticipation of whatever she was about to say. "What's your biggest turn-on and biggest turn-off?"

"A woman who's into hockey," one of the guys, Hayden, called out, cupping his hand around his mouth.

"Someone who knows their way around your stick," said another, and everyone laughed.

Finally, everyone quieted down, their attention on Frasier. When he answered, he looked me square in the eye and said, "Bryn." I swallowed hard, everyone else fading into the background. "Everything about Bryn is my biggest turn-on." My breath caught, and it no longer felt as if he was playing the game.

Or at least, I was left wondering which game we were playing. The fake relationship or the truth. My heart was pounding so loud it was a wonder everyone else couldn't hear it.

"Aw." Allie clasped her hands together beneath her chin. "That's so freaking sweet."

"But *boooring!*" shouted Elise next to her. Around the circle, people nodded. My skin was hot and tight, but I waited to see how Frasier wanted to handle it.

"Give us more," someone started chanting, and the others joined in. I covered my mouth with my hand, trying not to laugh. This was so ridiculous.

Frasier met my eyes again when he opened his mouth to speak, and everyone quieted down. "Biggest turn-on," Frasier said, "is a woman who's confident."

A few of the guys nodded.

"Really?" the maid of honor asked, shaking her head as if she couldn't believe what she was hearing. "It's that simple?"

Frasier nodded, and one of the groomsmen said, "One hundred percent, man." And he gave Frasier a fist bump.

"Biggest turn-off," Allie said, and I was grateful that everyone seemed to accept Frasier's answer.

Frasier dragged a hand through his hair. "When someone I've just met tries to call me by my nickname."

I laughed. "Oh. That's true." I could remember a few times when people, especially women, had tried to call Frasier or one of the guys by their nicknames. They always bristled at it.

Next, it was the best man's turn, and he had to tell us about the best sexual experience of his life so far. And then one of the bridesmaids had to choose her fantasy orgy guests from her boyfriend's contact list. That garnered some interesting reactions from said boyfriend and a few of the other guests.

Eventually, it was my turn again. "Okay," Allie said. "We've made it through one—relatively tame—round. So…" She glanced around the circle, and everyone seemed to lean forward as if in anticipation. "We're going to turn up the heat."

I was a little scared about what Allie meant by that, but I also wasn't going to back down. Not yet anyway. This time, I chose dare.

My sister smirked at whatever prompt was displayed on the screen, and I braced myself. Was I going to have to strip down and swim naked in the ocean? Pretend to have a loud, dramatic orgasm in front of the group or do something equally mortifying? Because the longer the game went on, and the more we drank, the more risqué it became.

"I dare you…" Allie frowned. "Bleh. That's too easy." She swiped again.

"Hey! You can't cherry-pick the dares," I protested. "You've never skipped to a harder one for anyone else."

"It was a dare to kiss someone for a minute. I mean, come on. Basic, especially since you're already in a relationship."

Everyone else booed in agreement, but the joke was on them because Frasier and I had never kissed. It wasn't as if I could fight her on it. And besides, the rest of the group seemed to be aligned with my sister.

Allie slowly lifted her gaze from her phone to me, and my stomach churned. "I dare you to show us your best audition for a burlesque act."

A few of the guys whistled, some whoops definitely rang out, and I was scared to look at Frasier.

"Good thing you took all those dance lessons when we were younger."

"What kind of dance lessons do you think Mom and Dad sent me to?" I teased. "It was ballet, not burlesque." Ballet, jazz, hip-hop, any type of dance, really—I'd loved it all. The creativity, the movement, the freedom.

"With burlesque, it's all about the tease." Allie giggled, sinking back down into her chair. "You have ninety seconds to prepare."

Ninety seconds was far from enough time. My dance training gave me an advantage, but I was out of practice and entirely outside of my area of expertise. That said, I'd attended a burlesque show once in college as extra credit for my theater elective.

It had all seemed so glamorous. The performers were so confident and in control of their bodies. Sometimes, their acts were about making a statement, but they were always body positive and empowering.

I supposed it was better than being challenged to a strip-tease. At least with burlesque, it was accepted that some acts didn't involve nudity. That said, it wasn't as if I had many layers that I could use as part of the "tease." I'd already ditched my shoes. I wasn't wearing a bra. I squeezed my eyes shut, trying to tune out everything else.

"Sixty seconds," Allie called out.

Think, Bryn. Think!

I needed music. A costume, even if it wasn't that great. An

act. It was all about captivating the audience, tantalizing them, regardless of how much or how little I removed.

I glanced around the circle for props, costume materials, *anything*. I stood and grabbed Allie's hat from her head before placing it on mine. I snagged one of the bridesmaids' pashminas before draping it around my shoulders.

"Thirty seconds," Allie taunted.

"What about music?" I asked.

"What song do you want?" I went to her side, nearly stumbling on the sand. I wanted to blame it on my haste, but maybe I was tipsier than I realized.

I grabbed Allie's phone and skimmed through her music selection. Even though the others were talking and laughing, I could feel their rising curiosity. My hands were shaking, but I knew, if I was going to do this, I was going to do it right. Once the music started, I would have to put aside my insecurities and embrace my inner badass.

I selected a Michael Bublé song with a sultry, big-band feel. I took a deep breath as Allie pressed play, preparing myself as if to step onto a stage. As the opening notes to "Feeling Good" began to play, I tried to channel all my inner confidence.

I grazed my fingers over the backs of several chairs, exaggerating the sway of my hips. When the jazzy beat kicked in, I sank down low. At first, it was clumsy. I felt awkward.

But if I thought of myself as a character in a show, I could push down the embarrassment threatening to heat my cheeks. I could imagine myself on a stage under a spotlight, with a top hat and a feather boa. Not...walking along the beach, with my sister and her friends watching as I dragged my hands seductively down my chest.

Several people let out a whistle, and I could feel everyone's eyes on me. But when my eyes locked on Frasier, I felt centered. And the way he was watching me made me feel like the confident, sexy woman I was trying to portray.

I was performing for him and him alone. I didn't dare scan the circle for reactions or opinions. In that moment, no one but Frasier existed. And his eyes were locked on mine, pulling me in.

As Michael Bublé sang about it being a new dawn, I felt some of my worries fall away. I hadn't danced in a while, but power oozed from my body with every step. I was practically vibrating with the force of it.

I held Frasier's eyes from across the circle, using my empty chair as a prop in my performance. I pretended the chair was my dance partner, and occasionally I'd grind against it or sit on it. I sank down, spreading my thighs apart, grateful for the long, flowy fabric of my dress. It hinted at my curves without revealing too much.

His nostrils flared, his hands gripping and releasing his own thighs. God, he was so hot. And if his biggest turn-on was a woman with confidence, I was going to do my best to give that to him. To be that for him, but also for myself.

I stood and removed my top hat, holding it over my face and pulsing it as I moved my hips and then shimmied my shoulders. I wasn't thinking about what was next; I wasn't *thinking* at all. I let the feel of the music guide me. I tossed the top hat aside, bending down before snapping up and whipping my hair around.

Maybe it was the rum or my audience, but I was enjoying myself. I flashed Frasier a flirty smile, really leaning into the role. His mouth popped open, and in the background, I could hear several people shouting their appreciation.

While I didn't typically crave the spotlight, I felt empowered. I was taking charge—of the performance, the energy, my sexuality. And I was embracing my sensuality, teasing with the pashmina, my body, my facial expressions. It was so freeing, like the smoke rising from the fire into the night air.

I tossed the pashmina aside, and I could feel all eyes on me as I crossed the circle to Frasier. When the music intensified, I dragged my hands up over my body, lifting them up my neck and through my hair before letting it fall. And then I sank down low, reveling in the way he watched me, thighs spread, lips parted.

As the music reached its crescendo, I lip-synched along with the final words about feeling good. I did feel good, and that was due in large part to Frasier. I wanted to touch him, needed to touch him and be close to him.

So I placed my hand on his shoulder, eyebrow raised in silent question. I couldn't flat out ask him for permission, not without giving it all away. He set his drink down beside him, and when he patted his thigh in response, I flashed him a grateful smile that he'd understood.

I lifted my dress slightly, slowly lowering myself onto his lap. He was so big, so imposing. And yet, I'd never felt anything but safe when I was with him.

Even now, when I knew I was pushing the limits, I trusted that he'd be there to catch me. He always was.

I draped my arms around his neck, thinking back to our dance at the beach bar. I'd never imagined that a man who was so powerful and physically aggressive could also be so sultry and sensuous, seductive even. All night, I'd found myself wanting him to touch me like that again.

I wanted him to want to kiss me. I wanted him to *want* me.

But right now, I had a show to finish. A dare to complete. So I locked my legs around his waist, and then I let go of his shoulders, reclining so that the ends of my hair dusted the ground. I brought myself back up to a seated position, draping one arm over his shoulder and then turning to wink at my audience as the final notes faded out.

For a moment, it was silent but for the snap and crackle of the logs on the fire. And then everyone burst into applause. Allie leaped to her feet. "Oh my god!"

"That was…" The girl next to me fanned herself. "So hot."

But the only opinion I cared about was Frasier's. I tapped his shoulder twice, our secret code asking if he was okay. He double tapped my thigh in response, his hand resting close to my hip and ass, encompassing me. *I'm good.*

"Damn." One of the guys was about to say something more but then stopped himself abruptly. When I looked back at Frasier, he was glaring.

"Grumpy bear." I played with the hair at his nape, trying not to laugh at his stern expression.

He leaned in, his lips trailing along my ear. "Can you blame me? That was fucking hot, and I don't like that anyone else saw you like that."

I shivered, both from his words and his possessive tone.

His hands were on my hips. And god, it felt so good—to be touched. Not by just anyone, but by him. My skin burned from his touch, my body reawakening as if from a long slumber. Frasier smoothed his hand up my spine, sliding it beneath my hair until he was cupping the back of my neck. I sighed aloud at the pleasure of it—his large, warm hands on my skin. The way he was looking at me, as if I were precious.

I watched him, dumbfounded, as he caressed my back, his eyes darting between mine. Searching mine. When he nuzzled my nose with his, I couldn't take it anymore.

"We should kiss," I blurted, soft enough so only he could hear.

Not for the sake of our fake relationship. Not for any reason except that I wanted to.

And yes, maybe I was a coward, using the situation to *lean in,* as Georgia had suggested. But I felt so empowered by my performance that I was willing to push the boundaries a little.

He chuckled, the sound low and deep like thunder rumbling over an open plain. My heart was galloping at full speed. I had no idea what he was going to say.

"Angel," he drawled. "I'm completely at your mercy."

I cupped his cheek, savoring the feel of his scruff scraping against my palm. He leaned into my touch, and something warmed in my chest.

In the back of my mind, I questioned whether this was a good idea. But I pushed those doubts away. I closed the distance before I could talk myself out of it, feeling a little thrill as I brushed my lips against his.

I'd planned for a quick kiss—just a taste, really. But the moment our lips locked, Frasier took control, cupping my nape as he demolished every plan, every thought in my mind.

There were no more games. No more lies or pretend.

I parted my lips, granting him access as he claimed me. He tasted of coconut rum and pineapples, comfort and wicked promises. He'd always made me feel safe, and right now, I knew I was in big trouble.

Because with every graze and glide and nibble, I was falling deeper and harder. I clutched his shirt, desperate for this man. Because, holy fuck, could he kiss. And I wanted more.

I didn't mean to, but I arched my hips against him. And that's when I felt it—his hard-on. I gasped at the sensation, seeking that friction despite all the layers separating us. He groaned, deepening the kiss.

We kissed for what could've been seconds or hours, I was so lost to him. At least until someone bellowed, "Get a room!"

The sounds of hoots and hollers broke through the haze,

and Frasier pulled back. His eyes were still locked on mine, tuning out everything and everyone else, just like he did on the ice. To be the center of his focus was…exhilarating.

I didn't want it to end. I didn't want to return to reality.

But it was unavoidable. And when I remembered that everyone was watching us, cheering for us, I buried my face in Frasier's chest. His woodsy citrus scent was grounding, and he cupped the back of my head, cradling me protectively and with tenderness.

"You ready to get out of here?" His voice rumbled through me.

I nodded, anticipation coursing through my veins. My nipples were hard, grazing against his chest. I had no idea what came next, but my body was alive for the first time in almost two years.

"More than ready." My voice was throaty, my pulse careening.

"Hang on tight," he said to me. Then to the group, he added, "And on that note—" Before I could even process his words, he stood with me in his arms. I wrapped my legs around his waist, enjoying the feeling of being weightless. Protected. Cared for. "We're off to bed."

That elicited another round of whoops, and I laughed even as my cheeks burned. I buried my face in his neck as he scooped up my shoes from the sand, quickly pocketing our phones from Kit's top hat. Frasier and I might have agreed this was pretend, but it was all beginning to feel a little too real. And as he carted me off to our room, carrying me in his arms, I found myself wishing it were true.

CHAPTER ELEVEN

Frasier

S ometimes I hated being right.

And this was definitely one of those times.

Because that kiss? With Bryn? Fucking incredible.

But she was drunk, and this was fake.

Unfortunately, my body didn't know any of that. And now I was hard and praying it was dark enough no one had noticed just how much I'd enjoyed being pressed up against her.

"You know I can walk, right?" she joked, her arms still around my neck, her head resting against my shoulder.

"Can you?" I asked, noticing she'd made no effort to move. She seemed surprisingly content in my arms, and my chest puffed up with pride. "You had quite a few drinks."

"Not *that* many," she said, drawing out her words in a lazy tone.

"Enough."

Enough to lower her inhibitions. Enough to play truth or dare. Enough to smile and let go.

"We're almost there," I murmured against her head, not wanting to let *her* go.

I could tell she was tired. It was in the way she rested against me, her limbs heavy with fatigue. The fact that she hadn't put up more of a fight about being carried.

After that, she was quiet, unusually so. And I worried that she regretted it. But hell, *she'd* sunk down onto my lap, seducing *me*. Kissing *me*.

And somehow, instead of being happy that I was right about the kiss, I was angry. With myself, for waiting so long. Mad that for Bryn, at least, it was fake.

But a part of me couldn't help but wonder, *was* the kiss fake? *Because it certainly didn't* feel *fake.*

I thought back to what she'd confessed at the beginning of the game.

I've been lying about our relationship, saying that we were just friends when we're so much more.

I was twisting myself in knots, trying to figure out what was real and what wasn't. If this was all an act, she was very convincing. I found myself questioning every look, every touch.

"Bear," she mused. Her speech was sluggish—either from drowsiness or alcohol, maybe both.

"Yeah, angel?" I asked.

"Are you okay?"

"What makes you think I wouldn't be?" I held on to her while grabbing my phone to unlock the door.

"I, um, I didn't know what to expect, and I'm sorry if you were uncomfortable."

Uncomfortable? I nearly laughed aloud. "That game of truth or dare was honestly kind of tame, compared to some of the shit I saw as a rookie."

Her eyes widened. "I don't know whether to laugh or cringe."

"It's best to just forget about it," I said. I certainly had.

Though I wouldn't be forgetting that kiss anytime soon—or ever.

Once we were inside, I crossed the bungalow and set her gently on the bed. She flopped backward as I moved about the room, plugging in her phone, grabbing some water and painkillers for her nightstand. She was so still and so quiet, I had to wonder if she'd fallen asleep.

I only wished I were half as tired as she, but I was fucking wired after that kiss. The entire evening, really.

It was so nice to be away from LA. Away from overzealous Hawks fans. Here, no one seemed to know who I was. Or if they did, they didn't care.

But it was so much more than that. I'd been able to let down my guard with Bryn as well. She might think it was all part of the act, but it was so nice to finally allow myself to look at her, touch her, dance with her, and not have to hold myself back.

I'd nursed two drinks the entire night, not enough to get buzzed. I'd wanted to keep an eye on Bryn. I'd wanted her to feel safe to let go and have fun.

And she had. I mean, that dance… Holy fuck, could she move. She'd had me completely under her spell, along with everyone else. And while I hated that she'd performed for anyone but me, I loved seeing her embrace her sensuality and confidence.

Bryn groaned, attempting to sit up. "I can't sleep in this dress. And my feet and legs are all sandy. I need a shower."

Since I wasn't willing to go digging through her stuff for another pair of those skimpy pajamas, and my self-control was already hanging on by a thread, I grabbed a clean T-shirt from my bag and tossed it to her. "Here."

"Mm." She held it close, snuggling it as she sniffed the cotton. "It smells like you."

She held up the shirt, looking at the front. "Wait." She scrunched up her nose. "Isn't this your lucky shirt?"

She didn't wait for my confirmation, merely folded it nicely and placed it gently on the bed. "I can't wear that. I know how superstitious hockey players are. What if I mess up your mojo?"

She was the reason it was lucky. But she didn't know that.

"Not possible," I said. "Now put it on so we can go to sleep."

She seemed to hesitate, and then she asked, "You're sure?"

"Positive."

She watched me a moment longer, perhaps waiting for me to change my mind. Then she pulled my shirt on over her dress, her arms disappearing into the sleeves. After performing some complicated-looking maneuver, she stood, wriggling before she flung her dress aside.

I chuckled, mostly to hide my reaction to how good she looked in my shirt. Toned thighs peeking out from beneath the hem. Smooth skin that I was dying to touch. "That was impressive."

"Bear, I've got moves you've never seen." She tried to wink, but it looked more like she had something in her eye. Yeah…she was definitely tipsy.

"Mm." I crossed my arms over my chest, staring down at her as I tried not to laugh. "Is that so."

I didn't doubt it, especially after her performance. But now was definitely not the time to be thinking about that, especially when I was going to share a bed with her. And she was drunk. Drunk—or tired enough—that her eyes were closing while she swayed on her feet. Considering how late we'd stayed up last night and how late it was now, it was probably a combination of the two.

"Take these," I said, handing her the bottle of water and some pain relievers.

She thanked me, then swallowed them down.

"All right. Time for bed," I said, pointing at the mattress.

She scrunched up her face. "I don't want to get sand in the bed."

"Fine," I sighed. "Come on." I lifted her into my arms once more.

I carried her to the bathroom and set her down gently on the side of the tub. I started the water, checking the temperature until it was nice and warm.

She crossed her arms over her chest, eyes closed. "Your shirt is comfy. Thanks."

"You're welcome," I said, biting back a comment about how good it looked on her. "Are you going to be okay in here for a sec if I go change?"

"Mm-hmm." She hummed, bringing my shirt up to her nose, using it to cover her mouth.

Unable to resist, I pressed a kiss to the top of her head. "I'll be quick."

I jogged into the bedroom, stripping down to my boxer briefs before slipping into some athletic shorts. When I returned to the bathroom, she'd turned so her feet were now soaking in the water, and her back was to me. I grabbed one of the complimentary makeup remover wipes from the counter before switching off the water and setting a towel beside her.

I told myself to take a step back, to leave, but I couldn't bring myself to do it. Instead, I stood behind her, smoothing my hand over her hair. She let her head fall back against my chest as I continued my ministrations, enjoying the way the silky strands flowed through my fingers. Watching her whip it around as part of her "audition" had been hot. But getting to spoil her after a long day, seeing her like this—unguarded and relaxed—was just as alluring, if not more so.

"That feels nice," she said.

Encouraged to continue, I started massaging her scalp, pleasure unfurling inside me as her shoulders relaxed. When she moaned, my cock definitely took notice. I had to stop and step back so I wouldn't poke her in the back with my hard-on.

I cleared my throat. "You should get to bed, and I need to rinse my feet. Are you ready to get out?"

She patted the edge of the tub, peering up at me with the sweetest expression. "Join me. Please?"

That "please" was my undoing. I adjusted myself, silently willing my erection to go down.

"Here," I said, handing her the package of wipes as a way to distract myself. Bryn had yet to take off her makeup, and I had a feeling she'd feel better if she did.

She shook her head, eyes closed. "I want to. But too tired."

Don't do it. Don't...

"Do you want me to help you?" I asked.

Her head bobbed slowly. I removed a wipe from the package, the crinkle of the container obscenely loud in the quietness of the bathroom.

I brushed her hair aside, tucking it behind her ear. She opened her eyes, and for a moment, we just stared at each other. She licked her lips, and I wondered if she was thinking about our kiss. I certainly was.

I cupped her jaw to hold her steady. I felt as if my heart might pound out of my chest. We were so close. And this was so...intimate.

"I don't deserve you," she whispered as I smoothed the makeup wipe along her skin.

She had it all wrong.

"You deserve everything." And I wanted to be the one to give it to her.

She shifted so her hand was on my thigh. "Thank you."

I stilled, wondering if her hand placement was accidental

or intentional. But one look at Bryn reminded me how tired she was, so I pushed those questions aside. I took my time, cleaning her forehead, then her cheeks. I catalogued each freckle, every contour of her face.

"Close your eyes," I rasped, feeling as if my control were slipping away the longer we stayed here.

She did as I'd asked, and I was so damn tempted to kiss her again. Every muscle in me was tight, and it took enormous willpower not to close that gap and press my lips to hers. But then she swayed, and I remembered how tired she was and how much rum she'd consumed.

"There you go." I cleared my throat. "Now I need to wash off my feet so I don't get sand in the bed."

"Exactly." She straightened, removing her hand from my thigh. "Because that's gross."

"But letting a dog sleep in bed with you isn't?" I teased, knowing she'd been the first to cave when it came to that rule.

I still liked to give her a hard time for it, not that I cared. Most of the time, Bacon and Biscuit preferred to sleep in their dog beds anyway. And if they brought her comfort, well…then who was I to complain? It was exactly why I'd suggested that we adopt them in the first place—to comfort Bryn.

"They're soft and cuddly. Sand is—" She scrunched up her face, and I tried not to laugh as I rinsed off my feet. "Gritty."

When I finished, I sat back up, enjoying the warm water on my skin. I craved these quiet moments with Bryn, especially after the chaotic fun of the past few hours.

"Bear." She slid her hand along the edge of the tub, her pinkie touching mine.

"Yeah?" I took it as an invitation and linked our fingers.

"Thank you." Her voice echoed gently off the bathroom tiles.

"For what?" I asked.

"For being there for me." She gave my hand a squeeze. "I don't know what I'd do without you."

"Bryn." I smoothed my thumb across the back of her hand. "I'm not going anywhere." I needed her to know that, to feel it. "Well, I *am* going to bed. And so are you." I gave her hand a squeeze and then released it. "Come on." I pulled the plug, watching the water as it spiraled around the drain.

Bryn

I WOKE WITH A START, BLINKING MY EYES OPEN AS I TRIED TO remember where I was. The clock on the nightstand said it was four in the morning, and I squeezed my eyes shut in frustration. *Why?*

As always, my mind started spinning. I thought about Frasier and how much had happened since we'd arrived in Anguilla. How much had changed in such a short span of time. And thoughts of my relationship with Frasier inevitably led to thoughts about Derek, as they so often did when I couldn't sleep.

I lay there, trying to settle my mind and to focus on something else. Anything else. Any efforts to get comfortable again were useless. It didn't matter how exhausted I was; my body wasn't going back to sleep. And the more I tried, the louder my thoughts became.

Derek—alone in a hotel room. He'd just won a game and was staying on the opposite side of the country. I wondered if he'd tried to call for help or if he'd even been able to. I wondered if he'd been in pain. If he'd been scared.

It felt as if a fist were clenching my heart, as if my windpipe were being squeezed. I couldn't…

Unable to handle it anymore, I slid out of bed and tiptoed over to peer out the French doors. I didn't dare open them for fear of waking Frasier, but I couldn't stay in bed either. I rested my forehead against the glass pane of the door, closing my eyes as I focused on my breathing.

I knew this was a bad idea. I knew I should've pushed harder for a separate room. But selfishly, I was glad Frasier was here, even if I was trying not to wake him. It made me feel less alone.

There was shuffling, and then Frasier said, "Can't sleep?"

I continued looking outside, even as I sensed him standing behind me. "No," I whispered, grateful he'd interrupted my thoughts. "Sorry I woke you."

"Can I help?"

I shook my head. "I don't know if anyone can."

I knew he had to be exhausted. We'd only gotten back from the bachelor/bachelorette party a few hours ago. But here he was, putting aside anything he was feeling to be there —for me.

"I'll be fine," I said, though it didn't feel like it at the moment. That said, I'd been through this before—many times. It might not seem like it now, but I would be fine. "I don't want you to lose sleep because of me."

"Angel…" He placed his hand on my shoulder. His touch was warm and reassuring, solid and sure. He wasn't going anywhere.

In the darkness, I found random thoughts spilling from my lips. "Do you ever feel like your body or your mind says one thing, but your heart says another?"

"I think most people experience that at some point or another. Why do you ask?"

"Because, lately, I feel like my heart or my body wants me to move forward with life, but my head will stop me."

"Is that what's keeping you awake?" he asked.

"Sort of. That's part of it, I guess. My body is exhausted, and I know I need rest. But my mind keeps spinning, spinning, spinning."

He slid his hand down my arm, and the touch was gentle and soothing. "Talk to me."

I wasn't sure I could or even wanted to. I hadn't even shared some of these thoughts with my therapist. But I also knew not talking wasn't working either. Lately, it felt as if I'd plateaued. I was stuck. I wanted to move forward, but something kept holding me back.

This trip was the first time in a while that I'd felt as if I'd made any progress. And then… Now…*this.*

I tried not to feel too discouraged, but it was disheartening.

"When I can't sleep, it's often because my mind goes to that night," I admitted.

"I get it. I think about that night a lot too." Frasier guided me over to the couch. He sank down onto it, tossing a blanket over my legs after I sat next to him. Then he grabbed my feet and pulled them into his lap. It didn't matter that we were in Anguilla. Suddenly, it felt like we were home.

"I think about what it was like for Derek, in those final moments—" My voice broke, a tear sliding down my cheek. "And I wonder not only why it happened, why his heart gave out all of a sudden. But also why, of all the times it could've happened, why it couldn't have been on a night when I would've been there. I'm a medical professional, for fuck's sake." I jabbed my chest with my thumb. "I have the training. If I'd been there..."

Frasier placed his hand on my knee, resting it there—heavy, reassuring. "Bryn." His tone was full of both pain and sympathy. "What happened was awful, but no one could have saved him."

"I hate that I'm even talking to you about this," I continued, angrily swiping away a tear. "Because I know how much he meant to you. And the last thing I want is to hurt you."

"You can always talk to me," he said in a solemn tone. "About anything."

I nodded. I knew that, but still...this conversation couldn't be easy for Frasier. It was gut-wrenching.

The medical examiner had determined that Derek had suffered a sudden cardiac death. SADS happened when the heart's electrical system malfunctioned, causing an arrhythmia that prevented effective blood pumping.

I knew it could occur with little to no warning. I knew it could affect someone at any time—during exercise, at rest, or, like Derek, in sleep. Just as I knew that it could result in death within minutes without immediate medical intervention. That was the point my mind always snagged on—*immediate medical intervention.*

"I just... I don't get it," I huffed. "Like even now, eighteen months later, I still can't understand it."

Frasier's touch was comforting. "I don't understand it either. We will probably never understand it. But at some point, I knew I had to make my peace with it, as hard as it's been."

"I've tried." The words felt as if they'd been ripped from my throat. "God, I've tried. But it just doesn't make sense. I've asked the staff, teammates, everyone. Derek didn't show any warning signs. No abnormal vitals. No chest pains. No fainting."

"True," Frasier said, but I sensed hesitation.

"What?" I asked.

"I don't know." He rubbed the back of his neck, and I could tell there was something he didn't want to say.

I was terrified to find out what that was, but I also had to know the answer. "Please just tell me."

"Just because none of us witnessed those symptoms doesn't mean he never had them."

I sucked in a jagged breath. "You think he was hiding them?"

"No." Frasier let out a deep sigh, and he looked so…tired. Weighed down by a deep exhaustion, a heaviness. Then he said, "I don't know. But if Derek didn't tell anyone, there was no way we could know."

I gnashed my teeth. "The autopsy also showed no structural abnormalities. *None.*"

"I know," Frasier said. He'd been with me when I'd read the report. He'd gone with me to identify the body.

"He didn't have an inherited disorder that could be linked to SADS." I tugged at my hair. "I get that it's especially common in athletes and young people, but he was in the best shape of his life. He was at the top of his career." My chest was heaving. "We'd just bought a house. We were going to start a family."

Frasier stilled, and I… I froze. *Oh shit.* I hadn't intended to mention that.

"Bryn…" Frasier's tone was soft yet guarded, as if he were tiptoeing across a frozen lake. Stepping carefully to avoid falling through the ice. "You were…" He swallowed hard. "Were you pregnant?"

I shook my head, wiping away another tear. "No, but we were trying."

"I—" He closed his eyes briefly, and I was grateful to have a moment to gather myself. "Come here." He shifted so I could get closer. "Come on, angel."

I moved so I was nestled in his arms, allowing him to hold me. He was warm and comforting, his heart beating steadily in his chest.

"Jesus, Bryn. I had no idea." His voice was gruff. "Thank you for telling me."

I curled up against him, feeling safe in his arms. Depleted and exhausted, but also…lighter somehow.

"I get that you want there to be an explanation. So do I," Frasier said, smoothing a hand over my hair. "But you can't let this consume you."

"I don't want to let it consume me," I admitted. "I've made so much progress, but lately, I feel stuck."

"Why do you think that is?" he asked.

I lifted a shoulder. "I guess I feel like maybe if I can just make sense of it in my mind, I'll be able to move past it."

"That's understandable. But you, of all people, know that a lot of times, medical things don't make sense."

"I know." My shoulders slumped. Because I did know that, thanks to my job.

"A child with a brain tumor never makes sense. And sometimes, the prognosis is bleak, and yet, you do everything you can to give them the best possible chance at life, despite the odds." He rubbed his thumb back and forth over my knee. "You make miracles happen every day."

"I'm not sure I'd go that far," I said.

"Don't downplay what you do or the hope you give to your patients and their families," he said. "We both know how important the mind is to the body's recovery."

I nodded. He was right. And I wasn't trying to downplay what I did, but I was part of a team. We all had a role to play, especially the patients and their families. And sometimes, no matter what we tried, something didn't work. It was heart-breaking and frustrating.

But then there were the times that treatment was even more successful than we'd hoped. That a patient's outcome was better than we could've ever envisioned. And those truly did feel like miracles.

"I guess I just wish some of those miracles had rubbed off on Derek. I feel like…" I swallowed hard, struggling to admit this. "I feel like I let him down."

"Bryn." Frasier's voice broke. "You didn't let him down." When I didn't say anything, Frasier held me tighter. "You *didn't*. I need you to know that. Because no one thinks that."

"Maybe *he* thought that," I whispered, confessing my deepest fear. "Maybe in his final moments, Derek wondered why I wasn't there to help him."

Frasier rubbed a hand over his eyes, clearing his throat before he spoke. "I can only believe that in his final moments, Derek was thinking of how much he loved you."

I sobbed, soaking Frasier's chest with my tears. I knew how much Derek had loved me. I had felt that love every day we were together, and even now, after he was gone. He was still with me, watching over me.

I clung to Frasier, and he held me, giving me the space to let it all out. To let go. All the while, he rubbed my back, whispering soothing words of support.

Eventually, when I had no more tears left, I let out a shaky sigh and rested my head against his chest, feeling calmer. I was emotionally wrung out, but it had been cathartic.

"Have you tried writing him letters?" Frasier asked.

"I…" I turned to look at him, only then realizing just how close our faces were. Our mouths. "No. Have you?"

He used his thumbs to dry my tears. Unlike my family, he didn't look at me with pity, but understanding. We were in this together. And just that simple act made me feel less alone.

"If I'm really missing him or wish I could tell him something, I'll call and listen to his voice on the phone before leaving a message."

Somehow that did and didn't surprise me, and I loved that Frasier wanted to continue talking to Derek, including him in his life, even if Derek was gone.

"Does it help?" I yawned, fighting to keep my eyes open.

"Sometimes, yeah."

"Huh." I hadn't even thought to check Derek's messages. I'd figured there was no point.

"But you could send him an email or write him a note. Whatever feels right to you."

"And what would I do with it?" I asked, thinking it wasn't as if I could actually give it to Derek.

"If it's an email, send it to one of his old accounts. A letter —" He lifted a shoulder. "Keep it in a box or burn it. There are no rules."

There are no rules, I thought. Wasn't that the truth?

CHAPTER TWELVE

Frazier

I blinked my eyes open and stared up at the ceiling. I was tempted to stay in bed, but I knew I'd feel better if I got my workout in. Besides, if I didn't go now, I wasn't sure when I'd have time. We were supposed to go snorkeling this morning, though I doubted that Bryn or the rest of the Bride Tribe would be up to it after last night's festivities. And then tonight was the rehearsal dinner.

For now, Bryn was still sleeping peacefully, so I left her another note and laced up my tennis shoes. The scenery was too beautiful to run inside on a treadmill, and I'd enjoyed taking various routes around the island, thanks to some tips from the concierge. Today was no different.

My feet pounded the pavement, keeping tempo with the music playing through my earbuds. The scenery was breathtaking as I passed along turquoise bays dotted with white boats. And yet, with each mile traveled, my mind kept circling back to Bryn.

Last night had been a roller coaster. I'd gone from kissing her to consoling her, and all of it had been intense and emotional. My chest squeezed as I thought about the pain she'd been carrying, the guilt. And suddenly, it didn't feel as if I could get enough air into my lungs.

I slowed, bending forward so that my hands were braced on my thighs. *Fuck.*

They'd been wanting to start a family. They'd been trying to get pregnant. I stood and tried to keep my body moving, even if it was just to pace.

All the…sorrow she'd been holding inside. All those thoughts, all that guilt, about Derek. Was it any wonder she was struggling to move forward?

Was it any surprise that I kept hesitating when it came to taking that next step with her? Deep down, maybe I'd sensed that she wasn't ready. And last night's conversation had only confirmed what I'd already known.

My phone buzzed, and I glanced at the screen, wanting to make sure I hadn't missed a message from Bryn. Boone had texted, but I didn't want to talk to him right now. Unfortunately, the only person I wanted to talk to was dead.

I tugged on my hair, feeling a wave of emotion rising within me, threatening to consume me. I knew it would pass, but god, it sucked in the moment. I took a few deep breaths, listening to the sound of the ocean, the sea gulls calling in the distance.

And then I picked up my phone. I navigated to my contacts and paused at the picture of Derek. It was just a small thumbnail, an older picture from college. But he looked so happy as confetti rained down from the rafters. Our team had just won the Frozen Four, and it had always been one of my favorite memories.

I hit the button to connect the call. He was one of the few people I called who still had a personalized voice mail greeting. I used to give him shit for it, but now I was grateful because it gave me a way to hear his voice.

"This is Derek—"

My knees sagged, and I staggered over to a nearby rock to sit.

"I can't come to the phone right now because I'm busy being amazing. Leave a message, and I'll get back to you when I'm done."

I couldn't help but laugh, despite the pain currently gripping me. When the phone signaled it was time to leave a message, I hesitated. I felt so many things, but I didn't even know what to say.

"Why?" I blurted.

I wasn't sure who I was really asking—Derek, the universe? Either way, I knew I wasn't going to get an answer.

"Why did you have to leave us?" I asked, as much for Bryn as myself. "And what am I supposed to do now?" I stood. "I don't fucking know where to go from here."

I used the neckline of my shirt to wipe away sweat and tears. Salt stung my eyes, but it was nothing compared to the anguish of what Bryn had revealed.

"I had no idea you were trying for a family."

I let the silence hang there as if waiting for an answer. But there was no answer because he was gone.

I'd never admitted this before, but I couldn't stop myself from saying, "Bryn is hurting, and what she really needs is a friend. And I am… I *am* that friend. But I'm also in love with her. I'm in love with Bryn," I repeated, feeling somehow calmer. "God, that feels good to admit aloud."

I took a deep breath in.

"I love her, and I have no idea what you would think of that. Would you be pissed? Pleased? Would you see it as a betrayal of our friendship?" My breath sawed in and out of me.

I was quiet, almost as if waiting for him to respond. Waiting for some sign. Bryn was always talking about seeing signs from Derek, and I could've really used one right now.

"I swear I didn't plan for this to happen. I just wanted to be there for her after…everything. I just wanted to help her. But she ended up helping me." I should've been telling Bryn this.

"It guts me to see her fall apart. I'm trying to be strong for her, but this is breaking me." My voice cracked with that admission.

The phone beeped, signaling that I'd run out of time. An automated message came on. "If you'd like to save…"

I hung up, sliding my phone into my pocket. I planted my hands on my hips and stared out over the bay. And then I took a deep breath and started running again.

BY THE TIME I RETURNED TO THE BUNGALOW, I FELT CALMER and more centered. I opened the door quietly in case Bryn was still sleeping, but the bed was empty. I wandered out to the patio, where she was sitting on one of the lounge chairs in a robe, a gentle breeze blowing through her hair.

She glanced over her shoulder, and when she saw me, she smiled. "Good morning." She seemed almost…chipper, which surprised me after the alcohol and the late-night emotional revelations.

She set aside the resort tablet, placing it on top of some papers, and I grabbed a glass of water.

"Morning." I gulped down the water.

"Good workout?" she asked as I took a seat on the lounger next to her.

"Yeah," I said, my heart rate finally getting back to normal. "How are you feeling?"

"Surprisingly good," she said, and I wondered if she was

referring to any lingering effects of the alcohol or her mental state. Hopefully, both. "You?"

I wasn't sure whether to bring up last night or not. So I said, "I'm good," and I meant it. After the run and my phone call, I felt calmer.

"Thanks for listening last night. I feel…" She stared out at the ocean. "I didn't mean to dump all that on you, but I feel more at peace now."

When she turned back to me, her gaze was clear. And I could see in her face and her features that she was more relaxed than she'd been even a few days ago. It settled something inside me.

I placed my hand over hers, and I couldn't help but smile a little. "I'm glad."

"I also had a short call with my therapist, and I wrote a letter to Derek." She smiled, and I realized that was what the paper under the tablet must be. "You were right. He would never blame me for what happened. And voicing it aloud to you helped me realize that. I was clinging to a need for answers, when there are none. And although I can wish things had happened differently, I also can't change them."

I nodded. "I think that's the hardest part. Finding acceptance."

"Sometimes, it's still hard to accept that he's gone. But I know there's nothing I could've done. Deep down, I've always known that. And I don't want to spend the rest of my life feeling guilty for something I had no control over."

I was so damn proud of her. I knew that hadn't been easy, just as I knew she would continue to struggle with grief. But the fact that she could release herself from the unnecessary burden she'd placed on herself was huge.

"I would hug you," I said, sensing she could use some comfort. I knew I could. "But I'm pretty sweaty from my workout."

She laughed. "You really think a little sweat will deter me?"

"Okay." I held open my arms. "Don't say I didn't warn you."

She stood and stepped into my embrace, and I wrapped my arms around her. "Bryn, you are one of the strongest people I know."

She peered up at me. "Because I can handle one of your sweaty, post-workout hugs?" she teased.

I chuckled, releasing her. "Absolutely. Now, what's on tap for today?"

"Depends on what you're in the mood for. I know we'd talked about going on the snorkeling excursion, but if you don't want to do that, there's always volleyball and lounging on the beach. Or if you want to get a massage or just need some time to yourself until the rehearsal dinner tonight, I get it. This trip has been…a lot." She dipped her head.

"What do you want to do?" I asked because I wanted—no, *needed*—to be where she was.

"Since you're stuck going with me to the rehearsal dinner tonight…" She batted her eyes. "I figured I'd let you pick."

I knew she'd been looking forward to snorkeling, and so had I. After growing up in Canada and then spending most of my adult life on the East Coast, I hadn't spent much time around the ocean. And LA wasn't really known for its snorkeling.

"Do you feel up to snorkeling?" I asked.

If she was, I figured it might be a good way to reset after last night. Get us both more present in our bodies and out of our heads. Plus, if my body was engaged, maybe I'd be less likely to do something stupid—like try to kiss her again. Because as much as I wanted to kiss her, last night's conversation had merely confirmed what I already knew—Bryn wasn't ready to date. What she really needed was a friend.

She nodded. "Yeah. I think as long as I stay hydrated today, I should be fine."

"Then my vote is for snorkeling," I said.

"Great!" She popped up from the chair. "I'll let my sister know we're coming. I think the van leaves in a little less than an hour. Will that be enough time for you to eat and get changed?"

I chuckled. "I should hope so. Just how long do you think my self-care routine is?"

She twisted the belt of her robe, a beautiful pink tinge coating her cheeks and neck. "I suppose it depends on what kind of self-care we're talking about."

I leaned in. "You tell me. You're the expert."

I'd told myself she needed a friend, and yet here I was flirting. But she'd opened the door. Who was I to close it?

"Oh, I'm not so sure about that." She laughed. "My efforts at self-care lately have been…hit or miss."

Wait. Was she talking about pleasuring herself? Or was she merely admitting that she wasn't as consistent with her skin-care routine as she'd like to be?

I was still pondering that when she said, "Go shower. We can eat when you're finished. I already ordered room service, and it should be here as soon as you're out of the shower. I hope that's okay."

"That's great," I said, appreciating her foresight and thoughtfulness. "Thanks."

I trusted Bryn to know what I would like, and I wasn't wrong. By the time I was out of the shower and dressed, breakfast was on the table. I dug into the food with gusto.

"I guess I was hungry," I said around a mouthful of eggs.

"I'll say." She stood and headed for the bedroom, a smile on her lips. "I'm going to get ready." She dragged her hand across my shoulder. It was just a whisper of a touch, so light I wondered if I'd imagined it. Even so, my mind lingered on it as I finished eating.

And by the time I was done with breakfast, I was no closer to figuring out what her touch or her comment about self-care meant, if anything. It was probably nothing, but it felt noteworthy. Maybe because she'd initiated it? Maybe because she'd done so when no one was around and it wouldn't benefit our fake-dating arrangement.

"Ready?" Bryn called.

I stood and turned to face her. "Just need to grab my..." *Damn.*

I tried to stop myself from swallowing my tongue because she looked edible. Her sand-colored crocheted dress gave the most tantalizing glimpses of a hot-pink-and-fuchsia swimsuit and bare, smooth, golden skin. It didn't hurt that she was wearing my baseball hat and a sexy little smirk.

"Just need to grab...?" She placed her hand on her hip, clearly enjoying my reaction. She was a damn snack, and it made me happy to see her feeling confident and sexy. Because she was, and she deserved to feel that.

"My hat." I plucked it off her head. "Thank you." I placed it on my own. "And sunglasses," I said, breezing past her.

I crouched down to grab my sunglasses from my bag. She leaned over me, draping her arms over my shoulders from behind. And then the little thief tried to steal my hat again. My Dartmouth hat. My *favorite* hat.

"Nice try, cheeky girl." I stood, spinning quickly and grabbing her waist. And then I tickled her sides.

She laughed and tried to counterattack. I removed my hat and shoved it in my waistband. She jumped, and I wrapped my arms around her thighs, hefting her up onto my back before she could try again. "Now, let's go before we miss our ride."

She squealed, clinging to me as I headed for the door. "Giddy up, cowboy."

I chuckled. "You know what they say about cowboys and their hats."

"Wear the hat, ride the cowboy." She pretended to swing a lasso. "Yeehaw!"

I mimed tipping an imaginary cowboy hat. "That's right, angel."

She laughed, and the sound was light and free. "I guess it's too bad you're not a real cowboy, then." I reached the door, and then she said, "Oh, wait. My bag!"

I turned back and grabbed it, throwing it over my arm. I loved seeing this playful, flirty side to her. I was glad that she seemed much lighter today. Happier.

I carried her down the boardwalk, reveling in the feel of her thighs beneath my palms. She was so strong yet soft, and last night's burlesque act had shown just how well she could blend the two. Touching her now only made me want to explore more of her curves.

Friend. What she needs is a friend.

When we reached the lobby, Bryn's mom laughed at the sight of us. I set Bryn down, and she stole my baseball hat *again* and placed it on her head. She looked good—wearing my hat and that smile. I almost didn't want to try to take it back from her, but I was enjoying the game too much. And I got the feeling she was too.

I planted my feet, arms crossed over my chest. "Yeah. I don't think so." I made a come-hither motion, but she didn't budge.

I took a few steps toward her, eating up the distance between us. "Come here." I snagged my arms around her waist, pulling her to me.

Her chest brushed against mine, and I tried to pin her arms behind her back. She laughed, struggling against me. It was hot and playful, and fuck, if I didn't love it. But I also wanted to know what it meant to Bryn and where we actually stood. We'd definitely need to talk about it at some point.

Fuck it.

For once, I didn't care. Not if it meant getting to see Bryn let loose like she was.

I grabbed her wrists, clasping them behind her back. She could escape my hold at any time, but judging from the way her eyes darkened, she didn't want to. Her chest was rising and falling, and then she licked her lips. *Fuck me.*

How was I supposed to be her friend when her body was broadcasting her desire for more? For me?

I leaned down and rasped, "I may not be a cowboy. But if you want to wear the hat, you've gotta pay the price."

"Is that so?" she asked, a slight uptick at the corner of her lips.

"Mm." I shifted so that we were standing close enough that there was no space between us.

"And what might that be?" she whispered.

"Welcome! Is everyone here?" a man said in a loud voice, startling us.

Bryn and I jumped back from each other as if we'd been doing something wrong. I looked at her and she looked at me, each of us biting back a smile.

She turned into my side, and I draped my arm over her shoulder. Everyone was casting us curious glances, including a man I assumed was our guide, judging from his T-shirt with the words "Island Boat Tours" printed on it.

Allie and Kit shuffled in, sunglasses on, energy levels low. I tried not to laugh. After how hard they'd partied last night, I was honestly surprised they were even here. I'd half expected them to stay in their room and not resurface until the rehearsal dinner tonight.

I leaned in, careful to keep my voice low as our guide explained what we could expect. "Maybe Kit will let me borrow his top hat since you seem so intent on stealing mine."

As the others lined up to sign the waivers, Bryn pressed up on her toes to whisper, "Good luck with that. I'm pretty sure one of the bridesmaids puked in it last night."

I cringed and reached for my baseball hat, but Bryn grabbed my wrist before I could take it. "Please?" She smiled up at me so sweetly, and then she said, "I'll pay the price."

"You don't even know what it is," I said.

Everyone filed out to board the van, some with more energy than others. Bryn grabbed her bag as she headed for the door. I was so distracted by the sway of her hips, her ass, that I nearly walked into a chair.

Jesus. Get it together, man. If I wasn't careful, I was going to injure myself.

"Whatever it is—" she grinned at me over her shoulder "—I'm game."

CHAPTER THIRTEEN

Frazier

"You missed a spot," Allie said, pointing at a place on my back.

I glanced over my shoulder, down at my side. After a short bus ride, we'd reached a small town where we'd be boarding the boat to Little Bay. The group had dispersed to use the restrooms and purchase souvenirs and snacks before we boarded the boat. I'd meant to put sunscreen on earlier, but I'd been a little distracted.

"Here," Bryn said, stepping closer. "Let me help you."

Her eyes were shielded by her sunglasses, the brim of my baseball hat casting a shadow across her face. She'd held my hand on the ride over, making conversation with her sister and the other guests as if it were all perfectly normal. As if our being a couple was nothing out of the ordinary.

I wanted to feel hopeful about our future, but I worried that, for her, it was all pretend.

That said, Bryn had been flirty. Affectionate. And not just when we were with her family. She'd been just as demonstrative when we'd been alone in our bungalow this morning, even when no one else was watching. Even when there had been no need to act like a couple.

She smoothed her hand over my shoulder, down my side. I inhaled slowly and let it out just as slowly, trying to maintain some semblance of control. She circled me so she was standing before me, drinking me in. When she grazed my ribs with the tips of her fingers, I shivered. Her lips quirked, and my cock jerked in response.

Not now. I groaned to myself.

I was used to shutting down my feelings on the ice so I could focus on the task at hand. I'd conditioned myself to present a certain side of myself in interviews. To don a mask in public. But this was a whole different level of compartmentalization. I was pretending we were in a relationship to everyone else, while also pretending I didn't have feelings for her when we were alone. Talk about a mindfuck.

She paused then, her eyes never leaving my torso. "When did you get this?" Bryn asked, her fingers gliding over the Roman numerals there.

My newest tattoo blended in with some of the others, and since it was on my ribs, I wasn't surprised she hadn't noticed it before.

"A few months after he died," I said in a quiet voice.

She furrowed her brow, her touch lingering. Everyone else was too busy to pay us much attention. I couldn't focus on anything but her.

"But it's his birthday?"

I held her gaze. "I prefer to celebrate the life he lived than commemorate the day he died."

"It's…" She peered up at me then, smiling. "I like that."

"Okay. Is everyone ready to board the boat?" our guide asked.

Bryn took a step back, and we followed the others on board. The water was so clear; I couldn't wait to see what it looked like beneath the surface. But for now, I was content to enjoy the ride with Bryn nestled in my side.

It wasn't long before we pulled up to a cove that felt more like a private beach. A few people stood along the top of the cliff, but otherwise, it was all ours.

"Wow." Bryn scanned the scenery, from the rocky cliff walls to the brilliant turquoise water.

After we'd anchored, our guide pulled out a bin of snorkel gear as well as some paddleboards. The boat rocked gently on the waves, but the water was pretty calm overall. I grabbed a mask and snorkel for Bryn and myself, and by the time I'd returned to our seats, she'd removed her cover-up. I was grateful for my sunglasses because my eyes felt as if they were going to pop out of my damn head.

Her swimsuit wrapped around her breasts, the fuchsia and hot pink popping against her tanned skin. But it was the way she was standing—the confidence and poise—that made her seem even hotter.

The boat rocked on the waves, and someone bumped into me. It was enough to shake me out of my thoughts.

"Ready?" I asked, holding up a mask and snorkel.

Bryn grinned, pushing up on her toes to kiss me on the cheek. "Thanks, babe."

I tried not to let my surprise show. Either the term of endearment was part of the façade, or it had slipped out. I could only hope it was the latter.

She removed my hat, tucking it safely in her bag along with her sunglasses. She'd braided her hair, letting it flow over one shoulder. For a minute, she looked the same as she had nearly ten years ago. And I felt as if we were back in college again.

I jumped into the water, grabbing on to one of the nearby paddleboards. Bryn approached the stern of the boat and then turned so her back was to me. She slowly descended the ladder there, and I tried not to groan aloud at the sight. I was grateful my lower body was concealed beneath the water because her ass was fucking phenomenal.

She swam over to me, latching on to the opposite side of the paddleboard. "Seen anything yet?" she asked, eyes blinking at me from behind the face mask.

"Been waiting for you," I said.

She grinned as I placed my snorkel in my mouth. And then we both held on to the edge of the board as we peered beneath the water.

Bryn pointed to something, and as it approached, I realized it was a turtle. It was so graceful as it swam through the water. We stayed that way for a while, pointing things out to each other and just taking it all in. Every so often, we'd resurface and talk about what we'd seen. It was unlike anything I'd ever experienced.

After a while, Bryn climbed on top of the board. She lay on her back, eyes closed.

"You okay?" I asked.

She smiled. "I'm great. This was just what I needed."

I placed my hand over hers. "Good."

"All right," our guide called out. "If anyone wants to jump from the cliff, now's a good time to go for it before it gets crowded."

"I think I'm going to do it," Bryn said, shocking me.

I hadn't expected her to *want* to do it. And I knew I *shouldn't* do it. Coach would kill me. And yet, I found myself saying, "Me too."

"Frasier, no." She turned on her stomach, water droplets clinging to her skin. She shook her head. "You can't. You could get in trouble with the team."

According to my contract—and that of pretty much every player in the league—we were prohibited from engaging in other sports that might impair our ability to play hockey without written consent from the club. It was a little late to ask for permission. And it was the off-season. If I couldn't do it now, when could I?

"It'll be fine. Besides, it's not technically a sport."

"Even so—"

"If you're going," I said, cutting off her argument, "I'm going."

She hesitated a moment then nodded. "Hop on so we can paddle over to the rope we need to climb up."

I was grateful Bryn and I had worn shoes in the water because the rock looked rough, and I didn't want it to tear up our feet. I climbed on the paddleboard behind her, leaving about a foot of space between us. She scooched back so her ass was cradled between my legs, and I just sat there for a moment in shock.

"You're going to do it?" Allie asked.

Right. Of course.

Bryn was cozying up to me so that we'd be believable as a couple. Yet again, my body didn't get the memo. Being around her lately was like living in a perpetual state of arousal. And as we paddled our way over to the cliff, every brush of her body against mine was both exquisite pleasure and torture.

We reached the base of the cliffs and handed off the paddleboard to some of our fellow guests. Bryn went first, scrambling up the rock. I was too focused on keeping both of us safe, my heart pounding in my chest as I followed her up to the opening where we were supposed to jump from.

I wasn't worried for myself. The climb was strenuous, but it wasn't anything I couldn't handle. But there were no safety nets, nothing to keep her from falling.

Bryn didn't look down, didn't look back. So I continued on until she pulled herself up over the edge. I joined her a moment later, unable to look away from the way her chest was flushed with color, heaving from exertion.

"You good?" I asked, scanning her body as if to check her over.

"Yeah." She grinned. She seemed almost…energized. Invigorated or something. "You?"

I nodded, and we both turned to look out at the water. When I'd been climbing, I hadn't looked back. And now that we were at the top, I was realizing it was a long way down.

"You don't have to do this," I said, noticing how quiet Bryn seemed all of a sudden. I figured she was rethinking her decision to cliff jump, and I wanted to give her a way out. "We can climb up the rest of the way and have someone pick us up at the top."

She shook her head, resolved. "I have to do this. I *want* to do this."

"Why?" I asked, genuinely curious.

"Because my head is screaming at me not to, and I'm sick of letting it run the show."

Well, I certainly couldn't argue with that.

We'd spent so much time together over the past year and a half, but it was only in the past few days that I'd felt this pivotal shift. Both in my relationship with Bryn, but also in our relationships with our grief over losing Derek.

Even so, I could see that she was trembling. Maybe she was cold, but I had a feeling it was nerves. There was no shame in changing your mind.

I found myself asking, "You're sure?"

She looked me in the eye. "Life is meant to be lived." And then she took a steadying breath and peered out toward the opening. "I'm ready."

Her words felt significant. As if she was ready to do more than jump off the cliff. She wasn't intending to fall; she was ready to fly. She was ready to live.

So, I held out my hand, wanting her to know that she had my support—both in jumping and in embracing life and all it had to offer. "Together?"

She placed her hand in mine, her gaze locked on me. "Together."

I found myself adding, "Always," as we took a step toward the edge.

I knew she was nervous. Hell, I was a little nervous myself —mostly for her. But I also knew this was something we needed to do. And we needed to do it together.

I couldn't explain it. And I knew that to anyone else, it would simply look as if we were having some vacation fun. But it was more than that. It felt…significant. Meaningful. And I could tell from the energy coursing between us that Bryn felt it too.

When we stepped into the sunlight, it was to a chorus of cheers and encouragement. The sun was so bright, they were barely more than specks on the water. It was a fifteen to twenty-foot drop, and I was more focused on keeping Bryn safe than pandering to our audience.

"Make sure to jump out away from the rocks," I said, trying not to let my worries for her undermine the courage it had taken her to make this decision.

"I will." Her hand was shaking in mine, and yet, she didn't waver.

"Tell me when you're ready." I rubbed my thumb across the back of her hand.

She turned to me, grinning this time. "Let's do this."

"One," I said, taking a step forward. "Two." A few loose rocks tumbled over the edge, plunging to the bottom, along with my stomach. We were really going to do this. *She* was really going to do this. "Three." And with that, we launched ourselves off the edge.

Bryn screamed almost the entire way down. I let out a

whoop, and before I knew it, I was hitting the water, the impact almost as shocking as the drop had been. I kicked my way back to the surface, only to find that Bryn was already there, waiting for me. She was laughing, and I could hear Allie cheering on her sister.

I swam over to Bryn, snagging the paddleboard on the way. I didn't even have to ask if she was good; I could tell from her smile.

"That was terrifying," she panted, smiling the entire time. "But also liberating."

I nodded. I couldn't have said it better myself. We hadn't just physically launched ourselves off a cliff; we'd taken a leap of faith. Our jump had been about so much more than just pushing our physical limits. Our mental ones had felt the impact as well.

I pushed the paddleboard toward her, and she hung on, the two of us facing each other in the shadow of the cliff. The water lapped at the rock wall, and it felt as if we were completely alone. Everyone else was snorkeling, not paying us any attention anymore.

I lifted my hand to Bryn's cheek. "That was incredible," I said. "*You* were incredible."

Part of me still couldn't believe she'd done that, and yet it also made complete sense. I thought about the way she'd looked at me when she'd said, *"Life is meant to be lived."* And I thought about her desire to stop letting her head run the show.

Maybe it was the adrenaline rush or the words she'd said, but I was sick of talking myself out of pursuing a relationship with Bryn. I wanted more, and her leap of faith emboldened me to take one of my own.

I inched closer, and she seemed to drift toward me as well. I dragged my thumb across her lips, imagining tasting the salt from them. I was done waiting to feel "ready." It was time to take the leap.

I cupped her cheek. I was about to brush my lips against hers when she said, "Frasier."

"Yeah?" Could she tell how nervous I was? Was she trying to stop me before I crossed that line? Was she trying to let me down gently?

"I know we kissed the other night as part of the dare. But I don't want you to feel like you have to kiss me or do anything that makes you uncomfortable because of…you know."

I barked out a laugh. "*Have* to kiss you?"

Was she for real right now?

The only reason I'd *had* to kiss her was because I'd been desperate to. Yes, the dare had been a convenient excuse. Just like our fake relationship was a convenient excuse. But I'd wanted to kiss Bryn.

Our legs tangled as we treaded water. "First of all, no one forced me to do anything I didn't want to do." I tucked her hair behind her ear.

She released her bottom lip, and I watched with satisfaction as it slowly lowered until she was sporting a little "o." Her gaze searched mine.

I trailed my knuckles down her jawline, and she sucked in a jagged breath. The moment felt fragile and delicate because the stakes were so high. Like jumping off the cliff into Little Bay but even more so.

"And, Bryn?" I said, feeling more confident as she licked her lips, her eyes darting to mine. "The next time I kiss you, there will be no doubts about me wanting you."

She flashed me a shy smile, peering at me from beneath her lashes. "I'm looking forward to it."

Thank fucking god. If we'd been standing on the edge of

the cliff right now, I would've been convinced I could fly. That was how light I felt in that moment.

It was so tempting to do it, to close the distance and take what I wanted. But her family was floating nearby, and I didn't want there to be any question in either of our minds. When I kissed Bryn again—and I would—I wanted her to know that it wasn't part of a fake relationship or a dare. It was real.

"So am I." I guided her hand to my mouth, watching her as I pressed a kiss to her palm. *So am I.*

CHAPTER FOURTEEN

Bryn

"Soo..." Allie hooked her arm through mine as we walked along the beach. We were waiting for a few more people to arrive so we could start the rehearsal. She was wearing a beautiful white dress, more casual than her wedding gown but still very bridal. "Are you and Frasier still taking things slow after last night?"

I laughed. "Real subtle, Al."

She laughed, leaning into me. "Well, we both know that subtlety is not always my strong suit."

It was a gentle nod to our conversation from yesterday—a reference to both the things she'd said and the fact that she'd been obvious about her teenage crush on Frasier. I smiled, feeling at peace for the first time in a long time.

The sun sparkled on the water as it faded into the horizon. It was a gorgeous evening, and it promised to be a fitting end to a fantastic day. After snorkeling, our group had been ravenous. We'd eaten lunch at a local place in town, and it had been phenomenal. I'd had the fried fish with pigeon peas and rice, and I couldn't remember enjoying food as much as I had on this trip.

"No, but I still love you."

"Love you too, sis. Did you have a good time today?"

I nodded. "I had a blast. The snorkeling was so much fun." But it was the fact that I'd shared the experience with Frasier that I cherished more than anything.

"I didn't realize you were such a daredevil." She nudged me.

"I don't know that I'm a daredevil," I said, thinking back on what it felt like to jump from the cliff in Little Bay. Terrifying. Exhilarating. Liberating.

"You're a badass. You jumped off a cliff."

It wasn't about jumping off the cliff, not really. It was about what it had represented—pushing myself outside my comfort zone. Taking a leap of faith.

And yet, I hadn't done it alone. Frasier had been there with me every step of the way. Just as he was always there with me—encouraging me, supporting me, loving me.

His words kept floating through my mind, as did the way he'd looked at me. As if he'd never wanted anything more.

"The next time I kiss you...there will be no doubts about me wanting you."

And my reply, *"I'm looking forward to it."*

I still couldn't believe he'd said it. Or that I'd been so brazen in response. But I'd meant what I'd said at the edge of the cliff. Life was meant to be lived, and I was done letting my head call all the shots.

I was ready to listen to my heart. And my heart led me to Frasier.

My dress blew about my legs, and I extricated some strands of hair from my lip gloss. "I'm surprised you didn't jump. You and your friends are definitely more daring than I am."

"Girl, you have no idea." She pressed her lips together as if trying to hold in a secret, which only piqued my curiosity.

I arched my brow. "What does that mean?"

Allie opened her mouth to tell me when Mom approached, effectively ending the conversation—at least for now. "Everyone's here now. Ready to start?"

"Promise to tell me later?" I asked Allie, and she nodded.

Allie headed up the beach to join Dad, while I hung back to walk with Mom. She draped her arm around my shoulder. "How are you holding up, sweetheart?"

"I'm…" I considered it a moment then said, "Good."

Apart from the fact that I'd been a bundle of excitement and anticipation all day. Ever since Frasier had essentially promised to kiss me again, I couldn't stop thinking about it. Wondering when it would happen.

I'd wondered about it all through lunch, when he'd smiled and flirted with me. All through the ride back to the resort, his arm draped around me, lips pressed to my temple. And I'd still been wondering about it as we'd gotten ready and joined everyone for the rehearsal.

Even now, my mind was on Frasier and the promise of another kiss. Because if it was anything like that first one, I was going to combust.

"You know it would be okay if you weren't, though, right?" Mom asked. "I'm sure this isn't easy for you."

I appreciated her saying that more than she could know. She'd given me space to feel my emotions without judgment. Without making me feel as if I needed to mask my pain for the sake of anyone else.

"Honestly, I wasn't sure what to expect. But I'm having a lot of fun."

She smiled, giving me a quick squeeze before releasing me. "I'm glad, Bryn. It's okay to be sad, but you deserve to be happy too."

"I know," I said, and I found that for the first time in a

while I actually believed it. More than believing it, I felt it was true. "Thanks, Mom."

We joined the rest of the party, and Frasier was waiting for me with a smile on his face. He greeted my mom then escorted her to a chair before sinking down beside her. The wedding planner herded all the bridesmaids and Allie to the hotel since we'd exit from the resort and onto the beach for the wedding tomorrow.

"Tell me now," I whispered to Allie once we were alone in the bathroom. She'd wanted to refresh her lipstick, and the other bridesmaids had stayed behind with Brooke, the flower girl.

Allie had barely finished telling me when someone else entered the bathroom. My eyes went wide, and we both tried to bite back our smiles and act normal as we headed back out to join the others.

The rehearsal was pretty straightforward, at least for the adults. The flower girl wasn't so sure she wanted any part of it. Her parents, our cousins, were trying to bribe her, coaxing Brooke down the aisle as everyone else tried not to laugh. She was adorable, a precocious three-year-old with dark brown curls that bobbed with every step. To her, this was all just a game.

"Hey, Brookie." Allie scooped her up, propping Brooke on her hip. "I'm so glad you're here."

"Me too." Brooke wrapped her arms around Allie's neck, and I smiled. "I like my big princess dress."

"I'm glad. You're going to look so pretty tomorrow," Allie said. "I even got you a special crown to wear."

Brooke peered up at my sister as if she were the fairy godmother herself. "Really?"

"Mm-hmm." Allie nodded.

Brooke ducked her head. "But...can I still have it even if...?" She trailed off.

"Of course," Allie said. "I'd love for you to walk down the aisle, but if you don't feel up to it, that's okay too. Okay?"

Brooke nodded. "I'll thinking about it."

"You do that," Allie said, trying not to laugh. "But just know this. I think you're very brave."

Brooke shook her head then whispered, "I'm scared."

"You know what?" Allie leaned in as if to share a secret. "I'm a little nervous too."

Brooke peered at Allie, wide-eyed. "You are?"

I could understand being afraid. As much as I told myself I wanted to live life, when it came down to it, I was afraid. But if anyone made me feel safe to be brave enough to try, it was Frasier.

Frasier slid his hand along my waist. "You good?"

"Yeah." I smiled. "Yeah. My sister's going to be a good mom someday, if that's what she wants."

Frasier nodded, guiding me down the beach as we followed the rest of the party to where the staff had set up several tables for dinner. The sun was setting, and a canopy of lights provided a warm glow. It was beautiful and romantic.

"Have I mentioned how much I like this dress?" he asked, toying with one of the thin straps on my shoulder.

My lips curled into a smile. "Once or twice," I teased. "I'll have to tell Georgia. She helped me pick it out."

"I'll be sure to send her some flowers as a thank-you when we get back."

I laughed, rolling my eyes. "Now you're just being ridiculous."

"I don't know." He leaned in. "Did Georgia pick your swimsuit from earlier? Because if so, I'm going to owe her a helluva lot more than flowers."

I rolled my lips between my teeth, enjoying this flirtier, more assertive side to Frasier. My cheeks heated, and I wondered how it was possible to feel both calm and excited in someone's presence.

Before I could answer Frasier's question about my swimsuit, someone was clinking their fork against their glass. Kit stood, a huge smile on his face.

"Thank you all for coming to celebrate our wedding." He held out his hand for Allie, and she stood, beaming at his side. "We know many of you traveled a long way to be here, and we appreciate it. I can remember the moment I knew I loved Allie. It was our first trip together, and honestly, it was a disaster."

Allie started laughing, and I loved watching them interact. I loved the way Kit loved my sister. I might have had some reservations when they'd first started dating. Kit was twelve years older than Allie. He'd been married once before. But as I'd gotten to know him, I realized what a great fit he was for my sister.

As I listened to him tell the story and saw how happy Allie was, I couldn't help but be delighted for them. Kit finished up by looking Allie in the eye and telling her how grateful he was to have met her. When they kissed, everyone was cheering, many of us wiping away tears.

And I realized that not only did I miss that, I *wanted* that—a partner.

I wanted what Allie and Kit had. What Derek and I had shared. And while I knew it wouldn't be the same as what I'd had with Derek, I was okay with that. I was open to the possibilities.

Frasier placed his hand on my thigh, and when I looked at him, I was struck by the gentle expression on his face. On the way he was there—always. I smiled at him, grateful for this incredible man in my life. Even if nothing more came out of this trip than an amazing kiss. Even if we ultimately went back to just being friends, he'd shown me what was possible. He'd made me remember what it was like to be cherished.

I leaned over, pressing my lips to his cheek. The scruff tickled, but I didn't mind. "Thank you."

"For what?" he asked, his grip on my thigh tightening ever so slightly.

"For…" I could barely speak around the lump lodged in my throat. "Everything."

He took my chin between his fingers, dragging my gaze up to his. "It's no less than you deserve."

He leaned in, and my pulse quickened. This was it. He was going to kiss me. And he did. Only, he pressed a chaste kiss to the corner of my mouth, bypassing my lips.

If the man was trying to torture me, it was working. I was so keyed up, so full of anticipation, I felt like a bottle of champagne that had been shaken up. If he didn't kiss me soon, I was going to burst.

When he pulled back, he had a wicked glint in his eyes. He knew exactly what he was doing, but two could play at that game.

"You never told me what I owe you for letting me borrow your hat."

"Borrow?" he spluttered. "I think you mean steal."

"Meh." I waved a hand through the air. "Semantics."

"Mm. I'm not so sure about that." He nudged me as the staff came out, bearing trays of dessert.

Everyone received one of two desserts. Frasier's looked like a key lime pie. And mine was a cup of ice cream with fried plantains and caramel sauce. Both looked equally delicious. He took a bite and groaned.

"You've gotta try this." He held up his fork with some of the pie for a taste.

I kept my eyes on his as I closed my lips around it. The

flavors were phenomenal—bursting on my tongue with a zest of citrus and the sweet, creamy filling. "Oh, that's good. Here." I held up my spoon with some of my dessert to give him a taste. It was equally delicious with more of a salty, sweet mix.

I laughed, and when I glanced up, my mom and sister were watching me with smiles on their faces. My sister looked like the cat that ate the cream. But my mom…she was practically glowing with happiness. Even my dad seemed pleased with the idea.

I bit the inside of my cheek and stared down at the table. While part of me felt bad for lying to them about my relationship with Frasier, I could see how happy they were. How relieved they all were that I was living life again.

For the first time since Derek's death, I felt like they saw me as Bryn—daughter, sister, friend. And not just a widow. It was both painful and a relief. Because I wasn't the same. And I could never go back to the person I once was—at least, not completely.

But I was coming to accept that, and I only hoped my family could too. And part of that acceptance included finally admitting to myself just how much Frasier meant to me. Not only as a friend, but as something more.

I made a quick, heartfelt speech, congratulating my sister and Kit. Everyone stayed for a while longer, laughing and drinking. At least until Brooke passed out and was carted off to bed. Soon after that, Frasier and I said our goodbyes.

"Oh," I groaned as we walked down the beach. "I'm so full. But that meal was so worth it."

"It was delicious." He linked our hands, gently rubbing his thumb over my wrist. "Has your family said anything about your tattoo?"

"Mom thought it was a beautiful tribute," I said, brushing

some of my hair away from my face. "Allie's trying to convince me to get a matching tattoo with her."

He chuckled. "Of what?"

"Who knows? I'm not entertaining the idea. And I should probably avoid playing truth or dare with her again. It would be just like her to dare me to get a matching tattoo with her."

"I wouldn't put it past her. She was definitely enjoying the game last night."

"She wasn't the only one," I muttered, thinking of what my sister had told me earlier. "I'm glad we left when we did."

He gave my hand a squeeze. "I had a feeling things were only going to get even more out of hand. Everyone seemed cool, but I don't want to get reamed by Coach or PR for something during the off-season."

Judging from what my sister had told me, Frasier was right about things getting out of hand. One of the bridesmaids had ended up having a threesome with two of the groomsmen. My face heated, and Frasier narrowed his eyes at me.

"What?" he asked.

"*What?* What?" I practically yelped.

"Bryn," he chided. "What aren't you telling me?"

"I, um—" I rolled my lips between my teeth. "Nothing."

He crossed his arms over his chest. "Nothing, huh? Why you blushin' then, Bryn?"

"No reason."

He stopped walking and peered down at me. "I dare you to tell me."

"Sounds to me like you're wanting to play another round of truth or dare."

"If that's what it takes to figure out what put that expression on your face. But I don't need to play a game to prove a point."

"Really? Isn't that what hockey is?" I taunted.

A muscle in his jaw twitched, and I tried not to laugh. So competitive. So serious. It was hot.

The tension between us built, pulling taut. When I wasn't sure I could take much more, he gritted out, "Do it. Ask me." He leaned in, practically growling, "Truth or dare."

Oh, he wanted to play? We'd play.

CHAPTER FIFTEEN

Frasier

Bryn typed something on her phone, the warm evening breeze rustling her hair. We'd made it back to the bungalow and had opted to sit on our private patio since it was such a beautiful night. The plunge pool glowed from within, and small solar-powered lights dotted the edge of the deck.

Bryn glanced up from her phone, a playful smirk curling her full lips. "Truth or dare?"

"Weren't you the one who said that using a website to generate questions feels a bit like cheating?" I pointed out.

"Yeah, but it's also more of a challenge."

"I like a challenge," I admitted. "But I also prefer using my imagination."

She laughed. "That's because you're old-school. You don't do social media. Your phone is practically a flip phone."

"You can't be focused in a world of constant distractions."

"I know." She looked up at me. "It's actually something I admire about you, even if I tease you for it."

"Thanks." I ducked my head. "And you can use the phone if you really want."

"Oh, I planned to. But you still haven't told me your choice. Truth or dare."

"Truth," I said, hoping I wouldn't regret this.

"Which do you enjoy more—cuddling or kissing?" Bryn asked.

"Both."

She gave me a look. "You have to choose one. You can't have both."

"Says who?"

"The question. The word 'more' requires a favorite."

My mind went to watching movies with Bryn, her nestled into my side. "Well, I like cuddling because it creates connection and it feels nice. I like holding a woman in my arms, making her feel safe, cherished. But I also like kissing because you can communicate so much with a kiss."

"Like what?" She leaned forward. It had the effect of pushing her tits together. And fuck me, what I wouldn't do to give them a squeeze.

Long game, Fizzy. Play the long game.

The Cup wasn't won in a game; it took a season. And there was so much more at stake here.

"Well…" I brushed her hair away from her face. "A kiss on the top of the head could mean, I'd do anything for you." I let my words hang in the air. Then, my touch was a whisper against her temple. "Here. I adore you. Behind the ear…" I dragged my finger there. "I want you." I held her gaze, speaking the words I felt about her, and hoping she would understand everything I was trying to communicate.

She leaned forward, lips parted. "Where else?"

"That's the beauty of a kiss. It can be placed anywhere." I watched her expressions as I said, "Lips," and dragged my finger down her lips. Down farther to her, "Collarbone."

I hesitated briefly, but the way her breath hitched made me continue my descent into the valley of her, "Breasts."

Her eyes were hooded, locked on mine as if she couldn't look away. "Stomach." And then I slowly lifted my hand before I could reach her waistline as I said, "Between your thighs."

She swallowed hard, pupils dilating even more. The black was so all-encompassing, it nearly swallowed the blue. We'd barely even touched, and I wasn't sure I'd ever been more turned on. To have Bryn finally looking at me in a way I'd only ever dreamed of… Shit. It felt as if my heart was going to pound out of my chest. And my dick was painfully hard, pressing against my zipper.

"Your turn," I rasped.

She swallowed hard. "Truth."

"What made you—"

"Nope!" She held up her hand, likely guessing what I was going to ask. "I change my mind. I want a dare."

I chuckled. "Fine. I dare you to tell me what had you blushing so hard earlier."

She let out a heavy sigh, shoulders dropping. She knew she wasn't getting out of this.

She peeked up at me from beneath her lashes. "Promise not to tell anyone?"

"Angel—" I tucked her hair behind her ear "—who am I going to tell?"

"Just…" She huffed. "Promise."

I held her gaze. "I promise."

"Last night, one of the bridesmaids had a threesome with two of the groomsmen." The words were said in a rush, like a confession.

"As part of the game?" I asked.

I wouldn't doubt it. If Allie had continued to increase the boldness of the game with every round, it was definitely likely.

"More like…as a result of the game," Bryn said.

"Is that something you're interested in?" I asked, thinking of the way her skin had flushed with color.

Her expression turned more serious. "No. I want whoever I'm with to be fully invested in me. When I'm with someone, I give myself one hundred percent."

I nodded. I hadn't expected anything else.

"Would you—or have you…" She trailed off, probably thinking of the stories about some of the other guys in the league.

"No."

"Wow." She laughed. "That was immediate and definitive."

"I don't share, and I'd never ask my partner to either. If I'm with someone, there's no one else for me."

"That's…admirable," she said, swallowing hard. Then, "Truth or dare?"

"Truth."

She glanced down at the screen of her phone. "If you had to have sex with any player in the league, who would you choose?"

I balked at her. "Seriously? That's what you want to know?"

"That was the prompt."

I scoffed. "That's an oddly specific prompt for a website that randomly generates truth-or-dare prompts."

She lifted a shoulder. "I might have tweaked it a little."

I chuckled. "This is what happens when you read *Heated Rivalry*."

"Answer the question, Bear, or take a shot."

I wasn't going to take a shot for that. I thought through the Hawks' roster as well as that of other teams in the league. "Don't laugh, and don't you dare tell anyone." I narrowed my eyes at her. "But I'm going with Keller."

"From Boston?" she asked, evaluating me. "Really?"

"Why not? He's won two Stanley Cups, and he has the all-time wins record for any goalie in the league."

"So you're picking based on stats, not looks or attraction?" She scrunched up her face.

"One." I held up a finger. "His stats *are* hot. And two." I held up another finger. "If I'm going to have to suck someone's dick, they might as well tell me how to become a legend."

She started laughing so hard, she was wheezing. "Oh my god, Frasier. You are ridiculous."

"What?" I lifted a shoulder. "You asked who I'd sleep with in the NHL. I told you."

She shook her head, still laughing. She covered her mouth as if to hide her amusement. "Sorry."

"No need to apologize," I said, gently grasping her wrist to lower her hand. "I love hearing you laugh. Seeing you smile." I traced her jaw with my hand. "Even if it's at my expense."

She let out a shuddery exhale, her eyes darting between mine as if searching for something. I let the moment hang there, waiting to see what she'd do. Finally, she said, "I suppose it's my turn again."

I dropped my hand and leaned back. "Truth or dare?"

"Dare."

Interesting.

"Where's the book you've been reading?" I asked.

"The one you gave me?" she asked, and when I nodded, she eyed me suspiciously. "Why?"

"Because I want to know what all the hype is about. I want you to read it aloud." I winked. "And be sure to pick a steamy scene."

Her cheeks pinkened, and she stood slowly. While she was gone, I switched on the hot tub before ridding myself of my tie and shoes. Then I rolled up my pants so I could put my feet in the water.

When Bryn returned, she sat on one of the chairs. "I can't believe you're going to make me do this."

I watched her, steam rising into the night air. "Take a shot or forfeit. You can end the game anytime you want."

But I knew she wouldn't. She was too competitive to do something like that.

"And be the first one to break?" She shook her head, confirming what I already knew. "I don't think so."

I loved that she didn't back down. I loved that she pushed herself outside her comfort zone. I loved that she felt comfortable enough with me to do so.

She opened her book to the midway point, thumbing through a few pages until she settled on one. She brushed her hair away from her face and began to read.

"She ran through the woods, the mask bobbing eerily behind her. Her heart was pounding, and she stumbled—"

"Wait." I held up a hand. "I specified that it needed to be a steamy scene."

Bryn peered down at me over the top of the book. "It is."

"She's running through the woods, and it sounds like she's being chased by a masked man. How is that steamy?"

"Trust me." Her eyes glinted, lips curling up at the corners. "It will be. I'm setting the stage."

"But why is she—"

"Frasier," she huffed. "Will you please just let me read it?"

"I need some context here, Bryn."

"Fine. She's a high-powered attorney, and he's trying to help her let go."

"By chasing her?" I shook my head. Seriously? What the fuck?

"By getting her to surrender." Bryn gave me a look. "Do you want me to read it or not?"

"It's your dare." I leaned back, resting on my palms. "It's your choice."

"Then stop interrupting."

I mimed zipping my lips.

She looked down at the book then back up at me. "And no judging or snide remarks." She pointed at me, and I shook my head. "Don't yuck my yum."

"Don't yuck my yum?" *Jesus.* I dragged a hand through my hair. It felt as if we were speaking a different language.

"Don't kink shame," she clarified.

"Is this a kink of yours? Being chased through a dark forest by a masked man."

She closed the book, keeping her finger between the pages as a bookmark. "You're missing the point."

"Which is…"

"You'd know if you'd just let me read you the damn scene." Oh, she was flustered now. It was pretty cute, actually. But telling her that would only piss her off even more. *Tempting.*

I smiled and shut my mouth, giving her my full attention.

She watched me a moment. Then, when she was satisfied that I wasn't going to interrupt again, she started reading once more.

I couldn't take my eyes off Bryn. Tendrils of hair curled around her face, heated from the steam of the hot tub. Her skin was flushed with color as she read the story. The filthy words on her sweet lips were making it difficult to concentrate.

My body felt like a live wire. One touch, and I was liable to explode. I pushed down on my cock, hoping she wouldn't notice. Secretly hoping maybe she would.

Because holy fuck, had she been right. The scene wasn't about the masked man in the forest; it was about the chase, the suspense and anticipation, the hunt.

And when he'd caught her, the things he'd done to her... *Fuck.*

And listening to Bryn read about them... I was about to come in my pants, and she hadn't even touched me.

She stopped reading, closing the book slowly.

"Wait." I was hanging on her every word, and she was just going to stop? "What happens next?"

She laughed. "I guess you'll have to read it to find out."

I tilted my head. *Touché.* I chuckled. "I guess I will."

"Truth or dare?" she asked. I'd been so caught up in the story, I'd forgotten all about the game.

I pressed my hands to my thighs. "Dare."

She tapped her phone. She grinned then rolled her lips between her teeth, watching me out of the corner of her eye.

"What is it?" I asked.

She showed me the screen where the dare was displayed.

No hands.

Turn someone on without touching them. How you do it is up to you, and the recipient can decide how to prove that your efforts have worked.

"If that had been your dare just now, you would've aced it," I said.

"Really?" she asked, and I noticed that her eyes darted quickly to my crotch then back to my face.

"You didn't touch me. And I can prove that your efforts worked," I rasped.

She smirked. "Good to know I aced a dare that wasn't even mine. I guess it's your turn now."

I thought about all the things I might do to turn Bryn on without touching her. I considered using dirty talk, but I thought it would be more impactful if we were touching or almost touching. I thought about what other senses I could invoke beyond touch or hearing. Taste was out as well, at least if it involved my tongue on her skin like I was currently imagining.

But I had vision and hearing to play with. I thought about how Bryn had lit up when we'd danced together at the beach bar. How surprised and impressed she'd been. I thought about her burlesque act and how she'd slowly seduced me without touch, without even removing any clothes, apart from a hat and wrap.

I scrolled through the music on my phone, looking for the perfect song. I settled on one with a good beat—not too fast. It had a sultry feel and lyrics that connected. Sure, I'd taken some dance classes when I'd lost that bet with Gabe or throughout my career to help with my flexibility, but never anything that had involved a striptease.

I stood as the music started playing. I had no idea what I was doing, but I kept my eyes locked on Bryn's as I moved my body to the beat. I remembered how she'd looked at me last night, connected with me during her burlesque "audition." And honestly, that had been one of the hottest parts, besides seeing her embrace her confidence and sensuality.

I slowly unbuttoned the top few buttons of my dress shirt, letting the music flow through me. I was more nervous than I'd been for my first NHL game. If Bryn wanted me to stop, all she had to do was say so. But she didn't, so I unbuttoned the rest, leaving my dress shirt hanging open.

Bryn grinned but quickly tried to hide her smile behind her hand.

I shook my head and tsked. "If you get to watch me, I get to watch you."

Her breath caught, and the temperature rose even more. I took my time, seducing her with every look, every move. I might not be able to touch her, but I was going to make damn sure she could imagine my hands all over her body.

I continued dancing, pushing past any embarrassment or insecurities. They all faded away when she was looking at me like that. It was almost as if she was seeing me for the first time. It was fucking exhilarating, the way she watched me with a mixture of disbelief and desire. I'd never hoisted the Cup over my head, though that had been a lifelong goal of mine. But even if I had, I couldn't imagine that it would even come close to this.

I strode toward Bryn, eyes locked on hers. I dropped to the ground, muscle memory pushing me into some of the warm-up stretches I ran through before a game. I took a split position, enjoying the way her mouth popped open in surprise.

Without my bulky pads on, my flexibility was even better, and I used that to my advantage. I moved to my knees, sliding them in a circular stretch that made it look as if I were rolling my hips to hit just the right spot.

"Holy shit," Bryn mouthed.

Her reactions emboldened me to continue, to push the line even more. I was determined to drive her as crazy as she made me.

I lifted my undershirt, giving her a peek of my abs, flexing my arms, my core. When the music shifted, I slowly dragged my hands over my lips, down my chest, past my cock. Her eyes tracked my every move, and I imagined what it would feel like to have her hands trace that same path.

I pulled my shirt up again, doing a few body rolls as I slowly lifted the material higher and higher. Her breathing grew ragged, and I tugged the shirt over my head before tossing it aside. When I saw her expression, I was so damn close to saying forget the dare and begging her to touch me.

"Damn, Bear. If this hockey thing doesn't work out, you might have a shot with Magic Mike in Vegas."

I chuckled low and deep, pleasure coursing through me. All this time, I'd held back with her. But I wasn't now, not anymore.

I dropped to the deck, sliding on my knees toward her in a move that was half crawl, half prowl. I traced up her legs without actually touching her, over her stomach, still hovering. Her chest. She sucked in a jagged breath, and my chest puffed up with a potent mixture of pride and satisfaction.

The entire time, our eyes were locked, and that was the hottest part of all. The connection. The intimacy. I'd never let myself be this vulnerable with anyone, but I trusted Bryn.

I stood, rolling my hips a few times as I catalogued her reactions. Flushed skin. Parted lips. Wide eyes.

I might be the one putting on a show, but I couldn't tear my eyes from her. "You're so fucking gorgeous."

Standing once more, I smoothed my hand down my chest until I reached my waist. The dare had been fairly vague— turn the other person on without touching them. It hadn't specified for how long or how far to take it. I was taking my cues from Bryn, and she was definitely into it.

Still, I didn't want to push too far, too fast. But I decided to test the waters. I slowly unbuttoned my pants, letting them rest loosely on my hips as I gauged Bryn's reaction. Her lips were parted, eyes drinking me in.

Fuck yes.

And now for a little tease.

I moved so I was standing behind her chair then leaned over to rasp, "I can't touch you, but if I could, I'd start with your lips."

She gripped the sides of the chair. "What about my lips?"

"I'd devour them because I've been dying for another taste." I imagined doing just that. "I'd get drunk on you, kissing until our lips were swollen. And then I'd kiss your neck." I leaned in so she could feel my breath on her skin. "I'd trace your collarbone with my tongue."

"Where else?" she asked, pressing her thighs together.

I was pretty sure I could've stopped then, and I would've accomplished the dare. But I didn't want to stop.

"Where would you want me to touch you?" I asked.

"Everywhere," she breathed.

"Your stomach?"

"Yes." It almost sounded like a hiss.

"Backs of your knees," I offered. When she nodded, I said, "The insides of your thighs."

"Where else?" she asked, impatient.

"Between your thighs," I said.

"More," she groaned, and my knees weakened.

I moved so I was facing her. Her skin was flushed, eyes glazed over. I straddled her chair, still dancing. Still *so* close to touching her but not quite.

"I can't touch you," I panted, as if I'd just completed a bag skate. "But you're welcome to touch me."

She peered up at me, and I wished I could capture this moment and lock it in my mind forever. She lifted her hands to my chest, her expression one of fascination. Her touch was delicate, and yet I felt it as if it were a brand on my skin. Singeing me as fire surged through my veins.

When she dragged her fingers back down my torso, I shuddered. My cock was fucking hard—it had been all night. And I felt as if it could pound through ice. And then Bryn hesitated above my waistline, fingers poised to unzip my pants and finish the job I'd started.

Fuck. Me. Was she really going to do it? All the blood left my brain, fleeing south. I was light-headed at the prospect.

She peered up at me from beneath her lashes. "Dare me."

I cupped her jaw. "I'm done playing games, Bryn. I want you."

She looked down then slowly met my gaze, a coy smile playing at her lips. "I want you too, Frasier."

Relief, excitement, and adrenaline surged through me. I crouched down, my smile meeting her smile as I pressed my lips to hers. She looped her arms around my neck, pulling me closer, eliminating the space between us.

Unlike our other kiss, neither of us had consumed any alcohol. We had no audience, no pretense. This kiss was real and raw and aching. We tangled and tempted and teased each other, until we drew apart, panting.

"I'll take that to mean I completed the dare to your satisfaction?" I asked, my body humming.

Her eyes darkened, tongue darting out to lick her swollen lips. "Touch me and find out," she husked. Followed by the unspoken words, *I dare you.*

I groaned, releasing her. She smelled so good. Tasted even better. And her coy smile was going to be my undoing. I took a step back, trying to compose myself before I blew my fucking load.

She gave my erection a pointed look. "That looks painful."

I grunted. She had no fucking idea.

I'd wanted her for so long. And to have her like this—finally looking at me like that—was everything.

She reached out and crooked a finger through my belt loop. I kept my hands at my sides, clenched to keep myself from grabbing her. I channeled the type of patience I used during an intense game. When I was on the ice, I had to react, but I also had to wait. I was always at the ready, but if I moved too early, if I tried to anticipate my opponent, I could end up letting in a goal instead of keeping it out. So even though I wanted to lunge for Bryn, I waited.

Slowly, she met my eyes, seeking permission. I nodded. *Fucking granted. Fucking yes.*

She hesitated, and I held my breath. It was like the final moments of overtime in the play-offs. My fate would be decided in the next breath. I would feel the agony of defeat as the puck slid past me and into the net. Or I would feel ecstasy as we clinched a win.

Whatever the result, it was up to Bryn now. Regardless of what she chose, I would always be there for her. That would never change.

Do it, I silently chanted, begging her to take that next step.

My breath shuddered, and then she pushed my pants down over my hips, dragging my boxer briefs along with them. My cock bobbed toward my stomach, hard and desperate for her touch. Her mouth. Her cunt.

I'd imagined this moment countless times. And somehow it was even better.

"Je-sus..." she whispered, dragging out each syllable as she stared at me with something akin to awe.

When she leaned forward, I could see straight down her dress. And unlike before—at the rehearsal dinner—I wasn't going to be a gentleman. I looked my fill, admiring her breasts, wondering what they'd feel like in my hands.

Hopefully I wouldn't have to wonder much longer.

"I want to touch you." I swallowed hard. "I *need* to touch you." If I sounded desperate, I didn't care.

She shook her head, and my stomach dropped. But then she said, "You always take care of me. Let me take care of you for once."

"You do take care of me—"

She gave me a brief, searing kiss. And it silenced me. "Please, Frasier."

As if I could say no to her. Especially not when she was looking at me as if I was the object of her every desire.

She took me in her hand, and my knees buckled. *Holy fuck.* Bryn was touching me. And it felt so fucking amazing. I grabbed on to the back of a chair, somehow managing to remain upright. But only just barely.

I smoothed my hand over her shoulder, marveling at the softness of her skin. I skimmed my fingers along her collarbone, keeping my touch light even as my hand shook. When I came to the strap of her dress, I paused, seeking confirmation. She met my eyes, and I held her gaze as I slid the strap down her shoulder.

I closed my eyes briefly, cursing under my breath. I was still in disbelief that this was real. *She* was real. And beautiful. And allowing me to see her this way.

I caressed her breasts, feeling their weight. Soft. Smooth. Full. "Perfection."

Her eyes fluttered shut, her lips parted ever so slightly. My breath caught. I wasn't sure I'd ever seen anything more stunning. But when she took the tip of me into her mouth, my eyes rolled back into my head.

"Fuck, angel." I continued touching her, exploring her. "You…" I shuddered. "You have no idea how good that feels." *How long I've wanted this.*

She took me deeper, using her hand to caress what wouldn't fit in her mouth. I nearly choked at the sensation. Warm. Wet. Perfect.

My muscles clenched, and I was trying so hard not to completely blow this. But it felt so damn good.

"Fuck, Bryn," I coaxed, threading my fingers through her hair.

She was setting the pace, not me, her blue eyes watching me the entire time. She tapped my thigh twice, checking in. I tapped her back twice.

"Yes," I hissed. "Oh my god. Look at you." I clenched my fists, my stomach tightening. It was too much. She was so beautiful, and I was so gone for her. I'd dreamed of this so many times, and now it felt like it wasn't even real. *"Fuck."*

I was quickly losing control of the situation. And then when she started touching herself…

It was tempting, oh-so tempting, to come. But I refused to come before Bryn.

I gave her shoulder a squeeze, and she popped off me. She peered up at me with such trust, her lips pink and swollen from sucking my cock. I grinned down at her, my cock leaking. I kicked my pants aside, and then I tugged on her hand, pulling her to a standing position.

"But I wasn't done." She pouted.

"Angel, in no world would I *ever* allow myself to come before getting you off at least once."

I cupped her cheeks, resting my forehead against hers. It felt so good to be able to touch her like this. Be with her like this. And I promised myself that I would show her just how good we could be together.

CHAPTER SIXTEEN

Bryn

F rasier's words sent a thrill through me.

Angel, in no world would I ever allow myself to come before getting you off at least once.

Oh god. Yes.

This was exactly what I needed. *He* was what I needed.

I reached for him, and he grabbed for me, and then we were kissing. Frasier tilted my head, and I opened myself to him, allowing him to deepen the kiss. In all the years I'd known him, I'd never expected him to be so passionate. Intense, yes. Dedicated and loyal. A team player. But damn, the man knew how to kiss.

Out here alone, with no witnesses but the stars in the sky, he took his time. This kiss was just as desperate as our first but also deeper. We were exploring each other, learning each other's preferences. With every brush of his hands on my skin, I felt as if I might implode.

For a man who was so large and imposing, he really was quite tender.

And even though he was naked and hard, his cock

nudging my stomach, he seemed in no rush to move on from kissing. He made me feel beautiful, cherished, and alive.

Part of me worried about what this would mean—for our relationship, for the future. If the last year and a half had taught me anything, it was how quickly plans could change. But if Frasier and I could survive everything that we had, I had faith that we could make it through almost anything together.

The only thing guaranteed was this moment.

I was done thinking. All I wanted was to feel. Frasier's hands on my skin. His lips on mine. Our bodies moving together.

He kissed down my neck, over my collarbone, across the tops of my breasts. I was on fire for him. When the remaining strap of my dress slid from my shoulder, I didn't fight it, leaving myself bare to him.

Frasier rubbed a hand over his mouth, watching me with the kind of intensity he usually reserved for the ice. I knew there was no going back after this, but instead of being scared, I was exhilarated. Free in a way. A bit like jumping off the cliff at Little Bay.

There was no awkwardness. No pretense. *No more games,* as he'd said earlier.

I let my dress fall the rest of the way until it pooled at my feet on the ground. I stood before Frasier in only my strappy sandals and lacy thong, and he looked at me like a man possessed.

He bent forward, resting his elbows on his knees. He took a few heaving breaths, eyes squeezed shut. I was about to ask if he was okay, but then he seemed to compose himself once more.

"Fuck, Bryn." He straightened, shaking his head. "You are something else. You have no idea how long…" He swallowed.

"How long?" I drank him in just as greedily, those

muscular thighs and glutes. So much power and strength in those quads. He had a light dusting of hair on his legs and stomach, and I couldn't stop thinking about the way he'd looked at me, danced for me, earlier.

"I've wanted this. Wanted *you.*" He guided me over to one of the lounge chairs, grabbing a towel and laying it down over the woven slats before saying, "Lie down."

His command sent a thrill through me, and I channeled my inner burlesque performer as I sank down into the chair, keeping my chest lifted. Letting him look his fill as I slowly reclined, my movements like those of a dancer. With my hands over my head, I stretched my hips from side to side, loving the way he looked as if he might pounce at any second.

"Spread your legs," he rasped. "Let me see you. See how wet you are for me."

With my feet perched on the chair, I slid my hands over my breasts then down my stomach and thighs until I reached my knees. I pressed my palms to the skin there, gently pushing them apart like he'd asked. I could feel how soaked my thong was, and I could only imagine what I looked like to him. Needy. Desperate. Wanton.

It's how I felt.

I *needed* Frasier. I was desperate for this man. I didn't want to restrain myself anymore, especially not with him.

He sank to his knees, watching me as I dragged my fingers back up my stomach and over my breasts, my throat and lips, until I linked my hands above my head. I was silently telling—no, begging—him to do whatever he wanted to me.

His eyes were hooded when they met mine, seeking my permission. He double tapped my thigh with his fingers, as if asking whether to proceed.

"Yes," I sighed, loving that he'd checked in. "Frasier, *please*."

"I could never refuse you anything, angel. Especially not when you ask so prettily."

I smiled, squirming with anticipation. It felt as if everything had led up to this moment. And I needed his hands—his mouth—on me.

His eyes remained on mine as he leaned in, kissing my ankle then the inside of my knee. He massaged my calf as he worked his way up my thigh, kissing the skin at the juncture of my hip. He leaned in, nuzzling me through my underwear before groaning deep and loud.

Oh god.

When he dragged his tongue up my slit, underwear still between us, my hips bucked. He groaned, using his arm to pin me, placing his palms on my thighs to spread me wider. I felt so…exposed. Bared to him in every way possible.

He took his time exploring me, reaching up to brush my nipple before tweaking it until I was writhing and begging for more. Everything felt *so* good. I just needed… "More," I said on a breathy sigh.

Finally, *finally*, he tugged my underwear to the side, and my entire body released a shiver of intense pleasure. I was already so close to the edge. It had been so long since I'd been touched, and I was aching for him.

I'd meant what I'd said the other day about self-care—my efforts had been hit or miss. And this was so much better than any toy in my arsenal. If his mouth and hands alone were this good, I could only imagine how incredible the sex would be. But I didn't want to just imagine…

"*More*," I pleaded, reaching up to cup my breasts. I pinched my nipples, and his eyes darkened even further.

"That's it," he said, inserting a finger, pumping in and out of me. "Look at that pretty pink pussy, glistening for me."

"Yes." Oh god, yes. The dirty talk. My toys certainly couldn't do that either.

"Show me what makes you feel good," he said, lips near my ear, trailing down my neck. "Show me what you need to get off."

"You," I croaked out. "I need. *You.*" The word came out breathy and desperate. I almost didn't recognize my own voice.

He softened, slanting his mouth over mine. I could taste myself on his lips. I could taste him. *Us.*

Slowly, he kissed his way back down my body, goose bumps rising in the wake of his ministrations. Then his mouth was back on my clit, licking and sucking and teasing. He was like a man possessed. And I wanted to be owned by him so completely that I could think of—and feel—nothing else.

When he inserted a second finger, my hips bucked. "So… close."

My body was rigid with anticipation, pulsing around him as he continued to worship me with his lips and his words. He was so tender and possessive, and every nerve ending was attuned to him.

When I started shaking, I knew I was on the verge of coming apart. I gasped and spluttered, instinct taking over. I'd almost forgotten what this was like—to give myself over to someone. To trust them with my body, my pleasure.

"That's it, angel." He used his free hand to link our fingers, his eyes locked on mine as he urged me to continue climbing, to reach that apex and then go over the edge.

I closed my eyes, crying out to the stars as I reached that point of no return. But Frasier didn't stop there. No, he kept going and going, pushing me for more, with his mouth, his hands, and his words, until I cried out again. Until I was breathless, my body limp and sated. I wasn't in control of anything, and it was glorious.

Slowly, I came back down to earth, floating softly like a feather. It was such a powerful release—physically and emotionally. And I couldn't help the tear that streaked down my cheek. Frasier hovered over me, kissing it away with such tenderness it made me ache.

"That…" He swallowed hard, Adam's apple bobbing. "…was the most beautiful thing I've ever seen."

My cheeks heated at the realization that he'd been studying me, watching me. I threaded my fingers through the hair at his nape, needing to ground myself. We'd just crossed a huge line. Part of me wondered if I should be apprehensive or filled with regret. Another part of me wondered why this didn't feel more awkward. Because it wasn't. If anything, this felt like a natural extension of our friendship.

I felt happy and light, effervescent almost. "Thank you."

He leaned his forehead to mine. "Thank you. For trusting me."

I pulled him to me, smashing my mouth to his. Infusing the kiss with everything I couldn't find the words to say. Thank you. Thank you. *Thank you.*

He brushed against me, and my nipples tightened. I wanted more. I wanted him. I reached down and gave his cock a few pumps. He was hard and heavy in my hand.

"Keep that up," he panted, kissing me sloppily, "and I won't last very long."

I smirked when his abs clenched, sensing he was already close. "Good."

"Jesus." He scrubbed a hand over his head, the movement agitated. He squeezed his eyes shut briefly, and I admired his long, dark lashes, the pink high on his cheekbones.

"Frasier." I tried not to smile as I continued pumping. Not

letting up. His body was a masterpiece, lean muscles and sinewy cords. I could watch him all day.

"Hmm?" He looked at me with a dazed expression, and I knew he was barely holding it together.

I slid his hand so it was covering my breast, needing that contact. He tweaked my nipple, making me gasp. In return, I cupped his balls, experimenting to see what felt good to him. What turned him on and sent him flying. He said something unintelligible, his movements jerky as I flicked his tip with my tongue.

"Let go," I said. "Make a mess of me."

He groaned, and with a few more strokes, he lost it. Warm ropes of come hit my chest as he gripped the edge of the chair, chanting, "Fuck. Fuck. *Fuck!*" until he slumped forward, spent.

He took a few deep breaths, and I felt as if I was waiting for the dust to settle. Waiting to see what happened now. Where we went from here.

And then his deep chuckle threaded through the night air. It was sexy as hell. Getting to see him like this—lost to me— was everything.

His eyes were dark when he took in my chest, covered with his release. He brushed his lips against mine. "Let's get cleaned up."

He grabbed my hand and towed me to the bathroom, looking back at me every few seconds as if to check I was still there. He flipped on the shower, and I balanced against the counter, trying to unbuckle my strappy sandals. I was still feeling off-kilter, still trying to wrap my head around this version of Frasier. Well, that and the fact that I'd seen my best friend naked.

I knew what he looked like when he came. I knew the sounds he made when his release overpowered him. And his come was still painted on my chest, marking me.

Frasier kneeled before me. "Let me."

I clutched the edge of the counter while he lifted my foot onto his thigh, sliding his hands down my calves to my ankle in a sensual move that had my body going haywire. It felt as if my earlier orgasm—powerful as it was—was merely a warm-up for something even bigger. He unbuckled my sandal, nostrils flaring. I ran my fingers through his hair, still getting used to the fact that I could touch him like this. Be with him like this.

He set my sandal aside then moved to my other foot, repeating the process from before but adding a kiss this time to the inside of my knee. He removed that shoe and then returned my foot to his thigh before smoothing his hands up to my hips. He dotted my hips with kisses, my lower abdomen. I relaxed into the intimacy of the moment, massaging his scalp.

When he peered up at me, it was with a question in his eyes and so much desire it made my chest ache. I nodded, and he used his thumbs to spread my folds. I tightened my grip on the counter, reveling in the groan that rumbled through him. It was so...possessive. So full of desire. For me.

And then, he leaned forward and licked up my slit, flattening his tongue against my clit. My body was hypersensitive, but Frasier was gentle. I dropped my head back, about to lose my grip on reality, not to mention the counter.

"I can't get enough of you." He lapped and sucked and feasted on me as if I were his favorite meal. "You taste so good. So sweet." He dipped his finger inside me then lifted it to my mouth, slick with desire. "Taste."

I opened my mouth, eyes locked on his as I sucked his finger clean. His hair was a mess from my fingers, his lips glossy with my desire. He moaned when I hollowed out my cheeks, his cock already growing hard once more. I blinked a few times, stunned by how quickly he'd recovered.

He picked me up and hauled me into the shower, kissing me roughly against the wall. The cool tile was a stark contrast to the warm water cascading over our intertwined bodies, making us hot and slick. His hands were everywhere. Caressing my back, my ass, cupping my breasts and pinching my nipples.

It was almost as if he couldn't touch enough of me fast enough. He growled against my lips, our movements no longer sweet and slow. But needy. Impatient.

I didn't want sweet and slow. I wanted wild and unrestrained. I wanted...

When his cock nudged my entrance, I gasped, then bit down on his lip. "That feels...so good," I said, barely able to force the words out. I was so close to sinking down on his length.

With my back braced against the wall, he reached under my leg to tease my clit. "You're so wet for me, angel. So perfect. Do you want to show me how well you'll take my cock?"

I bit my lip and nodded, loving his filthy words and the confidence with which he spoke them. He was a man who knew what he wanted, and he wanted me.

"Yes," I gasped. *"Yes. Please."* I didn't care that it sounded like I was begging.

He rested his forehead against mine. "Let me grab a condom. I saw one in the intimacy kit."

"Actually, Allie and Kit gifted us with an entire box."

He chuckled. "No shit?"

I nodded. "They're in the gift bag in the bedroom."

I trusted Frasier, and I didn't want anything between us. But I'd stopped taking birth control, and I hadn't restarted. There hadn't been any need to—until now.

I watched Frasier as he rushed across the bathroom, returning quickly with the box of condoms. I loved that he was just as desperate as me, and he wasn't even trying to hide it. He tore open a condom and rolled it on. His forearms and abs flexed from the movement. God, that was hot.

Frasier stepped back under the spray, grinning when he saw me waiting impatiently for him. I was running my hands over my breasts, imagining they were his. He'd said he couldn't get enough of me, and I knew exactly how he felt. Because I needed *him*.

He cupped the back of my neck, our bodies sliding against each other as we kissed and kissed and *kissed*. It could've been five minutes or five hours—I lost track of time. His hand was on my thigh, pulling me up on his hip. I tugged on his hair, drawing his lower lip between my teeth as he rolled his body against mine.

"Frasier?" I asked, growing impatient as we continued to rub against each other.

"Yeah." He sounded drowsy, almost drugged, his movements matching.

"Enough teasing. I want to feel you inside me." I gripped his ass, digging my nails into the rounded muscles there.

"I'm completely at your mercy," he said, repeating his words from the other day.

He mapped my curves with his hands, picking me up once more. His chest and shoulder muscles flexed from the effort, and I held on tight as he lined himself up with me. Then, I was sinking down onto him, groaning at the fullness.

"So good," I gasped. "So…much." The sensations. The intimacy. All of it.

"Fuck," he gritted out, resting his forehead against mine. "You feel incredible." He kissed me, drinking deeply before nipping at my lip. Then he began to move, slow and gentle. It was as if he was trying not to break me. "Are you okay?"

I wanted to laugh. I was more than okay. And while I appreciated his concern, it was unnecessary.

"Frasier." I tilted my forehead to his, meeting his eyes. Water droplets clung to his lashes, and he'd never been more beautiful than he was in that moment. "I don't want gentle." I cupped his cheek. "I want *you*. All of you."

"Fuck me," he murmured. And I grinned.

And then he started moving, pumping into me, and it was all I could focus on. Water rained down on us, and our bodies found their own rhythm. I could feel the force of his hips, the strength of his quads, glutes, and core. Part of me wished I could see our reflection because I could only imagine how hot he looked right now.

"That's it, Bryn. You feel so good." He grazed my shoulder with his teeth, and it felt like a million nerve endings lit up inside me.

I squeezed my eyes shut, holding on tight. Everything felt so intense. So full. The glide of his body. The warmth of the water and our slick skin. I was chasing that high again, and he was right there with me.

"Oh. My god. Frasier," I gasped.

"That's it," he coaxed. "That's it, angel."

He slid all the way out of me before pounding back into me, teasing my clit with every forceful thrust. It was wild and chaotic and beautiful.

When his teeth grazed my shoulder again, I was done for. I called out his name as my orgasm overpowered me. It bubbled up, fizzing through me like I had champagne in my veins. My vision went dark, my mouth going dry.

That first orgasm had been like a seismic shift—a rumble beneath the ground. But this one...this one was earth-shattering. It broke me apart, all the pieces of me floating away to be reshaped into something new.

Frasier followed me a moment later, his fingers digging into my hips as he grunted out his release. It was intense, the aftershocks still making me quiver.

Eventually, we stilled. His forehead was touching mine, his eyes closed. His breath was ragged, his face full of an emotion I couldn't quite place.

"Hey," I said in a soft tone. Was he having regrets? "Are you okay?"

He chuckled, the sound hoarse. "Yeah, angel. I'm okay. More than okay. Are you?"

I smiled as he set me back down, cupping my cheeks. "I'm…" I wasn't sure what the hell had just happened. How we'd gone from a flirty game of truth or dare to one of the hottest experiences of my life, but I wasn't mad about it.

"Bryn?" His eyes searched mine, concern at the forefront.

I smiled, partly to reassure him. But partly because it felt good. "I'm great."

He kissed me again, a quick peck. "Let's get cleaned up."

"Yeah." I smirked, giving the shower a pointed look. "I've heard that one before."

He gave my ass a playful smack. I stuck my tongue out at him. He narrowed his eyes and reached for me. I tried to dodge him, but he was too fast. He pulled me into his arms, holding me to him. And as our eyes met, something passed between us, and I found myself hoping he would never let go.

CHAPTER SEVENTEEN

Frasier

I opened my eyes as Bryn was climbing out of the bed. "Where do you think you're going?" I teased.

She smiled down at me, brushing my hair away from my face before giving me a quick peck. "Bathroom. I'll be back."

I released her before rolling onto my back and tucking my arms beneath my head. My dick was already growing hard at the sight of her. Her hair was mussed. My shirt draped over her body, stopping mid-thigh. It was my every fantasy come to life. I was one lucky bastard.

Last night had started with the game of truth or dare, and it had turned into a marathon of pleasure, each of us trying to outdo the other. We'd woken several times in the night, coming together, our bodies in sync. It had been intense—physically, emotionally. We'd probably be tired later, but I was too happy to care.

There was so much trust between us. And we'd been playful, having fun. In hockey, that kind of chemistry and combo made for an unbeatable team. And I could only hope Bryn would realize how good we could be together—not just in bed, but in life.

When Bryn returned from the bathroom, I asked, "How are you feeling?"

She yawned, stretching her arms over her head. It had the effect of lifting her—my—shirt even higher. Normally, I would've looked away. This time, I didn't.

She smiled. "I'm good. A little sore, but otherwise, I feel great. You?"

I cringed, only then realizing that maybe I should've eased into things more. But she'd never complained. If anything, she'd been the one asking for more. Harder.

God, now I'm *harder.*

"I'm amazing," I said, hit with a sudden pang of guilt, feeling it as if I'd been struck by lightning...

This is Derek. I can't come to the phone right now because I'm busy being amazing. Leave a message, and I'll get back to you when I'm done.

Derek. Fuck.

"Hey." Bryn frowned. "You okay?"

"Yeah." I shook my head as if to clear the thought and the pang of guilt that had accompanied it. "Yeah. I could use some food. Do you want some breakfast?"

"Yes, please."

I grabbed the hotel's in-room tablet from the nightstand so we could order room service. She grabbed her phone, gushing over the latest pictures our dog sitter had sent of Bacon and Biscuit. It was the first time I'd worked with the Hartwell Agency, a high-end placement agency for nannies, chefs, yacht staff, you name it. And so far, I'd been very pleased with their service.

Bryn sank down on the bed beside me as I paused on one

of the workouts on the hotel tablet. It wasn't the workout that had made me stop the scroll; it was the woman leading it.

"You know this is Coach's daughter, right?" I asked, pointing at the screen where an image of Emerson Thorne—Olympic Gold medalist—appeared.

"Wait." Bryn paused. "Is she a twin? Because I swear I've met her before at the Atlas Center, but her name was Astrid."

"Yeah." I laughed. "They're twins. Astrid is a doctor, and Emerson is—"

"Married to Nate Crawford, famous actor and producer."

"He's also one of the owners of the Huxley Grand empire."

"Interesting." She snatched the tablet from my hands. "You're thinking of doing a workout, aren't you?"

"After breakfast, if there's time. Want to join?"

"I suppose it depends on the type of workout." She eyed me, biting her lip before returning her attention to the device.

I arched my brow. "I thought you were sore."

She lifted a shoulder, peering up at me from beneath her lashes. "I know you'll make it feel better."

I rolled her over so I was lying on top of her. "Don't tease me, Bryn." I ground against her, dipping my head to her neck briefly to inhale her. Her amber fragrance was layered with notes of my own scent, and I loved that she smelled of me.

She groaned, eyes fluttering shut. "Frasier." She arched her hips against me. Nothing separated us as my dick glided through her folds.

I slid my hand up her stomach, under the shirt so I was cupping her breast. She gasped when I pinched her nipple. My phone buzzed, and we ignored it. The only person I wanted to talk to was here with me.

I ducked my head so I could tease her with my mouth. Then her phone started ringing.

She groaned. "I should get that."

If she thought that would deter me, she was wrong. I didn't stop what I was doing, kissing my way up her stomach.

She reached for the device, grabbing it from the night-stand. "Hey, Al. What's up?" Her voice was higher-pitched than normal, and I took it as encouragement to continue.

Bryn pushed on my shoulder, silently urging me to stop. She covered the speaker with her hand, smiling even as she asked, "What are you doing?"

She knew exactly what I was doing, and the fact that she was now clutching my shoulder encouraged me to continue. I kissed the underside of her breasts, circling her nipple with my tongue until I sucked one into my mouth.

"Mm-hmm." Bryn's pitch rose at the end, and I grinned to myself. "Yep. Sounds good."

I could hear Allie talking, but I couldn't make out the specifics.

"I'm fine," Bryn said. "Promise." After a few more mm-hmms and yeps, she said, "Great! See you soon!" and ended the call.

"You are evil," was the first thing she said to me after she got off the phone.

I adopted an innocent expression, peering up at her from between her thighs. "Me?"

She narrowed her eyes at me. "You knew exactly what you were doing."

"And you loved it." I grinned.

"I did, but now, I have to go." She moved to leave. "I'm supposed to get ready in the bridal suite with Allie and the other bridesmaids."

"Now?" I asked. "But the wedding isn't until the early evening."

She laughed. "Oh, Bear." She patted my bare chest. "You underestimate how long it takes to get ready for something like this."

"Probably." I swept her hair away from her face. "But you're beautiful just as you are."

She leaned into my touch, and I cupped her cheek. "I don't want to leave."

"Can you at least stay for a quick breakfast?" I asked.

Her phone kept buzzing, and I had a feeling it was all text messages from her family and the Bride Tribe. She shot her phone a dirty look then sighed. "I didn't realize how late it was, and I should really get going. They'll have food for us in the bridal suite."

"Yes, but—" I slid down her body, my intentions clear. "What I want isn't on the hotel menu."

"I—" Her breath caught, eyes hooded.

"Do you think you have time for that in your busy schedule?" I teased, nuzzling her mound.

"I—" She sighed, reclining against the pillows as I licked her in a slow, teasing motion. "I might be able to fit that in." She was smiling as she said it, and I wasn't sure she'd ever looked more at ease.

When I walked her to the door half an hour later, she wasn't just relaxed, she was satisfied. I was clad in one of the hotel robes, and she was in a pair of silk bridesmaid pajamas from Allie. The pale blue shorts showed off her toned, tanned legs. And the matching button-down shirt had her name monogrammed over the chest pocket.

"Have fun today," I said, drawing Bryn into my arms.

She smiled, draping her arms around my neck. "The day certainly started off on a high note."

After she'd come, we'd hopped in the shower, and she'd

made me see stars. I was so gone for her that when she'd dropped to her knees, I'd come embarrassingly quickly. Fortunately, Bryn didn't seem to mind that I couldn't get enough of her.

I leaned down to brush my lips against hers. "If it were up to me, we'd start every day like that."

I cupped her cheek, kissing her deeply, pouring everything I felt and everything I wanted to say into it. I knew she had to go, but I wanted to hold on to this moment of bliss. That's what this was. Peace and paradise and happiness.

She groaned, tilting her forehead to mine. "I have to go."

Her phone buzzed as if to reiterate her statement. "I'll see you later." I pressed a kiss to her forehead.

She nodded then turned to head down the pathway that led to the resort. I stood there, still in disbelief. She turned and glanced back at me over her shoulder, biting on a smile when she saw that I was watching. I grinned, waiting until she was out of sight to close the door.

I only wished I'd had more alone time with Bryn this morning. More time to check in and really see how she was doing after last night. Not that I had any concerns on the physical front. The sex had been fucking incredible, and I could tell just how happy she was. Sated and glowing. I was more concerned with her emotional state.

Bryn hadn't dated anyone since Derek's death, and she wasn't the type to have casual sex. I wasn't sure what she envisioned when it came to us, but our chemistry was electric and our connection was undeniable. Even so, I could only imagine how big a step it was to sleep with someone new after losing your spouse, and I was honored that she trusted me.

I grabbed the hotel tablet and was about to place an order for breakfast when my phone chimed. I submitted the order then grabbed my phone, frowning at the screen.

Mom: Please call me.

Another message came through on the heels of the first.

Mom: I wouldn't ask if it weren't important.

I dragged a hand through my hair, knowing I couldn't—shouldn't—put this off any longer.

Me: Give me five.

I slipped into a pair of athletic shorts. I'd already planned to do a workout, but I had a feeling I'd need to burn off some stress after this conversation. Not because of my mom but because of whatever my brother must have done now.

I took a deep breath and hit the number to connect the call. "Hey, Mom," I said when she picked up. "Sorry for not returning your call sooner. I'm out of the country."

"For hockey? Or…a sponsor, a photo shoot?"

I stood, pacing along the windows. "Bryn's sister's wedding."

"Oh, that's right. I knew you were going with her, but I didn't realize that's where you were now. When are you coming home?"

"We return to LA in a few days," I said, trying to buy myself a little extra time. I had two days left with Bryn in paradise, and I resented anything that intruded on my time with her.

I half hoped my comment would deter Mom from initiating a discussion about anything serious. I guessed that was too much to wish for because she said, "I'm sorry to interrupt your vacation, but I'm at a loss for what to do about Jules." She sniffled. "Oh, Frasier. He's a mess."

What's new? I sighed, hoping it wasn't too audible over the phone.

Unfortunately, he'd been a mess for a few years now. It was heartbreaking to watch him go through this and feel unable to get through to him. I loved my brother, but I felt helpless when it came to him. It pained me that I no longer had a relationship with him, just as it hurt that my parents didn't understand my need to set boundaries when it came to Jules.

I didn't ask about the specifics. I didn't need to. Because this was what had happened time and time again. And I hated it—for my brother, my parents, me. Our whole family.

I wanted off this toxic merry-go-round, and I thought I'd made that pretty damn clear.

"I hate to ask this," Mom said, and I realized I'd missed whatever she'd been saying before that. "But…"

I knew exactly where this was headed. My brother owed money to his dealer. His car was broken down—again. He'd gotten arrested. It was always something, and it was never his fault.

Sometimes, it really wasn't. And I didn't want my brother to struggle, but I also knew that I couldn't continue to enable him. It wasn't good for him, for me, or for anyone.

"I love Jules, and I absolutely want to help him. But I'm not giving him any more money." I was sick of him treating me like an ATM. I'd learned that lesson real quick.

"I just…" She sniffled again, and my heart broke a little. "Can you please just try talking to him? You've always been the cool older brother. Jules only listens to you."

"Jules doesn't listen to anyone." I wasn't trying to be callous, though my delivery probably wasn't the best. "He hasn't for a long time."

Not since his accident.

He'd been an Olympic-level snowboarder, at least until a career-ending injury. At first, he'd tried to ignore the doctor's recommendations. He'd convinced himself that he could return to competition just as he had every other time. He knew what it was like to train—to perform—through pain. We both did.

It was only after being airlifted off the half-pipe the last time that he'd realized it was over. And from that point, it had all been downhill. He'd gone from pushing his limits on the snow to pushing everyone away. If self-destruction were an Olympic sport, he'd have a gold medal.

I could understand why he'd had to try, even if I'd been concerned for him. If I'd been in his shoes, I probably would've done the same thing. But ever since then, he'd struggled with the injury, the pain. And he used painkillers to cope.

I'd tried to help him, I had. I'd given him more money than I cared to account for, time, emotional resources. And none of it had made a damn difference.

I could empathize with everything he'd endured. The idea of not being able to participate in the sport I loved was unthinkable. Hockey had always been an escape. And after losing Derek, it had helped me cope. Survive.

"If you won't talk to him, will you at least…"

"Mom," I said with as much strength and compassion as I could muster. "I've told you and Dad." Hell, even Jules when we'd still been talking. "If he wants to go to rehab, I would be happy to pay for it. Otherwise, there's nothing more to discuss."

"So, that's it?" Anger vibrated through her tone, and I hated that my brother's actions were putting a strain on my relationship with my parents. "You're just going to write your brother off?"

"No," I gritted out. It was heartbreaking not talking to my brother, but the alternative wasn't good for anyone. And I was sick of my parents pressuring me to help. "I always hope that he will find a better path. But we've tried and we've tried, and if he isn't willing to admit he needs help, then I'm not going to continue to enable him."

The line was silent for a moment, and when I glanced at the screen, I could see that the call was still connected. I guess neither of us had anything more to say. At least, I didn't. I hadn't wanted to go there, but she'd pushed me too far.

"I'm sorry, Frasier," Mom said, and the defeated tone of her voice broke me. "I'm…sorry."

I didn't want her to be sorry. I wanted my brother to stop hurting everyone and take responsibility for his actions.

"I don't want to continue enabling him either," she admitted. "But I'm at a loss for what to do. Your brother owes someone twenty thousand dollars, and I'm scared of what will happen if he doesn't pay."

My stomach churned. I knew that when she said "someone," she was referring to Jules's dealer. I also knew this wasn't the first time this had happened.

My parents had paid off Jules's debt before, and when I'd found out, I'd been furious. Jules had promised it would never happen again, and yet here we were.

"Please, Frasier." Mom was sobbing now, and my chest felt as if it were being cleaved in two. "I wouldn't ask if we had any other options, but there have been threats…"

I closed my eyes and pinched the bridge of my nose. What was I supposed to say to that? This was a no-win situation. If I helped, my brother might be safe. But for how long? How long would it be until he fucked up again? Until he—or my parents—expected me to bail him out again?

I wasn't trying to be insensitive. I cared about my brother, even if I was deeply disappointed and saddened by his actions. But if I helped, Jules's dealer would keep running up his credit. Taking advantage of my brother's addiction and demanding higher and higher sums of money.

And if I didn't help…

I shuddered, imagining the potential consequences not just to my brother but to my parents. But I wasn't sure that paying the money would solve anything. In fact, I had a feeling it would only make matters worse.

"You need to go to the police," I said.

"We can't. They told Jules if he went to the police…" She stopped talking, and I knew she was too upset, too rattled, to continue.

Fuck.

I sighed, knowing this issue wasn't going to be solved easily. And even though I was pissed, I felt obligated to help. I wasn't going to pay the debt, but there had to be another solution. One that didn't end in violence against my family.

There was a knock at the door, and I stood to answer it. "Mom, I have to go. Let me make a few calls," I said, tipping the hotel employee before carrying my food inside. "I'll get back to you."

"Okay." She exhaled, and it felt as if she'd dropped all the weight that had been on her shoulders onto mine. "Thank you, Frasier."

I said a terse goodbye and then hung my head. I removed the dome from my breakfast tray. It looked phenomenal, but I'd lost my appetite. I pushed the food away and stood, pacing as I thought through my options. Who to call.

Derek was one of the few people who had known about the situation with my brother, and I obviously couldn't talk to him. Bryn knew some of it, but I wasn't going to burden her with this information, especially not on her sister's wedding day. I didn't need to talk; I needed help. But I wasn't sure who could even assist me.

I scrolled through my contacts, landing on my agent, Talia. This type of thing wasn't in her usual purview, but I wanted to keep it as quiet as possible. And I trusted Talia to be discreet.

She'd signed an ironclad NDA. She was invested in my success. Plus, Talia was well-connected, and she might have some ideas as to who could help.

It was still early in LA, but I had a feeling she'd be awake. I inhaled and hit the button to connect the call.

"Frasier," she said, answering on the third ring. "To what do I owe the pleasure? Have you had a chance to look over that contract I sent you? Or were you calling because you need another personalized unreleased book?"

I chuckled, despite the depressing conversation with my mom and the reason for this call. I knew Talia had been curious about that request, and I appreciated that she hadn't asked me outright for more details. Besides, I was feeling better now that I was taking action. "Always straight to business, huh?"

"Well, I assume that's why you called me at seven o'clock on a Saturday morning."

"Yeah…" I rubbed the back of my neck. "Sorry about that."

She laughed. "It's okay. I was already up, thanks to the twins. So tell me what's going on?"

"I, uh—" I had no idea where to start, so I started at the beginning. I told her about my brother and his career, his accident, and what had happened since. She already knew some of it—mostly because when I'd come on as a client, she'd practically interrogated me to see if there was anything in my past or present that might be a liability when approaching potential brands. I'd been honest, but things were so much worse now.

When I finished, she was quiet for a few moments. "I'm sorry that you and your family are going through this."

"Thank you," I said. "I'm sorry to drag you into this, but I didn't know who else to call."

"No. It's good that you did. This doesn't seem like a job for a publicist," she mused.

I didn't have a full-time publicist. Most of the guys in the league didn't, apart from the heavy hitters like Holden Hansley. I worked with the Hawks' PR staff for most of my interviews, unless it was a larger campaign directed by the league. That said, I did not want to take this to the team or the league.

"Maybe a fixer. I know a good one, but I'm actually…" She clicked her teeth a few times then said, "I think this might be a job for Hudson Security."

I furrowed my brow. "The residential security company?"

"You know of them?"

"Some of the guys on the team use them," I said. "I've tried to talk Bryn into it." Not surprisingly, she'd refused.

"Mm. Hudson handles a lot more than just residential security. They offer executive protection services, and I think their expertise might be just what you need."

"You mean…like a bodyguard?" I asked, not sure that was the best fit for this scenario.

"Yes. They protect very high-profile clients, and I'm sure they've dealt with their fair share of blackmail and threats."

She made a good point. "Okay. Thanks, Talia. I'll give them a call."

"Mom!" one of her kids called for her in the background. "I'm hungry."

"I should get going before my kids tear the house apart."

I chuckled. "Oh. One more question before I let you go."

"What's up?"

"If I were to have a relationship with Bryn—"

"Mm-hmm," Talia hummed. She didn't sound at all surprised, not that I blamed her. I'd asked for an unreleased book to be signed to Bryn. Talia had to suspect something was up.

I rolled my eyes. "How would that look from a PR perspective?"

I didn't care what people thought of me, but I cared about how it might impact Bryn. I'd seen the toll the attention following Derek's death had taken on her, and I despised the media for profiting off her tragedy.

"First of all, congratulations. I love that for you." Talia paused, and I sensed hesitation. "It's something that would need to be handled carefully. In the world's eyes, she's Derek's widow."

I gnashed my teeth. "And she is, but that undermines everything she is as a person."

"*I* know that," Talia sighed. "And *you* know that. But you have to think about how this would be perceived. She was married to your best friend. Your teammate. When Derek died, people felt that heartbreak along with her. They've become invested in her story."

While I knew that Bryn was grateful for the support, she had been exhausted by the invasive questions, by people feeling like they knew her or were entitled to information about her or her relationship with Derek. Bryn finally felt as if she'd gotten her privacy back. Her life back. And here I was, threatening to upend it all again.

"She wouldn't want the attention," I said. "And neither would I."

"I completely understand." Talia's tone was gentle, and I sensed I wouldn't like what she had to say. But I'd asked her to give me her honest opinion, and she was. "But people are going to be interested."

Talia wasn't telling me anything I didn't already know— or fear. But that was a bridge Bryn and I would have to cross at some point. At least, if we wanted to be together. And I wanted that more than anything. I only hoped the potential media attention wouldn't deter Bryn from wanting to be with me.

CHAPTER EIGHTEEN

Bryn

I let out a happy sigh, drinking in the beautiful view as I peered at the ocean from the bridal suite. I eyed myself in a nearby mirror—the romantic half-up, half-down hairstyle was both relaxed and elegant, and I was excited to see how the makeup artist would finish my look. My eyes were bright. I looked relaxed, and I felt alive. I knew I'd be tired later, but I hadn't been this happy in a long time.

It wasn't just about the sex, though obviously, that had been phenomenal. Frasier made me feel cherished and adored, both in and out of the bedroom. But it was so much more than that.

I felt as if I'd walked through fire and come out the other side. Something had finally clicked—the months and months of therapy, the work I'd done myself, my talks with Frasier, all of it. For the first time in a year and a half, I was no longer surviving but thriving. The grief was still there—it would always be there, but it didn't feel as heavy as it once had.

My phone buzzed in my pocket, and I pulled it out to glance at the screen.

> Georgia: I know you're busy with wedding stuff, but I just wanted to check in to say I'm thinking about you!

I smiled, feeling so grateful for the women in my life. For Georgia and my mom and Allie, Kylie, and Logan. Each of our relationships was so special to me, and I loved how unique they all were.

> Me: Thanks! Getting ready for the wedding now.

I snapped a few quick pictures—of my view from the window, the bouquets lined up—and sent them to her. Allie's bouquet was particularly beautiful, taking inspiration from the island setting with the palm fronds and large green leaves that backed a cascade of white flowers.

> Georgia: Looks gorgeous. You know I'm here if you ever need to talk.

My chest warmed at her offer.

> Me: I know. Thanks. Lots to catch up on when I'm back.

Her response was almost immediate.

> Georgia: Ooh. Interesting. I'm definitely intrigued.

I knew she wanted more information, and I felt bad for being vague. But this wasn't the type of conversation to have via text, especially not on my sister's wedding day.

> Me: Girls' night in with the gang?

> Georgia: Definitely. I'll mention it in the group chat since I think Logan's coming to LA soon.

> Me: Awesome! Looking forward to it.

"Bryn," Allie called. "You're up next with the makeup artist."

"Thanks." I pocketed my phone.

Allie wrapped her arms around me from behind, and I laughed. I heard the click of a camera shutter. The photographer had been buzzing around, discreetly trying to snap some candid shots of the bridal party and my mom getting ready together.

"I've missed you," Allie said.

"Same." I turned to face her. "Actually, I have a conference in Boston this fall. I might be able to come a few days early on the front end and hang out if you're free."

"I'm free!"

I laughed. "You haven't even checked your calendar."

"Don't need to." She grinned. "If you're coming to visit, I'll make sure I'm available. The wedding has been fun, but I feel like I've barely seen you." She pouted.

"It's been a whirlwind, for sure."

"I know, but I'm so glad you're here," Allie said. "I can't tell you how much it means to me. And I'm glad you brought Frasier." She seemed to hesitate.

I tilted my head, sensing there was something more she wanted to say. "What?"

"When he's around, you just… Well, I can see how happy you are."

I was happy. But this happiness also felt…fragile and fleeting. Part of me was terrified something would come along and ruin it.

"And I know you're taking it slow," Allie continued. "But I know you, Bryn. And you wouldn't have jeopardized your friendship with Frasier unless you thought it was worth the risk."

"I…" I blinked a few times, stunned by how insightful Allie was. I wasn't even sure I'd consciously had that thought until she voiced it aloud. "Yeah." I swallowed hard, thinking of last night and the line Frasier and I had crossed. "You're right. It was a big risk. He's one of the most important people in my life."

This wasn't a vacation fling—at least not for me. And I didn't think it was for Frasier either. It was something we'd need to discuss at some point. But for now, I was content to just enjoy.

Allie's expression softened. "I'm delighted for you. Truly. You deserve to be happy again."

I pulled her into a hug. "Thanks, Al."

When I released her, she said, "I hope I'm not being insensitive by asking this. And you can totally tell me to fuck off if you don't want to answer. But do you think… Could you ever see getting…"

"Can I see myself getting married again?" I asked, and she nodded. "I think it's a little too soon to jump to that," I said, though I was surprised to find I wasn't as quick to rule out the possibility as I would've been in the past.

After Derek had died, I'd been convinced that I'd had my one and only love story. But now… I found that I was more open to the idea of a relationship. Of love. Maybe not marriage, but maybe I didn't have to rule it out either.

The future was undecided, and it was up to me to embrace it.

"Well, yeah," Allie laughed, seeming relieved. "You haven't even slept together. You definitely need to make sure he's good in bed before you shackle yourself to him. Though… how could he not be? That would be a crime." She looked horrified at the mere idea.

My cheeks heated at the memory of last night. His hands on my body. His mouth exploring me. The feel of him inside me, filling me.

"Wait. Wait!" Allie's eyes widened. "No way. Did you guys have sex?" When I nodded, she squealed. "Shut up!"

I laughed. Fortunately, before Allie could press me on it, the wedding planner approached with some questions.

"I want to hear the details," Allie said, pointing at me before she turned and walked away.

I sank down into the makeup artist's chair, chatting with them and my mom as I got my makeup done. It was relaxing, and it was nice to spend time with my mom. She'd been so busy helping Allie plan the wedding that we hadn't gotten to see each other in person as much as we usually did.

A light lunch was delivered, and the flower girl and her mom arrived to get ready. Brooke was excited, chatting happily with everyone. I hung out with her while she got her hair done, and we had an enlightening and entertaining conversation about unicorns and other mythical creatures.

Finally, it was almost time for the ceremony. Most of us were ready, apart from putting on our dresses, and the atmosphere was ebullient.

"A toast!" The maid of honor popped the cork on a bottle, and some spilled out before she started filling glasses.

She handed a glass to Allie and one to me. Allie gulped some down, and it was only then I realized that she didn't seem her calm, fun-loving self.

"Whoa there." I laughed. "Does someone have some wedding-day jitters?" I teased, mostly because I could tell she was tense, even if she was trying not to let it show.

"Not about marrying Kit, but…" Allie glanced around

then whispered, "I'm kind of rethinking my decision not to elope."

I nudged her, careful not to spill the remaining liquid in her flute. "What happened to the confident woman who gave Brooke a pep talk last night?"

"I—" Allie swallowed. "I know it seems silly to be nervous about walking down the aisle, but I am."

"It's completely normal," I said, rushing to reassure her. "And I'm pretty sure you'll feel much calmer as soon as you see Kit."

She nodded. "You're right. I'm sure you're right." She blew out a breath, her shoulders relaxing. "I'm so glad you're my big sister." She leaned her head on my shoulder.

I wrapped my arm around her. "Me too, Al. Me too."

The rest of the afternoon passed in a blur of champagne and laughter. At least until Allie gave each of us a necklace made with a freshwater teardrop pearl. She thanked each of us for the role we'd played in her life, and by the end, everyone was trying not to cry.

After a quick makeup refresh, I escorted Allie down to a small courtyard where she and Kit would share a private "first look" before she walked down the aisle. I fluffed her train, settling the hem of her dress so it laid just right. It was a simple but elegant strapless dress with a mermaid silhouette. The cathedral veil really gave it a dramatic flair.

She was a beautiful bride, and I wanted her to have that picture-perfect moment with her husband-to-be. When I glanced up at her, I realized that she was no longer my annoyingly lovable baby sister but a strong, independent, beautiful woman. I sniffled, quickly swiping away a tear.

"Bryn?" Allie peered down at me. "Are you okay?"

I stood, taking her hands in mine. "Yeah. I'm just—" I smiled wistfully. "I think I'm only just now realizing how grown-up you are."

She laughed, wiping away a tear of her own. I gave her hand a quick squeeze, then ducked back to the bridal suite to grab my bouquet and let Allie and Kit enjoy a moment alone together.

Before I knew it, it was time to walk down the aisle. The guests were seated facing the ocean—all azure waters and a white sandy beach. Large candles in hurricane glasses dotted the aisle along with bundles of baby's breath. Music floated on the salty air, the string quartet playing something that sounded like a rendition of a Sabrina Carpenter song.

Kit and the officiant took their places, along with the groomsmen. The floral arch was covered in more baby's breath, and it looked ethereal and romantic. I waited my turn, taking a deep breath when the wedding planner indicated it was time.

I proceeded up the aisle, searching for Frasier in the crowd. I spied him quickly, drinking him in, feeling anchored and centered. He wore a creamy linen suit that showed off his athlete's physique—broad shoulders, tapered waist, powerful thighs. And now I knew what he looked like beneath his suit. My cheeks heated, and I dipped my head briefly, biting back a smile as I took my place beside the floral arch.

When I lifted my head once more, our eyes met instantly, and Frasier placed his hand over his heart. Then he tapped twice. My smile broadened as I was filled with gratitude and relief. He was checking in, as always. I tapped the stem of my bouquet twice in answer. His shoulders relaxed, and something inside me did too.

Brooke flounced in, tossing rose petals like she had an endless supply. The guests gushed over her, and we all tried not to laugh too hard when she ran out midway up the aisle and then charged toward her dad. He scooped her up, making her giggle before tucking her into his side.

The song changed, shifting to something even slower and more romantic. And then my sister was standing at the end of the aisle, my parents flanking her. It made me think of my own wedding day.

But when everyone stood and turned to watch her procession, I couldn't stop looking at Frasier. Couldn't stop thinking about this enormous shift that had occurred in our relationship, altering it so fundamentally in such a short time. It wasn't just our relationship, though; it was a shift in my way of thinking.

Allie's question about getting married again, as well as my response, had shown me just how much had changed. How much *I* wanted to change.

I thought about what Meghan Hart and Penelope Glass had written in my signed copy of their latest book.

The best love stories have no end. Here's to your happily ever after.

I still loved Derek; I would always love Derek. But that didn't mean I couldn't make room for love in my life again. Just because that chapter of my life had ended differently than I'd hoped or expected didn't mean my story was done. Over.

My gaze landed on Frasier, and that was when I saw it. A gorgeous, bright-orange butterfly was hovering just above his head. I blinked a few times, positive I was imagining it. But then several other guests around him seemed to spot the beautiful creature, pointing at it and whispering.

Everyone else soon turned their attention to Allie, watching her progress down the aisle. But I couldn't look away from Frasier. Especially not when the butterfly fluttered down, landing on Frasier's lapel, just over his heart.

Frasier stilled, looking down at the delicate creature before carefully lifting his head to meet my gaze. His eyes were glassy, because he knew what butterflies meant to me. He knew that they represented Derek to me.

And it felt like a sign. Almost as if Derek were giving his permission for Frasier and me to be together. I dabbed at the corner of my eye, hoping everyone would chalk it up to the emotions of the day. But of all the people here, I knew only Frasier would understand the true reason for my tears or what they signified.

The longer I stood there, the officiant extolling the values of love and marriage, the more I realized something. I was grateful for the sign, but I hadn't needed it. Because my heart, mind, and body had already pointed me in the right direction —to Frasier.

Before I knew it, Allie and Kit had been pronounced husband and wife. The bridesmaid to my right nudged me, and I realized that the ceremony was over. Kit and Allie, the maid of honor and best man, had already proceeded down the aisle, and now all eyes were on me. I cringed, smiling awkwardly as I headed for the groomsman who would walk me out.

I leaned in, whispering, "Sorry," to Hayden.

He chuckled. "No worries. I find it difficult to stop looking at him too."

I laughed, giving Hayden's bicep a squeeze.

We joined the others farther down the beach, waiting for Allie and Kit and the rest of my immediate family. On the plus side, there were custom cocktails for the wedding party. But while the rest of the guests enjoyed a separate cocktail hour, we took photo after photo after photo.

I needed to be alone with Frasier, talk to him. And I wasn't the only one impatient to move on. Brooke—like all of us—was getting antsy.

"Are we done yet?" She pouted. "I want cake."

Poor Brooke. There wouldn't be cake for a while yet. But

I wasn't going to be the one to tell her that. Her dad handed her a piece of candy, coaxing her to smile.

My parents were released to join the party, along with some of the other family members. Then the groomsmen. Then, *finally*, the bridesmaids.

I made my way over to our assigned table at the reception. Frasier was sipping a rum concoction and talking with Kit's friend Hayden. Frasier stood as I approached, smiling, but something seemed off. I couldn't pinpoint what it was, but he didn't seem as relaxed as he had when I'd left the bungalow this morning.

My gaze darted between Frasier and Hayden, trying to determine whether there was some animosity between them. But Hayden seemed mellow enough, so I didn't think that was it. I wondered if some of the other guests had harassed Frasier for autographs or photos. Or maybe it was something else entirely. It probably wasn't obvious to anyone else, but I knew him well enough that I could tell something was bothering him.

"You are stunning," he rasped, pressing a kiss to my temple.

"Thank you." I held Frasier for an extra beat, pressing up on my toes to kiss his cheek before whispering, "You okay?"

Instead of answering, he stepped back, reaching into his pocket to remove his phone. "Sorry. I have to take this." He dropped a quick peck on my cheek. "I'll be back."

That was...*odd*. And now I was really worried.

A few of my cousins came over to say hello, but I excused myself, heading in the direction in which Frasier had disappeared. He was farther down the beach, and I couldn't hear the words he said over the roar of the ocean waves. But I could tell from his posture that he was upset.

What on earth is going on?

I debated whether to stay. Ultimately, I remained there,

ensuring no one else came by, while trying to give Frasier privacy.

When he ended the call, he stared out at the ocean. He linked his hands, placing them behind his neck before looking up to the sky. I studied him, my worry increasing the longer he remained. I'd inched closer, trying to give him space but wanting to be there for him. Finally, when I couldn't take it any longer, I closed the remaining distance between us.

I placed my hand on his shoulder. "Frasier?"

He straightened as if donning his armor. I'd never known him to act like that—at least, not with me anyway. On the ice, sure. In public, absolutely. But here with me? Alone on the beach in the middle of paradise?

He turned to face me, adopting a relaxed expression. But it didn't fool me. "Sorry about that."

"What's going on?" I asked. He opened his mouth, and I added, "And don't even try telling me nothing's wrong."

His jaw was set in a hard line. "We should be enjoying your sister's wedding. We can talk about it later."

"I'm worried about you." I softened my tone. "Talk to me, Bear. What's bothering you?"

When he still didn't answer, I said, "Come on." I tugged on his hand and led him over to a low stone wall overlooking the water. He placed his jacket on the wall before waiting for me to sit.

"Thank you."

He paced back and forth then stopped, and my blood pressure skyrocketed. Whatever was going on was…not good. I tried not to panic, but Frasier was usually so calm, even on the ice. Even when he had every right to lose his cool.

He took a seat next to me, lacing his fingers with mine. "Jules is in trouble."

"What kind of trouble?" I asked, my mind jumping to all sorts of conclusions based on what I knew about Frasier's brother and their complicated past.

"He owes someone dangerous a lot of money."

I grimaced. I could imagine what that meant. I placed my free hand over our clasped ones. "I'm sorry. You hadn't said anything about him for a while, so I'd hoped he was doing better."

Frasier shook his head then dropped it to his chest. "He's a fucking mess. I've offered to pay for rehab countless times, but he won't go. Instead, he keeps causing problems—for himself, my parents, me."

"That's hard," I said, wishing I'd realized how bad things had gotten. Wishing I'd been there more for Frasier.

"It fucking sucks." He dragged a hand through his hair. "And I promised myself that I wouldn't let it interfere with the wedding. Yet here we are."

Had Frasier been juggling this since before the trip? I mean, yes. Obviously. It was an ongoing situation. But I wondered how long he'd been dealing with this latest crisis.

"You know I understand, right?" I asked. "If you need to leave to be with your family. Or you need to make some calls. Or you want to head back to the bungalow and relax."

He shook his head. "I've done everything I can. For now, I just want to enjoy tonight and the time we have left here." He pulled me onto his lap, and I curled into him. "This trip has been wonderful, and I'm not ready for it to end."

"Me either," I whispered.

It was the perfect opening, and it would've been a great opportunity to bring up what this was. What it all meant. But Frasier was already dealing with so much, and I got the feeling that what he needed was a distraction.

I stood, holding out my hand. "I have an idea, but we'll have to be quick."

He quirked one eyebrow. "What kind of idea?" I bent forward and whispered in his ear. Then he said, "I fucking love this idea," in a gravelly voice.

I grinned, removing my shoes before taking off down the beach. Frasier chased after me, our laughter floating on the breeze.

CHAPTER NINETEEN

Frasier

Bryn's dress flowed around her legs, her hair flying behind her as she raced toward the closest beach cabana. I could've easily caught her, but I was enjoying the view too much. And based on the scene she'd read aloud from the novel, I had a feeling Bryn was enjoying the chase just as much as I was. I might not be wearing a mask or stalking her through a dark forest, but I was definitely going to catch her, pin her down, and make her beg for it.

The idea of pinning her down made my dick press against the zipper of my dress slacks. Though what I really wanted was to make Bryn mine both in and out of the bedroom. My earlier conversation with Talia came to mind, but I pushed those concerns away. Right now, Bryn and I were alone in paradise. And I wasn't going to let anything intrude on that—not my concerns for the future, the drama with my brother, or anything else.

Bryn glanced at me over her shoulder, laughing as her feet left little divots in the sand. I was gaining on her. I could've ended the chase, but I was taking my time. As we neared the cabana, she met my eyes, taunting me.

During the day, you could rent one for five hundred bucks a pop. But at night, they were unattended and unoccupied. Perfect for our current purposes.

"Got you," I said in a gravelly voice, snagging her around the waist and pulling her so her back was flush to my front.

She was breathing hard, our chests rising and falling in unison as I walked us inside the hut with my arms still around her. The wood floor was covered with a woven rug that softened the sound of Bryn's sandals when she dropped them at her side.

Three sides of the cabana were made of wooden slats meant to mimic the look of traditional island louvers, though they remained in a fixed position. It allowed for air to circulate and provided some semblance of privacy but not much. The side facing the ocean was fitted with thick white curtains that were currently tied back.

"Now that you've caught me…" she panted, and I knew it wasn't solely from the exertion of running across the beach. A lot of it was due to the anticipation. "What are you going to do with me?"

"Whatever…" I kissed her neck where it met her shoulder, prompting her to moan. "I…" I used my teeth to grab the strap of her dress and tug it down her arm, and goose bumps bloomed in my wake. "Want." I licked up her bicep, and she shivered.

I slid one hand up to cup her breast, using the other to unlatch the tie-back and close the curtain. I knew we were short on time if we wanted to avoid getting caught. Plus, the wedding toasts would be starting soon, and it would be noticeable if the sister of the bride were missing.

I gathered her dress in my hand, the fabric flowing over my arm. The material was lightweight, but there was a lot of it. And it was starting to annoy me, despite how hot she'd looked in it. Finally, touching skin, I smoothed my hand down her stomach and beneath her lace underwear. She groaned, swirling her hips, and I had to bite back a groan of my own.

"Shh." I nipped her ear with my teeth. But that only seemed to drive her even wilder.

She reached behind her back to tease me through my pants, rubbing my already-hard dick until I was positive it was leaking. All the while, I toyed with her clit, spreading her folds and running my fingers over that tight little nub in a way I'd learned would set her off.

"Oh god," she panted. "Oh fuck."

I kept one hand on her clit but slowed my efforts. "What did I tell you about being quiet?" I growled against her skin.

"I'll be quiet," she promised.

She placed her hand over mine, urging me to move once more. She was wet and desperate, and I ached to be inside her.

Since I was skeptical that she could, in fact, remain quiet, I slid my hand up her throat. She moaned and leaned into my hold, which made me want her even more. *Fuck.* Every time I pushed her limits, she pushed right back. It was hot.

I pressed two of my fingers against her lips, sliding them inside her mouth. I'd hoped that would keep her occupied while I resumed my efforts, but now I was the one having trouble staying silent. Because she sucked my fingers greedily, and I could so easily imagine her doing the same thing to my cock. I rocked against her, seeking the friction I so desperately craved.

Her movements became more frantic as I whispered filthy words of praise and encouragement. I loved seeing her let go like this. She was so uninhibited and unrestrained, so beautiful. And it wasn't long before she came, shuddering in my arms. A satisfied groan rumbled quietly through me.

She spun to face me, eyes wild and hungry. She looked

deliciously messy. Her lips were puffy. Her chest flushed with color. The top of her dress was barely hanging on, so I gave it a helpful tug before growling my appreciation.

"Fuck, angel. You are something else."

She preened, and I sucked her nipple into my mouth. She gasped when I swirled my tongue around the hardened peak.

"Too much?" I asked, peering up at her.

"Too *good*," she husked. Her movements were frantic as she unbuckled my pants. The hiss of the zipper seemed louder than normal. "I'm trying to be quiet, but I don't know if I can."

Fortunately, the crash of the waves provided some background noise. But if anyone happened to walk by the cabana, they would have no doubts about what we were doing.

"You seem to do better when your mouth is occupied."

She draped her arms around my neck, pulling me to her until our mouths met in a sloppy, desperate kiss. I growled my appreciation, struggling to remain quiet, especially when she reached inside my pants, taking my cock in her hand. A zing of pleasure shot down my spine.

It felt so good. I was already *so* close.

"Fuck." I swallowed, wanting to make it last. Wanting to make it good for her.

She smirked. "You were saying something about being quiet?"

I smashed my mouth to hers, ravishing her with every stroke of my tongue. And she was just as eager, just as aggressive. I fucking loved it. Loved that we could be slow and sensual or fast and flirty or whatever we wanted to be.

I didn't even realize she'd guided me over to the couch until it was pressed up against the backs of my knees. She placed her palms against my chest, giving me a gentle shove. It didn't do much to move me, but I took the hint and sank down on the cushions. When she began to lower to her knees, I grabbed her wrist and shook my head. As much as I would love to see her take me in her mouth, we were short on time, and I wanted to make us both feel good.

"But I wanted to…"

"Later," I rasped. When we'd have more time. "I want to kiss you. Come 'ere."

She grinned and stood, straddling me before sinking down on my lap. Her dress billowed around us, blocking my view, which was a damn shame. She was still wearing her underwear, but they were soaked.

I ran my hands over her body, loving how disheveled she looked. It matched how I felt.

When she'd stepped onto the aisle, the sight of her had sucked the air from my lungs. She was gorgeous, radiant in a pale blue dress that matched the color of her eyes. And with every step she'd taken toward me, the dress flowed around her, providing tantalizing glimpses of her thighs, thanks to the deep slit.

As much as I'd loved her dress earlier, I liked it even more now. The top had long since been abandoned, fluttering around her waist. Her tits bounced as she swiveled her hips, creating the most torturous friction. My hands were on her waist, and my eyes rolled into the back of my head. I was going to lose my damn mind.

I swirled my tongue around her dusky pink nipple, loving her quiet mewls of desperation. She clutched at me as if trying to hold on to reality. I wasn't even inside her, and we were both out of control.

"Please tell me you have a condom," she said, gasping as she slid along my length.

Her hooded eyes and the impatient rocking of her hips said it all. This was going to be fast and wild, a little out of control. And I wouldn't have wanted it any other way.

"I…" I squeezed my eyes shut, gripping her hips. "Fuck. No. I didn't grab one." Because I hadn't expected this.

"My recent physical came back with no issues, so I would say eff it. But…" She glanced away. "I'm not on birth control."

Oh fuck. Oh… I ground my molars in an attempt to keep my mouth shut. I wanted that so badly. I wanted to be inside her. I wanted no barriers between us—physically or emotionally. And I was honored by the trust she placed in me.

But I also didn't want her to have regrets. This wasn't the kind of decision you made in the heat of the moment. Yes, Bryn wanted kids, and I'd always wanted a big family. And the idea of Bryn carrying our child was one of the hottest things I'd ever imagined. But there was no way we should consider having a baby together when I wasn't even sure if we *were* together.

It merely reaffirmed what I'd already known—Bryn and I needed to discuss what this was. What we wanted our relationship to look like after we returned home.

Now wasn't the right time, but I wasn't going to put off this conversation much longer. We needed to talk, and I vowed that I would do just that—tomorrow. For now, I was going to do everything in my power to show her just how much she meant to me.

"Frasier?" she asked.

"I, uh—" I cleared my throat, struggling to hold it together. "Sorry. My physical was also good." But this was all so new, and I had no idea what she was thinking about us or our future. "You could sit on my face, or…"

"Could we keep doing this?" She glided over me, her slick underwear providing a flimsy barrier. "I'm not ovulating, but I understand if you aren't comfortable with the risk."

I wasn't an idiot. Even with my lust-addled brain, I knew there was still a chance that she could get pregnant.

Which was why I'd given her the option of doing something else.

I gripped her ass, pulling her over me again. "Angel, we can do whatever you want."

"Are you sure?" she asked, hands on my shoulders. "Because I want to make you feel good."

"Trust me," I chuckled. "I do feel good, and I'm not worried about coming." If anything, I worried about coming too soon.

I grabbed a clean beach towel from nearby, so I wouldn't make a mess when that inevitably happened. We were supposed to return to the wedding after all. "Now, ride me."

She grinned, leaning forward to cover my lips with hers. As our tongues tangled, she slid against me, using my cock and the friction from her underwear to drive her to the brink.

"Take what you need," I said, palming her breast, one then the other. I sucked her nipple into my mouth, teasing and tasting, coaxing out her pleasure. Using every means available to make her feel good, while trying to hold on for as long as possible.

I was reciting stats in my head, toying with her breasts, praying that she would come soon before I embarrassed myself. I gripped the towel, hoping my reflexes would be as fast as they were on the ice. Because as soon as she came, I was going to fucking explode.

Bryn's speed increased, our kisses growing sloppier and more desperate. When she started to moan my name, I covered her mouth with my hand.

"I'm beginning to think you want to get caught."

And then she was shuddering on top of me, her head thrown back in ecstasy. Mouth open to form a silent "O." She was glorious—wild and untethered.

I held off for as long as I could, letting her ride out her

pleasure. But I was losing control, unraveling. Bryn moved to my side, crouching down to take me in her mouth.

Whatever I said, it wasn't intelligible. I placed my hand on the back of her head, gently holding her hair to the side.

"Fuck, angel." I watched her, wishing I could make it last longer. "You look so pretty sucking my cock."

She used her hand to pump me, lavishing the tip with attention. And I was done for. I gave her shoulder a gentle squeeze, a warning. But she didn't stop, didn't back off, and I finally let go. Pleasure surged through my veins, a rush of satisfaction washing over me.

And she swallowed it all down then licked me clean. When she sat back up, she wiped at the corner of her mouth. She grinned, and I chuckled, so damn in love with her.

"Come here," I said, pulling her to me for a kiss. A quick cuddle.

She let out a happy sigh and laid her head on my chest. It felt better than any shutout game, any play-off win, even winning the Frozen Four. Because Bryn was finally in my arms—exactly where she was meant to be.

I forced myself to stand, knowing we needed to get back to the reception. I tucked myself back into my pants. And then I offered Bryn my hand, gently pulling her to a standing position before helping her fix her dress.

"Thank you." I kissed her temple. "That was exactly what I needed."

"Me too." She smiled. "Though I'm pretty sure it will be obvious what we were doing."

"Maybe. But you look even more beautiful." I kissed her nose.

"What does that mean?" she asked, tilting her head.

"Exactly what it sounded like," I said.

"No." She pointed at her nose. "That kiss. What are you trying to communicate?"

Ah. So she remembered what I'd said last night about kisses. I didn't know why I was surprised.

I leaned in so my lips hovered beside her ear. *I love you. I'm obsessed with you. You make everything better.* "You're cute."

"Mm." I could hear the smile in her voice. She liked my comment, but she didn't love it. No woman wanted to be referred to as "cute" after sex. They wanted to be pretty, sexy, desirable. And she was all of those and more.

I kissed the spot just below her ear, inhaling her warm, rich amber scent. "Remember what that means?"

She sucked in a jagged breath. "Yes."

I want you.

Because I did—want her. Today. Tomorrow. Always.

"Expecting company?" I teased, surveying the feast as Frasier rolled a room service cart outside to the table overlooking the ocean.

It was the morning after my sister's wedding, and Frasier and I had stayed up late into the night dancing. Everyone had. It had been a magical evening, one of those perfect nights when people truly connected and had fun.

Even after we'd come back to the bungalow, Frasier and I hadn't gone straight to sleep. We'd undressed each other slowly, making love beneath the stars.

This morning, we'd opted to sleep in, wanting to enjoy our last full day in paradise. We were supposed to fly home tomorrow, and if I weren't so eager to see Biscuit and Bacon, I would've begged Frasier to stay longer. That said, we both had to get back to work. Back to real life.

The muscles of his back rippled as he steered the cart, and I couldn't resist watching the way he moved, his body a study in contradictions. He was powerful, especially his quads and ass. But he was also graceful. His large size could be intimidating, and yet he'd only ever made me feel safe.

He lifted a shoulder. "I ordered for both of us."

I barked out a laugh. "Just how much do you think I can eat?"

"Trust me, you're going to thank me when you try the French toast." He lifted the silver dome to reveal one of the plates. My stomach rumbled in appreciation.

He smirked as if to say, "See. I was right." I stuck out my tongue at him.

He guided me to a chair, pulling it out and waiting for me to be seated. I resisted the urge to pull my legs into my lap and wrap his T-shirt around them. To bury my nose in the neckline and inhale.

He pressed his lips to my neck, giving my shoulder a squeeze before moving to the chair beside mine. We were both facing the ocean, and his hand was already resting on my thigh. I loved his constant need to be touching me.

Frasier placed the French toast in front of me. Always taking care of me. Focusing on my needs before his own—both at breakfast and in the bedroom.

I placed my hand on his arm, pulling him closer so I could kiss his cheek. "Thank you."

He turned, giving me a kiss on the lips. "You're welcome."

I sliced into the thick bread and dipped it in some syrup. When I took a bite, the flavors and textures exploded on my tongue. Crunchy. Packed with cinnamon and vanilla. Soft. Sweet.

"Wow. That is good."

He leaned in, eyes alight with pleasure. "Want to know the secret?"

"Um. Yes. Are you kidding?" I dug into another bite, relishing the taste of it. Everything about it was unexpected and delicious.

"They use Portuguese sweet bread soaked in an egg mixture. And then they dip the thick crust in crushed cornflakes."

I shook my head, marveling at the man before me. "How do you know all that?"

"Boone."

"Boone?" I asked, referring to one of the defensemen for the Hawks. I hadn't realized he was such a foodie.

Frasier lifted a shoulder. "He dated a line cook at the Huxley Grand LA for a while."

"Boone." I stared at him. "Boone Parks *dated* someone?" He was one of the biggest players on the team, and I wasn't referring to his role on the ice.

Frasier chuckled, his entire face lighting up. I hadn't seen him this relaxed since...well, it had been years, really. "Shocking, I know."

I shook my head, still in disbelief. I couldn't picture it. "Boone," I mouthed.

"Mm." Frasier licked his lips. He held up a croissant. "You've gotta try this *pain au chocolat*."

I leaned forward, taking a bite. My eyes closed as the flaky, buttery shell fell apart in my mouth, oozing with rich, creamy chocolate. "Oh my god," I said, covering my still-full mouth. I laughed then dabbed my lips with the corner of my napkin. "That is *so* good."

"More?" he asked, his eyes homed in on mine.

It felt as if he were asking about more than just the food, and I nodded. Because I wanted more of this. More lazy mornings spent feeding each other. More late nights spent in each other's arms. More dancing. More laughter. More fun. More everything with Frasier.

He held the croissant to my lips, our eyes locked. I took another bite. When some chocolate filling escaped, he used his finger to wipe it up. He held it to my mouth, and I parted my lips. But then he turned his finger to his mouth and sucked it between his lips, cleaning it.

"Hey! That was mine." But I couldn't be too outraged. I was honestly too distracted and more than a little turned on, despite how many times we'd had sex in the past forty-eight hours.

I narrowed my eyes at him then lunged for the *pain au chocolat*. He was faster than me—no surprise there. The man's reflexes both on and off the ice were unreal.

He caged me to him with one arm, while taking the most obnoxious bite. Moaning around it loudly. I narrowed my eyes at him.

"You're a tease," I said, though my tone lacked bite. "Getting me addicted, only to take it away. Is that the kind of thing I can expect when we get back to LA? You got me addicted to sex, and then you're going to cut me off?" I was joking, sort of. But I wished I could take back those words. Because while I'd meant to broach the topic of our relationship with Frasier, I'd hoped to use a little more finesse. And now I was kicking myself for taking a sledgehammer to our last morning in paradise together.

"I, um—" I squeezed my eyes shut briefly, trying to backpedal. "Sorry. I don't…" I sighed, and he gave my thigh a reassuring squeeze. "That came out all wrong."

"I'm glad you brought it up," he said, and I couldn't get a read on him. Probably because I was trying not to completely freak the fuck out. "Because we both know that things will be…different when we get back to LA. With the preseason ramping up, and…"

"Frasier." I glanced up at him. "I get it. Trust me. You don't have to explain. I know how busy you're going to be. I have no expectations about what this is." I gestured between us, my skin heating and my heart sinking.

This conversation wasn't going at all how I'd hoped or planned. I was bumbling through, saying the opposite of what I actually meant.

"Bryn." His voice was a command, compelling me to look at him. "I don't do casual," he rasped, and his confession sent a flutter through my belly. Or maybe it was the intense way he was looking at me. Studying me.

"And I know this started as a fake-dating situation, but I meant what I said the other day," Frasier continued. "If it were up to me, we'd wake up together every day and start our mornings talking, touching, tangled up in each other."

"I want that too," I admitted.

"So we're agreed?" he asked. "No more pretend relationship?"

I nodded. "No more pretending."

He pulled me into his lap, brushing my hair away from my face. His blue eyes swirled with affection, sucking me into their depths. I cupped his cheek, and when he kissed me, it was with both tenderness and passion.

I was elated. I was scared. I was a bundle of emotions. But Frasier made me feel safe, loved, cherished. And I clung to that feeling, growing light-headed as he slid one hand down to my neck, moving the other to my nape. And even though it wasn't our first kiss, it felt like a new beginning. A promise.

When we reluctantly pulled apart, we were still touching. My heart was racing, but my mind was quiet. And my heart felt whole.

CHAPTER TWENTY

Bryn

"What's all this?" Georgia asked, stepping daintily over the bags of dirt that I'd hauled to the back-yard but had yet to move from the pathway.

Today had been my first day off since returning from Anguilla a week ago, and I'd spent it in the garden.

"Sorry. I ran out of steam." I was resting on top of a stack of them, still trying to get myself up and moving.

Bacon and Biscuit were lounging in the yard, acting as if they'd done all the hard work. They'd certainly run around a lot, chasing me every time I dragged in something new. Sniffing and investigating.

I hadn't realized how late it had gotten. Perhaps I'd been a little overambitious. There were raised-garden beds to be assembled, plants to be planted, string lights to be hung, new patio furniture to be arranged. I couldn't wait to see it when it was all done, even if it was going to take me a lot longer than I'd anticipated.

"You look cute," I said to Georgia, admiring her cotton sundress and cork wedge sandals. She held a bottle of wine in one hand, reaching down to pet Biscuit when she wandered over.

"Girl, you need a wheelbarrow," Logan said, crouching down to give Bacon a cuddle. Her shirt rose up, showing a sliver of her toned stomach and the Olympic rings tattoo that rested on her side.

"A wheelbarrow?" Georgia laughed, glancing around at the destruction that was my backyard. "What Bryn needs is a professional landscape architect."

"Maybe," I admitted, groaning when I stood. "Or maybe a massage."

My massage in Anguilla last week seemed like a lifetime ago. So much had happened since then.

I brushed my hair away from my face, taking some dirt along with it. This project was a long time coming, and I was sick of looking out at a sad yard and even sadder flower beds.

"Let me rinse off and change," I said, my muscles aching in protest. "There's food in the kitchen. Help yourself."

The dogs trotted inside, and the rest of us followed.

"Kylie's coming, right?" Logan asked.

It was so good to see Logan. I was so happy that she'd found a great team and friends in Minnesota, but I missed her. Fortunately, she had a photo shoot in LA, so she was visiting for a few days. I'd offered to let her stay with me, but the brand had put her up in the Huxley Grand LA. While I didn't blame her for wanting to stay at a luxury hotel, I suspected Logan was hooking up with someone who lived in LA, though she wouldn't tell us who it was.

"Yeah. I think she's just running a little late. She got caught up dealing with a client emergency."

Logan cringed, and I laughed. We both knew that in Kylie's world, a client "emergency" could mean anything from a comment being taken out of context to a sex tape.

I ran through the shower and debated putting on something cute, but this was a casual girls' night in. Besides, I was tired after working all week. So, I settled on some comfy cotton shorts and a matching top.

When I returned to the kitchen, it was to the sound of hushed whispers that stopped abruptly. Georgia smiled brightly when she saw me, and I narrowed my eyes at her.

"Wine?" She offered me a glass.

"Thanks," I said, eyeing her suspiciously as I accepted it from her.

There was a knock at the back door, and I went over to answer it when I saw Kylie standing there. "Sorry about the mess." I hugged her.

"Looks like you've taken on quite the project."

I linked my arm with hers. "That's an understatement. Come on, Logan and Georgia are here. We just opened a bottle of wine, and you look like you could use a glass."

She laughed, though the sound was bitter. "Another understatement."

"That bad?" I asked.

She huffed. "You have no idea. Please promise me that you'll always come to me first with anything that might affect your brand."

My brand. I wanted to scoff, but I knew she was right. My brand was "Derek's wife." "Widow to a famous hockey player who died tragically." And her comment made me feel even worse for waiting to tell her about Frasier and me.

We joined the others in the kitchen, and a generous glass of wine was soon offered to Kylie.

"To…" Georgia lifted her glass, looking from me to Logan to Kylie.

"Making messes," I offered.

Logan laughed, and she and Georgia repeated the toast, while Kylie said, "And cleaning them up." And then we all clinked our glasses together before taking a sip.

The flavors settled on my tongue, buttery and rich and

yet fruity somehow too. It tasted like apricots. "Oh. That's good," I said, admiring the color of the wine and the way it coated the glass when I swirled it. "Did you get that on your trip?" I picked up the bottle, inspecting the label.

Georgia nodded. "There's a great little winery there that's owned by a former LA Leatherbacks player, Lorenzo Mancini."

"I've been wanting to go to the Alondra Valley," I said. "I hear they have the cutest bookstore, Bibliolater. They host an annual Meghan Hart celebration day."

"It definitely sounds right up your alley." Georgia grinned. "I assume you're going to read her upcoming release with Penelope Glass."

"I—" I bit my lip and glanced away. "I sort of already did."

"What?" Her eyes bulged. "How? It's not even out yet."

"Yeah," Kylie chimed in, leaning her hip against the counter. "How did you manage that? I tried to get a few copies for some of my clients for promo purposes without success."

I toed the floor with my slides. "It was a gift."

"From whom?" Kylie leaned forward, clearly intrigued.

Georgia's wineglass scarcely concealed her knowing grin. "I have a pretty good idea who."

Kylie and Logan turned to her, then the three of them turned to me. "Frasier might have given me an advance copy."

"Shut. Up." Kylie stared at me as if to assess whether I was telling the truth. When I laughed nervously, she said, "Oh my god. You're serious."

"Yep." I went to get it from my room, where it had pride of place on my nightstand even though I'd already finished reading it.

Kylie's eyes widened when I returned with the book in hand. "Holy shit." I handed it to her, and she opened the inside and paused when she came to the inscription. "And they signed it too? And wrote a personalized note?"

I nodded. On the flight home, I'd learned that Frasier had asked his agent to give Meghan Hart and Penelope Glass a handwritten letter telling them why the book was so important to me. Apparently, they'd been touched by the story and excited about the signed jersey he'd offered in return. He'd specifically asked them to write what they had. It made it even more special.

"I'd ask to borrow this," Kylie said, watching my expression. "But I'm guessing you'd say no."

"I thought you preordered a copy," I said, reluctant to part with it. Any other book—signed or not—sure. A book was meant to be read and enjoyed. But this one was special.

"I did." She sighed. "It should be here any day now. But we're getting off topic." She arched one eyebrow. "What's up with you and Frasier?"

"Yeah. I'm surprised Frasier isn't helping with your latest project." Georgia glanced around as if waiting for him to appear.

I laughed. "Way to be subtle, G. And no, Frasier's not here."

We'd been inseparable since the trip to Anguilla, and now it felt strange to be without him. Part of me was scared by how quickly I'd become attached to him. And the other part couldn't wait to see him again.

He'd spent every night here for the past week, but he'd gone home early this morning to catch up on laundry and check in on the situation with his brother. Plus, he knew I was hanging out with the girls tonight, so he planned to come over tomorrow. Since it was only for one night, we'd figured Bacon and Biscuit would be more comfortable here. And I was more than happy to keep them with me.

"Can you blame me for asking?" Georgia lifted a shoulder. "He practically lives here."

"Ha-ha," I deadpanned. It wasn't the first time our friends had said something to that effect, but it definitely hit different this time.

Frasier didn't live here, but would he want to? If we kept dating, would he want to move in together? And would he want to live here or at his place or somewhere else entirely? Would I be okay sharing the home Derek and I had made with another man? Conversely, would I be okay selling it and letting it go?

Whoa. I shook my head as if to clear it. I was getting ahead of myself.

"You guys do share two dogs." Logan popped a piece of prosciutto into her mouth.

I couldn't argue with that. so instead, I carried the charcuterie board into the living room. Everyone grabbed something as the dogs followed us. Logan sank to the floor, and Bacon immediately climbed into her lap. Georgia sat on the couch, and Kylie and I joined her.

I imagined what it would be like to enjoy the charcuterie in my garden. I wanted to get a large retractable screen and a projector. I envisioned lounging out there on a quilt, watching movies or even hockey games. The preseason was starting soon, and it seemed overly optimistic to think I could have it done in time. But maybe I could finish before the season kicked off.

"Okay, So..." Georgia leaned in. "I've been dying to hear all about what happened at your sister's wedding. You told me we had a lot to catch up on, and I could—and have—read a million possibilities into that after the whole 'only one bed' in a romantic bungalow situation."

"She definitely has," Logan muttered darkly. "Trust me."

"Wait." Kylie furrowed her brow. "I knew Frasier was

going with you to the wedding as your plus-one, but…did something happen between the two of you?"

"Are you asking as my publicist or my friend?"

She lifted a shoulder. "Both."

Either way, she needed to know, and I wanted to tell her. So I explained how Frasier had gotten roped into being my fake date.

Once I'd finished, Georgia said, "Okay. Now that we're all caught up, enough stalling."

I laughed. "I know. And I'm sorry for being vague and for making you wait *so long*," I joked, as if it were a huge hardship. "But it's not entirely my fault." I gave her a pointed look.

"Yes. Yes. I was out of town." She waved a hand through the air. "And we had to wait for Logan."

"Plus, I had work, and I haven't even been back that long. I'm pretty sure I'm still jet-lagged."

"And yet you had time to go buy an entire nursery worth of plants." Georgia gestured to the back door and the garden beyond. Logan and Georgia shared a look.

"What?" I asked, annoyed that they seemed to be having a private conversation about me without ever saying a word.

"Did something…happen?" Georgia asked in a gentle tone. "Something…bad?"

"What?" I glanced between them, trying to determine where they'd gotten that idea. "No. Why would you think that?"

"Because you're totally dopamine loading," Georgia said as if the answer were obvious.

"With the garden?" I asked, brow furrowed. When they nodded, I said, "I'm not dopamine loading. I'm doing a project."

"To avoid uncomfortable feelings? To make yourself feel better?" she asked. I appreciated her honesty and concern, even if it was unwarranted this time.

"I'm not doing it to avoid my feelings. I'm doing it because I'm sick of looking out at that sad excuse for a garden and thinking of what could've been. It's time for a change."

"So let me get this straight. You come back from a vacation where you and Frasier pretend you're dating, and you have a sudden and intense desire to grow a garden."

"Maybe it seems sudden," I said, knowing that I could just as easily be talking about my feelings for Frasier. "But I've been wanting to make a change for a while, and something clicked on the trip." Now I was definitely talking about Frasier. And myself. My journey with my grief.

"Clicked...how?" Kylie asked. "Clicked for you, or between you and Frasier?"

"Both," I said, fiddling with the stem of my wineglass. I rolled my lips between my teeth, trying not to smile too hard.

"Oh my god." Georgia gasped. "You had sex with Frasier, didn't you?"

"I..." My cheeks heated. "Yeah." The word came out as more of a squeak.

Logan arched one brow. "Details, please."

So I told them everything. Well, not *everything*. There were some things I wanted to keep between just Frasier and me. But I told them about truth or dare, eliciting whoops of delight about my burlesque number. I told them about cliff diving and our first real kiss. Our conversation the morning before we came home.

"Damn," Logan said, blinking a few times as if to process it all. "That was a lot to pack into one trip."

"Yeah." Georgia shook her head. "I mean...I know I told you to lean in, but girl, you *jumped*."

"It was scary," I said. It still was. "But it felt right."

"I'm happy for you," Kylie said. "Truly, Bryn." She gave me a hug.

"Does this mean we get to attend home games again when I'm in town?" Logan asked. Because, of course, she was thinking about how this affected hockey.

I laughed, though her question certainly gave me pause. I hadn't thought about that until now. But the season would be starting before we knew it.

"I don't know," Georgia said. "Is Levi going to be pissed if you start attending his rival's games?"

Logan lifted a shoulder. "It's not like it would be the first time I've gone to a Hawks game."

Georgia leaned forward. "I was referring to Kovalsky, not the Hawks."

"Yeah," I said. "What's the deal with those two? Your brother seems to really hate Carson."

"You're never going to believe this," Logan said. "But they played together in Juniors, and Levi even lived with Carson's family part time."

"What?" Georgia gasped.

"I know, right?" Logan shook her head. "It's difficult to believe it now, but for a while, they were actually really good friends."

We all stared at her, stunned, but it didn't seem as if she was going to elaborate.

"Back to Bryn." Kylie polished off her wine before refilling her glass. "Regardless of whether you want to attend the games, we should probably work on a plan."

My skin felt tight. "My family knows. My friends know. They're the only people who matter." Besides, we'd just started dating; there was no way I was ready to announce it to the world.

"I get that." Kylie gnawed on her bottom lip. "But wouldn't you rather have the story come out on your own terms?"

I'd rather not have it come out at all. Not because I wasn't proud of Frasier or our relationship, but it was really no one's business.

Georgia nodded. "She's right, Bryn."

"We've been together for a little more than a week," I said, feeling as if it was all happening way too fast. "We want to keep it quiet for now." I was trying not to get too ahead of myself or get too in my head. "We're just enjoying being with each other."

Frasier already had enough on his plate with the preseason starting. Not to mention the situation with his brother. I was relieved that he'd hired Hudson Security.

"I get it," Kylie said in a gentle tone. "I'll work on some options for when you're ready."

"Thanks, Ky."

Selfishly, I wanted to keep our relationship a secret as long as possible. Part of me worried about what people would think—the media, the fans, the staff and players of the Hawks. I didn't want to care what anyone thought, but I also wasn't ready for our new relationship to be dissected under a microscope. I'd just reclaimed my happiness, and I wanted to enjoy it for as long as I could.

CHAPTER TWENTY-ONE

Bryn

Three Months Later

"Come on." I stood, barely catching the bowl of popcorn before it fell from my lap and onto the floor. "Come on!" I called again, louder this time, pushing all my encouragement through the screen and onto the ice.

Bacon and Biscuit sniffed around, eating the kernels I hadn't been able to save. I didn't even try to stop them, I was so engrossed in the game.

"Let's go, boys!" Georgia cheered, and Kylie clapped, the three of us riveted to the screen while we watched the second period of the game.

The Hawks were playing one heck of a game against Dallas, especially Frasier. He might be a sweetheart off the ice, but he was intimidating as hell between the pipes. He had to be. He was one of the best goalies in the league. And he guarded that net like a mother bear protecting her cubs.

He'd kept out twenty shots on goal over the past two periods, and several of them had seemed like impossible saves. He was on fire tonight, and I wasn't the only one who'd noticed. The commentators had said as much, and so had Logan when she'd last texted.

Kovi stole the puck and headed for the net, passing it to Gabe, who passed it to Holden. Holden made the shot, threading the needle with the puck, through the legs of one of the other players and right over the top of the shoulder of the opposing team's goalie. It was a beautiful play, and the crowd went wild.

Dallas won the next face-off. They were good, but our guys were dominating. When it was time for the second intermission, we were in the lead by one. Logan texted us in the group chat.

Georgia, Kylie, and I refilled our drinks and snacks, talking about some of the highlights until play resumed. Allie texted me about the game. We'd texted or talked on the phone almost daily since I'd returned from Anguilla, and I felt closer to her than ever. I was really looking forward to visiting her in Boston.

As soon as the teams skated onto the ice for the third period, you could feel a shift in the energy. Both teams wanted to win. Allie might have texted again, but she'd have to wait for a response because my focus was on the game.

The third period was intense. There were a few times that I'd thought Dallas would score, but the Hawks had a strong defensive line. And anytime Dallas was able to make it into the crease, Frasier kept them from scoring.

With two minutes left in the game, one of the Dallas players sent the puck toward the crease. I held my breath, releasing it with a smile when Frasier caught it in his glove. The buzzer rang, announcing the end of the game. The score was one-nothing; the Hawks had won.

Georgia, Kylie, and I jumped around, the dogs barking and joining into our celebrations.

"Jesus." Georgia laughed. "That was a good game."

"The team is on fire this season!" Kylie said.

"No joke." Georgia grabbed the popcorn and started carrying things to the kitchen.

We weren't that far into the regular season, but if the Hawks kept this up, they'd have a real shot at the play-offs this year. Part of me wished Derek were here to see it. He would've gotten a kick out of playing with Holden Hansley. And I would've loved to have heard what he had to say about Carson. Kovi was cocky and mouthy, but the fans loved him. And our rivals loved to hate him.

Frasier and I were still flying under the radar, though Kylie had convinced me to post a few images of us. It wasn't clear that it was Frasier in the pictures with me, just close-ups of our hands linked on my thigh. Another with two breakfast dishes and a simple caption. So far, most of the comments had been positive.

People speculated that Frasier and I were together. Our close friends and family knew the truth, including Derek's parents, who had been sweet and supportive. But it was as if they'd all formed a protective bubble around us. I loved them all the more for it.

I followed Georgia to the kitchen, where she bustled around, wiping down the counters. "Thanks, but you don't have to clean up."

"It's fine," she said. "I'm happy to."

My phone chimed with a new text from Logan—a picture of Frasier as he shook hands with one of the Dallas players. Logan's season wouldn't start for another month or so, so she'd gone to Dallas to watch the game and visit her brother, Levi. We'd missed her tonight, but we'd texted in our group chat the entire game. She'd been rooting for Dallas—her brother's team—of course. And it had been an aggressive game from start to finish.

Kylie called out from the living room, "Bryn, your man is being interviewed."

I raced into the living room, eager to see Frasier. I had been missing him like crazy since the season had started. We made every minute count, but between his training and my work schedule, we hadn't gotten to spend nearly enough time together. During the week, I had work. When I was off on the weekends, he often had games.

I had yet to attend any home games—I didn't want to draw attention to myself or the fact that we were dating. And this was his first away game.

On-screen, the reporter asked him some questions, and Frasier slicked back his hair, sweaty from the game. He was still dressed in his pads, and I knew he was probably more than ready to shower. But he spoke eloquently, praising his teammates for their defensive and offensive maneuvers while also commending the Dallas team for their competitive level of play.

My chest swelled. I was so proud of him for the way he'd played this past season, the fire he'd brought to the ice. It was a testament to his mental strength, to his resilience. But then the interview ended, and I was left feeling his absence again.

"Oh boy," Georgia said, shaking her head. "You've got it bad, huh?"

I'd been so convinced that it wouldn't be possible to feel this way again. That I wouldn't love again. And here I was, staring at an image of the man who'd changed my mind, feeling both excitement and trepidation.

Frasier supported me unconditionally, not that he'd ever said those words. Not that he needed to. It was in his actions, in everything he did.

Kylie smiled, and Georgia pulled me in for a hug. I didn't have to say anything because they knew. They'd been there for all of it, and they saw how happy I was with Frasier.

"Don't let anyone else see you looking at him like that, or there will be no more keeping this secret." Georgia was grinning as she said it.

"Everyone already suspects that you're dating," Kylie said, though that was no surprise. People had speculated on our relationship ever since Derek's death because of all the time we spent together. "And they're excited for you. Most of the comments fielded by my team have been supportive. People want to believe in finding love after loss, and you're proving it's possible."

That was a relief. And even if she hadn't said the words aloud, I heard the subtle push: *it's time.*

I knew Frasier was ready to go public; he'd been ready. He'd been nothing but patient—letting me dictate the timing. And yet...I continued to hesitate.

Biscuit scratched at the back door. I'd never been so eager to let the dogs out. "Come on," I said, opening the door for her and slipping into my garden shoes. "I need to water the garden." And then to my friends, I added, "Do either of you want to take home some tomatoes and basil? They're growing like crazy."

I was talking a million miles a minute, but I couldn't help it. I knew Kylie was right, but I was scared.

"I wish," Kylie said, quickly masking the disappointment that had overtaken her expression. "And thanks for the offer, but I never have time to cook."

Biscuit bounded through the door, and Bacon followed, with Georgia last. "I still can't believe you grew all of this."

I laughed, taking it all in. "Neither can I."

But I loved having a garden, especially the fresh produce. I'd gone down the rabbit hole of social media garden influencers, and I was obsessed. And my garden was flourishing. I had almost more produce than I knew what to do with. And there were flowers everywhere. I'd planted a ton of native varieties that attracted pollinators, and butterflies visited almost daily.

The space had transformed from something depressing that I wanted to avoid into my happy place. It was magical out here, especially at night. Frasier and I loved hauling out a bunch of blankets and pillows and watching a movie while we cuddled with the dogs. We might not have much time together, but we certainly made every moment count.

Georgia and I harvested some produce for her to take home. "How do you know when the tomatoes are ready?" she asked.

I explained what to look for, pointing out some that were overripe or underripe.

"So, timing is important," she said.

"Very." I narrowed my eyes at her. I could read through the lines, and she wasn't being all that subtle.

"You might be an expert at harvesting tomatoes—"

"An expert." I laughed, tossing some of the ripe ones into my basket. "Hardly."

"Kylie's an expert too."

"At harvesting tomatoes?" I asked, intentionally misinterpreting Georgia's statement.

"Bryn," Georgia chided.

I blew out a breath. Frasier and I had talked about our relationship and how we wanted to announce it, the potential public response. Despite what Kylie had said about the mostly positive comments, I was still nervous to take that next step. To go from speculation to confirmation.

"Do you have reservations about Frasier or your relationship?" she asked.

"No." I shook my head. "None." I took a deep breath. "I'm finally happy again, and I don't want anything to ruin it."

"What if it doesn't ruin it? What if it's actually better? Aren't you sick of sneaking around? Frasier's been really patient, but keeping this secret might be hurting him. Don't you want to go to his games?"

I swallowed hard. I hated the idea of hurting Frasier, but the games were a sticking point for me. Because, of course, I wanted to support Frasier. But I also didn't know how to do that without feeling as if I were betraying Derek. And I was afraid that if I voiced that aloud, no one would understand.

"Bryn?" she asked in a gentle tone, stepping closer to place her hand on my shoulder. "Are you okay?"

"I—" The words got stuck in my throat. "I want to go to the games, but it's complicated."

She nodded, patiently waiting for me to elaborate.

"This is going to sound ridiculous, but whose jersey would I even wear?"

"Only you can answer that." She smiled then, guiding me back inside. "But I'm sure Kylie would have a few ideas."

We headed back into the house. I talked with Georgia and Kylie for a while longer, grateful for my friends. I'd known they would never judge me, even as I grappled with the complicated feelings that accompanied grief. Instead, they'd been compassionate and supportive, listening and helping me work through my thoughts.

By the time I wished Georgia and Kylie a good night, I felt better. I might not have a concrete plan for how to juggle my past with my present, but I knew that Frasier was my future.

I headed upstairs to get ready for bed. After a long, hot shower, I felt even more relaxed. Maybe I didn't have to have all the answers so long as I kept an open mind. I'd just finished slipping into my pjs when my phone rang. I reached for it, smiling when I saw Frasier's name on the screen with a request for FaceTime. I hit the button to connect the call and rested my phone against the bathroom mirror so I could see him while getting ready for bed.

"Congratulations!" I beamed at him, and he smiled back

at me from his hotel room. He was shirtless, and the lighting was low, almost as if he was getting ready for bed too.

"Thanks, angel. I take it you watched the game."

"Of course." I reached for my under-eye cream, dabbing it onto my skin. "You had some really nice saves in the second period. And that final attempted goal—" I clutched my chest. "Ugh. That was a nail-biter. Good save, Bear."

He chuckled, running a hand through his hair, now damp from a shower. "Thanks. Doing some self-care?"

"Yes." I smirked as I applied my lifting oil. "But not like *that.*"

"Mm." He leaned his head back against the upholstered headboard, his lips curving into a smile. His bare chest was on display, and I wanted to run my fingers down the muscles. Rest my head over his heart. "It could be like *that*. I did just win a game. Feels like we should celebrate."

"You didn't want to go out with the team?" I applied my last layer of oil. I stood back, peering at my reflection. I looked like a glazed donut. *Perfect.*

"A few of the younger guys went out, but I didn't feel like it."

I wasn't surprised that Frasier had elected to stay in, but something in his tone caught my attention. I leaned closer to the screen, noticing the dark circles beneath his eyes. "You okay?"

I knew the games and all the travel were physically exhausting, but this seemed to go deeper than that. At the very least, I figured he'd have been happy that the team had won. But he seemed distracted, down or something.

"Jules checked himself in to rehab," he said, surprising me.

Frasier hadn't mentioned his brother in weeks. The last I'd heard, Hudson Security had worked with the local authorities to conduct a sting operation. The dealer had been arrested, and we kept hoping Frasier's brother would finally get the help he needed. But I'd been afraid to mention it, taking the lead from Frasier.

"That's good, right?"

"Yeah. Yeah." He shook his head as if to clear it. "I just hope it sticks."

"Me too." I knew how painful this was for Frasier, and I wished I could crawl through the screen and hug him.

"I miss you."

"I miss you too." I grinned. "And I'm counting down the days until you're home again."

"Me too." He tucked his arm beneath his head. "Thanks for the good-luck note, by the way. And the self-care kit."

"You're welcome." I beamed. "I hope you liked it."

His eyes were locked on mine when he said, "I loved it." And it felt as if he was saying so much more. After a long pause, he asked, "How are Biscuit and Bacon? Behaving, hopefully."

I smiled. "They're good. Biscuit is sniffing around downstairs, and Bacon was already getting into bed when I hopped in the shower."

"I wish I were there. Cuddling in bed with you."

"Is that all you wish we were doing?" I teased.

"No. If I were there, you'd already be naked."

I took a few steps back so he could see more of me. And then I dragged my silk tank top over my head, casting it aside. When I looked at the screen again, Frasier's eyes had gone wide. I turned so my back was to him, taking my time to tease him as I lowered my matching silk shorts.

"Better?" I asked.

"Fuck yes," he said, scrambling to remove his own shorts. "Turn around. Show me everything."

It was his first away game, our first time being apart since we'd started dating. And it was the first time I'd dared to do something like this.

I turned slowly, running my hands over my body and imagining they were his. My mind went back to Allie's bachelorette party and that night on the beach. Then, as now, his eyes were hooded as he watched me.

"That's it, angel." He adjusted his phone, letting me see how hard he was, see the way he was gripping his cock. "You know I love it when you give me a show."

My lips curved upward, and I knew he was thinking about that night too. I dragged my hand down my neck, over my breasts, goose bumps rising in its wake. As he watched me, I felt sexy and desired.

"Need you, Bryn," he rasped, fisting his cock, giving it a few lazy strokes.

"Mm. Don't stop," I said, referring both to his words and what he was doing with his hand. I bit down on my lip. Watching him was hot.

"Look at what you do to me," he hissed, letting me see just how aroused he was. The low lighting cast shadows over his chest and abs, his muscles clenching with every pump, every groan.

"So hot," I whispered, as if in a trance.

"Get on the bed. I want to see you—all of you."

I grabbed the phone and carried it with me to the bed. "Tell me what you wish we were doing now."

› CHAPTER TWENTY-TWO

Frasier

"Hey, angel." I buried my face in Bryn's neck, inhaling her warm, amber scent. "God. I missed you."

As soon as the team plane had landed, I'd sped over to Bryn's house. I'd been gone for three days, but it could've been three years for how long it felt. Texting and talking on the phone had helped, but I hated being away from Bryn.

I'd barely gotten through the door, and then she was there, jumping into my arms, kissing me. I'd laughed and held her tight, my bag still slung over my shoulder as we devoured each other, rediscovering each other until I cast my duffel aside.

She slid down my front, my cock jerking to attention at the feel of her in those damn yoga pants. She'd been taking dance classes again, and I loved watching her grow stronger each week. But all I wanted to do right now was hold her. Her arms were wrapped around me, her cheek pressed to my chest.

"I missed you too," she sighed. "So much."

I didn't want to let her go, but the dogs were pawing at my legs, begging for my attention. I cupped Bryn's cheeks and gave her a quick peck before brushing her hair away from her face. And then I paused. Frowned.

Now that I'd taken a closer look at Bryn, she seemed exhausted. When we'd talked last night, she'd seemed fine. Same thing the night before. But the dark circles beneath her eyes spoke to a string of sleepless nights. I guided her over to the couch, pulling her into my lap.

"You look tired. Are you feeling okay?"

"I didn't sleep well last night. I'll be fine," she said, but she didn't sound convinced. I definitely wasn't.

"Talk to me, Bryn," I said in a gentle tone. When she tried to get up, I caged her in my arms. "Angel, please. Tell me what's going on."

She was silent for a moment, then she said, "Being away from you was harder than I expected."

"It sucked." I'd totally underestimated just how difficult it was for the guys on the team to be apart from their significant others.

"And I'm scared," she whispered. When she met my gaze, it was with tears in her eyes. The effect was devastating. *She* was devastating. "I'm terrified because I'm so happy." She choked on a sob. "I'm so happy with you, and I'm scared of losing you."

I cupped her cheek, drying her tear with my thumb. "Bryn."

I didn't know what else to say. Her fears were understandable, considering what she'd been through. And I wasn't willing to make a promise I couldn't keep. Because none of us could guarantee that we'd be here tomorrow.

But I also couldn't sit back and do nothing. I held her, trying to comfort her while brainstorming possible solutions. I'd tried to check in regularly during the trip. I'd shared my location with her on my phone. But I knew that no matter what I did, that fear might never go away, not completely.

"I'm glad you told me," I said.

"I didn't want to." She tugged at the corners of her eyes.

I pulled back to look at her. "Why?"

"Because I don't want you to be distracted this season. And we have so little time together lately, and I don't want to spend it on…this." She frowned.

"Angel." I held her chin. "I'm just happy to be with you. I don't *ever* want you to feel like you have to hold back or hide what you're feeling. Not with me."

"I know." A tear slipped out, tracing its way down her cheek before I caught it with my thumb. "It just…" She sucked in a jagged breath. "I just want to be happy and live life. I was making such good progress. I was doing so well."

I nodded, understanding her frustration. Her disappointment. I brushed her hair away from her face, wishing I could take away her pain. "Have you talked to your therapist about it?"

"Yeah. And she reminded me that grief and healing are nonlinear. We worked on some coping strategies to calm my anxiety when you have to travel."

"That's good," I said. "I'm glad you reached out for support."

I wasn't surprised that Bryn had felt triggered by my trip. I'd tried to check in when I could, but perhaps I'd underestimated how difficult this would be for her. I hated it for her. Hated that every time we were apart for a night, she worried that something would happen to me, like it had happened to Derek.

"Is there something I can do to make it easier on you?" I asked, knowing this would continue to be an issue.

The team was on the road a lot. We had forty-one away games during the regular season, and we were usually gone more than one night. But even if I didn't have a job that involved travel, this fear would probably always be there, given what she'd experienced. Hopefully, with time, it would get easier for Bryn.

For now, I would do whatever it took to help her through this. Flying her to every away game wasn't feasible with her job, not to mention the dogs, her garden, and her dance classes. But maybe she could come to some of the out-of-town games.

"Come to my next away game," I said. "Come watch us play in Seattle."

"I'd love to, but…" She hesitated, and I took that as my opening to persuade her.

"The game is on a Saturday. You could fly up that morning. After the game, I'll sneak you into my room." I waggled my brows.

She laughed, and I could tell she was considering it. But then she said, "As much as I love that idea, it doesn't solve the issue of all the other away games. I won't always be able to attend."

I knew that, but I also hoped this might help ease us into the transition of my being away.

"Bryn." I cupped her cheek. "I know that, but I'd do anything to spend time with you. And I'd do anything to take away your fears, even if only temporarily."

She kissed me. It was slow and tender, but it quickly turned passionate. Possessive. Hands and teeth and tongues. A claiming.

"Is that a yes?" I asked when we eventually broke apart.

"It's a maybe," she said, shifting so she was straddling me. "Can I think about it?" She swept my hair away from my face.

"Of course." I kissed her temple. "Just know that I'd love having you there."

She gnawed on her lip, and I could see the hesitation

written across her features. I wanted to understand the reasons behind it, but more than anything, I wanted to assuage her fears.

"Are you worried someone will recognize you?" I asked.

"Actually—" She laughed, wiggling tantalizingly on my rapidly hardening cock. "I was thinking it might be time to launch our relationship."

"Mm." I grasped her chin, trying not to get my hopes up. All these months, I'd been letting her take the lead. I'd been trying not to push, but I was ready. I'd been ready. And her suggestion was making me even harder. "Is that so?"

She nodded, smiling as she ground against me. Bryn had been subtly posting pictures on her social media for months now. But this was the first time she'd given any indication that she was ready to go public with our relationship.

"What's responsible for this change of heart?" I asked.

Bryn lifted her shoulder, a sort of nervous-playful energy coursing through her. "It's time."

Before I could delve into that, Bacon whined, pawing at the back door.

Damn.

Bryn groaned and moved to stand, but I said, "I'll go."

"I should start dinner." She slid off me, but not before giving me one more kiss.

I stood, adjusting myself before removing my button-down shirt. When I glanced over at her, she was watching me with a dazed expression.

"Right. Dinner." She nearly tripped over the rug on the way to the kitchen, and I tried not to laugh. "I'm going to work on dinner."

I took the dogs out to the backyard, marveling at the lush space Bryn had created. It was welcoming and vibrant—full of life. I threw a ball to the dogs a few times and then gave them a cuddle before we headed back inside. Bryn was standing at the counter chopping vegetables, and I stood there a moment just watching her.

The sun drifted through the window, dust motes floating in the air. She hummed softly to herself as she prepared the items for dinner. I smiled, feeling more at home and at peace than I had maybe ever.

She glanced up and caught me looking at her. She flashed me a lopsided grin, knife still in hand. "What?"

I stepped closer, and it felt as if my heart was going to burst out of my rib cage to get to her. "I love you."

It wasn't elaborate or planned, but it was genuine and heartfelt. And saying it felt more natural than holding it in any longer.

"I know." Bryn set down the knife and wiped her hands on the towel.

I chuckled, some of the tension easing out of me. "Okay, Han Solo."

She rolled her eyes, but she was smiling as she came over to me. "I didn't mean for it to sound cocky. I meant..." She draped her arms around my neck. "I meant that I feel your love. Every day. Because you're always there, quietly supporting me. Loving me."

I nodded, tilting my forehead to her. She used to believe that she'd already had her love story, but I hoped that was no longer the case. I hoped she'd realized that she could find love again—with me.

"And I love you. Not," she added, toying with the hair at the nape of my neck, "because of what you do for me. But I love you because of who you are. Because of how I feel when I'm with you."

I felt as if I were floating, relieved and so fucking happy. And then I hauled her into my arms, kissing her as I made my way toward the stairs. I planned to spend the rest of the night showing Bryn just how much I loved her.

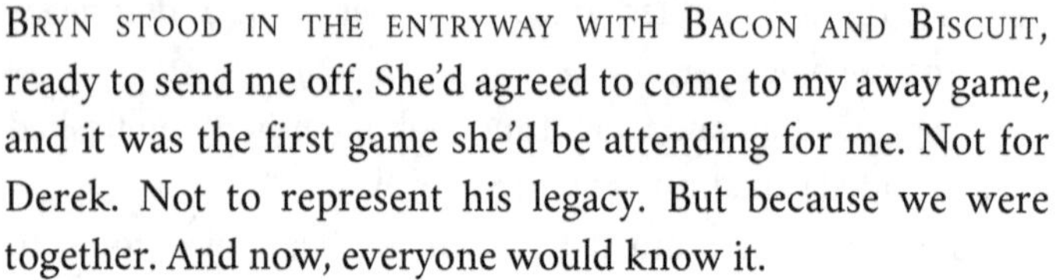

BRYN STOOD IN THE ENTRYWAY WITH BACON AND BISCUIT, ready to send me off. She'd agreed to come to my away game, and it was the first game she'd be attending for me. Not for Derek. Not to represent his legacy. But because we were together. And now, everyone would know it.

She'd posted a picture the other night of the two of us and our dogs. And the internet had flipped out. The post had gone viral, and Kylie had been fielding requests for interviews from everyone hosting podcasts about navigating grief to morning shows.

So far, the response had been overwhelmingly positive. And while I knew Bryn hated the attention, I was grateful that everyone seemed so supportive. Kylie said everything was going according to plan. She and Georgia were going to attend the game with Bryn, and I was glad she'd have her friends there.

I knew they were looking forward to making a girls' weekend out of it. In addition to attending the game, they planned to visit the Chihuly Museum, take a harbor cruise, and go to Pike Place. And even though I'd joked about sneaking Bryn into my hotel room, we both knew it was against team rules. The league was strict about privacy and security when the team was traveling. If someone's family wanted to attend a game, the player had to buy them tickets. And they needed to stay in separate accommodations.

It sucked, but I wasn't going to break protocol, as much as I might be tempted. The rules were there for a reason, and I respected them. But maybe there'd be time…

"I have something for you," Bryn said, interrupting my thoughts. She handed me an envelope with my name written on it, just as she had before every game. Sometimes the note was long, sometimes it was short, but it was always heartfelt.

"Thanks, angel." I gave her a quick peck before sliding it into a safe spot in my carry-on. "I also have something for you."

I used my left hand to give her a small bag, hoping this gift would land well. I'd been racking my brain for ways to help her feel less anxious when I was on the road, and this was the best I'd come up with. It might seem a little cheesy, but I didn't care so long as it would ease Bryn's worries.

She removed the tissue paper and then pulled out a heart-shaped stress ball. Her lips quirked to the side as she removed the accompanying paper and read it aloud. "My heart beats for you—and only you." She smiled at that. "Cute."

Oh, come on. Give me a little credit, angel.

"Turn the paper over," I said, my right hand still in my pocket.

She did as I asked, brows creasing in confusion as she stared at the QR code and log-in information. "What is this?"

"It's a link to an app that tracks my heart rate twenty-four seven."

Her head snapped up, gaze meeting mine. "What?"

I removed my hand from my pocket, holding it up to show off the dark gray, matte band that rested on the ring finger of my right hand. "It's a smart ring that will track my sleep, heart rate, and a bunch of other stuff that no one cares about. And I'm giving you access to the app. So you can check in on me in real time, anytime, day or night."

"Frasier…" Her expression wobbled, and then she covered her face with her hands.

It was as if a dam had burst, and tears streamed down her face. I stood there a moment, wondering if I'd made a mistake. And then I snapped into action, wrapping my arms around her.

Shit. Shit!

I'd intended to help her feel more at ease about being apart, not upset her. Especially not when I was about to walk out the door to leave for the airport.

"I'm sorry. If you don't like it, we can forget all about it," I said, rubbing circles on her back.

She lifted her head from my chest. She cupped my cheeks, her eyes rimmed with red. "You are so incredibly thoughtful." She kissed me. "Thank you." She kissed me again, the salt of her tears mingling with the taste of her. "Thank you for not acting like I'm over the top. Thank you for trying to give me peace of mind. I love you."

Hearing those words from her lips would never grow old.

"I love you." I kissed her, holding her close.

"Thank you," she said again after a few minutes, seeming calmer. "Sincerely. What you did was incredibly thoughtful." She gave me a quick peck.

I pulled her into my arms, soaking her in. "I don't want to go."

"What time do you have to leave?" she asked in a husky voice that made my cock thicken.

I glanced at my watch and groaned. "Five minutes ago."

"Are you sure you can't stay a few more minutes?" she whispered in my ear, dragging her teeth down the lobe.

"Mm." I squeezed my eyes shut, humming as she smoothed her hands down my back, teasing my waistband. "Angel," I groaned, wishing I weren't already running late. And with LA traffic, you really never knew how long the drive would take.

I grabbed her ass, pulling her so she was flush with me. Letting her feel just how hard I was for her. I plundered her mouth, ravishing her lips. She moaned, arching her hips against mine.

My phone chimed, and I cursed the time and the reminder that I had to leave. "I don't want to go, but I have to."

She smoothed her hands up my back then down over my shoulders until she was clutching my shirt in her hands. "I guess I'll just have to give you a proper thank-you tomorrow night after the game." She dragged my lips to hers for a searing kiss.

"I guess you will," I said, forcing myself to take a step back before I was even later. I pressed down on my cock before throwing my bag over my shoulder.

She walked me to the door, and I pulled her to me, kissing a spot on her neck just behind her ear. "See you tomorrow."

"Tomorrow," she whispered before letting out a long sigh.

I hate saying goodbye.

CHAPTER TWENTY-THREE

Frasier

As I suited up for the game, I couldn't help but be excited. Bryn would be in the stands cheering for me. I wasn't sure I'd ever been more jacked up for a game.

Gabe clapped a hand on my shoulder. "Ready to go out there and dominate?"

I nodded. "Let's do it, Goldie."

Kovi blasted through the locker room in only his compression shorts and some athletic tape after visiting the trainers. Other guys were in various states of undress as we geared up to play Seattle. The game started soon, but before that, we'd take to the ice for warm-up and stretches.

Coach entered the locker room once we were dressed, a small sheet of paper in hand as always. "Tonight, we're going to go out there and play whistle to whistle. Focus on the details. Execute."

All the players started chanting, "Execute! Execute!"

Coach held up his hand. "Okay. Starting lineup. We've got Gabe."

Everyone clapped once and called back, "Yeah."

This continued as he read down the line, until Coach said, "And Fizzy between the pipes."

The team roared, and I could feel their energy surging through me as I stood and led the team down the tunnel toward the arena. The stands were already filling in, and as I skated onto the ice, I searched for Bryn. I'd purchased her tickets close to center ice, close to the floor, wanting to be able to find her in the crowd.

I finally spotted her and stilled when I realized what she was wearing. A bright-blue Hawks jersey with the number thirty on it—*my* number. *Holy shit.* A surge of pride and possessiveness had me nearly falling to my knees on the ice.

I placed my hand over my heart, feeling the significance of the moment. When I skated closer, I realized that her jersey, like mine, also had a black circle with the number six on it in honor of Derek. I rubbed at my chest to ease the pang there, sadness mingling with joy.

I'd had no idea that she'd planned to wear my jersey, and it struck me hard. That she was here with me, cheering me on, with my name and number on her back. It wasn't something I took lightly, and I wanted to gather her in my arms and hold her.

I would, after the game. But for now, I had to settle for the fact that Georgia was sitting next to her, with Kylie on the other side. Bryn's eyes met mine, and I double tapped my chest over my heart. Checking in. She smiled and double tapped over her heart in response.

After that, I found it easier to focus. And as we proceeded through the warm-up, I started to get more into the zone. By the time we returned to the ice for the start of the game, I was ready. Amped up.

The crowd was just as fired up, and it was going to be a good game. A challenging game. The home team always had an advantage, so I tried not to let it get to me when Seattle scored a goal midway through the first period. We continued to struggle to get any shots on goal. Seattle was determined to win, but we were just as motivated.

The second period was just as tough as the first. Seattle's offense was on fire tonight, weaving past our guys to get within close range of our goal. Kovi and Boone stayed on them, but Seattle still managed to score a second goal. A fake shot that pissed me off because I should've known better.

Fortunately, with minutes until the end of the second period, Gabe scored a goal with Kovi assisting. Gabe went down the line of the bench, high-fiving our guys. And when the buzzer went off a few seconds later, the score was two to one in Seattle's favor.

During intermission, I toweled off and hydrated, taking a minute to rest before the final period. Coach gave us some pointers, and then we retook the ice. I stood in front of the net, scraping the ice with my skates to give me more friction and control. I checked the net, making sure it was secure, tapping the goalposts for luck before performing a series of stretches.

As soon as the period started, you could feel the way the aggression and intensity had increased. Seattle was eager to close out this game with a win, but we weren't going to give up. Handy scored a sick goal, tying up the score.

And then we scored another on the heels of that, dropping the puck in the net with a sweet shot and stunning everyone. I couldn't fight the grin on my face. It was fucking on.

With only eight minutes left in the game, one of the Seattle players, Wilson, aka "Willy," skated near the net.

His body was turned away from me, but I heard his words all the same. "I heard your girl has a thing for hockey players."

I shifted beneath my pads, seething. I knew he was chirping, trying to get a rise out of me. But he'd crossed a line, and there was no way I could let what he'd just said stand.

"The fuck you just say?" Kovi asked before I could even respond. Kovi was a mouthy motherfucker, but in that moment, I loved him for it.

"First your teammate, now you, huh?" Wilson said, undeterred.

"Shut your fucking mouth, Willy," I growled, cracking my neck from side to side. He wanted a fight, and if he kept that up, he was going to get one.

Everything in me strained forward, as if urging me toward him, to fight him. I wasn't going to give him the satisfaction. I was going to focus on the game.

"Did you two ever share? I don't usually go for someone else's sloppy seconds, but I'd make an exception for her. Give her a hat trick." And then Willy winked at me over his shoulder.

My vision tunneled on him, pulse pounding in my ears. He had no idea what Bryn had gone through, what I had gone through. And for him to both tarnish Derek's memory and disparage Bryn... I saw fucking red.

I didn't even think about the consequences; all I cared about was teaching him a lesson. I tore off my gloves, tossing them aside. The crowd made a sound of surprise, encouragement, I wasn't sure. Either way, didn't fucking matter. This fucker was going down. I wouldn't let anyone talk about Bryn that way.

I removed my helmet, and Willy removed his. He spat onto the ice, grinning like a fucking idiot. Like this was exactly what he'd wanted. Fuck. Maybe it was.

"It's just a joke, bro," he said, acting as if he hadn't just insulted the woman I loved and my late best friend. *This asshole.*

Kovi was there in an instant, gloves thrown as well. I

threw the first punch, getting in a good one, before one of Willy's teammates jumped in, piling on.

"It's not funny, *bro*," Kovi growled, attempting to punch Willy, while one of the other Seattle guys went after Kovi.

"We don't talk about women—or anyone—like that," I ground out. I reared back to punch Willy again, enraged at his words. At his insinuation.

Chaos erupted on the ice. Players from both sides joined the fray. The shrill sound of multiple whistles cut through the air as the refs attempted to wrestle us apart. Willy and I were locked together. I wouldn't—couldn't—release his jersey from my grip. Not until he'd apologized.

I didn't care that Willy had blood running down from his nose. Didn't fucking care that the refs wanted this to end.

"Let go!" the ref yelled, skating between us, trying to break up the fight like a bouncer at a nightclub. "End this. *Now.*"

Another ref came to escort me away, and I was forced to release Willy's jersey. I continued glaring at him as the ref escorted me toward the bench. Willy grinned, face bloodied and nose bent. *Serves him right.* I spat on the ice in his direction.

Kovi was bleeding, but he seemed more concerned with talking to one of the other refs. I was still trying to talk myself down from committing murder.

Coach's expression was stern, disappointment radiating off him. But he said nothing—for now. I was positive I would get reamed once the game was over. By him. By management.

Whatever. I blew out a breath.

While we waited for the refs to make a call, a trainer checked me over. The fight had shifted the energy of the game, and I wondered if that was what Willy had been after all along. Or if he really was just a dickhead.

My heart was pounding. The refs seemed to be confer-
ring for a long time, and I couldn't even bring myself to
look at Bryn. I wanted to, but I knew what I'd see there—
worry. And I couldn't play the rest of the game if I was
distracted.

The head ref skated to center ice, switching on the microphone on his headset. He made the hand motion for
roughing as he announced the penalty. "Seattle number five,
five-minute penalty for fighting." That was good at least.
"Additional two-minute penalty for instigating." There was a
lot of booing at that one, and I felt vindicated that the ref had
taken our side. Then he said, "LA number thirty. Five-minute
penalty."

Fuck.

I kept my head held high. I would not apologize for the
fight because I'd done nothing wrong.

I knew Coach would demand an explanation later, but for
now, my sole focus was on winning. I took my position in
front of the goal, trying to get my head back in the game. I
would not let one fucker and his disgusting comments ruin
my focus. I would not let that be the reason we lost the game.
If anything, it made me want to win even more. This was
personal now.

And the rest of my team seemed to think so too. Some of
them had heard what Wilson had said, and they were livid.
Fuck winning, we had something to prove. Gabe practically
flew across the ice. He acted as if he was going to take a shot,
but then he passed to Holden at the last second. The puck
slid right into the net, a beauty of a shot.

Seconds later, the buzzer went off, announcing the end of
the game. *Fuck yes!* We'd won. And the win tasted all that
much sweeter after what Willy had said.

We lined up to shake hands with the opposing team.
Fortunately, Willy had returned to the locker room after the

fight, likely to check if his nose was broken. I hoped it was. It was the least he deserved for everything he'd said.

I glanced up at the stands one more time before I headed into the locker room. Bryn was still standing there, brow creased with concern. I hated that I couldn't immediately go to her, reassure her.

In the locker room, the celebration was more subdued than usual, even as the lyrics of our celly song played through the speakers. I started removing my pads, tossing my uniform into the bin to be cleaned.

After I'd showered, Coach pulled me aside. "How are you feeling?"

I clenched and unclenched my fists at my side. "Pissed."

He nodded. "It's not like you to fight. Can you walk me through what happened out there?"

I explained about the chirping, about what the Seattle player had said. Coach's expression darkened with each passing moment. Finally, he said, "Thank you for telling me. I'm going to speak with management to see how they want to handle this. But you did the right thing."

"Thanks, Coach." I hadn't needed his approval, but it meant a lot to me.

Coach excused himself, and I went over to Kovi and fist-bumped him. "Thanks for having my back out there, man."

"Of course. You're my teammate. And even if you weren't, what he said was so fucking wrong."

I nodded, and Gabe slung his arm around my shoulder. "You know, you're not so bad, Kovi."

Carson barked out a laugh. "You're not so bad either, Goldie."

Gabe gave Carson a playful shove, and then we resumed getting ready. The NHL may no longer require players to wear suits to and from a game, but the Hawks continued to insist on it. Coach always told us that we had to look like champions on and off the ice.

It was uncomfortable at times—having to wear a suit during a flight. But he was right. I'd sometimes see pictures of the other teams getting off their bus for a game, and they looked sloppy.

"Fizzy. Kovi," Coach called out, beckoning us over. The rest of the guys grew quiet, and I could feel their attention on us. "Daniel and I are going to answer questions at the press conference, but we'd like to have you join us. If you think you can answer questions calmly and factually."

Shit. This was an even bigger deal than I'd feared if Daniel was joining the press conference. Though GMs like Daniel usually traveled with the team for away games, it was rare that they spoke at postgame press conferences.

I was going to have to find a way to be calm. So, I took a deep breath and nodded. "Yes, Coach."

Kovi looked at me then nodded as well. We followed Coach into the media room, and the lights seemed extra bright tonight, the shutter of the cameras extra loud. I shuffled behind the table, taking a seat next to Kovi. Daniel, our GM and Georgia's brother, was already there, and Coach took a seat beside him.

"I'm sure you all have questions about what happened tonight," Daniel said, and the room immediately went quiet. "What happened on the ice was unfortunate, and we are grateful to the referees who saw and understood the situation for what it was."

Daniel toyed with the cuff of his dress shirt. "One of the members of the opposing team made some inappropriate comments about a person we all care deeply about."

"Who was it?" called out a reporter.

"It doesn't matter." Daniel waved a hand through the air. "What matters is that the Hawks have a zero-tolerance policy for 'locker-room talk,' on or off the ice. It is not part of our team culture nor the culture we want for the league."

"Do you think Wilson from Seattle should be punished?" someone asked.

"He was given a penalty, both for fighting and for instigating the fight, which we think was fair under the circumstances."

Fair? I clenched my jaw to keep from saying anything. It was the bare minimum.

"Yes, but do you believe he should be punished by the league?" someone else asked.

It was a good thing Daniel was doing most of the talking, because there was no way I would've remained as composed as he was.

"That's up to the league to decide," he said. "Personally, I am committed to changing the culture of our sport."

"Frasier, this was your first-ever fight on the ice. Do you think violence was the best way to handle the situation?"

I rubbed the back of my neck but didn't apologize. Because I had absolutely no remorse or regret for what I'd done. "Ordinarily, I'd say no. But Wilson's comments were completely unacceptable."

"Could you shed some light on what those comments were?"

They weren't going to let this go, were they?

Daniel answered that one. "No. They do not bear repeating." His tone was curt, his impatience clear.

Just thinking about it had me clenching my fists, wishing I could hit the bastard again. Harder. *Fucking hat trick.*

"Frasier, were you and Wilson fighting over Bryn Morgan? Your current partner, who was previously married to your teammate."

I took a slow, deep breath, but it did nothing to calm me. I was beginning to think it was a bad idea for me to be here.

But I leaned forward and spoke into my mic. "No comment."

"Coach," someone in the audience said. "What are your thoughts after the game?"

Declan leaned forward. "I'm proud of my team. Do I condone fighting? No. But I stand behind my men's decision. They might have done the 'wrong' thing, but they did it for the right reasons."

I'd always respected Declan Cross, but I'd never been more grateful to have him as the leader of our team than in that moment. He'd been a legend on the ice himself, a player for the Hawks years ago, before his career had been cut short by an injury. And while his stats were impressive, it was his courage to be himself that had always made me admire him on a personal level.

He'd been the first NHL player to come out publicly. At the time, it had been huge. I could only imagine the strength it had taken him to do so. He was committed to his family. He'd proposed to his husband, James Thorne, on the ice. And he'd coached one of his twin daughters, helping her win an Olympic gold medal. I was touched by his comment, grateful that he had my back.

I didn't know what the culture of the Hawks had been like before I'd been traded. Declan had come on as head coach around the same time that I'd joined the team, and it seemed like he was part of a much bigger culture shift for the Hawks. I'd played on other teams, and I'd been close to my teammates. But I'd never been as proud to play for an organization as I was in this moment.

After a few more questions, we exited the room.

"Good job tonight, boys," Daniel said, clapping me on the back. "I believe there's someone waiting for you."

I glanced down the end of the hall where Bryn was standing with Georgia and Kylie. Daniel motioned for security to let them through. I sprinted toward Bryn, wrapping her in my arms.

When I released her, she searched me over as if inspecting for any injuries. "Are you okay?"

"I'm fine," I said. "The trainer checked me out, and I'm good."

"Are you sure? Do you have a headache? Any dizziness?" She grabbed a penlight from her pocket and shone it in my eye like she would one of her patients.

"Bryn." I grasped her wrist, gently lowering her hand. "I'm okay. I promise."

I placed our clasped hands over her heart. Over the number six patch that represented Derek. I tapped twice. *I'm okay.*

Her shoulders relaxed, but only a little. She continued to keep a watchful eye on me, as if unwilling to believe it was true.

I leaned in, keeping my voice low though my tone was rife with innuendo. "If you're concerned, you can do a *thorough* examination later."

She smiled, even as she gripped my shirt, holding me close. "Trust me. I will."

CHAPTER TWENTY-FOUR

Bryn

I followed Kylie and Georgia down the hall to the restroom. "That meal was so, so good."

After the game, we'd gone to dinner with some of the guys from the team at Alchemy. The atmosphere of the restaurant was moody and dark, sultry even. And the food was phenomenal. It had been a while since I'd hung out with so many of the guys from the team at once.

I'd gotten to know Carson better, and it was always fun to see Boone and Gabe. Holden had tagged along, but he'd seemed more reserved than I'd expected. Frasier had rested his hand on my thigh or the back of my chair throughout the entire meal, occasionally leaning in to whisper something in my ear.

Despite the win, everyone seemed more solemn tonight. I had a feeling that had to do with the fight. I'd never seen Frasier react like that, so whatever Wilson had said must have really gotten to him.

I was just glad Frasier was okay. And fortunately, it didn't seem like he was in trouble with the management or the league. I figured they might be more willing to let it slide since it was so out of character. But also, the team had won.

Georgia pushed open the door to the restroom. I glanced around, taking in the swanky lounge area. The velvet-covered chairs and side tables looked as if they'd be at home in a luxury penthouse, not the bathroom. Though I guessed, we weren't in the bathroom just yet since the stalls and the sinks were in another area beyond this.

"Did Frasier tell you what Wilson said?" Georgia asked me, cheeks flushed pink from the wine.

I'd assumed the fight was like most fights during a game—guys too jacked up on adrenaline and a chirp that had gone too far. That said, Frasier typically kept his cool on the ice. So he had to have been really pissed to risk a fight, especially when the score had been so close.

Kylie typed out a message on her phone before tossing it into her purse. She disappeared into a stall. I shook my head and took the stall next to Kylie's, closing the door behind me.

"I couldn't get anything out of my brother," Georgia huffed. "Even though I'm technically a member of the staff and signed an NDA. Not to mention the fact that I'm his freaking sister."

I laughed, flushing the toilet and zipping my jeans before joining Georgia at the sink, where she fluffed her hair and reapplied her lipstick. Daniel was notoriously tight-lipped when it came to the Hawks. And I appreciated his loyalty to the team, even if I figured it was mostly because he was responsible for the organization. That said, I knew not everything was about the bottom line for him.

The Hawks had been nothing short of incredible in the wake of Derek's death. They'd paid out a million dollars as basic protection plus his entire salary for the season in which he'd died, as well as the following one. It was more than was required by Derek's contract. I'd been stunned by their generosity, and I had a feeling Daniel had a lot to do with it.

"Frasier seriously said nothing?" Georgia asked.

I shook my head, applying another coat of lip gloss. "I was too focused on his well-being to ask. He claims he's fine, but I'm worried he has a concussion."

Georgia frowned, her eyes meeting mine in the reflection of the mirror. "The trainers checked him out, right?"

"Yes." And I knew they were the best in the field. I'd even examined him briefly myself. Yet still, I worried. "But the effects can be delayed."

Georgia wrapped her arm around me, saying nothing but offering her support, nonetheless. I hugged her back, appreciating the fact that she didn't try to reassure me or, worse, tell me I was overreacting. She just...let me know she was there for me.

"Did you get anything out of Carson?" Georgia asked Kylie as she exited her bathroom stall.

Kylie stepped up to the sink, glancing from me then back to Georgia. She'd been checking her phone on and off all evening, but that wasn't unusual. She was often keeping an eye on things or putting out fires for her clients.

"That's a yes," I said, my stomach churning. "But you don't want to tell us. Or rather, you don't want to tell me."

"Wilson is an ass," Georgia said. "Always has been. It was nice to see him taken down a peg."

"Oh, the internet is definitely giving him a dressing down." Kylie's grin was wicked.

Interesting. But I wasn't going there. The internet could be a dangerous place. I'd learned that after Derek's death. Most people were supportive, but others could be judgmental, even critical. I didn't need their negative energy.

"You know Wilson?" I asked Georgia.

"He got drafted to the Hawks years ago. The team traded

him because of his attitude and shitty performance. Since then, Wilson has had an axe to grind when it comes to the Hawks."

That didn't surprise me. From what little I knew of him, Wilson seemed like the type of man to hold a grudge. Petty. Vindictive. Small.

"Even so..." Georgia seemed to be considering it. "For Frasier to throw down, whatever Wilson said must have been bad."

"What he said was wrong," Kylie gritted out. She switched off the water and grabbed a towel from the stack. She dried her hands and turned to face me. "And as your friend, I really don't want to tell you. But as your publicist, I feel like I have a duty to inform you."

Georgia sighed. "I really wanted it to be something fun and juicy. But this sounds like it's going to piss me off."

I laughed, but there was a nervous edge to it.

"Okay. I changed my mind," Georgia said, clearly sensing my unease. "I don't want to know. Besides, does it matter what that asswipe said?" Georgia crossed her arms over her chest. "I'm sure Frasier's actions were justified."

I could think of very few reasons Frasier would fight during a game, and I was one of them. "The more you say without telling us what was actually said, the more concerned I am. I think I'd rather you just tell me so I don't have to keep wondering."

"You sure?" Kylie asked, worry creasing her brow. "We can enjoy dinner and then discuss it after we return to the hotel."

I nodded. "I'm sure."

With a resigned sigh, Kylie relayed what had happened on the ice. By the end, Georgia was fuming. And I was...shell-shocked.

A thing for hockey players?

Had they ever shared me?

Hat trick? I'd nearly gagged when she'd told us that part.

"And then Frasier clocked him. This is unconfirmed, but I'm pretty sure Wilson has a broken nose. Serves him right," she muttered.

"Fuck yes." Georgia fist-pumped the air. "As if I didn't already love Frasier. He and Carson showed that our team won't stand for the kind of 'locker-room talk,' 'boys will be boys' bullshit that's plagued the league for far too long."

Kylie nodded. "And the fans are loving it."

It was nice to know we had the fans on our side and that people were sick of the misogynistic, exclusive boys club of the past. And while, yes, the entire exchange was disgusting, I couldn't have been more proud of Frasier and Carson for how they'd handled it. They had shut it down. They'd called him out.

That said, I didn't understand how someone could be so callous. Especially a fellow hockey player, regardless of the fact that he had an axe to grind.

I knew Wilson was likely just trying to get a rise out of Frasier. And it had obviously worked. But it made me wonder what other people had been saying about our relationship. I'd been content to live in a bubble, and now I worried that I should've paid more attention.

I pulled my phone out of my pocket, navigating to social media to check on my latest post. It was a picture of me at the game with Georgia and Kylie, smiling and ready to cheer on the team. Even though I'd posted it just a few hours ago, the photo already had thousands of comments. I scrolled through the top few to see what had been liked the most.

Georgia leaned over my shoulder, peering down at my screen. "Are you sure that's a good idea, Bryn?"

Good idea or not, it was something I needed to do.

@sillymillymama So happy for you! I've followed your story since you lost your husband. I'm a young widow too, and I'm so glad you've found happiness again.

@bookishreading The cutest! Enjoy the game.

@goaliegirlies Love the custom jersey. A nice way to honor your late husband, while celebrating your new relationship.

@puckbunny69 I'd have a threesome with Morgan and Holmes. Get it, girl. That's hot.

I GROANED. I'D BEEN OPTIMISTIC AFTER THE FIRST FEW comments, but they only got worse after the one from @puckbunny69. I rolled my eyes at her incredibly *unoriginal* handle. And then I continued reading, even though I had a feeling I'd regret it. Still…I needed to know what people were saying—about me, but mostly about Derek.

As his widow, I took my responsibility as the steward of his memory very seriously. It was why I'd agreed to interviews and attended tribute games when all I'd wanted was to curl up in a ball and die. It was why I'd told Derek's story in partnership with the SADS Foundation to promote awareness, even when it gutted me to relive that trauma. And it was a big reason why I'd struggled so much with wearing a jersey with anyone else's last name and number.

@puckboys responding to @puckbunny69 Me too.

@puckboys responding to @puckbunny69 Do you think they had a threesome while he was still alive? They've known each other since college.

@puckbunny69 It's possible.

@mat706 Now that she collected all the money from his endorsements, she's ready to move on to her next victim.

@backdoor22 I don't get why they're fighting over her. She's not that hot.

@Hockeyfan301 Let's hope she's not a black widow, or the Hawks will lose their best goalie in addition to a talented defenseman. FML. We're never going to get a Stanley again at this rate.

My hands were shaking so badly, I dropped my phone. Kylie picked it up, holding on to it. Georgia was saying something—at least, her lips were moving. But it felt as if I were underwater, and I couldn't decipher the words.

I knew that comments of strangers on the internet shouldn't—didn't—matter. But in that moment, it felt as if a hot knife had sliced through my chest, cutting me wide open.

Was this truly what people thought about me? That I'd profited off my husband's death, and now I was so easily moving on? As if I'd never loved him. As if losing him hadn't been so incredibly painful.

I hated feeling as if I'd betrayed Derek. I hated that anyone was questioning my motivations, my love for him. And the idea that the piece I had left of him—his legacy— might be tarnished beyond repair was heartbreaking.

"I can't—" I clutched my throat, unable to draw a full breath. "I can't. *Breathe.*"

"Hey." Georgia's voice was soothing. "Hey." She guided me to one of the seats in the lounge area of the bathroom. "Slow down. In through your nose…" She waited until I did just that. "Out through your mouth. That's it. There you go."

I clawed at my shirt. It felt too tight and all wrong. Ever since I'd put on the custom jersey, my skin had felt itchy and hot. I yanked it over my head and tossed it aside.

I'd betrayed Derek. I'd failed him—again.

I wasn't there for him when he needed me. When his heart had failed, I couldn't save him. And now, I was letting him down once more.

And this wasn't just about Derek; this affected Frasier too. In all the years he'd played hockey, he'd never gotten into a fight on the ice. I was negatively affecting his focus, his safety. Hell, I was lucky that the team had stood behind him. Otherwise, his career might be on the line as well.

"Bryn," Kylie said, crouching down beside me. "It's going to be okay."

I gathered my knees to my chest, resting my head against them. "I betrayed Derek. Our marriage. His memory."

"You didn't," Georgia said. "Everyone knows how much you loved each other."

They had, but now people were questioning if I'd been unfaithful to him. The mere suggestion of it made my head swim and my stomach churn.

"They think I cheated on him," I cried.

Georgia rubbed my back in a soothing motion. "No one believes that."

"Clearly, they do." I sniffled, gesturing to my phone. "And they think I capitalized on his death."

"No one who *matters* believes that bullshit," Kylie said.

Whether they believed it or not, it was out there now. I stood, scrambling over to one of the stalls. And then I heaved over the toilet until there was nothing left. I rested my head on my forearm, wishing the room would stop spinning.

I should've been careful what I wished for, because the spinning stopped. And then everything went black.

Frasier

Georgia: You need to come to the bathroom now. Bryn fainted.

I STOOD AND PUSHED BACK MY CHAIR SO FAST THAT IT TOPPLED over. My teammates all turned to me with looks of concern.

"What's wrong?" Gabe asked.

"Bryn." I headed for the bathroom, ignoring the curious looks of nearby diners.

I raced down the hallway, nearly colliding with a server and their tray. I apologized but continued on. I pushed open the door, not even bothering to knock because I was so focused on getting to Bryn.

Her eyes were open, which was a relief. But her skin was pale, and she was resting on a chair.

"Frasier?" She blinked a few times.

I went over to her, kneeling on the floor. I took her hands in mine. "Angel, what's wrong? Are you okay?"

I checked her over, relieved that she showed no signs of injury. But it was concerning that she'd fainted. Why had she passed out?

Was this what it had felt like for her to see the fight? To worry that I'd been injured.

"I'm fine," Bryn said, rubbing her forehead.

Georgia gave me a worried look, and Kylie shook her head. Bryn had recently eaten, so I didn't think it was a blood sugar issue. She'd been drinking wine, but she'd also had just as much water, so I wasn't too worried about hydration. Still, I didn't understand why she'd fainted.

"What happened?" I asked Kylie, trying to remain calm and not freak the fuck out.

Kylie chewed on her lip. "Bryn threw up, and then she passed out."

"Bryn," I sighed, cupping her cheek. Her skin was pale and clammy.

I squeezed my eyes shut briefly. Now I was really worried.

I opened my phone, debating the best course of action. I could call one of the team doctors to see if they'd help me. But if Bryn needed an IV or some type of intervention, a hospital was the best bet. Maybe I was blowing things way out of proportion, but I wasn't taking any chances where she was concerned.

I opened my ride-share app and requested a car. It was supposed to arrive in about five minutes, which was a relief.

"Angel. Do you feel up to walking or should I carry you?"

"Carry me where?" Her eyes went wide. "You're not carrying me through the restaurant." She shook her head but then stopped, lifting a shaky hand to her forehead.

I frowned. Only then did I realize that she'd removed her —*my*—jersey. She was wearing a tank top and jeans, the jersey cast aside.

"Come on," I said. "Up you go." I gathered her in my arms then headed for the door. "Can one of you get her purse and things?" I asked Bryn's friends.

Georgia jogged over, jersey and purse in hand. "Where are you taking her?"

"The hospital."

"Would you please stop fussing over me?" Bryn said. "I'm fine."

"Bryn." I glared at her. She couldn't be serious.

"What about curfew?" she asked, knowing I had to be back at the hotel, back in my room, before eleven.

I gnashed my teeth. "Fuck curfew." The team could fine me for all I cared, because I was not leaving Bryn's side. Not now. Not ever.

HOT AS PUCK

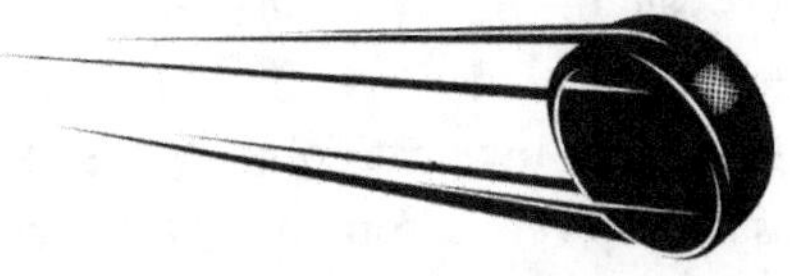

Original Air Date: October 5
@ The Hive Sports and Entertainment

Logan: So…

Levi: So. Yeah. Wow. That was one hell of a game between Seattle and LA. Everyone's talking about it.

Logan: Oh, come on. No one's talking about the game. They're talking about the fight.

Levi: The fight between…well, pretty much the entirety of both teams.

Logan: I haven't seen a pile-on like that in a while. I'm surprised the ref didn't give everyone on the ice a five-minute penalty.

Levi: It wouldn't be unprecedented. For anyone who didn't

see it, Wilson got five minutes for fighting and an additional two minutes for instigating the fight, but Holmes threw the first punch. Hardly seems fair.

Logan: Wilson crossed the line. What he said…

Levi: Which brings me to my next point. Who's to decide what qualifies as a chirp versus something that's crossed the line to the point of penalizing a player for instigating a fight?

Logan: Chirping is meant to be witty, sarcastic, or a personal dig at an opponent's skill. *Not* a dig about someone's family.

Levi: I agree. Family is off-limits. But Wilson got his punishment on the ice in the form of a fight. Hell, he got a broken nose. That's always been how these situations are handled—between the players. Not by the refs.

Logan: He disrespected a former player. Someone who *died*.
Levi: And he should apologize so we can move on. Speaking of moving on, let's talk about the Boston game.

Logan: No. I don't think we should move on. I'm over the bro culture that has dominated this sport. I'm tired of being expected to ignore sexist and misogynistic comments. If anything, what Holmes and Kovalski did makes me respect them even more.

Levi: You're not the only one. Maybe you should join their fan club.

Logan: Maybe I will.

Levi: Good.

Logan: Good.

Levi: Can we talk about the Boston game now?

Logan: I suppose we could…

CHAPTER TWENTY-FIVE

Frasier

"How's Bryn doing?" Kovi asked, towel wrapped around his waist, fresh out of a post-practice shower.

It had been a week since the Seattle game, and since then, everything had felt…off.

On the ice, I felt as if I were going through the motions. We'd played two games since then, and we'd lost one and barely eked out a win in the other. Off the ice, I was a mess. I couldn't stop thinking—worrying—about Bryn.

Not that I'd gotten to spend much time with her, apart from when I'd taken her to the ER. They'd run some tests but had ultimately released her. Even so, I couldn't help but be concerned.

She might be fine physically. But she'd been distracted and distant ever since.

"She's good. Thanks," I said, because I didn't know what else to say.

I felt like I knew nothing. Not why she'd fainted—supposedly it was stress-related. Or even why I got the feeling that she was avoiding me.

Hell, maybe it was all in my head. I'd been in three different time zones within the past five days, and I was exhausted. From the travel, but also from the added attention in the wake of my fight with Wilson. Talia and her team had been fielding so many requests for interviews and sponsorships and endorsements, it made my head spin.

I could only assume the increased attention was weighing on Bryn as well. Someone had leaked what was said during the fight, and the public had been swift to defend my actions, along with Kovi's.

But when it came to Bryn, people had some strong opinions about our relationship. Both for and against. Not that it would change anything when it came to my feelings for her. But I worried about the impact on Bryn.

I saw what the media had put her through when Derek died. It felt as if they expected something from her. And it was wrong. I was scared that this incident was dragging her back to that time.

I told myself she was just busy—with work and preparing to go to the conference in Boston and to visit her sister. But it felt like there was something more going on.

"Let us know if there's anything we can do to help," Gabe said as I finished getting dressed.

"Thanks," I said. "She's about to leave for Boston for a week, but I'll let you know."

"Holmes," one of the assistant coaches barked. "Coach wants to see you."

I sighed, pushing off the bench, all while wondering what this was about when I really just wanted to go home and see Bryn.

I headed down the hall toward Coach's office. Georgia was coming my direction, and I paused.

"Hey. Do you have a sec?" I asked, knowing I didn't have long.

"Yeah. What's up?" She grinned.

I glanced around, relieved to find the hallway empty. "Have you seen Bryn much this week?"

She lifted a shoulder. "We watched the game together the other night. And we've texted a few times. Why?"

"How did she seem to you?"

"Tired, maybe?" She furrowed her brow. "I know she's looking forward to seeing her sister. Maybe a break from LA is just what the doctor ordered."

I nodded, hoping Georgia was right. Hoping that once some of the excitement from the fight died down, everything would go back to normal.

That hope was short-lived. At least if my meeting with Coach was anything to go by. But I put his words aside and headed home. Well, to Bryn's house. I'd been meaning to talk to her about us moving in together, but then the fight had happened, and it hadn't felt like the right time.

I let myself in the back door using the key she'd given me. "Bryn?" I called out, frowning when Bacon and Biscuit jogged up to me, but there was no sign of Bryn.

I crouched down, scratching them behind the ears. "Hey, there. Hey, buddy."

Bacon licked my cheek, and I chuckled. I stood and headed for the family room. "Bryn?" I called again. In the bedroom, I found her suitcase, packed and ready to go. The bathroom was empty. I frowned. "Bryn?"

"In here," she said, and I followed the sound of her voice to the guest bedroom.

I found her in the closet, a mound of Derek's jerseys and paraphernalia spread out on the bed. "Hey, angel." I pulled her in for a hug, dropping a kiss on the top of her head. "What are you working on?"

"There's a charity auction coming up to raise awareness for SADS, and they asked if I'd donate something of Derek's."

"That's generous of you." I took a seat on the edge of the bed, one of the few spots not covered by his jerseys or other mementos from his career.

She lifted a shoulder. "Seems like the least I can do."

One of his Dartmouth jerseys caught my eye, and I picked it up, smiling. "Oh man. This brings back memories."

"From winning the Frozen Four?"

I nodded, setting it back down gently. "One hell of a win."

"That it was," she said with a wistful smile.

"Are you sure you're okay with parting with some of his things?" I asked, knowing it couldn't be easy.

"It's for a good cause," was all she said in reply. She went back to the closet, returning the Dartmouth jersey to the rod.

"Speaking of a good cause," I said, wondering how my news would go over. "Coach called me into his office today to talk about the fight."

She stilled, her shoulders bunching. And then she resumed sorting as if nothing was out of the ordinary. "What about it?"

"Apparently, the NHL reached out to him." When she turned to face me, I was struck by how exhausted she looked. I stood, going over to her, cupping her cheek. "Bryn, are you sure you're feeling okay?"

"Just tired," she said, brushing away my concern.

"Did you follow up with your doctor?" I asked, aggravated that we still didn't know why she'd fainted, other than a vague diagnosis of "stress."

She glanced away, busying herself with something in the closet. "I scheduled an appointment."

"Good." I stepped closer, rubbing her shoulders. She moaned, closing her eyes and sinking into my touch. I guided her over to the bed, continuing to massage her tight muscles.

"That feels so good." She tilted her head back.

"Maybe you should stay home from the conference." I

leaned forward to rasp in her ear. "Call in sick and let me take care of you."

"While I love that idea..." She moaned again when I hit another knot of muscles. "You have a game tomorrow night."

"Maybe I'll call in sick too," I said.

She laughed. "Frasier, when have you, or any of the guys, ever called in sick?"

We both knew the answer: never. Unless we were dying, we were on the ice.

"Okay, but—" I smoothed my hands down her arms. "I've missed you." I pressed a kiss to her neck. And I wasn't solely referring to physical distance. Lately, it felt as if she was pulling away from me, and I didn't understand why.

"I've missed you too." She gave me a peck. "But that's what life during the season is like." She shrugged, and then she stood.

Was that all this was?

I wasn't used to having someone waiting at home for me. Someone I wanted to come home to. Even when I'd been with Sheree, it hadn't been like *this*.

I ached for Bryn when we were apart. When I was on the road, I couldn't wait to come home to her. When I was home, I couldn't get enough of her.

"I don't know how the guys with kids do it," I said. It was hard enough to be away from Bryn. Let alone feeling like you were missing out on your family's milestones.

She straightened. "I'm sure it's not easy. On the players or their partners."

I nodded, knowing she was right. It wasn't easy to be on the road, to be away from her. But I could only imagine how difficult it would be to be the one at home, taking care of everything. It seemed like the perfect segue into something I'd been wanting to talk about for a while.

"So, you know how it never feels like we have enough

time together?" I asked, and she nodded. "And I'm always over here when I'm not traveling."

"Yeah."

"I was thinking…what if we moved in together? I could sell my condo, and we could live here or find somewhere else. Whatever you want."

She was silent for a moment that stretched on and on. And on.

Shit. I rubbed the back of my neck. Had I totally misread the situation?

"Bryn?" I finally asked, my chest tight with anticipation.

"Can I—" She cleared her throat. "Can I think about it?"

"Of course," I said, trying not to let my disappointment show. This had seemed like a no-brainer. And I wasn't asking her to move. Even so, her hesitation gave me pause.

"I, um—" She shook her head. "I'm sorry, Frasier." She placed her hand on my arm. "I just need some time to work through something."

"You'll let me know if I can help in any way, right?" I asked. I told myself to be patient, to have faith in Bryn and in our relationship. But it was difficult to sit by and do nothing, not being able to help when I knew she was hurting.

She nodded. "So what did the league have to say?" she asked, clearly wanting to change the subject.

"Apparently, they want to start a new campaign to send a clear message that locker-room talk has no place in hockey. They plan to train players and others in the league how to be upstanders—to speak up even when it feels difficult. Plus, get this, they want to draft new rules with fines attached to them."

"Wow." She blinked a few times. "That's huge. They're finally going to do something about the bro culture." She grinned. "Good."

"And…" I was most nervous about this next part. "They want me to be the spokesperson. Well, Kovi and me."

She stopped and looked at me. "What did you say?"

I tried to tamp down my excitement. I didn't want to influence her decision, though I had a difficult time imagining Bryn saying no to something like this. "I said I'd think about it, but that I needed to talk to you first."

"Talk to me?" She tilted her head.

"Of course I'd consult you. We're partners, and we make decisions together."

"Right." She nodded woodenly. "Together."

"And this affects you, not just as my partner but because of what Wilson said. The opportunity arose out of the fight in Seattle. So there's a good chance it—and what was said— will continue to be discussed if I take on this role."

"Ah." She lifted her chin. "I see."

"And I worried that you might have felt triggered by some of Wilson's comments or what happened in the…aftermath," I said, alluding to internet trolls. "So I wanted to see what you thought, because of that and the time commitment. My hope is that everyone will focus more on this positive change than the fight, but I can't promise that. And while I appreciate them offering it to me, I don't have to accept."

"What?" She jerked her head back. "Frasier. No." She came closer. "If it's something you want to do, you should absolutely accept. I'm just surprised, that's all. I know how much you hate being the center of attention."

"You're right. I'm not a fan of the spotlight." And I hated when its harsh glare was directed at Bryn—using her tragedy, her pain, to sell stories. "But I am a fan of using my platform to make positive change. And this opportunity could show the world that there's space for everyone in hockey."

"Then you should do it." She gave me a watery smile. "If

that's what you want. Because you'd be a wonderful role model."

I was humbled by her comments. "Thanks, angel." I gave her hand a squeeze. "I wish Derek were here. He was always talking about growing the game for the next generation. He would've supported this initiative wholeheartedly."

She nodded, her eyes glassy as she glanced down at the floor. "Yes. He would've."

Later, after she'd finished going through Derek's jerseys, we ate dinner. Took the dogs for a walk. I'd set up the projector in the backyard, cueing up a movie. Less than ten minutes in, she'd fallen asleep.

I studied Bryn, gently brushing her hair away from her face. Her eyes were closed, blond lashes soft against her skin. Her lips were slightly pursed, face relaxed. She was breathtaking and completely exhausted.

I frowned. The only other time I'd seen her this tired was after Derek's death. The shock of it, the aftermath, the trauma had completely depleted her.

I understood that grief was nonlinear, but I didn't get the impression that this was about Derek. For the past few months, everything had been great. And I couldn't understand what had happened or even how to fix it.

Was it the fight? The response? The travel?

I couldn't change my travel schedule, and I'd tried to alleviate her fears. When I was home, I did everything I could do to maximize our limited time together, which was why I'd suggested moving in together. I'd been so certain she'd agree that I'd reached out to a Realtor about listing my condo.

But Bryn had seemed surprised by my suggestion. Hesitant. She'd asked if she could think about it.

I didn't know what there was to think about. We loved each other. We wanted to be together. Right?

I sighed, falling onto my back on the quilt. I stared up at

the sky, tucking my arms beneath my head. Bryn said she needed to work through something, but in the past, Bryn had always come to me, relied on me. It killed me—not knowing what was bothering her or how to fix it. And when the credits eventually rolled on the movie, I was no closer to having any answers.

"THE WIND WHISTLED THROUGH THE CAVE, MAKING HER SHIVER and the fire flicker. He laid her down on their jackets, ignoring the storm that continued to rage outside—"

"What the fuck are you listening to?" Gabe asked, entering the room where the ice baths were located.

I was about to step into the freezing water but quickly hit pause on the audiobook, hoping my expression wasn't guilty as fuck. "Hammy feeling better?"

The only reason I'd selected that book was because I'd assumed he'd be with the trainers a while longer. Gabe's hamstring had been bothering him since a hit he'd taken in the last game, so he'd been spending more time with the trainers—doing stretches, getting it massaged.

"Yes, but—" He narrowed his eyes at me. "Why are you being so cagey? And what was that book?"

I rubbed the back of my neck. "It's, um…" God, there was no getting around this. Was there? "Have you heard of Meghan Hart?"

"No." He removed his sweat pants, leaving him in his compression shorts. "Should I know her?"

"She's one of Bryn's favorite authors."

He arched one brow. "Interesting. What does she write?"

"Romance."

He leaned his head back and guffawed. "Fizzy, if you wanted some tips, all you had to do was ask."

I rolled my eyes. "I've been missing Bryn. I thought this might help me feel closer to her." And I was still thrown by her reaction to the idea of us moving in together.

I could understand if she wasn't ready to leave behind the home she'd shared with Derek, but I wasn't asking her to do that. I would never ask that of her. Maybe I'd been wrong to think she was ready for this next step.

Gabe leaned his elbow on the edge of the cold tub next to mine. "She's been gone, what? A day?"

"Two," I said, but it seemed like so much more than that because of the distance she seemed intent on putting between us. "And I feel like I haven't seen her at all since the season started."

Now that I was the one at home and she was out of town, it was even more disorienting. I didn't like it.

"But the two of you are good, right?"

I lifted a shoulder, not entirely sure what to say to that.

"Fine." Gabe yanked his shirt over his head. "Since you're so mopey and pathetic, let's give it a try."

I pressed play, sinking into the water as I focused on my breathing. The narrator's voice carried through the room, describing the scene in great detail. It was definitely a good distraction from the ice water.

About five minutes in, the door opened, and Boone came striding in. He paused, glanced between Gabe and me, and then said, "Oh shit." He covered his mouth, a huge fucking grin on his face as the narrator continued to describe how the main character slid inside her... "What are you two listening to?"

Gabe and I glanced at each other, then Gabe pointed at me. "It was his idea."

Traitor.

"Is this Meghan Hart?" Boone asked, leaning against the wall.

I whipped my attention to him. "You know her?"

He lifted a shoulder. "I slept with this girl once who was a huge fan. She asked me to act out one of the scenes from the book."

I arched an eyebrow. Gabe started laughing. "You pretended to be trapped in a cave in the middle of a snowstorm?" He laughed some more.

"No, fucker. Just wait until later in the book." Boone winked. "She asked me to tie her up and blindfold her."

"Damn," Gabe said just as my timer went off, and the narrator ceased talking. "That sounds hot."

Boone smirked. "It was. So did you guys start a book club or something?"

I laughed, climbing out of the tub. "No. Though I guess we do a lot of buddy reads."

"Buddy reads?" Gabe asked, toweling off.

"Bryn told me that's what it's called when you read a book with a friend at the same time. Like we do with our audiobooks."

"Aw." Boone batted his eyes. "Aren't you two too cute." He hooked a thumb over his shoulder. "Should I tell the guys we need to start workshopping your couple's moniker?"

I gave his shoulder a playful shove. "You going to take your ice bath or just stand there and pretend?"

Boone crossed his arms over his chest. "Why are you even still here?"

"Bryn's out of town," Gabe offered.

"Oh. That explains it," Boone said, tilting his chin up.

I frowned. "Explains what?"

"Why you've been such a grumpy bastard lately." He pushed off the wall, following us to the sauna.

"I am not—" I looked to Gabe for confirmation, but he

scrunched up his face. "Fine." I pressed the heels of my hands into my eyes. "I am."

Because I didn't understand what was going on. Because I didn't understand Bryn's hesitation when it came to our future.

Gabe opened the door to the sauna, and the three of us filed in before taking a seat. "What's going on? You've been distracted and playing like shit all week."

Boone nodded.

Fuck.

"I'm worried about her," I admitted.

"Because she fainted?" Gabe asked. "Because, fuck. That was scary."

Gabe had followed me to the bathroom after it had happened. I hadn't known it at the time, hadn't realized he was waiting in the hallway until I'd carried Bryn to the back exit of the restaurant.

"That, and I feel like she's pulling away from me," I admitted.

"Why do you feel like she's pulling away from you?" Boone asked.

"Because I know her, and she's been withdrawn lately. Plus..." I hesitated, not sure I wanted to admit this, even to two of my closest friends.

"Plus..." Boone prompted.

I... *Shit.* "I suggested that we move in together, and she said, 'Can I think about it?'"

"Oof." Gabe cringed, and Boone sucked in air through his teeth.

"Right." I used a towel to dry the sweat from my face.

I was fucked.

Did she need to think about it because she had reservations about us? About our relationship? I pressed the heels of my hands to my eyes, sick of asking myself the same questions with no answers.

I knew I was spiraling, but I couldn't seem to stop. If only she would just talk to me. Tell me what she was thinking.

"Did she say why?" Gabe asked.

I shook my head, dropping it to rest in my hands. I groaned, wishing I knew what was wrong.

"I don't get that," Boone said, interrupting my thoughts. "I know she loves you. It's obvious to anyone who sees the two of you together."

I knew she did too, which was why I couldn't make sense of it.

"How did you ask her?" Gabe asked.

I told them about the conversation. When I finished, Gabe scrunched up his face. "I hate to say this, but it wasn't the most romantic way to go about it."

I barked out a laugh. "I didn't realize I needed to make a big deal out of it, an elaborate declaration."

"Dude, have you seen what guys do to ask a girl to prom these days?" he asked. When I shook my head, he said, "My nephew came up with this whole 'promposal' with two of his friends, where they did an elaborate dance number and everything."

"You're shitting me."

He shook his head, but it was Boone who responded. "No. There's whole TikTok videos on it. It's insane."

I had a full-body shiver. "This is exactly why I avoid social media."

Even so, it wasn't like me to sit around stewing in my head and doing nothing. I was a man of action, and I could remind her of why we were so good together.

It was time to start phase two of Operation Woo.

CHAPTER TWENTY-SIX

Bryn

"Another package arrived from Frasier," Allie said, eyebrow raised as she carried in the large box.

Packages in varying sizes had started arriving a few days ago. The first one had included a friendship bracelet he'd made with our initials and a heart on it. Plus, he'd included a picture of us from college. I hadn't even remembered taking that photo, but there we were, his arm slung over my shoulder, huge smiles on our faces. I'd wondered if Derek had been standing behind the camera.

A handwritten note had accompanied the bracelet and photo. I reread the note every night before bed. I'd check Frasier's stats on the health app, then read his words. I practically had it memorized by now.

You are my best friend, and I will always be there for you. We are better together.

I love you.

Love, Frasier

Better together.

THE WORDS KEPT RINGING IN MY EARS BECAUSE HERE I WAS, freaking out on my own.

The next day, there'd been an adorable stuffed teddy bear dressed in a Hawks jersey with the number thirty on it and Holmes on the back. The accompanying note had read, "I know how much you love my bear hugs, so I sent you a friend to cuddle with. I love you. F."

The following day, he'd sent some Polaroids of Bacon and Biscuit, as well as a note they'd "written," telling me how much they loved, appreciated, and missed me. It was all so incredibly sweet. And it only made me feel worse about how I'd been acting lately.

Sullen. Withdrawn.

And when he'd suggested that we move in together, I'd said, "Can I think about it?"

Can I think about it? I wanted to go back and kick myself for that answer.

What was there to think about? I loved him. He loved me. We wanted to be together.

And yet…I'd hesitated.

And I *hated* that I'd hesitated. Because I saw how much it had hurt Frasier, when that was the last thing I'd wanted.

Here he was, reaching out. Despite how I'd pushed him away, Frasier kept showing up, kept showing me just how much he loved me.

I stood, going over to the kitchen to open the latest missive. I had no idea what could be inside, but I was excited to find out.

I grabbed a pair of scissors from a kitchen drawer and

sliced open the box. Inside was a gorgeous bouquet that had been grown by local farmers. While Allie set to work putting the flowers in a vase, I plucked the card from the inside.

Apart from the occasional text, Frasier's notes had been our only source of contact since I'd arrived in Boston. I'd been busy with Allie and my conference, and the time change didn't help. But I sensed that he was giving me space while trying to reassure me that he was there for me. I loved him all the more for it.

> Bryn,
>
> I chose these flowers because they symbolize resilience, growth, hope, and love.
>
> We have grown through so many challenges together, and I am always amazed by your strength and resilience.
>
> Love,
> Frasier

I burst into tears. Allie guided me over to the couch, setting the bouquet on top of the coffee table.

"Okay," she huffed, hugging me to her side. "I've been patient all week. With the gifts and the notes and the puffy eyes. I've tried to give you space, but I can't take it anymore. What is going on? Why is Frasier love bombing you?"

"I—" I shook my head, covering my face with my hands. I couldn't stop crying, even though the idea that Frasier was love bombing me was laughable. "He's not love bombing me."

"Okay," Allie said, dragging out the word as she placed her

hand on my back. "Did he do something stupid? Are you guys fighting? Did you break up?"

"No." I sniffled. "No. Nothing like that."

If anything, I should be the one sending him gifts and love letters. I'd been all over the place lately, and it wasn't fair to him. Every time a new gift or note arrived from Frasier, I felt equal parts guilt and relief. And every day, I melted a little more, falling even harder for this man.

"I'm glad to hear that, because I really did not want to have to hurt him." She pounded her fist into her palm.

I laughed at that, but it came out as more of a snort. The idea of Allie even trying was comedic. She was a foot shorter than him.

"Frasier's done—" I hiccupped around a sob "—nothing wrong and everything right."

"Okay," she said, dragging out the word. "So then, why all the daily gifts? Why all the tears?"

"Because apparently that's what happens when you're pregnant." I threw my hands into the air. "You turn into an emotional mess."

My eyes widened when I realized what I'd just admitted. Not to Frasier, the father of my child. But to my sister.

Allie stilled. "Bryn," she whispered. "You're...pregnant?"

I nodded. It felt so strange to finally admit that aloud. It made it more real somehow.

"Oh my god," she squealed. "That's the best news! Or at least..." She dialed back some of her enthusiasm. "*I* think it's the best news ever. But how do you feel?"

"How does it look like I feel?" The tears fell freely. "I'm a mess. Everything is happening so fast, and I'm happy, sad, scared, conflicted."

"That's understandable," she said, scooting closer to wrap her arm around me. "Having a baby is a big deal." She gave me a squeeze, and something in me eased.

"Yeah, but I can't help but think about Derek. And how if he were alive, I'd be having this baby with him. Then I feel guilty because I love Frasier too. I love him so much. But I never would've realized that, never would've had this gift." I cradled my stomach. "If Derek hadn't died."

"Oh, Brynnie." Allie pulled me into a hug. She rubbed my back, comforting me until I'd calmed down a little. "That's a lot that you've been holding on to."

I nodded, letting her hold me. The fear was still there, the worry, but I felt better now that I'd told someone.

I'd been carrying this secret around for weeks. And while Frasier should've been the first person I'd told, I'd been trying to process all my complex feelings about the pregnancy. Because beneath it all, there was happiness. So much happiness. Shock, yes. But also, joy.

"Here." Allie grabbed some tissues and handed them to me.

God, I'm such a mess.

After a muttered, "Thanks," I blew my nose then leaned back against the couch cushions.

"Okay. Why don't you break it down for me? Tell me what's going on in your head." She shifted on the couch. "But first, how are you feeling? Physically."

I shrugged. "I'm exhausted all the time, but otherwise, I feel okay."

"Are you and Frasier considering your options?" she asked, and I appreciated that she didn't simply assume I was keeping the baby. Though, I was. "Or have you already decided what you want to do?"

"I've decided what I want to do, but..." I chewed on the inside of my cheek. "I sort of haven't told Frasier yet?" It came out as more of a question.

"Haven't told him what you want to do, or..." She trailed off.

"Haven't even told him that I'm pregnant." I cringed. "I've been low-key avoiding him for the past two weeks." I said the last part in a rush, my cheeks heating with my admission. "And he might have asked me to move in with him." I rolled my lips between my teeth. "But I asked him if I could think about it."

"Ah." She tilted her head back. "Suddenly, the gifts make a lot more sense."

"They do?" I asked.

"He's worried about you, and he wants to reassure you that he's there for you."

I frowned. And how would Allie know that, infer that, especially without seeing the notes from Frasier? I narrowed my eyes at her.

She bit her lip, a guilty expression on her face. "He might have texted me to ask how you were doing."

"He did?" I didn't know why I was surprised.

He'd been there for me every step of the way. When I was breaking, he'd held me together. When I'd wanted to reminisce, he'd joined me. And when I was happy, he was there, smiling along with me. Even now, after I'd put distance between us, he was still there for me. Still loving me.

"And…I might have glanced at one of his notes. Just in passing," she rushed to add.

"Oh my god." I grabbed a pillow and whacked her with it. "What are you? Twelve?"

She laughed, covering herself as if to shield her body from my attack. "Okay. Okay. I'm sorry. I shouldn't have done it, but I was worried about you. You showed up tearful and exhausted, and I was afraid you'd broken up."

"No." I dropped the pillow to my lap, hugging it to me. "But he might break up with me once he realizes I've been keeping this huge secret from him."

"Bryn," Allie chided. "Frasier loves you. He's not going to

break up with you, especially not when he finds out you're carrying his baby."

"Still…" I frowned. "I should've told him. I was just so shocked at first."

It was a moment I'd never forget. Frasier had rushed me to the hospital, holding my hand as they'd asked a million questions and run a variety of tests. I'd squeezed his hand, hoping to reassure him and wipe away the worry creasing his brow.

Through it all, I'd felt nothing but his care and concern. His love.

"WILL YOU BE OKAY IF I STEP OUT FOR A MINUTE?" HE ASKED. "I should call Coach."

I nodded. I'd given up arguing that he should go back to the hotel.

He leaned over, pressing a kiss to my forehead. "I won't be long." And then he left.

A few minutes later, the doctor returned. And my whole world had changed in the blink of an eye.

"Congratulations, Mrs. Morgan. You're pregnant."

I'd clutched at my throat. Pregnant? Mrs. Morgan?

Derek's last name.

Frasier's baby.

And then I'd thrown up again.

"AND NOW?" ALLIE ASKED. "HOW DO YOU FEEL?"

"I'm still in shock," I admitted. I hadn't believed it at first. We'd been using condoms. But the bloodwork had confirmed it then, as had the appointment last week with my OB. "At first, I needed to digest the news. I needed confirmation from my doctor. And then, I'd told myself to just tell Frasier. But there also hasn't really been a good time."

"You seem reluctant to tell him," she said. "Are you worried about how he'll respond?"

"I mean, yes and no. It's not like we were planning this or even trying for it. But I know he loves me."

"True, but I know Frasier, and he adores you. Don't you think he'll be happy about the baby, even if the timing is a bit of a surprise?"

Of that, I had little doubt. I knew Frasier loved me, just like I knew he would love this child. I nodded, feeling even more selfish for keeping this secret from him for as long as I had.

I should be happy. I *was* happy. I knew that things didn't always go according to plan, and this was a gift. I'd found love again with an amazing man, and we were going to have a baby together.

And yet...I couldn't help thinking of Derek. I peered down at my tattoo, stuck between the past and the future. Derek and Frasier. The two men I loved.

I counted out the little sixes to calm myself. Thirty.
Thirty. Sixes.

I blinked a few times. Thirty was Frasier's lucky number, his jersey number, just like six had been Derek's.

And together, they formed the most beautiful butterfly.

Butterflies were a symbol of transformation and rebirth. Every time I saw one, it felt as if Derek was saying hello. But now, I'd also come to realize that butterflies were a reminder of everything I'd overcome, always with Fraiser at my side. Butterfly was also the position a goalie often adopted in defending the net.

Maybe I was looking for meaning where there was none, but it seemed crazy to me that I'd never made those connections before now. Never realized that my tattoo was a perfect representation of the two men I loved.

I was still thinking of that as I talked to my therapist. Got ready for bed. Formulated a plan.

The following day, another package arrived. This time, it was Frasier's lucky shirt. The note read, "I don't need luck. All I need is you."

And I needed Frasier, and it was time to show him that. It was time to go home.

"So…" Allie glanced over at me as we neared the line for airport security. "How are you feeling?"

I held a hand to my stomach. "Like I'm going to throw up."

"Well, yeah—" She grinned. "You're pregnant. I hear that's a common symptom."

I glared at her.

"Okay. Okay." She held up her hands. "Jeez. I was just trying to make you laugh. Clearly, pregnancy-related jokes are off the table."

I rolled my eyes and pulled her into a hug. "Thank you for this week. Thanks for always being there for me." I could already feel a tear threatening to leak out. *Damn it.* "I love you, Al."

"Love you too, Brynnie." She pulled back, placing her hand to my stomach, though it didn't look much different from normal. "And I love you too, baby."

I smiled, softening. "You're going to be the best auntie." She grinned, and I felt compelled to add, "And a bad influence even if I know you'll love this kid like crazy."

She elbowed me. "Hey."

"You made us all play truth or dare at your wedding."

"And you totally enjoyed yourself. You know—" she looped her arm through mine "—you should be thanking me for making you play."

"How do you figure?" I asked.

"Because I'm pretty sure that little burlesque number has something to do with your current situation." She gave my stomach a pointed glance.

I squeezed my eyes shut, though she might not be entirely wrong. I was only ten weeks along, but it was funny to think that a game of truth or dare had been the catalyst for, well, everything.

I'd embraced my confidence, rediscovering myself and my love for dance. I'd ended the dance by suggesting we kiss. It had forced me to admit that I'd wanted Frasier. And then when we'd played our own private game of truth or dare... I nearly had to fan myself just thinking about it.

I took myself back to those moments, to the feeling of freedom and empowerment I'd experienced. Both from the burlesque dance to the cliff diving and everything that had led up to those moments. Every step of the way, Frasier had been by my side, supporting me, loving me.

I'd promised "together," and I'd meant it. Deep down, I knew we were better, stronger, together. Yet I'd distanced myself the past few weeks, freaking out alone.

No more.

Yes, I'd needed time to process. But I should've trusted him with my feelings. He'd been there for me all along.

I smoothed my fingers over my tattoo, smiling. *Derek. Frasier. Me. All of us.*

Allie took my hand in hers. "You're going to be a great mom. Now, go catch your flight so you can surprise your man."

My conference had ended sooner than expected, and I'd been able to switch to an earlier flight. Frasier had spent all week showing me how much he loved me, sending me surprises. Now it was my turn to show him.

I took a deep breath, hoping I could pull this off. Hoping it would all go over as well as I hoped. "Fingers crossed."

"He's totally going to rail you after." An older woman passing by shot Allie a scandalized look, which my sister ignored.

I laughed, grabbing my bag and rolling it toward the security line. "Never change, Al. Never change."

"You've got this!" She gave me two thumbs up.

"You are so cheesy." I rolled my eyes, but I was smiling the entire time. "But I know."

Because I did. I had faith in myself. And I knew that with Frasier by my side, we could handle anything—*together*.

CHAPTER TWENTY-SEVEN

Bryn

"How was your trip?" Georgia asked, hugging me.

"Good." I smiled. Allie had really shown up for me this past week. "Thanks again for picking me up a day early. And keeping it a secret from Frasier."

"No problem. So, I'm dying to know. What's this big surprise you have planned?" She waggled her brows.

I mimed zipping my lips. I'd already told Allie about the baby—albeit accidentally. I wasn't going to tell anyone else until I'd had a chance to talk to Frasier first.

"Aw. No fun." Georgia pouted. "But fine. I understand. How can I help?"

"Can you drop me at my house?"

I needed to pick up a few things—some I had, some that I'd ordered. And I needed to do that and make it to Frasier's condo in LA traffic before he finished practice. I glanced at the darkening sky, trying not to stress about how long it was going to take to get there.

"Of course."

Georgia and I chatted during the drive—about the season, about my visit to Boston, about everything and nothing.

When she pulled up to my house, she shut off the engine and walked with me to the gate that led to the backyard.

"Thanks again for the ride," I said, hugging her. "I would invite you in, but—"

"I know. I know." She grinned, backing toward her car. "Surprises and all that. Let's do something together soon," she called as she waved goodbye.

I nodded then turned to the gate, releasing the latch. The string lights were on, but that wasn't unusual since I had them set on a timer. I took the path that led down the side of the house, annoyed every time my bag got stuck between the large pavestones. But when I rounded the corner, I dropped the handle to my bag, my jaw following suit.

Frasier was standing in the middle of my backyard, but it had been transformed. I didn't know where to look first. At him—standing there with a warm smile and a question in his eyes. Or at the yard, which had become something else entirely.

As much as I wanted to go to him, touch him, I remained rooted to the spot. He looked so handsome, and he was wearing the outfit he'd had on the night of the beach bar bachelor/bachelorette party. The night of truth or dare. The night of our first kiss.

Beside him was a pergola with lanterns hanging down from the crossbeams. Three sides were draped in gauzy curtains that flowed gently in the breeze. And my eyes snagged on the bed nestled underneath. It all looked so inviting.

The sound of a wave crashing drew my attention to the large screen, where the projector displayed a video of the beach. "What is all this?" I smiled, completely blown away.

"Welcome," Frasier said, closing the distance between us, "to Anguilla."

So much for the surprise I'd planned for him.

I laughed, completely in awe of this man and everything he'd done. "I love it." I wrapped my arms around him, and he held me tight. My entire body relaxed in his hold, knowing that I was safe and cherished.

"I'm glad." He released me and held out his hand, a sheepish smile playing at his lips. I placed mine in his, allowing him to lead me over to the bistro table we often ate at.

Together, I reminded myself, despite my trepidation over the conversation I knew we needed to have.

"Does this mean we're going to play truth or dare?" I teased, wanting to live in this magical world he'd created for a while longer.

His eyes heated. "If you want. But first, how about some dinner?"

I nodded, not even sure what to say. How was he so perfect?

Okay. Not perfect. Nobody was perfect. But Frasier was pretty damn close.

He pulled out my chair, waiting for me to be seated. And then he leaned in, pressing a kiss to my temple. *I adore you.*

"Be right back."

He grabbed my suitcase and carry-on bag and took them inside. A minute later, he returned with two drinks that looked suspiciously like the ones we'd been served at the beach bar—rum punch.

Oh shit.

"Here, angel." He handed me a glass. "I know we've both been busy and stressed lately. As silly as it sounds, I kept thinking—I wish we could just go back to Anguilla. Back to when everything was fun and easy, and we got to spend all our time together."

I held out my hand, and he placed his in mine. "I absolutely love it. Thank you."

"So…" He lifted his glass. "To Anguilla."

What the heck was I supposed to do? I couldn't drink alcohol, but I didn't want to just blurt out the news now. I wanted to apologize and explain what I'd been feeling, resolve things with Frasier before I told him about the baby. I didn't want to have anything hanging between us when I delivered that news. But if I didn't drink after the toast, Frasier might think I didn't share his sentiment.

"To Anguilla." I clinked my glass against his, and then I held it to my mouth, pretending to take a sip.

"Have you eaten?" he asked, and when I shook my head, he added, "Good."

He disappeared into the house once more, and this time when he returned, it was with two silver-domed plates that looked suspiciously like the ones room service would deliver at the Huxley Grand. He placed them on the table before me, and when he lifted the domes with a dramatic flourish, I gasped.

I glanced up at him, fighting back tears. There was no way I was going to make it through this evening without crying. He was so sweet and thoughtful. And he'd gone to all this effort…for me.

"How?" I asked, holding a hand to my mouth. How had he gotten one of the exact meals we'd had in Anguilla?

He lifted his shoulder, a small smirk playing at his lips. "I have my ways."

I shook my head, stunned by it all. "Thank you. I have felt so loved this entire week, and tonight is…" I swallowed hard. "Really special."

He took the seat across from me, smiling. "Good. Because I do love you, and you deserve to feel special."

"So do you," I said, wanting him to know that he was special to me, loved beyond compare.

The corner of his mouth lifted. "Let's eat before this gets cold."

As we ate, I watched Frasier from beneath my lashes. Despite the setting, he didn't seem as relaxed as usual, or maybe I was projecting my own nerves onto him.

I was anxious to tell him about the baby. I was pretty sure he'd be happy, but it was still big news, unexpected news. News that I'd known for weeks and hadn't shared with him.

"How and *where* are Bacon and Biscuit?" I asked before taking a bite.

"They're good. I left them with the dog sitter so we could have some uninterrupted alone time."

I nodded, trying to reassure myself that I had nothing to worry about. Frasier loved me, and I loved him. We would figure the rest out—together.

"Did you have a good visit with Allie?" he asked, and it felt as if we were both dancing around the topics we really needed to discuss.

"I did." I smiled, toying with my friendship bracelet, the one Frasier had sent me. "Though it's good to be home. Or in Anguilla, as it were." I gestured to our surroundings.

"I would've taken you to the real Anguilla if we'd had time."

"I don't know." I glanced around, taking it all in again. I realized the pergola was meant to mimic the cabana. It was our own private paradise, and the fact that he'd gone to so much effort made it even more meaningful. "This might be even better."

He smiled, but it didn't quite reach his eyes. And I hated the uncertainty I saw there. I hated that I'd made him question my feelings for him or our future together.

"But maybe we could go back to Anguilla," I said. "After the season's over." Would I even be able to fly at that point?

He nodded. "I'd like that."

We were both in our heads. Both walking on eggshells. If Frasier and I wanted to go back to Anguilla, back to that time of ease and connection, I knew what needed to be done.

"Truth or dare?" I asked, trying to keep the mood light even as I eased into a heavier conversation.

He sighed. "I'm not sure I'm in the mood to play games. To be honest, Bryn, I've been wanting to—"

"Please?" I pleaded, interrupting him. "Just humor me."

He grinned, the expression both wary and indulgent all at once. "Fine. Truth."

"Do you still want to move in together?"

He tilted his head, evaluating me. And then he leaned back in his chair, dragging his hand through his hair. "Yes, but only if it makes sense for both of us. I'm sorry if I pushed for too much, too soon by suggesting that we move in together."

"Thank you," I said. "And I'm sorry if I made you question my love for you or my commitment to this relationship by asking if I could think about it."

It was tempting to rush to tell him about the baby, but I wanted to heal the wounds I'd caused first. I wanted him to *know*, without any doubt in his mind, that I wanted him for him. Not because I was pregnant, not because of any reason other than that I loved him.

"Bryn." He took my hand in his, and I clung to him, grateful for his touch. "You have nothing to apologize for. You can take all the time you need."

"I appreciate your saying that." I dabbed at the corner of my mouth, setting my napkin aside. "But I don't want to wait. I know I said I needed to think about it, but I don't. I didn't then, and I don't now. I want to live with you, Frasier. I want to share a life together. I love you."

He pushed his chair back, and I settled on his lap. I draped my arms around his neck, and I could feel the tension leave him. I felt the same, so much more at peace now that I was in his embrace.

He brushed my hair away from my face, cradling me in his arms. "I love you, Bryn. And I know this isn't easy—navigating a relationship in the public eye, especially after everything that happened with Derek. But you are my number one priority."

I kissed him then, sweet and slow. It was a homecoming, a promise.

I knew that. He'd shown me that time and time again. But I needed to show Frasier that he was mine.

"I love that we talk about Derek and share memories of him, and I hope we always will." Frasier nodded, and I felt encouraged to continue. "I think a big part of why I pulled back was because I was struggling with how to be a supportive partner to you while also continuing to honor his legacy. And then there were the comments that led to the fight, and everything that followed…" I hung my head. "I guess I felt like I was letting you both down."

"Bryn." Frasier placed his finger beneath my chin, forcing my gaze to his. "If Derek were here, I'm pretty sure he would agree. You could never let me down."

"You say that, but I already have. You've never lost your cool on the ice. And you got into a fight—because of me."

"I got into a fight," he gritted out, "because Wilson's a dick who crossed the line."

I hated to admit it but, "He only said what so many other people were thinking."

"Fuck them. I couldn't give a shit what people think about our relationship. We know the truth. Derek knew the truth."

"I know," I sighed. "And I don't *want* to care, but I do. Because I feel responsible for safeguarding Derek's legacy. I'm happy to do it, proud to do it. But I don't know what that looks like now that we're together."

"It looks like whatever you want it to," Frasier said. "I know it's important to you, and it's important to me too. Derek was like a brother to me. But if you're worried that honoring his memory will make me feel somehow…less important to you or less loved, you're wrong."

I didn't realize how badly I'd needed to hear those words. And it only made me wish I'd talked to Frasier about this sooner.

I nodded. "Thank you."

"Wear my jersey, wear his jersey, come to the games, don't. Regardless of what you do or which jersey you wear, I know you love me."

I held him tight, my arms draped around his neck. "I do. I love you so, *so* much."

I didn't realize I was crying until he cupped my cheeks, catching my tears with his thumbs where he held me.

"I'm sorry I didn't talk to you about this until now." I sniffled. "I was just trying to process everything." Including the pregnancy.

"You can always come to me," he said, meeting my gaze. "Always."

"I know." I appreciated that he hadn't tried to make me feel guilty about it. He'd been patient and understanding all along. "And you can come to me."

He tilted his forehead to mine. "Together."

"Together," I echoed.

We stayed there for a while, listening to the crash of the waves on the screen, safe and whole in each other's arms.

Eventually, I said, "So…I had a surprise planned for you. But, um, well—" I gestured to the backyard. "There was a change of plans."

He chuckled.

"Who told you I was coming home early?" I asked. He

pressed his lips together and shook his head. I narrowed my eyes at him. "Was it Georgia or Allie?"

He shook his head again, looking as if he was trying not to laugh.

"Mm." I crossed my arms over my chest. "Okay. I see how it is."

"I just wanted to do something nice to reconnect."

"You did nice things for me all week. I loved all my surprises, and now I have a gift for you." He moved me so I was straddling him, allowing me to feel how hard he was. I laughed. "Not that." I swatted his chest playfully. "Well, not yet."

He kissed my collarbone, the top of my breast. I moaned. It felt so good to be touched by him. Loved by him. I moaned at the feel of his hands on my body, worshipping me. I'd missed this, missed *him.*

He groaned, gripping my hips as he guided me over him. "You sure?"

"I—" I squeezed my eyes shut. No, I wasn't sure. But I had to do something first. I pressed a kiss to his cheek then stood. "Yes. I just need to do something real quick."

He wrapped his hand around my wrist, attempting to pull me back to him. I cupped his cheek, knowing if I kissed him, I wouldn't want to stop. "I'll be right back." I held his gaze. "Promise."

He sighed and released me. "I'll be here"

I dashed inside, grabbing a package from the counter and carrying it to my bedroom along with my carry-on bag. I closed the door and ripped open the package, smiling when I saw it. It was perfect.

I opened my suitcase, swapping out my shirt. Then I grabbed an empty shoebox and placed the items inside before heading toward the back door. I took a deep breath, watching Frasier through the glass.

I placed my hand on my stomach. "Okay, baby. This is it."

I stepped outside, trying to remain calm, cool, collected. Frasier's eyes were tracking me, and I could tell he was wondering why I was wearing his jersey. And not just any jersey—a custom, one-of-a-kind Dartmouth jersey, thanks to the rhinestones that covered his name and number. Hopefully, it would all make sense soon.

I took a seat and placed the shoebox on the table. "I, um, I know we always say that we're better together, and I truly believe that. And I'm sorry. I'm sorry I pushed you away when I should've talked to you. We are a team, and I promise to do a better job of showing you that in the future."

I placed the box on the table in front of him, holding my breath. He tilted his head, the edge of his mouth curling up ever so slightly.

"What's this?" he asked, lifting the lid.

And then he stilled. My heart was beating like a drum, and I wouldn't have been surprised if he could hear it.

Frasier picked up the tiny Hawks jersey. His eyes darted to mine and back to the jersey. And then he turned it over, swallowing hard when he noticed his name and number on the back.

"Bryn..." he whispered, a question and a prayer.

I flashed him a watery smile. "I hope you're okay with adding another member to our team," I said, trying not to cry as I handed him the sonogram pictures. "Because you're going to be a dad."

CHAPTER TWENTY-EIGHT

Frasier

You're going to be a dad.

Holy shit. I stared at the sonogram images again, then I looked to Bryn for confirmation, then to her stomach. Everything looked the same, but it wasn't. Because she was carrying my child. *Our child.*

"I'm going to be a dad?" My voice cracked.

She nodded then let out a shaky, "Surprise!" complete with jazz hands, but it sounded more like a question.

Had she been worried about how I'd react? Because I was fucking elated. And clearly, I was doing a shitty job of showing it.

I was up and out of my chair, pulling her into my arms. "This is the best news." I kissed the top of her head. Her temple. Her lips, wanting to both reassure her and shower her with love. "I love you."

She smiled, cupping my cheek. "I love you too, Frasier."

"We're really…" I placed my hands on her stomach. "You're really pregnant?"

She nodded, biting back a smile.

"Oh my god. I can't believe this." I picked her up and

spun her in my arms. She giggled, and then I panicked, setting her down gently. "I'm sorry. Was that too much? Are you okay?" I looked her over as if checking for an injury.

She laughed again, rolling her eyes this time. "I'm fine. You're not going to break me. Promise."

"I know, but—"

"The baby will be fine too," she said, placing her hand over my heart.

Everything in me softened at that. "We're going to have a baby." I cupped her cheek. The reality of it was still sinking in.

Bryn. Me. A baby.

She leaned into my hold, smiling. I guided her over to the cabana, needing to hear more about it. To hear everything.

I helped her down onto the cushions then sank down beside her. I had a million questions, but Bryn's well-being was my primary concern. "How are you feeling?"

She brushed my hair away from my face. "Tired. Emotional. But otherwise, okay."

I nodded, still trying to process this incredible news. How had I not realized or even considered this as a possibility?

The fainting. The exhaustion. The lack of appetite. What I'd thought was stress—and maybe some of it was—must also be symptoms of early pregnancy.

"And the baby?" I asked.

She placed her hand over her stomach, and I wasn't even sure she was aware of it. She was going to be such a good mom. "My doctor says the baby looks healthy."

"How far along are you?" I asked, placing my hand over hers, over the life we'd created—together. I swiped away a tear, and I was choked up just thinking about it.

"Frasier." Her smile was soft, her eyes swimming with emotion as she caught another tear.

"I just never expected this." I was unable to contain my smile. "I'm so happy."

"I was just as surprised," she said. "I'm still surprised. I mean, we were careful. We used condoms."

"Yeah, but there was that one time…"

"Yeah…" Her cheeks pinkened, and I knew we were both replaying that night. She'd picked me up at the Atlas Center after an away game, and we hadn't even made it out of the parking lot without having sex in the back of my car. Needless to say, we'd been a little reckless.

"Do you think…?"

She nodded. "The timing lines up. I'm about ten weeks along."

Eight? My eyes practically bugged out of my head. I felt as if I'd already missed so much.

"You can go with me to my next appointment if you want," she said.

"Of course I'm fucking going," I growled. That wasn't even a question. I wished I'd been able to go with her to the first appointment.

"I'll try to schedule it around your games and practice."

"I'll be there," I said, and I meant it. I didn't care what was on my calendar; there was no way I was going to miss this.

We still had so much we needed to plan and do. But for now, I just wanted to revel in this gift.

"I know this isn't what we planned…" She trailed off, seemingly at a loss for words.

"Bryn." I brought her hand to my mouth, pressing a kiss to her knuckles. "We both know that things don't always go according to plan, but I'm thrilled. Are you—"

"So am I," she said, shoulders relaxing. "I mean, yes, it was a big shock at first. And I'm sorry I didn't tell you sooner."

I frowned, not understanding. "How long have you known?"

"I, um—" She glanced down and away. "I found out when I was in the hospital in Seattle."

My eyes widened. *Seattle?* She'd known since *Seattle?* That was weeks ago.

"I kind of freaked out a little."

"And now?" I asked, hating that she'd been dealing with this all on her own.

It hurt that she felt the need to keep this, or anything, from me. But I was trying to respect the fact that she'd needed time to work things out on her own. My first inclination was always to rush in and fix things, but sometimes that wasn't the best option.

"I was always happy about it," she said. "Please don't ever doubt that. I just… It was such a big surprise. And there was so much going on that night and since."

"I wish you'd told me, but I'm glad I know now." I leaned in, brushing my lips against hers.

She cupped the nape of my neck, holding me in place. It was sweet and tender, expressing everything our words couldn't quite convey. *I'm sorry. I love you. I'm here for you—always.*

"I missed you," she said when I leaned my forehead to hers. "Missed this."

I nodded. I'd missed her more than words could say. And now that she was pregnant, I had no idea how I was going to handle being away from her when I had to travel for games. I squeezed my eyes shut, already dreading it. Because I loved hockey, but I loved Bryn more.

"You okay?" she asked, and I didn't want to think about anything else in this moment.

"Happy," I said, running my thumb over her bottom lip. "So happy."

I glanced down at her jersey, plucking at the front. "Also…where'd you get this?" Seeing her wear my name and number was always hot, but especially so tonight. I felt possessive, primal. Maybe it was because it was my college jersey, or maybe it was just because it was Bryn. The woman I loved. The mother of my child.

She cleared her throat, though it sounded almost as if she was trying not to laugh. "Allie had it."

I sensed there was more to that story, but I didn't push. What mattered was that Bryn was here in my arms, right where she belonged.

"Are we okay?" she asked, and she seemed so uncertain. I hated it.

"Bryn." I cupped her cheek, softening. "We're good. At least on my end."

She nodded. "I'm sorry. I know I screwed up, and these pregnancy hormones make me feel..." She shook her head. "Like my emotions are all a little too close to the surface or something."

"Are we good on your end?" I asked. "Or do you need me to provide some reassurance?"

She arched one brow, a mischievous smile playing at her lips. "What kind of reassurance?"

I chuckled, brushing her hair away from her face. "You tell me. I'm at your service."

She tugged on my shirt, pulling me back down to her. "Well, since we are in Anguilla, it would be a shame to waste such a nice cabana."

"We can't have that." I slanted my mouth over hers, pulling her on top of me.

I placed my hands on her hips, my cock already aching to be inside her. Her hair fell down, shielding us in a golden cocoon.

"Hi." She smiled.

"Hi." I returned her smile. I'd never imagined that I could be this happy.

"Are you waiting for a personal invitation or something?" she teased, kissing my cheek, my brow, my nose, my lips.

"I'm just not sure where to start. I want you naked, but I want to see you in only my jersey. I want to be gentle and tender and loving, but I want to pound into you."

She laughed. "Do it all. We have time."

"What do you want?" I asked, skimming my hands up her sides so I was cupping her breasts. She moaned, pressing into my hands.

"You," she whispered. "Only you."

GABE SMIRKED AT ME FROM ACROSS THE LOCKER ROOM AS WE laced up for morning skate. "I take it from your huge, dopey smile that your 'trip to Anguilla' went well."

"Something like that," I said, trying to play it cool, but failing miserably.

I couldn't stop thinking about the fact that I was going to be a dad. I was bursting to tell everyone the news, but Bryn and I had decided to wait a little longer, at least until the end of the first trimester. Keeping this secret was going to kill me.

"We're moving in together," I said, grinning. *And we're having a baby.*

Gabe patted my shoulder. "My man. That's awesome."

"Congrats." Carson held up his hand for a high five.

I could only imagine how excited the guys would be when I told them we were expecting. *One step at a time.*

I slapped his palm. "Thanks, Kovi."

Practice went well enough. I felt invincible, as if nothing could touch me. That said, I knew I wasn't superhuman. And considering what had happened to Derek, and the fact that I had a child on the way, I was determined to put things in place to protect Bryn and our baby. They were my priority, and they always would be.

I planned to call Talia on my way home, but first, there was someone else I needed to talk to. After practice, I got in my car and pressed the button to connect the call. It rang and rang, finally going to voice mail, not that I'd expected anything else.

"Derek, hey. I, um—" I tucked my wet hair behind my ear. "I'm going to be a dad."

The bridge of my nose stung, and yet, I smiled. "Can you believe it?"

I let out a shaky exhale, feeling as if my heart might explode from sheer happiness.

"Anyway, I know I usually call to bitch on here, but I wanted to give you some happy news for once. I hope that wherever you are, you're cheering us on. And I promise to take good care of our girl."

HOT AS PUCK

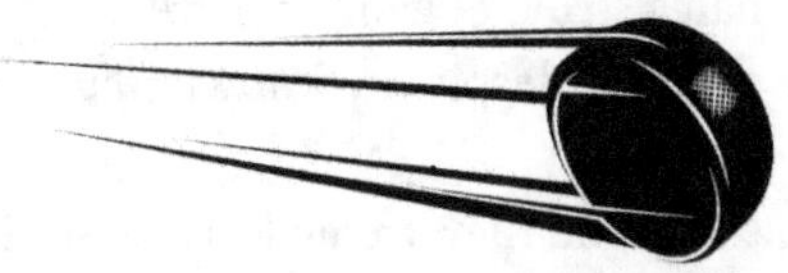

Original Air Date: April 2
@ The Hive Sports and Entertainment

Logan: [Singing] It's the most wonderful time of the year...

Levi: Play-off season. Yeah, baby.

Logan: That's right, we're entering the play-off season for the PWHL and the NHL. We have some teams we expected and some surprises.

Levi: Like the Hawks.

Logan: I didn't think that was all that surprising.

Levi: You're biased.

Logan: And you're not?

Levi: Either way, it's going to be epic.

Logan: That it is. The Hawks had a few games where it seemed like they might blow it.

Levi: That's an understatement. Everyone has off days, but Frasier Holmes had a string of games where he was playing far below his usual level, despite no known injuries.

Logan: After the big fight, they seemed to lose some of their momentum. But they are on fire once more.

Levi: Yeah. Not sure what got into him, but something seemed to really light a fire under his ass for those last few games.

Logan: We can't talk about the fight without mentioning Wilson. Seattle dropped him at the end of his contract.

Levi: He's been a free agent for months, and yet no one has claimed him.

Logan: It's looking like he might be out of the game for good.

Levi: Nah. He could always go play for a team in Europe.

Logan: Or a beer league.

Levi: I could use a beer right about now.

Logan: Okay. Let's talk top three beers.

Levi: Like our favorite brands?

Logan: No. Like the best memories or times to drink a beer.

For example, I love nothing more than that first beer after a win.

Levi: Oh. Fuck yeah. That beer tastes amazing. So does shower beer after a bag skate.

Logan: For sure. Beer in a hot tub after a day of skiing.
Levi: Beer after a play-off win.

Logan: Hopefully I'll get to experience that one soon because my team's going to the play-offs, baby!

Levi: Yes, you may have mentioned it once or twice. And congratulations to your team for making it to the play-offs.

Logan: Thanks. The PWHL works a little differently than the NHL when it comes to our cup.

Levi: Do you want to explain what that looks like? For any fans who are new to the PWHL?

CHAPTER TWENTY-NINE

Bryn

F rasier and I held hands as we headed down the hallway of the Huxley Grand LA. The Hawks were throwing a party to celebrate the end of the regular season, and I was looking forward to spending time with all our friends before the play-offs took over everyone's lives.

We stopped just before the closed doors to the ballroom, and I could already hear music and conversation from the other side. Frasier raised my hand to his mouth, pressing a kiss to the inside of my wrist. I shivered from the contact and the way he was looking at me.

"Angel, you look beautiful."

Georgia had recently suggested shopping for maternity clothes, and she'd helped me pick out this gorgeous dress. It was pastel, and something about the pattern reminded me of butterflies. It was comfortable but also sexy, showing off my growing baby bump. Judging from the way Frasier kept looking at me—touching me—he was a fan.

I looped my arms around his neck, and his hands naturally dropped to my waist as if they were made to fit there. I pressed up on my toes, and he leaned forward, our mouths meeting for a kiss.

I kissed him again, short and sweet. "I love you, and I'm so proud of you."

For the way he'd played this season. But even more than that, I was so impressed by the work he and Carson were doing in partnership with the league to train others to be upstanders. They'd received so many wonderful messages from the next generation of players—and their parents—thanking them for their leadership.

"Love you, angel." He pressed a kiss to the spot behind my ear. *I want you.*

I nodded emphatically, my pulse quickening. I wanted him too.

"Maybe we should just skip the party and get a room upstairs," he rasped, eyes darkening.

"Tempting," I said, even though he'd already made me come twice this morning before we'd left the house.

The man was determined to spoil me—with orgasms, back rubs, you name it. Anytime I even mentioned a pregnancy craving, he was on it. I felt his love for me and the baby in every single thing he did.

"Mm." He slid his hands over my hips, down to cup my ass. And then he pulled me closer so I was flush with him. "*Very* tempting."

He claimed my lips, coaxing me even closer, making me want even more. He gave my ass a squeeze, and I moaned when I felt his hard-on pressing against me. "Yes," I said. "More," I whispered. "Please."

He groaned. "You're killing me, Bryn." And then, with a shaky exhale, he pulled back.

I pouted, my body still on fire for this man. He'd gotten me all hot and bothered, and now he was just going to…stop?

"Later." He kissed me on the nose. I narrowed my eyes at him, and he chuckled. "Come on." He linked our fingers, practically dragging me toward the ballroom. "We'll just make a quick appearance, and then we'll leave."

"Promise?"

As much as I wanted to see our friends, alone time with Frasier was in short supply. And I didn't feel like sharing him.

"Promise." He kissed the top of my head.

Frasier held open the door to the ballroom, and as soon as the two of us were inside, everyone turned to us and shouted, "Surprise!"

I looked to Frasier for answers, but he seemed just as stunned as I was. He lifted his hands. "Don't look at me. I had nothing to do with this."

I smiled a few times, blinking rapidly as if to stop the tears I knew would fall.

Georgia was the first to approach, a huge smile on her face. "We wanted to throw the two of you a baby shower to celebrate! Surprise!"

I laughed, and as I looked around, the beautiful pink and white flowers suddenly made more sense. It felt like a spring-time garden, with blue silk butterflies interspersed. It was so sweet.

"Georgia." I pulled her in for a hug, trying so hard not to bawl. "This is beautiful. And so over the top."

She sketched a little bow. "You're welcome."

I laughed. "I love it. Thank you."

I spied Kylie and, "Logan?" I gasped as she stepped forward to hug me. "Oh my god. I can't believe you're here." I thought she was supposed to be back in Minnesota, preparing for her own play-offs.

Logan held me tight. "Of course I'm here. So happy for you, Bryn."

And then I noticed just how many people were here, for us. Coach Cross and his husband, Daniel and the staff from the Hawks. Carson, Gabe, Holden, Zayne, Boone, and so many of the other guys from the team. Friends from my work. Frasier's agent, Talia. His parents. Derek's parents. *My* parents.

"Mom! Dad!" I hugged them. I'd had no idea they were even coming to town.

"So excited to be a Nana!" Mom said as Dad shook Frasier's hand. They'd visited a few times since Allie's wedding, but I was so happy they could be here for this.

"And an Auntie!" Allie said, jumping in. I launched myself at her. My family had been nothing but supportive—and enthusiastic—since we'd told them about the baby.

I couldn't seem to stop crying. I was so grateful and happy and stunned, really. And through it all, Frasier was at my side.

It was so nice to have everyone together to celebrate such a happy occasion. And as we ate and talked and laughed, I couldn't help but think about how much my life had changed. How much *I* had changed.

When I finally found Georgia again, I leaned in and said, "You could've given me a little warning," in a teasing tone.

She laughed. "Why do you think I was so insistent on taking you shopping for a nice dress for the party?"

"Well, thank you. You did an amazing job." I glanced around, taking it all in.

I loved how casual and low-key the baby shower was. There were no cheesy games. No awkward opening of presents, though there was a huge pile of gifts that I had no idea how we were going to *get* home, let alone find a place for. The party was more about spending time with friends and family than anything else, which was exactly the way I would've wanted it.

"I'm glad you like it. Though, I can't take all the credit."

"I love it." I gave her shoulder a squeeze, meeting her eyes. "Sincerely. The flowers, the butterflies…" I trailed off. I couldn't think of butterflies without thinking of Derek, and it felt as if he were here in some small way.

I was still trying to find that balance between honoring the past, living in the present, and looking toward the future. But it was getting easier. I attended home games when I could, supporting Frasier and the team. And I continued working with the SADS Foundation to raise funds and awareness for the condition that had claimed Derek's life.

Georgia said nothing, wrapping her arms around me for a hug. Allie joined us, handing me a plate of food.

"You're just as bad as Frasier," I teased, though I appreciated that everyone was looking out for me.

"That man is so far gone for you it isn't even funny. And when he meets your baby girl…" She shook her head.

Sometimes I still couldn't believe this was my life. I'd been so convinced that my love story was over, and yet I couldn't have been more wrong. I'd never been happier to have been proven wrong.

Yes, there were still times that I worried about Frasier when we were apart. I still talked to my therapist. I still missed Derek. But everything I'd gone through only made me more grateful for the blessings in my life. My friends and family. Bacon and Biscuit. Frasier. And a baby on the way.

I SAT IN THE GLIDER IN THE BABY'S FUTURE NURSERY, WRITING thank-you notes while Frasier assembled the crib. Our friends and family had gone above and beyond, and this kid was so spoiled. Bacon was sniffing around, inspecting all the new items as if she couldn't quite figure out what—or whom—they were for. Biscuit was napping at my feet, bored by the whole thing.

I was just happy to be relaxing at home, with Frasier and the dogs for once. The past few months had passed in a blur of games, doctor's appointments, work, and so much more. Frasier had sold his condo and moved in with me, and I loved being with him all the time. At least, when he wasn't out of town for a game. When he was home, he was working on his latest project—preparing a room for our baby girl, who still didn't have a name.

Frasier and I had hired a local artist to paint one of the walls as a woodland scene, and it was like an "I Spy" straight out of a fairy tale. Foxes and other animals were hidden throughout the forest, including a family of bears to represent Frasier, me, and the baby. I adored all the details—the little birds and flowers, even a hawk for the team. But my favorite part was all the butterflies in varying shades, shapes, and colors. It was beautiful and meaningful, and I absolutely loved it.

I placed my pen down for a moment, watching Frasier as he attached one of the sides of the crib. He already loved this baby so much, and it only made me fall even harder for him.

Life was good. Better than good.

He glanced up at me, sunlight streaming through the window. We'd have to get some blackout shades, but for now, I was enjoying all the natural light.

"So, I was thinking," he said, returning his attention to the crib. Which meant my attention returned to his forearms. *So hot.*

"Bryn?" he asked, brow raised.

"Mm."

"I was thinking about names for the baby."

We knew she would take Frasier's last name, but we hadn't decided on a first name yet. Nothing had felt right.

"What if…" He shifted. "I was thinking Morgan, in honor of Derek."

"Morgan." I nodded as a tear streaked down my cheek. "I love that."

Frasier set aside his tools, coming over to me. And then he was kneeling before me, cupping my cheeks, wiping my tears.

"Morgan Holmes." I smiled, loving that Frasier wanted to honor someone who was so dear to both of us. "It's perfect."

I thought back to the book Frasier had given me, and the inscription from Meghan Hart and Penelope Glass.

The best love stories have no end.

Because I'd never stopped loving Derek, but I'd also made room in my heart for Frasier and, now, our child.

The baby—*Morgan*—kicked as if to show her approval. I laughed, placing Frasier's hand over my stomach. When he felt her movements, his expression softened even more. He was such a goner for our daughter. He hadn't even met her yet, and he was already wrapped around her little finger.

"Hi, baby." He spoke to my stomach. "It's your daddy, and I can't wait to meet you. But if you could please try to time it so that I'm not at an away game, I'd really appreciate it."

I laughed, but it was no joke. The play-offs were starting soon, and depending on how the Hawks played, they'd last for months. I wanted success for Frasier—for everyone on the team. But selfishly, I wanted him home for the birth of our child.

For now, I was trying not to stress. I still had a few months until my due date. I might not be able to travel to the away games now that I was in my third trimester, but I would attend every home game possible. And the ones I couldn't attend, I'd watch from the comfort of our couch.

Allie had already offered—insisted, really—on coming to stay for the last few weeks of my pregnancy. And I was looking forward to spending some time with her.

"So…" Frasier said, seeming nervous all of a sudden. "You know how we were talking about names?"

I nodded, assuming he wanted to discuss a middle name for Morgan now that we'd decided on her first name.

"I was wondering what you'd think about changing your last name so we'd all have the same one."

I considered it a moment. I'd loved being married to Derek. I'd loved sharing his last name. But I wanted to have the same name as my children.

"I'm not opposed to the idea," I said. "But the only real reason I'd do it is—"

I realized then that Frasier had shifted from two knees to one. He was kneeling before me, a plastic Easter egg in hand like the ones that were often thrown on the ice after a shutout game.

"This egg contains a promise, but it will only open when you're ready for it."

I had a pretty good feeling I knew what was inside that egg, and it wasn't chocolate candy. A swell of emotion rose inside me, and I loved the fact that he'd given me a choice. He hadn't put me on the spot; he hadn't pushed. He was patient, as always.

And even though I knew I could've told him I wanted to wait, that wasn't what I wanted. I wanted him, and I wanted this life—together.

I swallowed hard and whispered, "I'm ready."

The corner of Frasier's mouth lifted into a hint of a smile. "I love you, Bryn, and I want to spend the rest of my life showing you that. Marry me?" He popped open the egg, revealing…

"Is that a ring pop?" I laughed, removing the candy from inside.

When I glanced up again, he was holding out another ring with a gold band and two large stones—an emerald-cut diamond hugging a pear-shaped one. My eyes widened. I'd never seen anything like it.

"It's called a *moi et toi* ring. It's French for 'me and you,' and I liked that it symbolized us—together."

I met his eyes and vowed, "Together." He slid the ring on my finger, and it sparkled and sparkled. "I love it. It's perfect."

He brought my hand to his mouth, pressing a kiss to the back of it. "We can get married whenever you want. I'm a patient man, but I can't wait to make you mine."

I leaned forward, cupping his cheeks as tears ran down my face. "I already am."

CHAPTER THIRTY

Bryn

Two Months Later

"Holy shit," Georgia said, eyes focused on the players as they raced across the ice at the Atlas Center. "Holy shit! Come on, Holden!" she yelled, cupping her hands to her mouth.

"Give us a handy," Logan shouted, and I started laughing from our seats at center ice.

Logan looked at me, as if to say "what?" but Georgia bent forward, clutching her stomach as she laughed.

"Give us a handy?" I mouthed at Logan, waiting for her to replay her words. But then Holden was charging toward the opposing team's goal, lining up to take that shot.

I held my breath along with most of the arena as the puck sailed through the air, landing squarely in the net. The buzzer went off, and the crowd went wild—the atmosphere in here was electric. I'd attended many home games over the years, but they'd never felt quite like this.

The Hawks were in the lead in the sixth game of the Stanley Cup finals. If we won today, we *won*. And we were now one step closer to clinching that W.

"Oh my god! Oh my god!" I was bouncing up and down—well, as much as I could this late into my pregnancy. And then—*oof*.

"Oh god." I gripped the back of the seat in front of me, panting as a more intense contraction hit.

"Are you okay?" Allie asked.

I'd been in early labor for the past eight hours. I hadn't told anyone, but I'd been diligent about monitoring my symptoms. Cramping. Backache. The adrenaline from the game certainly helped.

"Yeah." I breathed through it. "Yeah." It was the second period of the biggest game of Frasier's life. "I'm fine." I smiled, but she didn't seem convinced.

It passed, and I straightened. *I've got this.*

"Your hubby is killing it out there," Logan said after Frasier blocked another shot.

I grinned, glancing down at my rings, loving the way the two diamonds complemented each other. They were tight on my swollen fingers, but I hadn't wanted to take them off. Now I couldn't take them off even if I'd wanted to.

As the game paused for a commercial break, my mind flashed back to that day. Frasier and I had gotten married about a month ago in our backyard. Georgia had helped me find a beautiful dress that was simple, elegant, and surprisingly sexy. And she'd done my hair and makeup, standing witness at the ceremony along with both sets of our parents, my sister and her husband, and only our closest friends.

I'd never forget Frasier's expression as I walked down the aisle toward him—the love and tenderness and devotion that had shone from his eyes. I'd carried a bouquet of flowers from our garden, and he'd worn a new suit that had shown off his athletic form. The day had been absolutely perfect and exactly what we'd wanted. Small, intimate, and meaningful. We might have another, bigger celebration later. But I was just happy to be Frasier's wife.

After the ceremony, we'd celebrated with dinner in a private dining room at 76, one of the Huxley Grand LA restaurants. The night had been full of laughter and love. Frasier had surprised me by renting one of the suites at the hotel. And he'd proceeded to spend the evening showing me just how much he loved and cherished his wife.

Another contraction hit, knocking me out of the memory and into the present. As it gained strength, I bent forward, groaning. *No. No. No. No. No!*

I did not want to leave now. It was the middle of the game. Maybe if I just…stayed calm and breathed through it, baby would sit tight a little longer.

"Bryn," Georgia said in a calm voice. "I think we should get you to the hospital."

I waved a hand through the air, even as my teeth were gritted against the pain. "They'll probably just turn me away since my contractions aren't close enough yet."

My friends and sister eyed me skeptically, but I ignored them to focus on the game.

I could feel the next contraction building, and I tried to slow my breathing. In through the nose, out through the mouth. In… I ground my molars, the pain becoming more intense. I breathed through it, trying to focus on the game as the pain eventually crested and then waned once more.

"Okay. Let's go," Allie said in a no-nonsense tone.

I shook my head. "Who's the medical professional here?" Though I was a little concerned with how quickly the contractions were coming. Since this was my first pregnancy, I'd thought it would take a little longer to progress.

Allie rolled her eyes. "Frasier would kill me if he knew you were in labor and I didn't take you to the hospital."

"I just…" *Ugh!* I wanted to watch this game. I wanted him to be there for the birth of our child. I looked to Logan for support. "Back me up here, Lo."

Even Logan seemed hesitant to side with me. But ultimately, she said, "Bryn's tough. She knows what she's doing. Give her until the end of the period," she said to Allie and Georgia.

Georgia frowned. "I don't like it."

"Neither do I," Allie said, but she didn't fight me on it.

The game continued, and Kovi raced down the ice. I tried to follow the puck as I kept an eye on my watch, monitoring the contractions. They were getting more intense. Coming closer together. And then, close to the end of the second period, I felt it. Pressure. The most intense need to push.

I squeezed my eyes shut. *Oh shit.*

In that moment, I knew… "I'm not going to make it to the hospital."

Allie looked toward the rafters and sighed, muttering something to herself. Logan looked like a deer caught in the headlights, but Georgia sprang into action. She was talking on the phone, but I wasn't paying any attention.

"Okay," Georgia said as the buzzer signaled the end of the second period. "We're going down to the ice. One of the team doctors is going to meet us there and assess the situation in the medical room. There's an ambulance waiting outside."

"Damn," Logan said, clearly impressed.

Allie and Logan helped me back down the stairs since we were closer to the rink than the exit at the top. By that point, people had started to notice that something was going on. Logan growled at anyone who dared to take a photo, and I was just trying to hold it together until we'd made it to the med bay.

Georgia smiled at security, and they waved us through. Some of the maintenance staff brought out carpets, laying them down on the ice so we could safely cross it to the medical room. Inside, a female doctor was waiting. I blinked a few times, trying to place her.

"I'm Dr. Thorne," she said, putting on her gloves. My eyes widened. Coach's daughter? "How close are your contractions?"

I squeezed my eyes shut, bracing for the next one as Allie said, "Too close."

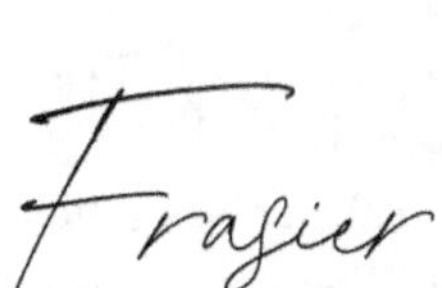

Frasier

SOMEONE CAME INTO THE LOCKER ROOM AND WHISPERED IN Coach's ear. Whatever it was made him go stock-still.

"Holmes," he barked.

I raised my head, exhausted from two grueling periods on the ice. Sweat beaded on my forehead, and I was trying to cool down so I could go back out there feeling strong when intermission ended. "Coach?"

He waved me over, and my brow furrowed. Was he about to pull me from the pipes? That wouldn't make any sense. It would be fucking insane to put in a cold goalie in the final period of the sixth game of the Stanley Cup finals. Especially in a game where the score was this close. Besides, I was playing at my best.

"I hesitate to tell you this because I want your focus to be on this game." My stomach dropped at his words. "But as a dad, I feel that you should know. Bryn's in labor."

"She…what?" I turned as if to leave, to grab my keys and run to the car. But then I realized I was dressed out in full pads, and it was the middle of the Stanley Cup final. *Fuck!* I tugged on my hair.

The locker room quieted, and some of the guys asked, "What's wrong? What's going on?"

"Bryn's in labor," I said to my teammates, pacing. "I have to…" I couldn't leave, but I also couldn't let her do this on her own. "I have to talk to her."

"She's in the med bay," Coach said, shocking me. "You have fifteen minutes until intermission is over."

"What?" I choked out.

I blinked a few times, trying to process it all. Stanley Cup finals. Bryn was in labor. Holy *shit*.

And then I was sprinting—as much as I could in all my gear—to the med bay. The chants of my teammates echoed behind me, spurring me on. "Fiz-zy. Fiz-zy. Fiz-zy."

When I reached the door to the med bay, I was panting, but it was more from adrenaline than anything else. I knocked on the door, and Georgia answered.

"Oh, thank god." She sagged and then stepped aside.

Bryn was on one of the tables with a sheet draped over her bottom half. Allie was holding one hand and Logan the other. Bryn's eyes darted to mine, and I rushed over to a sink, washing my hands thoroughly before rushing to her side. Was she okay? And why did they act as if she was having the baby here? *Now?*

Logan stepped aside, and I took Bryn's hand, smoothing her hair away from her face. Her cheeks were red, sweat dotting her forehead. She looked as if she'd been working just as hard as I'd been playing on the ice.

"Angel." I kissed the top of her head. "How are you doing?"

Before she could answer, her face contorted, skin turning even redder as she squeezed the shit out of my hand. My eyes widened, and I looked to Astrid for reassurance. But she wasn't paying attention to me; she was already peering beneath the sheet.

"I can see the baby's head," Astrid said.

What? I tried not to panic. We should be at the hospital, not...the med bay of the Atlas Center during Stanley Cup finals.

I opened my mouth to ask what I could do to help, but Astrid emitted a calm, focused energy that made me realize she had this in hand. And when I looked to Bryn, she seemed equally in the zone. So I closed my mouth, trusting that she'd tell me if she needed anything. And I focused on lending Bryn and Morgan all my love and support.

Bryn turned to me, and her eyes locked on mine. "I'm so glad you're here."

I clasped my hands around hers, kissing her knuckles. "So am I, angel."

Bryn's muscles tensed, and I sensed another contraction. Bryn looked to Astrid. Something unspoken passed between them, and a sense of peace washed over me. It only reaffirmed what I already knew: Bryn was in good hands.

"You're almost there. Take a deep breath, then give me one more big push like the last one," Astrid said. And then she nodded.

Bryn squeezed her eyes shut, giving it her all. I could see the exertion, the pain, the everything that she was pouring into this moment.

"That's it, Bryn." I held her hand, wishing there were more I could do. "You've got this. You're almost there."

And then I heard it, Morgan's cry. I couldn't hold back my

smile as relief washed over me. Bryn dropped her head against the pillow, exhausted.

She looked at me, and I looked at her, so many emotions flowing between us in that moment. Relief. Joy. Understanding. Gratitude. And so much love.

I pressed a kiss to her temple. "You did it, angel." I could barely get the words out, I was so choked up. "You did it."

"*We* did it."

I kissed her then, sweat and tears mingling with joy and love. When I pulled back to cup her cheek, she'd never looked more beautiful to me. *My wife. The mother of my child.*

"Congratulations, Mom," Astrid said, wrapping up the baby and handing her to Bryn. "And Dad." Astrid smiled at me.

Dad.

Holy shit. I'm a dad.

I stared down at Morgan and her impossibly small features. I was dying to hold her, to touch her to confirm that she was real. She was ours, and she was beautiful. But I was drenched in sweat and covered in hockey gear, so I settled for offering her one of my fingers. She grabbed it, and I tried to soak it all in. Her tiny little fingernails. The dark lashes framing her eyes. Her sweet little mouth that stretched into the most adorable little yawn.

Someone banged on the door. "Holmes. Time's up!" Coach called.

I couldn't leave Bryn, not when she'd just had our baby. But my team—my brothers—needed me. I'd never felt as torn as I did in that moment.

I went to the door, wrenching it open. "Ten minutes. Please." I pressed my palms together. "I'm begging for a game delay, and then I promise I'll be back on the ice, completely focused."

He nodded brusquely. "I'll see what I can do, but I'll be lucky if I get a five-minute delay."

"Okay." I let out a breath. "I'll take anything."

I went back to Bryn's side, brushing her hair away from her face. She smiled up at me, our daughter in her arms. "It's okay, Frasier," Bryn said, clearly sensing my hesitation. "I'm okay. Morgan's okay. You were here for us. Now you need to be there for your team."

"She's in good hands," Allie said, perhaps sensing my need for reassurance. "I promise I'll take good care of her."

"Thank you," I said to Allie, then again to Logan, Georgia, and especially Astrid. How could I ever possibly convey my gratitude for everything they'd done for Bryn?

I bent down to Bryn, who was still holding Morgan. Even though I knew they were in good hands, it felt impossible to wrench myself away from them.

"I love you." I kissed Bryn, hard, the bridge of my nose stinging. "I'm so proud of you."

"I love you," Bryn said, smiling through her tears. "Now, go. Bring home the Cup."

A tear slipped out, and I quickly wiped it away. I could've stayed there, with them, all day. But I knew that even if Coach had secured the game delay, I was out of time.

With one last kiss for Bryn and a quick glance at our baby girl, I headed back into the hallway, back to the locker room. My body might be with the team, but my heart was firmly back in that room, with Bryn and Morgan. When I entered the locker room, all conversation immediately quieted. Everyone was looking at me, full of apprehension.

"She's here!" I shouted, and they all raised their towels in the air, spinning them in circles.

Carson nudged me. "Looks like Morgan arrived just in time for her daddy to win a Cup."

I chuckled as my teammates started chanting, "Daddy Fizzy. Daddy Fizzy."

My smile was huge, and I couldn't help but laugh. And as I looked around the room at each of my teammates—at my family—I was filled with so much gratitude. Gabe came and hugged me, then Kovi, each of them tapping the number six over my heart, silently telling me that Derek would be proud.

As we headed back onto the ice, we were buzzing. Despite all my gear, I'd never felt more weightless. I double tapped the six on my chest, looking up to the rafters where a banner displayed Derek's name and number in his honor. I hoped that Derek knew he was with me, always.

When I scraped up the ice in front of the net, it was with a focused determination. I had even more motivation to bring home the Cup. For Derek and my teammates. For Bryn and for Morgan. But regardless of what happened in the game, I knew I'd already won.

Frasier

Two Months Later

Morgan whimpered, and I knew she was seconds away from building up to a full-blown cry. I jumped out of bed to get her before she could wake Bryn. I headed over to Morgan's bassinette, scooping her up into my arms. Her wide blue eyes blinked up at me—sleepy and sweet—and I smiled down at her.

She opened her mouth, seeming to debate another protest. But then she yawned instead, making me melt all over again as she settled contentedly in my arms.

"Is someone hungry?" I whispered, carrying her down the hall to the kitchen. Past the pictures of Bryn and me on our wedding day, past the picture of me hoisting the Cup over my head, past Morgan's newborn photos and a photo of Bryn, Derek, and me from college. Our home was filled with so many memories.

I opened the fridge and pulled out a bottle that Bryn had already pumped. I hummed to Morgan as I moved about the kitchen, warming her bottle. Bacon lifted her head from her bed in the corner, then went back to cuddling with Biscuit.

"Do you know what today is?" I asked Morgan, checking the temperature of the milk before holding the nipple up to her mouth. She sucked it right in. "Hm, hungry girl?"

She blinked up at me, dark lashes and beautiful blue eyes. Just like her mama.

"Today..." I grinned. "Today is Daddy's day with the Stanley Cup, and we're going to have so much fun."

She drank her milk, gulping it down with soft little suckling noises. "You see," I said, carrying her over to the back door. We went outside, nestling beneath the "cabana." It was Morgan's favorite place, and I loved spending time out here. "It's tradition. Each member of the team that wins the championship gets to have their day with the Cup. And today is mine." I smiled. "Maybe one day, you'll play hockey too."

She grunted as I removed the bottle, gently patting her back to burp her. Even though she was eight weeks old, she still seemed so small. And yet, it felt as if she'd already grown and changed so much. She'd recently started smiling, and she was so expressive.

Sometimes she'd scrunch her nose in a way that reminded me of Bryn. At times, her stare could be so intense that it made me think of Derek. I saw Bryn, Derek, me, all of us wrapped up in this tiny little human.

I'd never felt as content as I was now. When she was resettled in the cradle of my arms, I resumed feeding her. Life was good, and I loved being a dad.

I felt so fortunate that Morgan had been born at the end of play-offs. I got to spend the off-season with my favorite girls, and I was soaking up every minute with them. My parents had come to visit, as had Bryn's family, and everyone was so in love with Morgan. The Hawks organization had been so supportive, everyone showering us with love, food, and help. It was nice to have a community, a family, that was more than just a team.

"Do you think you'd like to play hockey, sweet girl?" I asked. "It's in your blood and your name. You have the names of two famous hockey players." I told her about Derek and what an amazing athlete and friend he'd been.

I still missed him. I would *always* miss him. Just as part of Bryn's heart would always belong to Derek. But I also felt like he'd be happy for us—for the life we'd built, the home we shared, and the daughter we cherished.

Morgan made a little gurgling sound, and I traced her features, loving the way her eyelids fluttered shut every time I slid my finger down the slope of her nose. I could watch her all day.

"It's too bad your mom didn't agree with the middle name I wanted to give you." I was joking, mostly.

Since Morgan had been born at the rink during the Stanley Cup finals, I'd suggested Stanley. But Bryn had had her heart set on Rose after her grandmother. Hell, after she'd given birth to our daughter—at the Atlas Center, no less—I would've given her anything she'd wanted. Still would.

After Morgan's surprise entrance into the world, an ambulance had taken Bryn and the baby to the hospital to be checked out. She'd watched us win the Stanley Cup from the hospital, with Allie at her side.

I was just thankful that she and Morgan were okay. More than okay. Astrid had done a phenomenal job of keeping them both healthy. And I would be forever grateful to her for watching out for my girls. We'd invited her over for dinner a few times since, and she and Bryn had become friends, bonding over their shared interest in the medical field.

As always, our friends and family had been nothing short of incredible. They'd brought food, helped run errands, cuddled with Morgan so we could rest. Even Coach had stopped by, and he'd been smitten with Morgan. How could he not be? I glanced down at my daughter, overwhelmed by the love I felt for this tiny human.

A breeze rustled the curtains surrounding the cabana, and I glanced around the backyard. The garden was in full bloom, and we spent a ton of time out here. A butterfly flitted from one flower to another, and I smiled. *Hi, Derek.*

The back door opened, and Bacon and Biscuit trotted out into the yard, Bryn behind them. The dogs curled up beside me, sniffing Morgan before lying down. From the moment we'd brought her home from the hospital, the dogs had been her protectors.

"Hey." Bryn smiled, joining us. Her silk robe fluttered about her bare legs, giving me a tantalizing glimpse of her thighs. She looked so damn sexy. Motherhood suited her.

"Good morning, angel." I leaned over to kiss her. "Did you get some rest?"

She nodded. "Yes. Thank you."

She looked more relaxed, and I loved seeing her well-rested and well-fed. She leaned against me as we both stared down at our baby girl.

Now that it was the off-season, I was trying to take as many of the night feedings as I could to give Bryn a break. I knew that once the season started again, I wouldn't be around as much, and I wanted Bryn to rest and recover.

She was doing well, especially after how quickly everything had happened. She'd been cleared to resume physical activity at her six-week checkup, and she'd been slowly returning to her dance classes and gardening.

"You seem happy." I could hear the smile in Bryn's voice.

"I'm always happy when I'm with my girls."

"And..."

"And," I chuckled, "it feels like Christmas morning."

We'd both been eagerly anticipating my day with the Cup.

In the meantime, I'd enjoyed watching my teammates cele-brate our win.

Gabe had taken the Cup to Disneyland and spent the day with several kids from the Make-A-Wish Foundation. The pictures had been fucking adorable. Gabe looked as if he'd had as much fun as the kids. Boone had hosted an epic brunch at the Huxley Grand LA, where they'd filled the Cup with mimosas. Supposedly, the tab for that party had been six figures.

Bryn and I had discussed how we wanted to celebrate. While some players took the Cup to their hometowns, LA was the place that felt like home to us. So, we were going to start with a visit to the children's hospital where Bryn worked, escorted by an NHL employee, of course.

Then we'd invited Dartmouth hockey players from the men's and women's teams to come help us celebrate, in honor of the time Derek, Bryn, and I had spent there. We were going to fill the Cup with hearts to raise funding and awareness for SADS. But for right now, I just wanted to enjoy this moment of peace and tranquility. Because as excited as I was to show off the Cup and celebrate the win, spending time with the people I loved mattered most.

"You hungry?" I asked, tucking her hair behind her ear.

She nodded. "Starving."

Bryn was almost always starving. She was breastfeeding and sometimes supplementing with formula because Morgan was such a voracious eater. Bryn looked healthy and happy and strong. I was in awe of her body and her strength, captivated by her beauty and her heart.

"Mm." I leaned in, brushing my lips across hers once more. "Me too."

She'd only recently been cleared to have sex again, and I'd been waiting for her to tell me she was ready.

She smiled against my lips. "It's your day. You can have whatever you want."

"Is that a promise?" I asked, hoping like hell she'd say yes.

She placed her hand over my heart, the sunlight catching on her rings and making them sparkle. "It's a promise."

"Because what I want," I rasped, "is you."

"You have me." She smiled. "Always."

We'd overcome so much in the past few years, and although I knew life wasn't always sunshine and butterflies, I felt like it could be when I was with Bryn and Morgan. And I was confident that no matter what storms came our way, we'd weather them—together.

Not ready to say goodbye to Frasier and Bryn?

Me either. Which is why I wrote an extended epilogue showing a glimpse into their future. I just love seeing them get their happily ever after, especially after everything they've been through! Plus, gain some more insights into some of the other characters in the Hawks world and guess whose story might be next!

Sign up for my newsletter and have the exclusive content delivered straight to your inbox!

Scan the QR Code below to sign up!

CRAVING MORE FEEL-GOOD FORBIDDEN ROMANCE?

The Tempt Series features high stakes, billionaires, and forbidden Love. Dive into a whirlwind of emotions as boundaries blur and passions ignite.

Temptation

Knox is a billionaire who can have anything he desires... except *her*. Kendall used to date his son, but he's always wanted her for himself.

Reputation

Emerson thinks her boss, billionaire celebrity Nate Crawford, can't stand her. Secretly, he can't stand the fact that he wants her. But when it comes to Nate's daughter, they'd both do anything for her. Even, pretend to be engaged.

Redemption

She's the billionaire; he's her bodyguard. They used to be in love, and now they're sailing the Caribbean alone together. What could possibly go wrong?

The Exception
He needs a wife to maintain control of his family's company. She needs money, and a lot of it, to restore a French chateau. So, they strike up a bargain: a marriage of convenience for this grumpy/sunshine duo.

Discretion
This single mom values her independence and won't sacrifice anything for a man, not after everything she went through with her ex-husband. He's her boss's brother, and she absolutely should not get involved with him.

Love big city romances with strong female friendships and swoon-worthy men? Check out the Love in LA Series!

Irreplaceable
After Harper returns from her vacation fling she realizes she's pregnant, and…she has no idea who the father really is because he lied about his identity.

You'll love this if you're a fan of surprise pregnancy, sports romances with a hot alpha baby daddy. Enzo is a player on the Hollywood Heatwaves—the soccer team Knox owns.

Inevitable
Sumner's always crushed on Wolfe despite their age gap, and now he's her boss for the summer. There's just one problem…he's also her dad's best friend.

Unexpected

Single mom and boss babe, Alexis, needs a new nanny for the summer. But when Preston shows up, she vows not to fall for the hot, younger man who's great with her daughter.

Irresistible

An interior designer and her wealthy client mix business with pleasure in this steamy friends with benefits romance.

Undeniable

Military pen pal romance between a former Navy SEAL turned bodyguard and a curvy bookworm. Sparks fly in this fun, steamy, opposites attract romance.

Unpredictable

Wedding planner, Juliana, is struggling to move on after losing her fiancé. So when her one-night stand walks in as her new client, she doesn't know how to proceed. But the sexy silver fox father of the bride is determined to win her over.

Or if you're a fan of small town romances with lots of steam, check out the Alondra Valley Series!

Feels Like Love features single mom, Wren, who's terrible at dating. So when her older brother's best friend needs a place to stay, she asks him to be her dating coach. But the more they "practice," the more real it feels.

Love Like No Other kicks off at Harper and Enzo's winery when a jilted-bride seeks solace in the arms of a hometown hottie with one big secret.

A Love Like That is a grumpy single dad, small town romance packed with the angst that comes for falling for your late wife's much younger sister.

Acknowledgements

This story hit different, and I'm not exactly sure why. I can't put my finger on why it's so special to me, I simply know that it is. Thank you for joining me on this adventure.

Grief isn't an easy thing to experience. I feel like this past year has been a year of conflicting emotions for me. Sorrow and gratitude, fear and hope, and so much more. I experienced a major upheaval in my life—personally with a health issue, with a family member who experienced major health issues, and with the situation in the world at large.

And through it all, the glimmers, the microjoys, the friends and family supporting me, got me through it.

Jade — Where to start. You have been such an incredible friend—*always*. But especially this past year. If writing a book is like birthing a baby into this world, you were the mid-wife helping me deliver this story.

You make me a stronger writer, and you challenge me on pacing. You are so clever and always provide great insight. I know I say this with every book, but this story absolutely wouldn't be the same without you. Sincerely, you've had the biggest impact on this book after me, and I thank you for holding my hand, for giving me your honest feedback despite all the other obligations you have.

I so appreciate you, and I'm not sure how I could ever adequately express that.

A huge thank you to all my beta readers. Thank you for making me a stronger writer, for offering your unique insight and advice. You each bring something different to the table, and I'm always amazed and impressed by your suggestions. I'm so incredibly honored to have you on my team!

A huge thank you to Kristen for being such an amazing friend. I value your judgment and honesty, and I so appreciate your support. We've been through so much together, and I treasure your friendship and advice. Seriously, I cannot thank you enough for all that you do. You are my "hype girl." You always pump me up and make me feel fabulous.

Beth, thank you so much for your encouragement and support. I always have so much fun with you. I'm not sure I've ever had a friend who makes me laugh as much as you do.

Thank you to Ellen, as always. Thank you for sharing your incredible eye for detail. Your comments are always priceless.

To my editor, Lisa with Silently Correcting Your Grammar. I so appreciate your attention to detail, and your patience with my questions. You always go above and beyond and this time was no exception.

Thank you to Angela for always being encouraging and supportive. For helping me with all the details, so I can focus on the big picture.

Thank you to my husband for always encouraging me. For always supporting my dreams and believing in me. You are better than any book boyfriend I could ever imagine. You constantly build me up, and I couldn't ask for a better partner.

And to my daughter, for always putting a smile on my face. You are spirited and independent, and I wouldn't have it any other way. Dream big, my darling.

Thank you to my parents for always being so encouraging. For reading my books. For being my biggest fans!

And to my mother-in-law, who is always cheering me on and lending a willing ear to listen to my writing adventures.

A huge shout out to all my fellow authors. Sometimes this job can feel so solitary, but I know you're all out there. And we're all cheering each other on.

A big thank you to Shauna for helping me pivot, but also for being so supportive the past few years. For helping me get the word out about my stories.

Also, a big *t*hank you to @caropalmier and @TakeALookAt-MyBookshelf for coming up with the name for the hockey team—Hollywood Hawks. Definitely much better than my original idea: Hollywood Hummingbirds. LOL

To the Hartley's Hustlers and my Sweetharts. You rock! I cannot possibly tell you how much your support means to me! I appreciate everything you do to promote my books and to encourage me throughout my writing journey.

A HUGE thank you to all the readers who share your love for my stories. I could not do this without you, and I'm honored that you've taken the time to read my words.

About The Author

Jenna Hartley is *USA Today* bestselling author who writes feel-good forbidden romance, much like her own real-life love story. She's known for writing strong women and swoon-worthy men, as well as blending panty-melting and heart-warming moments.

When she's not reading or writing romance, Jenna can be found tending to her growing indoor plant collection (pun intended), organizing, and hiking. She lives in Texas with her family and loves nothing more than a good book and good chocolate, except a dance party with her daughter.

www.authorjennahartley.com